The Book

of

Lost Fragrances

Also by M. J. Rose

FICTION

Lip Service

In Fidelity

Flesh Tones

Sheet Music

Lying in Bed

The Halo Effect

The Delilah Complex

The Venus Fix

The Reincarnationist

The Memorist

The Hypnotist

NONFICTION

Buzz Your Book (with Douglas Clegg)

The Book of Lost Fragrances

~ A Novel of Suspense ~

M. J. ROSE

ATRIA BOOKS

New York   London   Toronto   Sydney   New Delhi

ATRIA BOOKS
A Division of Simon & Schuster, Inc.
1230 Avenue of the Americas
New York, NY 10020

First Atria Books hardcover edition March 2012

ATRIA BOOKS and colophon are trademarks of Simon & Schuster, Inc.

For information about special discounts for bulk purchases, please contact Simon & Schuster Special Sales at 1-866-506-1949 or business@simonandschuster.com.

The Simon & Schuster Speakers Bureau can bring authors to your live event. For more information or to book an event, contact the Simon & Schuster Speakers Bureau at 1-866-248-3049 or visit our website at www.simonspeakers.com.

Designed by Jill Putorti

Manufactured in the United States of America

10 9 8 7 6 5 4 3 2 1

Library of Congress Cataloging-in-Publication Data

Rose, M. J.
    The book of lost fragrances : a novel of suspense / M. J. Rose.—1st Atria Books hardcover ed.
        p.   cm.
    1. Perfumes industry—Fiction. 2. Missing persons—Fiction. I. Title.
    PS3568.O76386B66 2012
    813'.54—dc22
                                                                2011014137

ISBN 978-1-4516-2130-3
ISBN 978-1-4516-2149-5 (ebook)

To Judith, who dwells in possibility

But when from a long-distant past nothing subsists, after the people are dead, after the things are broken and scattered, taste and smell alone, more fragile but more enduring, more unsubstantial, more persistent, more faithful, remain poised a long time, like souls, remembering, waiting, hoping, amid the ruins of all the rest; and bear unflinchingly, in the tiny and almost impalpable drop of their essence, the vast structure of recollection.

—MARCEL PROUST, *REMEMBRANCE OF THINGS PAST*

Prologue

**China Tells Living Buddhas To Obtain Permission
Before They Reincarnate**
Beijing
April 4, 2007

Tibet's living Buddhas have been banned from reincarnation without permission from China's atheist leaders. The ban is included in new rules intended to assert Beijing's authority over Tibet's restive and deeply Buddhist people.

For the first time China has given the Government the power to ensure that no new living Buddha can be identified, sounding a possible death knell to a mystical system that dates back at least as far as the 12th century.

China already insists that only the Government can approve the appointments of Tibet's two most important monks, the Dalai Lama and the Panchen Lama. The Dalai Lama's announcement in May 1995 that a search inside Tibet . . . had identified the 11th reincarnation of the Panchen Lama, who died in 1989, enraged Beijing. The boy chosen by the Dalai Lama has disappeared.

Excerpted from an article in the Times *(UK) by Jane Macartney.*

Who looks outside, dreams; who looks inside, awakes.

—CARL JUNG

One

Giles L'Etoile was a master of scent, not a thief. He had never stolen any-thing but one woman's heart, and she'd always said she'd given that willingly. But on this chilly Egyptian evening, as he descended the rickety ladder into the ancient tomb, each tentative footstep brought him closer to criminality.

Preceding L'Etoile had been an explorer, an engineer, an architect, an artist, a cartographer, and, of course, the general himself—all the savants from Napoléon's army of intellectuals and scientists now stealing into a sacred burial place that had remained untouched for thousands of years. The crypt had been discovered the day before by the explorer Emile Saurent and his team of Egyptian boys, who had stopped digging when they unearthed the sealed stone door. Now the twenty-nine-year-old Napoléon would have the privilege of being the first man to see what had lain lost and forgotten for millennia. It was no secret that he entertained dreams of conquering Egypt. But his grand ambitions went beyond military conquests. Under his aegis, Egypt's history was being explored, studied and mapped.

At the bottom of the ladder, L'Etoile joined the assembled party in a dimly lit vestibule. He sniffed and identified limestone and plaster dust, stale air and the workers' body odor, and a hint of another scent almost too faint to take in.

Four pink granite columns, their bases buried under piles of dirt and debris, held up a ceiling painted with a rich lapis lazuli and a silver astronomical star chart. Cut into the walls were several doors, one larger than the others. Here Saurent was already chiseling away at its plaster seal.

The walls of the antechamber were painted with delicate and detailed murals, beautifully rendered in earth-toned colors. The murals were so vibrant L'Etoile expected to smell the paint, but it was Napoléon's cologne he breathed in. The stylized motif of water lilies that bordered the crypt and framed the paintings interested the perfumer. Egyptians called the flower the blue lotus and had been using its essence in perfumes for thousands of years. L'Etoile, who at thirty had already spent almost a decade studying the sophisticated and ancient Egyptian art of perfume making, knew this flower and its properties well. Its perfume was lovely, but what separated it from other flowers was its hallucinogenic properties. He'd experienced them firsthand and found them to be an excellent solution when his past rose up and pushed at his present.

The lotus wasn't the only floral element in the paintings. Workers took seeds from sacks in storerooms in the first panel and planted beds in the next. In the following panel, they tended the emerging shoots and blooms and trees and then in progression cut the flowers, boughs, and herbs and picked the fruit. In the last, they carried the bounty to the man L'Etoile assumed was the deceased, and laid it at his feet.

As more plaster fell and chips hit the alabaster floor, Abu, the guide Saurent had brought, lectured the men about what they were seeing. Abu's recitation was interesting, but the odors of perspiration, burning wicks, and chalky dust began to overwhelm L'Etoile, and he glanced over at the general. As much as the perfumer suffered, he knew it was worse for Napoléon. So great was the commander's sensitivity to scent, he couldn't tolerate being around certain servants, soldiers, or women whose smell disagreed with him. There were stories of his extended baths and his excessive use of eau de cologne—his private blend made of lemon, citron, bergamot and rosemary. The general even had special candles (they lit this dark chamber now) sent over from France because they were made with a wax obtained by crystallizing sperm whale oil that burned with a less noxious odor.

Napoléon's obsession was one of the reasons L'Etoile was still in Egypt. The general had asked him to stay on longer so he could have a perfumer at his disposal. L'Etoile hadn't minded. Everything that had mattered to him in Paris had been lost six years before, during the Reign of Terror. Nothing waited for him at home but memories.

As Saurent chipped away at the last of the plaster, the perfumer edged closer to study the deep carvings on the door. Here too was a border of blue lotus, these framing cartouches of the same indecipherable hieroglyphics that one saw all across Egypt. Perhaps the newly discovered stone in the port city of Rashid would yield clues as to how to translate these markings.

"All done," Saurent said as he gave his tools to one of the Egyptian boys and dusted off his hands. "Général?"

Napoléon stepped up to the portal and tried to twist the still-bright brass ring. Coughed. Pulled harder. The general was lean, almost emaciated, and L'Etoile hoped he'd be able to make it budge. Finally, a loud creaking echoed in the cavern as the door swung open.

Saurent and L'Etoile joined the general on the threshold, all three of them thrusting their candles into the darkness to enliven the inner chamber, and in the flickering pale yellow light, a corridor filled with treasures revealed itself.

But it wasn't the elaborate wall drawings in the passageway, the alabaster jars, the finely carved and decorated sculptures, or the treasure-filled wooden chests that L'Etoile would remember for the rest of his life. It was the warm, sweet air that rushed out to embrace him.

The perfumer smelled death and history. Faint whiffs of tired flowers, fruits, herbs, and woods. Most of these he was familiar with—but he smelled other notes, too. Weaker. Less familiar. Only ideas of scents, really, but they mesmerized him and drew him forward, tantalizing and entreating like a lovely dream on the verge of being lost forever.

He ignored Saurent's warning that he was entering uncharted territory—that there could be booby traps, serpents coiled and waiting—and Abu's admonitions about lurking spirits more dangerous than the snakes. L'Etoile followed his nose into the darkness with just his single candle, pushing ahead of the general and everyone else, hungry for a more concentrated dose of the mysterious perfume.

He walked down the highly decorated corridor to an inner sanctuary and inhaled deeply, trying to learn more from the ancient air. Frustrated, he exhaled and inadvertently blew his candle out.

It must have been all the deep breaths, or perhaps the pervasive darkness. Maybe it was the stale air that made him so dizzy. It didn't matter. As he battled the vertigo, his awareness of the scent became more powerful, more intimate. Finally, he began to identify specific ingredients. Frankincense and myrrh, blue lotus and almond oil. All popular in Egyptian fragrances and incenses. But there was something else, elusive and just beyond his reach.

Standing alone, in the dark, he was so deep in concentration he didn't hear the footsteps of the rest of the party as they came closer.

"What's that odor?"

The voice startled the perfumer. He turned to Napoléon, who'd just entered the inner chamber.

"A perfume that hasn't been breathed for centuries," L'Etoile whispered.

As the others entered, Abu set to explaining that they were now standing in the funeral chamber and pointed out the brightly colored murals. One showed the deceased dressing a large statue of a man with a jackal's head, placing food at the man-beast's feet. Slightly behind him, a lithe and lovely woman in a transparent gown held a tray of bottles. In the next scene, she was lighting a censer, the smoke becoming visible. In the next panel, the jackal stood among jars, presses, and alembics, objects that L'Etoile recognized from his father's perfume shop back in Paris.

L'Etoile knew how important fragrance was to ancient Egyptians, but he'd never seen this much imagery relating to the making or using of scent before.

"Who is this man buried here?" Napoléon asked Abu. "Can you tell yet?"

"Not yet, Général," Abu answered. "But we should find more clues there."

Abu pointed toward the center of the room.

The stylized black granite sarcophagus was five times the size of an ordinary man. Its polished surface was carved with cartouches and inlaid with a turquoise and lapis portrait of a beautiful, catlike man with blue water lilies around his head. L'Etoile recognized him. He was Nefertum, son of Iset. The god of perfume.

The scenes in the murals, the motif of lilies, the censers in all the corners of the room, suddenly made sense to L'Etoile. This was the tomb of an ancient Egyptian perfumer. And judging from its majesty, the priest had been revered.

Saurent barked out orders to his team of workers, and after a brief struggle, the young men lifted the stone lid. Nestled inside was a wide wooden coffin painted with still more scenes of the two people represented in the murals. This cover they were able to pry off without much difficulty.

Inside was an oversize mummy, oddly shaped—the right length but too wide by half—blackened with asphalt from the Dead Sea. Instead of only one, it wore two elaborate gold masks. Both were crowned with headdresses of turquoise and lapis and wore carnelian, gold and amethyst breastplates. The only difference between them was that the one on the right was male and the one on the left, female.

"I've never seen anything like this before," Abu uttered in hushed astonishment.

"What does it mean?" Napoléon asked.

"I don't know, Général. It's most unusual," Abu stammered.

"Unwrap him, Saurent," Napoléon ordered.

Despite Abu's protestations, Saurent insisted the young men cut through the linen and expose the actual mummy. The Frenchman was paying them, so they agreed. As L'Etoile knew, ancient embalming techniques using fragrant oils and unguents along with the dry air should have prevented the deceased's soft muscles and tissue from decaying. Even the hair might have been preserved. He'd seen mummies before and had been fascinated by their sweet-smelling corpses.

It took only a few minutes to cut and peel back the blackened cloth.

"No. Like nothing I have ever seen," Abu whispered.

The corpse on the right didn't have his arms crossed on his chest, as was the custom. Instead his right hand was extended and holding the hand of a woman with whom he'd been mummified. Her left hand was knotted with his. The two lovers were so lifelike, their bodies so uncorrupted, it appeared they had been buried months ago, not centuries.

The assembled crowed murmured with amazement at the sight of this couple intertwined in death, but what affected L'Etoile was not what he saw. Here at last was the fountainhead of the odor that had begun to tease him as he'd climbed down the ladder.

He struggled to separate out the notes he recognized from the ones he didn't, searching for the ingredients that gave the blend its promise of hope, of long nights and voluptuous dreams, of invitation and embrace. Of an everlasting covenant ripe with possibility. Of lost souls reunited.

Tears sprang to the perfumer's eyes as he inhaled again. This was the kind of scent he'd always imagined capturing. He was smelling liquid emotion. Giles L'Etoile was smelling love.

The perfumer was desperate. What gave this fragrance its complexity? Why was it so elusive? Why couldn't he recognize it? He'd smelled and memorized over five hundred different ingredients. What was in this composition?

If only there were a machine that would be able to take in the air and separate out the components it contained. Long ago, he'd spoken to his father about such a thing. Jean-Louis had scoffed, as he did at most of his son's inventions and imaginings, chastising him for wasting time on impractical ideas, for indulging in foolish romanticism.

"Perfume can evoke feelings, Papa," L'Etoile had argued. "Imagine what a fortune we'd make if we were selling dreams and not just formulations."

"Nonsense," his father admonished. "We are chemists, not poets. Our job is to mask the stench of the streets, to cover the scent of the flesh and relieve the senses from the onslaught of smells that are unpleasant, vile and infected."

"No, Father. You're wrong. Poetry is the very essence of what we do."

Despite his father's opinion, L'Etoile was certain that there was more that scent could offer. That it had a deeper purpose. It was why he had come to Egypt. And he'd discovered that he was right. Ancient perfumers had been priests. Perfume was part of holy rituals and religious customs. The soul rose to the heavens on the smoke from incense.

The general came closer to inspect the mummies. As he reached down into the coffin, Abu muttered a warning. Napoléon waved off the cautionary words and lifted a small object out of the male mummy's hand. "How extraordinary," he said as he extracted an identical piece of pottery from the female's hand. "They are each holding one of these." He opened the first pot, then the second. A moment passed. He sniffed the air. Then he lifted each pot to his nose, smelling one and then the other.

"L'Etoile, they seem to contain an identical perfumed substance." He gave one of the pots to him. "Is this a pomade? Do you recognize it?"

The container was small enough to fit in his hand. Glazed white, it was decorated with elaborate coral and turquoise designs and hieroglyphs that encircled its belly. The lost language of the ancients no one could read. But one L'Etoile could surely smell. He touched the waxy surface. So *this*, here in his hand, was the wellspring of the odor that had drawn L'Etoile toward the chamber.

He wasn't prescient. Not a psychic. L'Etoile was sensitive to one thing only: scent. It was why at twenty he'd left Marie-Genevieve and Paris in 1789 for the dry air and heat of Egypt, to study this ancient culture's magical, mesmerizing smells. But none of what he'd discovered in all that time compared to what he held in his hands.

Up close, the scent was rich and ripe, and he felt himself float away on its wings, away from the tomb, out into the open, under the sky, under the moon, to a riverbank where he could feel the wind and taste the cool night.

Something was happening to him.

He knew who he was—Giles L'Etoile, the son of the finest perfumer and glove maker in Paris. And where he was—with general Napoléon Bonaparte in a tomb under the earth in Alexandria. Yet at the same time, he was transported, sitting beside a woman on the edge of a wide, green river under the shade of date trees. He felt he'd known this woman forever, but at the same time, she was a stranger.

She was lovely, long and lean with thick, black hair and black eyes that were filled with tears. Her body, enrobed in a thin cotton shift, was wracked with sobs, and the sound of her misery cut through him. Instinctively he knew that something he'd done or hadn't done was the source, the cause of her pain, and that her suffering was his to quell. He had to make a sacrifice. If he didn't, her fate would haunt him through eternity.

He removed the long linen robe he wore over his kilt and dipped a corner into the water so that he could wipe her cheeks. As he leaned over the river, he glimpsed his face in its surface. L'Etoile saw someone he didn't recognize. A younger man. Twenty-five at most. His skin was darker and more golden than L'Etoile's. His features were sharp in places where the perfumer's were round, and his eyes were black-brown instead of light blue.

"Look," a voice said from far away, "there is a papyrus here."

Dimly, L'Etoile was aware that the voice was familiar: Abu's. But more pressing was the sudden clatter of horses' hooves. The woman heard them, too. The panic evident on her face. He dropped the robe and took her hand, raising her up to lead her away from the river and find a place to hide her and keep her safe.

There was a shout. Someone fell against him. He heard pottery shattering on the alabaster floor. L'Etoile was back in the tomb, and instead of the woman's lovely, melancholy face, he was looking at Abu, clutching a thick scroll to his chest and staring down at a broken clay pot.

The scent had sent everyone into a trance, but L'Etoile had come out of it first. All around him, chaos had erupted. Men whispered, wept and screamed, speaking in languages L'Etoile couldn't understand. They seemed to be battling invisible demons, struggling with hidden foes, comforting and taking comfort from unseen companions.

What had happened to him? What was happening to the men around him?

One of the young Egyptian workers was slumped against the wall, smiling and singing a song in some ancient language. Another was lying on the ground moaning; a third was striking out at an invisible assailant. Two of the savants were unaffected but watching in horror. Saurent was kneeling in prayer, a beatific expression on his face, speaking in Latin, reciting a mass. The cartographer was beating on the wall with his fist, crying out a man's name over and over.

L'Etoile's eyes found Napoléon. The general was standing, frozen, by the sarcophagus, staring at a spot on the wall as if it were a window onto a distant vista. His skin was paler than usual, and sweat dotted his brow. He looked sickly.

There were scents that could cure ills and others that could make you ill, poisons that seduced you with their sweetness before they sucked the breath out of you. L'Etoile's father had taught him about all of them and warned him about their effects.

Now, here, he was afraid for himself and for his commander and for the men in this room. Had they all been poisoned by some ancient noxious scent?

He had to help. Grabbing a small gold box from a pile of treasures against the far wall, he opened it, dumped its contents—gold and colored glass—onto the floor, and then hastily thrust the still-intact clay pot inside. Scooping up the shards of the pot that the general had dropped, L'Etoile added them and slammed the lid shut.

The scent was still conspicuous, but now that the perfume containers were enclosed, the air slowly began to clear. L'Etoile watched as first one man and then another stood and looked around, each trying to get his bearings.

There was a loud crash as Napoléon fell onto the wooden coffin, smashing and splintering its cover. The perfumer had heard the rumors that the general suffered from epilepsy, the same nervous disorder that had affected his hero, Julius Caesar. Now froth bubbled from the general's mouth, and he shook with convulsions.

His aide-de-camp rushed to his side and bent over him.

Had the strange perfume brought on this episode? It had certainly affected L'Etoile. The dizziness and disorientation he'd been experiencing since he'd entered this tomb were only now starting to dissipate.

"This place is cursed!" Abu yelled out as he threw the papyrus scroll back inside the coffin and on top of the desiccated bodies. "We must leave here now!" He rushed out of the inner chamber and down the first corridor.

"The tomb is cursed," the young workers repeated with trembling voices as they followed, pushing and shoving each other out through the narrow entryway.

The savants went next.

Napoléon's aide-de-camp helped the general—who had recovered his faculties but was still weak—escorting him out, leaving L'Etoile alone in the burial chamber of the perfumer and the woman who had been entombed with him.

Bending over the lovers, he grabbed the papyrus scroll that Abu had thrown into the coffin, added it to the contents of the small gold box, and then shoved the box deep inside his satchel.

Two

When Jac L'Etoile was fourteen years old, mythology saved her life. She remembered everything about that year. Especially the things she'd tried to forget. Those she remembered in the most detail. It was always like that, wasn't it?

The teenager waiting for her now, outside the TV studio on West Forty-ninth Street, couldn't be much older than fourteen. Gangly, awkward, but excited and jittery like a young colt, she stepped forward and held out a copy of Jac's book, *Mythfinders.*

"Can I have your autograph, Miss L'Etoile?"

Jac had just been on a network morning talk show promoting her book, but she wasn't by any means a celebrity. Her cable show, also titled *Mythfinders*—exploring the genesis of legends—claimed under a million viewers, so encounters like this were both unexpected and gratifying.

The town car she'd ordered idled at the curb, the driver standing at the ready by the passenger door. But it didn't matter if she was a little late. No one but ghosts waited for her where she was going.

"What's your name?" Jac asked.

"Maddy."

Jac could smell the light, lemony cologne the girl was wearing.

Teenage girls and citron were forever finding each other. Uncapping the pen, Jac started to write.

"Sometimes it helps to know there really are heroes," Maddy said in a hushed voice. "That people can really do amazing things."

The noisy and crowded street across from Radio City Music Hall was an odd place for a confession, but Jac nodded and smiled at Maddy in complicity.

She'd known the same hunger far too long.

When Jac first started exploring the genesis of myths—traveling to ancient sites all over the world; visiting museums, private collections and libraries; searching the ruins of civilizations long gone—she'd imagined her findings would entertain and educate. To that end, she sought out and found the facts at the center of the great fictions, looked for and discovered the life-size versions of the giants in legends. She wrote about how celebrated deeds had in actuality been small acts, sometimes even accidents. Jac reported on how rarely the deaths of mythology's heroes were grand, metaphoric or meteoric, but instead how storytellers had exaggerated reality to create metaphors that instructed and inspired.

She believed she was debunking myths. Bringing them down to size. But she wound up doing the opposite.

The proof that myths were, in fact, based in fact—that some version of ancient heroes, gods, fates, furies and muses really had existed—gave readers and viewers hope.

And that's why they wrote Jac fan letters and thank-you notes, why Jac's TV show was in its second year, and why teenagers like Maddy asked for her autograph.

And it was why Jac felt like a fraud.

Jac knew that believing in heroes could save your life but also knew that such belief in grandiose fantasy could destroy it just as easily. She didn't tell Maddy that. Instead she finished the inscription, handed back the book, thanked her, and then slipped into the waiting car.

Forty-five minutes later the aroma of towering pines and newly blooming redbud trees informed Jac they'd reached the Sleepy Hollow

Cemetery, nestled in the lush Hudson River Valley. She looked up from her reading just as the looming wrought-iron gates came into view.

As the car passed through the entrance, Jac undid and retied the ribbon that kept the wayward curls off her face. Twice. She'd been collecting ribbons since she was a child and had boxes of them: satin, grosgrain, velvet, moiré and jacquard—most found at antique stores in baskets of trimmings. There had been seven yards of this creamy satin on a water-stained spool stamped "Memorial Black."

The chauffeur drove down the cemetery's center road until he came to a fork, and then he took a right. Watching out the window for the familiar granite orb-and-cross rooftop ornament, Jac knotted and unknotted her long white scarf as the driver navigated narrow lane after lane of tombstones, mausoleums and monuments.

For the last 160 years, all of her mother's family had been buried in this Victorian cemetery that sat high on a ridge overlooking the Pocantico River. Having so many relatives asleep in this overgrown memorial park made her feel strangely at home. Uncomfortable and uneasy, but at home in this land of the dead.

The driver pulled up to a grove of locust trees, parked, and came around to open Jac's door. Her resolve fought her anxiety. She vacillated for only seconds and then got out.

Under the shade of the trees, Jac stood on the steps to the ornate Greek-style mausoleum and tried the key. She didn't remember having trouble with the lock before, but there hadn't been a river of rust flowing from the keyhole last year. Maybe the keyway had corroded. As she jiggled the blade and put pressure on the bow, she noticed how many joints between the stone blocks to the right of the door were filled with moss.

On the lintel were three bronze heads corroded by the elements. The faces—Life, Death and Immortality—peered down at her. She looked at each as she continued to jiggle the key in the lock.

The pitting that had attacked Death had, ironically, softened his expression, especially around his closed eyes. The finger he held up to his lips, silencing them forever, was rotting. So was his crown of poppies—the ancient Greek symbol for sleep.

Unlike his two elderly companions, Immortality was young, but the serpent winding around his head, tail in its mouth, was mottled with black and green deterioration. Inappropriate for an ancient icon of eternity. Only the symbol for the human soul, the butterfly in the middle of Immortality's forehead, was still pristine.

Jac's struggle with the key continued. She was almost giddy at the thought that she'd be denied entry. But the tumblers clicked solemnly, and the lock finally yielded. As she pushed it open, the door's hinges moaned like an old man. Immediately, the chalky smell of stone and stale air mixed with decayed leaves and dried wood wafted out. The "scent of the forgotten," Jac called it.

She stood on the threshold and peered inside.

The midmorning light that passed through the two stained-glass windows of purple irises saturated the interior space with a melancholy cobalt wash. It spilled over the stone angel who lay prostrate on the altar. Her face was hidden, but her grief was visible in the way her delicate marble fingers hung over the pedestal and how her wings drooped down, their tips brushing the floor.

Under each of the two windows, alabaster urns contained Jac's offerings from last year: long-dead branches of apple blossoms now withered and dried out.

In the center of the small enclosure, on a granite bench, a woman sat waiting, watching Jac, smiling a familiar, sad smile. Blue light passed through the woman's form and splashed on Jac's legs.

I was worried you weren't coming. The soft voice seemed to come from the air around the translucent specter, not from within it.

She's not real, Jac reminded herself as she stepped inside, closing the door behind her. Her mother's ghost was an aberration. A delusion of her imagination. A holdover from her illness. The last relic of those terrible times when the face Jac saw in the mirror wasn't her own—but belonged to someone unrecognizable looking back. When she'd been so sure the crayon drawings she made weren't imaginary landscapes but places she'd lived that she went searching for them. When she could hear the screams of the people she saw being buried alive . . . burned alive . . . even though no one else could.

Jac was fourteen the first time her dead mother spoke to her. Often in the hours after she'd died. Then daily, then less frequently. But after Jac left France and moved to America, she only heard her voice once a year. Here in the sepulcher on each anniversary of her mother's internment. A mother who, in essence, had abandoned her daughter too early and with too much drama. Literally *in essence*—because Audrey had died in the perfume workshop, surrounded by the most beautiful smells in the world. It would remain for Jac, who found her, a gruesome and shocking sensory memory. The scents of roses and lilies, of lavender, musk and patchouli, of vanilla, violets and verbena, of sandalwood and sage, and the image of those dead eyes open, staring into nothingness. Of an always-animated face now stilled. Of one hand outstretched in her lap—as if, at the last moment, Audrey had remembered she was leaving something important and reached out for it.

Still hugging the fresh apple blossoms she'd brought with her, Jac crossed the vault and put down the flowers on the marble floor beside the antique urn. She had a job to do here. As she lifted out last year's dead branches, they fell apart, making a mess. Kneeling, she used the edge of her hand to sweep the debris into a pile. She could have hired perpetual care for things like this yearly ritual of cleaning up, but it kept Jac occupied and tethered to something tangible and concrete during her annual visit.

She wasn't an only child, but every year she was alone in the crypt. She always reminded her brother of the date, hoping—but never assuming—that Robbie would come. Expectations lead only to disappointments. Her mother had taught her that, cautioning the little girl not to fall prey to life's tempting promises.

"Survivors," she used to tell her, "face facts." It was a tough lesson—and possibly a poisonous one—to inflict on a child who wasn't yet old enough to consider from whence the advice came: a woman who wasn't able to follow her own counsel. *You come from a family of dreamers, but there's a difference between real and pretend. Do you understand? This will help. I promise.*

But there was a difference between Jac's childhood dreams and everyone else's. Hers were full of nasty noises and ugly visions. Threats that were impossible to escape. Robbie's were fantastical. He'd believed that one day they would find the book of fragrances that their ancestor had brought back from Egypt, and use its formulas to create wonderful elixirs. Whenever he talked about it, she'd smile at him in the condescending way that older siblings have and say: "Maman told me that's just make-believe."

"No, Papa said it's true," Robbie would argue. He'd run off to their library to find the antique leather-bound history book that by now fell open to the right page. He'd point to the engraving of Pliny the Elder, the Roman author and philosopher. "He saw Cleopatra's book of fragrance formulas. He writes about it right here."

She hated to disillusion her brother, but it was important he understand that it was all just an exaggerated story. If she could convince him, then maybe she could believe it herself.

"There might have been an inventory of the perfumes Cleopatra's factory had manufactured, but we don't have it. And there's no such thing as the Fragrance of Memory. There can't be a perfume that makes you remember things. It's all a fairy tale our ancestors made up so that the House of L'Etoile would seem more exotic. For over two hundred years, our family has created and manufactured perfumes and sold them from our store. Just perfumes, Robbie. Mixtures of oils and alcohol. Not dreams. Not fantasies. Those are all made up, Robbie. To entertain us."

Her mother had taught her all about stories. The ones you made up on purpose. And the ones that came unbidden. "Even when they are frightening and hold you in their grip, you can control them," Audrey would say with a knowing look in her eye. Jac understood. Her mother was giving Jac clues. Helping her deal with what made the two of them different from the others.

Despite her mother's advice, make-believe had still nearly driven Jac insane. As bad as her visions had been when Audrey was alive, they intensified with her mother's death. And there had been no way Jac could convince herself they weren't real.

After months of doctors who prescribed treatments and drugs that not only didn't help but sometimes made her feel even crazier, one finally saw inside her and understood her. He taught her to distill the terrors the way perfumers took flowers and extracted their essences. Then he worked with her to make sense of all those droplets of screaming, bleeding hallucinations. He showed her how to find the symbolism in her delusions and to use mythological and spiritual archetypes to interpret them. Symbols, he explained, don't have to relate to a person's actual life. More often, they are part of the collective unconscious. Archetypes are a universal language. They were the clues Jac needed to decipher her torment.

In one of Jac's most horrific recurring delusions, she was trapped in a burning room high above an apocalyptic city. The fourth wall was all windows. Desperately, as the smoke threatened to overwhelm her, she tried to find a way to open the casements. If only she could get out, she knew she could use the great translucent wings strapped to her back to fly to safety.

Somewhere beyond the room, she could hear people—albeit impossible over the roar of the fire. She screamed for help. But no one came to her rescue. She was going to die.

With the doctor's help, Jac examined her unconscious and was able to identify threads of the myth of Daedalus and Icarus. An important difference—that proved to be the clue to understanding the significance of the dream—was that in her nightmare she was alone. Both her father and her mother had forsaken her. Even if Icarus ignored his father's advice, his father was there, offering it. But no one was warning Jac not to fly too close to the sun or to the sea. She was abandoned. Imprisoned. Doomed. Fated to burn to death.

Learning about archetypes and symbolic imagery was the first step in a long road that led her to writing *Mythfinders* and then to producing the cable television show. Instead of becoming a perfumer like her brother and her father and his father before him, Jac had become an explorer, tracing the origins of ancient myths. She brought myths to life so that she could bring them down to earth. Traveling from Athens to Rome to Alexandria, she sought out archaeological landmarks and historical records, searching for proof of the people and events that had grown into myths.

Jac wanted to help people understand that stories existed as metaphors, lessons and maps—but not as truths. Magic can be dangerous.

Reality was empowering. There were no Minotaurs. No monsters. There were no unicorns or fairies or ghosts. There was a line between fact and fantasy. And as an adult, she never took her eyes off of it.

Except when she came here, each year, on the tenth of May, on the anniversary of her mother's death.

The light shifted. Jac knew it was the clouds moving, but the impression it created was that the angel was breathing. How lovely it would be to believe a stone angel could come to life. That there were heroes who never disappointed. That her mother really did speak to her from the grave.

Ah, but I do, came the whispered response to Jac's unspoken thought. *You know I do. I know how dangerous you think it is for you to believe me— but talk to me, sweetheart, it will help.*

Jac stood and began to unwrap the apple blossoms she'd brought. She never spoke to the specter. Her mother wasn't actually here. The manifestation was caused by an abnormality in her brain. She'd seen the MRI on her father's desk and read the doctor's letter.

Jac was fourteen at the time—but she'd have to look up some of the words in the dictionary even now. The scan showed what they called a very slight reduction of volume in frontal white matter, the area where evidence of psychotic disease was sometimes found. Proof it wasn't her overactive imagination that made her feel as if she was going crazy but an abnormality doctors could see.

Although, it wasn't one they could treat with any certainty. The patient's long-term prognosis was uncertain. The condition might never become more pronounced than it was already. Or she could develop more severe bipolar tendencies.

The doctor recommended immediate therapy along with a cycle of psychopharmaceuticals to see if it relieved Jac's symptoms.

Jac tore off the cellophane packaging and crumpled it, the crackling loud but not loud enough to drown out her mother's voice.

I know this is upsetting for you, sweetheart, and I am sorry.

Once the branches were nestled in the urn under the stained-glass window on the west wall, they began to scent the air. Jac usually preferred shadowy, woodsy scents. Sharp spices and musk. Moss and pepper with only a hint of rose. But this sweet-smelling flower was her mother's favorite, and so she brought it year after year and let it remind her of all that she missed.

The sky darkened, and a sudden rainstorm beat against the glass. Crouching in front of the urn, Jac sat on her heels and listened to the drops hitting hard on the roof and pounding the windows. Usually she was impatient to get to the next appointment. To change the scenery. Not to linger. Anything to avoid the boredom that invited excess contemplation of the wrong kind. But here, in this crypt, once a year, Jac felt a kind of sick relief in giving in to her fear, grief and disillusionment. Here, in this abyss, in the sad blue light, she could just be still and care too much instead of not at all. She could allow herself the visions. Be frightened by them but not fight them. Just once a year. Just here.

When I was a little girl, I used to believe this light was a bridge that let me walk from the living to the dead and back again.

Jac could almost feel her mother stroking her hair as she spoke in that soft whisper she'd used when putting her to bed. Jac shut her eyes. The sound of the storm filled the silence until Audrey spoke again.

That's what it is for us, isn't it, sweetheart? A bridge?

Jac didn't speak. Couldn't. She listened for her mother's next words but instead heard the rain and then the whine of hinges as the heavy wrought-iron and glass door opened. She turned as a gust of wet cold wind blew in. Jac saw the shadow of a man and for a moment wasn't sure if that was real, either.

Three

The young monk bowed his head for a moment, as if in prayer, and then lit a wooden match. His stillness and calm were almost beatific, a moment of profound inner peace. His expression hardly changed, even as he touched the lit match to his ceremonial dress, doused in kerosene. Flames, the same color as his saffron robe, engulfed him.

Xie Ping turned away from the website and looked into Cali Fong's eyes, not surprised to see them bright with tears.

"It's an outrage," she whispered, her lower lip trembling. At just under five feet tall, twenty-three-year-old Cali could pass for a teenager. She seemed the most unlikely creator of her sophisticated, oversize paintings—sometimes twenty feet tall. And the passion with which she discussed human rights and artistic freedom likewise belied her tiny frame. Someone that outspoken wasn't Xie's smartest choice for a close friend, but he'd decided long ago that avoiding the relationship would be just as suspect as entering into it.

"You should get off the computer," Xie said. "And don't cry, please. Not in public."

Although many students and teachers were discussing their feelings about the newest spate of unrest in Tibet, it could be especially dangerous for him to attract attention.

"But this is important, and—"

"Cali, I need to get back," he said, trying to focus her. "I have a project due and am going to have to work half the night as it is. Why don't you wipe your browser now so we can go?"

Every PC bought in China came with preinstalled Web-blocking software to ensure no one could visit the BBC, Twitter, YouTube, Wikipedia, and blogger sites. The government claimed that the effort was instituted to ban pornography, but everyone knew it was to stop the public from getting news about democracy, Tibet or members of the banned Falun Gong spiritual movement. Surfing politically subversive or pornographic websites was a crime, as was taking advantage of any of the ways around the internet policing.

Ways that Cali had become expert at. While she erased her history, Xie closed his eyes and traveled inside his mind to find a place of stillness and silently intoned a mantra that he'd learned when he was just six years old.

Om mani padme hum.

He did this slowly, four times, and the bustle of the internet café disappeared for the few seconds Xie allowed himself. He was more shaken up by the footage than he could afford to show Cali or—worse—anyone else who might be watching.

Cali touched his arm and brought him back to the present. "How much more tragic is this going to get before the international agencies step in?"

"They can't step in. There are too many financial ramifications. They all owe us too much money. China holds everyone hostage." Xie sounded rational. He felt anything but. The travesty playing itself out in his homeland was exacerbating daily. It was time to get involved. He had no choice. Not any longer. No more hiding. No matter how hard the path ahead would be. No matter how dangerous.

Through the window, he spied a group of police in blue drab headed their way. There were regular crackdowns and searches for subversives, and he didn't want to get caught in one. "Let's go," he said, standing.

"Already in the last six days, a hundred and three monks have set themselves on fire."

"I know, Cali. I know. Let's go."

"A hundred and three monks," she repeated, not being able to process the number.

He grabbed her arm. "We have to go."

As they walked out the door, the four policemen he'd seen from the window crossed the street and headed toward the café. Safely clear of the threat, Cali asked the question that Xie had been thinking but wouldn't voice. "How is any of this going to help that poor little boy? Will anyone ever find him? Why crack down on Order Number Five now? Didn't they know it would just stir up more trouble? And how could they be so obvious about how they handled it? How dangerous can one little boy be?"

"When it's a little boy like Kim? Very dangerous."

Order Number Five was a regulation that came into effect in 2007 and gave the government the right to regulate the reincarnation of living Buddhas by requiring everyone to register in order to be reincarnated.

Approving incarnations was not the endgame. Disallowing incarnations that interfered with China's oppression of Tibet and Tibetan Buddhism was. The order required that "living Buddha permits" be registered with the state and at the same time banned any incarnations from taking place in certain delineated regions. Not surprisingly, the two most holy cities in Tibet, Xingjiang and Lhasa, were on that list.

Xie remembered his grandfather telling him about hearing the news when the present Dalai Lama, the spiritual leader of Tibetan Buddhism and head of state, had been identified in 1937. The toddler had been only two years old when he was found by a search party looking for the reincarnation of the thirteenth Lama, Thubten Gyatso, who had been Dalai from 1879, when he was three, until he died in 1933.

Their first clue as to the whereabouts of the child came to light when the head of the embalmed lama's body turned. The corpse that had faced south was suddenly facing northeast.

Next a senior lama saw a vision of buildings and letters in the reflection of a sacred lake. These hints led them to a specific monastery in the Amdo region where monks helped them find the child.

And then they administered the final test used to reveal the veracity of a possible reincarnate: a group of objects, some belonging to the dead lama, some not, were given to the boy.

"This is mine, it's mine," he said as he selected only the relics that had belonged to the dead lama, ignoring the others. First prayer beads, then the dead leader's glasses.

Thirteen years later, in 1950, the Communist Party of China invaded Tibet and took control of the government. Nine years after that, the fourteenth Dalai Lama, still only twenty-four years old, fled his homeland to live in exile in India. Since then—more than fifty years later—the unresolved conflict had grown more violent. This latest incident had led to a spate of aggravated restlessness and brutality.

The action that had sparked this newest and tragic rebellion had occurred in Lhasa two weeks ago, when a three-year-old child went missing twenty-four hours after being identified as an incarnated lama.

Since then, there had been rioting in the streets of all of Tibet's cities, and heavy-handed and merciless police tactics had pushed the situation into a full-scale crisis more violent than any since the horrific protests and killings during the 2008 Olympics.

"This is the same thing that happened before, isn't it?" Cali asked.

"Yes, almost exactly."

More than twenty years before, days after a four-year-old Tibetan child was identified as the new Panchen Lama, the boy, along with his entire family, had disappeared.

For hundreds of years, the Panchen Lama helped to identify the next Dalai Lama. The Chinese government still officially claimed that boy was alive and well and was working as an engineer in Beijing. Unofficially, most people assumed that he'd been killed. Only a few held out hope that, one day, he'd resurface.

The two friends were quiet as they walked the last few blocks back to the Nanjing Arts Institute, where both were graduate students and teaching assistants.

At the entrance to the building, Xie kissed Cali good-bye on the cheek. "I'll see you tomorrow?"

She nodded.

He took her arm gently, speaking in a low and determined voice. "I know how upset you are, but please don't talk to anyone about what you saw. It's dangerous, and I want you to stay safe."

"I wish you were just a little bit brave."

There was so much he wanted to say. Of all the sacrifices required of him, none made him ache more than not being able to explain the truth to Cali.

"I need you to stay safe," he repeated.

four

Jac was shocked to see her brother standing in the doorway. It was a long trip from the Rue des Saints-Pères in Paris to a limestone mausoleum in a cemetery thirty miles outside of New York City.

"You frightened me," she said instead of telling him how happy she was he'd come.

"I'm sorry," Robbie said as he stepped inside. He was smiling at her in spite of her greeting.

Water dripped off the extravagant bunch of apple blossom branches he cradled in his left arm and streamed off the burl-handled umbrella that had once belonged to their grandfather. Despite the rain, he was wearing his signature handmade leather shoes. Her brother was always meticulously dressed but wore his clothes with a lack of concern. Robbie was comfortable with himself in a way that Jac had always envied. Too often she felt as if she wasn't living in her own skin.

Like Jac, Robbie had almond-shaped light green eyes, an oval face and wavy mahogany hair, but he wore his slicked back in a ponytail. In his left ear, an emerald stud sparkled, and raindrops glinted on the platinum rings he wore on nearly all of his fingers except his thumbs. When Robbie entered a room, something magical always happened. The light took notice. The air became redolent with new smells.

They never used to fight, but that had changed in the last few months, and she hadn't forgotten the argument they'd had on the phone three days ago—their most serious to date. She watched her brother, whose presence had filled up the small space. From the smile still on his lips, she knew he wasn't thinking about the fight any longer. He just looked quietly pleased to see her.

She waited for him to say more. But like their father, Robbie often preferred to communicate with gestures rather than words. It sometimes frustrated her as much as it had Audrey. Jac glanced over at the marble bench. The apparition was gone. Had Robbie chased Audrey away? She looked back at her brother.

Jac used to resent that of the two of them, she was merely handsome, while Robbie was beautiful. They had similar features, but his were too refined for a man, and hers, she felt, were slightly too coarse for a woman. Looking at him was like looking into a mysterious mirror and seeing another version of herself. Their androgyny, she thought, made them closer to each other than most brothers and sisters. That and their shared tragedy.

"I'm surprised you came," she finally said. Instead of being glad that Robbie was here now, she was resenting all the times he'd left her to do this alone. "Aren't you the one who always tells me that we shouldn't commemorate the anniversary of anyone's death? That you don't even believe Maman is really dead?"

"Oh, Jac, of course I believe she's dead. Of course I do. The mother we had is gone. But what I believe . . . what I know . . . is that her spirit isn't gone and never will be."

"It's a charming sentiment," she said, unable to keep the sarcasm out of her voice. "It must be comforting to have such a life-affirming belief system."

For a few seconds, he searched her eyes, trying to communicate something that she couldn't read. Then Robbie walked over to her, bent down, and gently kissed her on the forehead. "I thought I'd keep you company. It's always a sad day, isn't it?"

Jac closed her eyes. It was a relief to have her brother here. She took his hand and squeezed. It was hard to stay angry at Robbie for long.

"Are you all right?" he asked.

Robbie spoke to her in French, and Jac automatically responded in the same language. Both were bilingual—with an American mother and a French father—but she preferred English, and he, French. For better, but mostly for worse, she was her mother's daughter, and he was his father's son.

"Fine."

She'd never told him about hearing their mother's voice, though for most of her life she'd shared everything else with him. Despite being so different, they'd always been desperately connected, the way children of damaged parents can be.

Robbie tilted his head again, and Jac saw the doubt in his eyes. He didn't believe her, but she knew he wasn't going to press her. It wasn't her brother's style to push. He was the patient one. The calm one. The one who never argued.

Or at least he had been until recently.

Jac was fourteen and Robbie was eleven when Audrey died. The next year was the lost year, when her delusions had become even more serious and she'd been shuffled from doctor to doctor, first diagnosed as delusional by one, then as schizophrenic by another. Finally, she'd gone to a clinic in Switzerland that did help, and a year later, she emerged almost whole. After that, at fifteen, she'd come to live in America with her mother's sister and her husband, while Robbie had stayed in Paris with their father. But every summer, brother and sister each traveled to Grasse in the south of France and spent twelve weeks together at their grandmother's house, where their bonds were renewed.

Six months ago, their father had been declared incompetent—due to Alzheimer's disease—and the two of them had inherited the family business. They'd had no idea it was so close to bankruptcy. Robbie had been working on his own line of niche perfumes. Jac wasn't in France or part of the day-to-day business. Both were shocked at the state of the company's finances. They were unable to agree about what path to take, and too often lately, their transatlantic phone calls ended bitterly and without resolution. The critical problems plaguing the House of L'Etoile had driven them apart in a way the ocean between them never had.

"They're lovely." Jac nodded toward the apple blossom branches Robbie still held.

He looked over at the urn she'd already filled with the same flowers. "Doesn't look like there's any room left for them, though."

"That one is empty." She pointed behind him to a second urn.

She watched Robbie take in the rest of the space. As far as she knew, he'd never been here before. He looked at the life-size stone angel, the stained-glass windows and the marble wall with its inscriptions of names and dates carved in neat rows. Scanning them, he reached up and ran his fingers across the crevices and edges of the letters engraved on the middle row, three from the top. Their mother's name. The gesture tugged at Jac.

"When she was happy," he said, "there was no one more loving. No one more lovely." Then he turned back and smiled at his sister. The months of bickering by telephone melted in the face of his deep, soothing calm. Even before Robbie had become a student of Buddhism, he'd been contemplative and centered in a way she wasn't. She wanted nothing more than for the two of them to stop arguing and stay like this: together, remembering.

"Did you come to sign the papers?" she asked. "There's really no other solution. We need to make the sale."

Don't push him, baby.

The intrusion startled Jac, and she had to force herself not to turn toward the direction of her mother's voice. She'd thought Audrey was gone.

It was almost as if he was echoing their mother. "Don't, Jac. Not yet," Robbie said as he unwrapped his flowers. "We have lots of time to talk. Can we just be us for a while?"

But we haven't been us for a long time, she thought.

Like their father, when they were children, she and her brother dreamed of doing with fragrance what sculptors did with stone and painters did with pigment. To become poets of scent. Jac had given up the lofty goal when she saw how both her parents suffered for their artistic ambitions.

Their father had been consumed by the idea of creating one true, perfect scent that would capture the imagination. First his determination and then his frustration embittered him. They all suffered for it. Especially their mother. Audrey was a well-respected poet with demons so strong they left her too weak to fend off her husband's darkness. To escape him, she went jumping from one destructive affair to another, finally throwing her life away over one.

Your father and I might have given up. You might have given up—but not Robbie. He's never given up. He never will.

Jac felt the sting of the comment. Yes, her mother was right. Jac had abandoned the effort before she'd even started. And Robbie had persevered. He was determined to make up for their father's failures, their mother's suffering.

And the burden to save him from that folly was all hers.

An errant blossom was hanging off one of the branches he'd just placed, its white, pink-tinged petals a grayish lavender in the blue light. Jac picked it off, leaned forward, and inhaled its scent.

"How did a man who created complicated and sophisticated fragrances put up with a wife who favored such a sweet-smelling flower?" she asked. "There was an irony to that, wasn't there?"

"So much about our parents was ironic."

He hesitated. Took a breath. And then said, very softly—as if whispering would lessen the impact—"I saw Papa yesterday before I left for the airport."

Jac didn't respond.

Your father should have been a novelist. At least then, his imagination might have brought him some success. Instead his delusions drained the famous and venerable perfume House of L'Etoile almost to the point of extinction . . . Audrey laughed. The sound had a bitter cast to it that belied the beauty she'd been with her sparkling green eyes and shining gold-brown hair, with her heart-shaped lips and high, sharp cheekbones.

In these *mausoleum conversations,* as Jac had come to think of them, Audrey never called her husband by his name—never said Louis, or Louie, which was how the French pronounced it. It was always *your*

father, as if that distanced him further. As if his being on the other side
of the grave did not keep them far enough apart.

From Audrey, Jac had learned that when people hurt or disappoint
you, erase as much of them from your memory as you can. Wipe them
out. And she'd mastered the technique. She never wondered what had
happened to Griffin North. Never imagined what he was doing. Or
what he'd become.

Except aren't you doing that right now? Audrey teased. *Anyway,* she
added, *he wasn't good enough for you.*

Jac and Griffin had met in college. He was two years ahead of her.
When she went to graduate school, she was three hours away from the
school where he was getting his PhD. Every other weekend, he drove
to see her. But Jac wasn't a good driver. The idea of being alone in a car
terrified her. What if the shadows came back while she was behind the
wheel? So on alternate weekends, she took the bus to visit him. And,
hungry to spend every last second with him, she'd catch the latest bus
home—Sunday at seven. She always forgot to eat before she left, and by
the time she got back to her school, the cafeteria was closed.

One night, as she stepped onto the bus, Griffin thrust a brown paper
bag into her hand. Once seated, she opened it. Inside was a sandwich
wrapped in wax paper tied with a white ribbon she must have left at his
place. On it he'd written, "I didn't want you to be hungry because of me."

Her mother was wrong. Griffin was good enough for her. The problem was he didn't *think* he was. That's why he'd left.

Jac had carried the ribbon in her wallet until it started to fray. Then
she'd tucked it away in a jewelry box. She had it still.

Her mother's suicide had started Jac's education in loss. Griffin—a
young man who shared her love of mythology, smelled of ancient woods
and touched her as if she was something precious—had been her final
lesson.

Robbie had just said something, but Jac had missed it.

"I'm sorry. What?"

"I don't think the doctors are right about how little he can remember."

"Of course, you don't. You're Count *Tourjours Droit.*" Jac laughed.
She'd given him the nickname—Count *Always Right*—and it had

caught on with her parents and grandparents. "How could the doctors know what you know?"

Now Robbie laughed. As a kid, he changed rules and regulations so that he was never wrong. It was either endearing or infuriating, depending on the situation. When he was eight and she was eleven, she'd held an elaborate ceremony in the garden courtyard that separated the house from the perfume shop. Knighting him with an umbrella, she'd given him his nickname.

"Did our father know who you were this time?"

"He clearly knows I'm someone who cares about him." Each word was an effort laced with pain. "But I can't be sure he knows I'm his son."

Jac didn't want to hear this. The image of their father that Robbie was painting was going to haunt her for days, seeping under the wall she put up, through the cracks.

"Despite everything he's forgotten, he still can recite perfume formulas and remind me about the little secrets involved in mixing the different fragrances," her brother continued. "He doesn't remember how to read, but he knows exactly how many drops of rose absolute to mix with essence of vanilla. And when he talks about the formulas, he always says, 'Mix up one bottle especially for Jac.'" Robbie's smile was expansive. Her brother's kindness was his best attribute. But as much as she admired his ability to find some good in everyone, it annoyed her when it came to their father. He'd been a selfish man who'd caused all of them unbearable pain.

"Can we talk about something else?" Jac asked.

"We need to talk about him."

Jac shook her head. "Not now. Not here. It doesn't seem respectful."

"To our mother?" Robbie seemed perplexed.

"Yes. To our mother."

"Jac, she's not here listening to us."

"Thanks for explaining that. Go ahead, then. Finish what you wanted to tell me about our father. He doesn't know who you are but he remembers my name—"

"I need to talk to you about this."

She took a deep breath. "Okay, I'm sorry. Tell me."

"Sometimes, there's a fierce look in his eyes, like he's trying to get all his synapses firing at the same time. Using all his concentration to connect to a thought. And sometimes, for a moment, he does. But when he can't, he's overwhelmed by his failure. Jac, sometimes he cries." Robbie whispered the last words.

Jac was quiet. She couldn't imagine seeing her tough, demanding father weep. "I wish you didn't have to see that. I wish it wasn't so hard on you."

"I'm not talking about how it is for me. It's how it is for him that I want you to understand. Please come see him. Yours is the only name he still knows. Not mine. Not Claire's. 'Don't forget to make up a bottle of Rouge for Jac,' he'll say as I leave."

Robbie's smile was one of the saddest she'd ever seen.

"Forgiveness is the greatest gift anyone can offer, please come see him."

"When did those Buddhists teach you to preach, baby brother?" she said with a too-bright laugh that betrayed her when it caught in her throat. Jac wished she could make him happy. Wished everything he believed in was real and everything he hoped for could come true. That she could forgive their father. That there was an easy way out of their financial crisis. That there really was a book of ancient formulas for incenses and unguents used in the ancient Egyptian rituals and that it had been brought back from Egypt and hidden away somewhere on the family's property in Paris.

But reality was safer. And above all else, she had to keep Robbie safe. He was the only family she had left.

Jac glanced over at the angel of grief. "She looks as if all the years of missing people have weighed down her wings and they're too heavy to lift her up again."

Robbie came over to her, put his arm around her shoulders, and pulled her close. "An angel can always fly."

She inhaled the complicated cacophony of scents that clung to him. Cool air, rain, the apple blossoms, and more. "You smell," she said, wrinkling her nose, "of such wonderful things." She could at least give him this.

"They're my samples. What I've been working on. What I've been telling you about on the phone. I set up meetings. Bergdorf. Bendel. Barneys. We have relationships there."

"For our classic perfumes."

"They're interested in seeing what I have, Jac."

"Even if they are, the House of L'Etoile doesn't have the money to start up a new division."

"I'll find a backer."

She shook her head.

"I will," he insisted.

"There are a thousand niche perfumers not succeeding. Consumers aren't buying any of the new creations twice. And every day there is another report about ingredients being banned for environmental reasons."

"And in a few years, perfumers won't even be able to use alcohol because of global warming . . . I've heard every argument. There are always exceptions."

"You're wasting your time," Jac insisted. "The marketplace is over-crowded. If the House of L'Etoile was hot and chic right now, maybe, but we're not. We have a line of timeless perfumes. We can't afford to experiment with our reputation."

"No matter what I say, you're going to argue with me, aren't you? Can't you suspend your cynicism for just a little while? What if I have a solution here? What if we don't have to divest any of our classics?"

"Robbie, please. You have to sign the papers. It's the only chance we have of saving the company, of keeping the store and the house in Paris, of going on."

He walked around the angel, resting his hand on the back of her wings as if consoling her—or giving himself ballast. Jac had once seen a photograph of Oscar Wilde taken when he was just twenty-eight years old, Robbie's age now, wearing a fine velvet jacket and elegant shoes. A beautiful young man sitting on an opulent chair, surrounded by Persian rugs, holding a book, his head tilted and resting on his hand, looking out at the viewer with an expression of intimacy and promise.

Her brother was looking at her like that now.

"We owe the bank three million euros. We can't mortgage the build-ing on Rue de Saint-Pères. Our father already did that. We have to divest," she said.

"The House of L'Etoile belongs to us now. You and me. It's lasted intact for almost two hundred and fifty years. We can't break it apart. Just smell what I've been working on."

"You've spent the last six years in Grasse in a magical kingdom of lavender fields working on crystal vials of scent as if you lived a century ago. No matter how wonderful your new scents are, they won't raise the kind of money we owe. We have to sell Rouge and Noir. We'll still own over a dozen classics."

"Not without you even smelling what I've done, not without me trying to get orders and find a backer."

"We don't have the time."

"I have a plan. Please just trust me. Give me the week. Someone is going to fall in love with what I've made. The time for these scents is right. The world is aligned with essences like these."

"You're not being practical."

"You have no confidence."

"I'm a realist."

Robbie nodded toward the silent angel. "And that's what she's really mourning, Jac."

five

The studio was empty when Xie returned. And he was thankful for the quiet. He arranged his tools in front of him and went back to work on the painting he'd started that afternoon. All of his consciousness was concentrated in his fingers. He quieted his mind and let go of the tormenting, doubting thoughts. Xie withdrew into the sweep of the movement. He lived on the edge of the line of ink that seeped into the paper. Soon he stopped thinking, stopped hearing the sounds coming in through the open window or down the hall and was aware only of the gentle whoosh the brush made as it danced across the white paper.

The ancient art of calligraphy, unlike so many other traditions, had survived into the modern age, mostly because Mao Tse-tung had recognized that in a country with hundreds of different dialects, calligraphy—despite its elitist history—was an effective communications device worth adapting. The regime's appropriation of calligraphy as a communications tool took it out of its original high-art status and moved it into the realm of the ordinary.

Some artists imbued their work with rebellious overtones and opined with their brushes and inks. Xie didn't. His paintings weren't political expressions. He didn't shout with his calligraphy. But he did whisper. And there were those outside of China who had heard.

Xie's style broke away from the traditional with his use of seals. Typically, these carved blocks contained the characters of the artist's name and were used with red paint or cinnabar ink. He used the seals to add narrative to his work. Over the years, he'd cut hundreds of blocks, incising each with different illustrative elements: from naturalistic leaves, flowers, clouds and moons, to human forms, faces, hands, lips, eyes, arms and legs.

The young calligrapher's work was expressive, intricate and delicate. And with each painting, he risked his life. Because hidden somewhere in every seal's design was one tiny jagged line: a thunderbolt. His second signature.

A message to anyone who knew what to look for that he had not been killed; that he was still alive.

Despite Xie's efforts, in the midst of his meditative state, images of the burning monk broke his concentration. It was rare for him to lose control like this. Struggling to still the noise of his mind, Xie suppressed his awareness, swirled it into the dense black ink. Usually when he painted, he was free. Not today. Today the burden of the tragic violence was too heavy.

With so many artists sharing the studio, someone was always coming in or going out, so when the door opened and he heard two sets of footsteps, Xie didn't glance up. Not yet. Holding on to the last flourish of a curve, he stepped away only when he heard his name spoken and looked up with a feeling of dread. He'd recognized Lui Chung's voice. While he'd expected this meeting would take place sometime in the next week, he hadn't anticipated it would transpire tonight.

"Over a very good dinner, Professor Wu here"—Lui Chung nodded at his companion—"has been telling me wonderful things about your recent work." He came close, leaned over Xie's shoulder and looked down at the unfinished painting. "And I can see why."

Chung was always eating, chewing and swallowing, making little spitting noises. As usual, the sound of him masticating the candy in his mouth nauseated Xie.

Surprise visits from the baby-faced and pudgy Beijing official were never welcome, but this one was especially unsettling coming on the heels of the illegal footage Xie had just looked at on the internet. "Thank you," Xie murmured in a reserved, low voice, keeping his eyes down, being respectful, as he had been taught so long ago.

"Would you like one?" Chung asked as he held out the bag of confections wrapped in edible paper. "It's your favorite. Rice candy."

Xie took the awful sweet and put it on the taboret behind him. "I'll save it for later. I don't like to eat while I'm working."

When he was a child at the orphanage outside of Beijing, Xie had many teachers. They taught him math, history, geography, language, natural and social sciences, drawing and violin. But Lui Chung was a special kind of teacher. Starting when Xie was six years old, and continuing for six years, every day for two hours, Chung educated the boy away from the other students in what was called "moral training," which included ethics but stressed love of the motherland, the party, and the people. These sessions always began with Chung playing music for ten minutes and ended with the programmer praising Xie and offering him a rice candy as a reward for doing so well.

At that moment, reaching his hand into the bag, Xie would always feel a flush of fear. Somehow he imagined he was going to lose his fingers; that they were going to break off and Chung would take the bag away before Xie could get them out.

Om mani padme hum.

As wise a child as he was, when the sessions started, Xie didn't know the word for brainwashing. But he understood that Chung was trying to change how he thought, and the sessions scared him. So during the two-hour episodes, Xie learned how to split his consciousness. While he remained aware of the present—enough so that he could hear Chung spouting his propaganda and respond when necessary—he was able to use his mantra as a shield. As he repeated the phrase, a humming started deep inside him that emanated outward, pushing all the intrusions—noises, words, worries—away and keeping his inner core inviolate.

Om mani padme hum.

And in the process, he learned how to hold two separate consciousnesses at the same time.

"Will you have one?" Now Chung offered the bag of candies to Professor Wu.

"Thank you, yes," Xie's mentor said as he reached for a sweet. At eighty, Wu, the head of the calligraphy department, was as sprightly and vital as a man thirty years younger. His work, he professed, was what kept him healthy and satisfied. He often lectured his students about the spiritual and psychological benefits of calligraphy—of any art—about how it connects you to history and the continuum of the universe, how it bypasses politics even when it is political, and how it speaks directly to the best in man.

"Most delicious," Wu said, popping the delicacy in his mouth.

Chung dipped in and took another for himself.

With both men eating, it wasn't long before a sickly smell permeated the work area. Xie's impulse to gag was strong, but he controlled it.

"We're honored to have you visit the studio," Wu said respectfully to Chung.

Xie had been reluctant to tell Professor Wu about his past. Better to be silent than take risks. Xie had a karmic responsibility to fulfill. To draw attention to himself for any reason other than his prowess with the brush and ink could ruin his chances of accomplishing his goal. But Wu was perceptive. He was wise. He'd known the boy was hiding a terrible secret that weighed on him.

"Professor Wu also tells me that your work won the first prize in the graduate competition," Chung said, talking as he chewed. "Congratulations."

Xie nodded and again averted his gaze, as if humbled by the compliment. "Thank you."

"Do you still find your studies here at the art institute satisfying?"

Always the same questions. Always the same answers.

"Yes, I'm very satisfied here."

"Nature is a good subject to concentrate on," Chung said.

"I'm glad you are pleased." Xie had chosen his specialty precisely for its neutrality. No one ever was accused of subversive thinking by painting a mountain, a stream, or clouds. And the poetry that graced his work was ages old.

While artists were still encouraged to glorify the state, in the last decade socially critical artists had emerged and even flourished. The most extreme, who created sexually explicit art or overtly challenged government decisions, lived off the radar, but the more moderate were now accepted as part of China's cultural establishment and even held positions in universities. Despite the changes, Xie could ill afford suspicion, and he avoided politically charged messages.

Or so it appeared.

"And Professor Wu has also told me you are one of only four graduate students from this university whose paintings have been chosen to go on an exhibition tour in Europe. This is quite an honor. We are all very proud of you."

Xie intoned yet another thank-you.

Chung sighed. "That's all? Thank you?"

Xie knew his silence frustrated his old Beijing tutor, but it was hard to say the wrong thing if you said nothing at all. Or next to nothing. From the time he had arrived at the orphanage, he'd spoken little.

When Xie had first smelled the flames, he wondered why the monks had lit the sacrificial fires before dawn. But as much as he wanted to investigate, he didn't get up. The six-year-old, who then was called Dorjee, had been living in the Tsechen Damchos Ling monastery for a few months, learning the practice of *dzogchen*. At the heart of the ancient and direct stream of wisdom was discipline. Dorjee was engaged in a meditation. Nothing was supposed to disturb that.

But he couldn't block out the screams. Or the sounds of running feet.

"Dorjee, come with me." Suddenly Ribur Rinpoche was at the door. "Quickly. The monastery is on fire."

The hallway was thick with smoke that smelled of burning rubber. That was what their fuel smelled like. The blaze was consuming the yak chips. How would they stay warm though winter?

Outside, the Rinpoche settled Dorjee under a snow-capped tree and warned his young student to stay clear of the burning buildings. "You could get hurt. It's dangerous. You understand, don't you?"

Dorjee nodded.

"If you're afraid, use your mantra and engage in mindfulness."

It was the last thing the Rinpoche said to him before he ran back to join his fellow monks trying to save the sanctuary, the centuries-old *thanka* paintings, the holy relics and the rare scriptures.

Om mani padme hum.

Dorjee repeated the mantra again and again, but it wasn't working. The flames had eaten through the temple's roof and were reaching toward the sacred Mount Kailash. What was happening inside the monastery? Was the Rinpoche all right? Why hadn't he come outside again?

Then a hand clamped roughly over Dorjee's mouth. Fingers grabbed him around the waist. He tried to scream, but his lips moved against flesh. He tried to kick and get loose. The man's grip was too tight.

"We're saving you from the fire, you fool. Stop trying to fight us."

Chung and others believed that the fire, the immolation of his teachers, and the boy's ensuing "rescue"—which was how they all referred to the kidnapping—had traumatized him and made him almost a mute.

Xie, as they had renamed him when they hid him in the Beijing orphanage, knew better. But it was convenient to allow them to think so.

Chung had tried to encourage the boy to converse, telling him he'd never be able to find a wife or have children if he didn't speak. The threat didn't scare Xie; the Rinpoche in Tibet had explained to him that he wasn't fated to have a traditional life.

Now Chung's voice brought Xie back to the present. "Professor Wu has made a formal request that you be allowed to travel along with your fellow artists to Europe on the exhibition tour. That's why I'm here. To talk to you about that. Is it something you want to do?"

Xie didn't blink, didn't move a muscle in his face, and didn't look up from the drawing. He dipped his brush in the ink and then dragged it in a leisurely movement that created half a character. The spirit of the letter was like a bird flying high above the mountain. Xie knew that Chung was waiting for an answer. He couldn't hesitate too long.

When Chung became impatient, he could get angry, and Xie didn't want to invite his rage.

"If my government wants me to go, I'd be pleased."

Chung smiled. A ten-word sentence from Xie was like a lengthy ballad from anyone else. As if in celebration, he plucked a third rice candy from the red cellophane bag and popped it in his mouth. He offered another to Professor Wu and to Xie, in turn, who accepted it with another soft thank-you. And set it aside on the taboret.

In the orphanage, there were two types of children. One accepted Chung's candy and ate it on the spot, hungrily, desperately, not savoring it as much as absorbing it, trying to gain some comfort from the treat, from its specialness, from the break in the routine and the delight in the moment. The other group took their candy and carefully, as if it were made of glass, put it in the pockets of their smocks and saved it for later.

Some were clever, hoarding the candies and trading them for favors. Others just saved them for when they were alone, and used the candy almost like a memory tool to take them back to a time before the orphanage, when they had families and knew love.

Xie did none of these. When another of the children was especially sad, he would give him a piece from his cache. He got pleasure from knowing that for a few minutes, the little boy was a bit happier.

All he asked of the other children was that they promise not to tell the matron what he'd done. He was worried Chung would hear about his acts of kindness and suspect that the brainwashing wasn't working.

Wu believed if calligraphy was going to thrive as a modern art form, its young masters had to open themselves to new techniques and inter-pretations. Under his tutelage, students were trained not only in poetry, music and the brush and ink arts, but also in Western materials, colors and concepts. He encouraged them to be creative—to play with the shapes and structures of the characters they used. He encouraged them to be brave and break the rules.

But the worst rule he broke was the yearly conversation he had with Xie.

Before the professor accepted students into his program, he took them to a waterfall in an ancient park and asked them to create a spontaneous drawing expressing the mood of the sacred spot.

Wu studied how the prospective student interacted with nature, brush and ink and then, based on this one effort, made his final decision on whether or not to allow the young artist into his program.

When Xie had finished his waterfall test, Wu had complimented his work by inviting him to study with him. Xie had bowed his head and said he'd be honored.

Then Wu put his hand on the boy's shoulder. It was the first time anyone had touched him like that since his Rinpoche so long ago.

"I can see there's great suffering in your eyes. What happened to you, son?"

In halting, whispered phrases, as water rushed over primordial rocks, Xie, who had never said a word to any living being about what he'd experienced as a child, never alluded to his past or what he knew about himself, told his professor who he was.

Later he would wonder what had made him so confident that he could trust in the elderly man. Had he sensed a kindred spirit? Or been desperate to find someone who could help? Or was it simply the long-forgotten and comforting touch of someone who cared enough to reach out to him?

Once a year, Wu and Xie hiked out to the waterfall. And there, with the water's roar blanketing their words, they discussed Xie's options. Coming up with a plan. Slowly. Patiently.

"You mentioned a glass of wine before I go back to my hotel. Is that still possible?" Chung asked Wu.

Xie returned to his brush and ink. As usual, his "special" tutor was hungry. Hungry, and in a hurry, and slightly lazy—always on the lookout for a shortcut.

"Yes, if you could just take care of this first?" Wu handed Chung the document giving Xie permission to take the trip to England, Italy and then to France. Ten days of traveling with a dozen other Chinese artists.

Hungry, lazy, in a hurry. Would Chung read the document carefully?

Xie averted his eyes, afraid to watch, and focused on his painting, but his mind wasn't still. Was his old programmer going to note the dates? Write them down to take them back to Beijing and check them against some master document that kept track of the comings and goings of heads of states? Was this trip going to get caught up in inexhaustible bureaucratic red tape or be allowed?

Again Xie dipped the brush into the ink that was the color of a moonless sky and touched the point to the fine paper. He let his wrist and his fingers go where they wanted, let them soar across the page.

"Now, about that wine?" Chung said as he placed the document on the table.

Xie's eyes slid to inspect it.

The signature was sloppy. There was no grace to his letters, just as there was no grace to the man. But it was signed.

Six

Robbie approached the Queen Anne–style villa with its gables, pitted stone gargoyles, and scrolled wrought-iron railing. He was pleased that the Manhattan developers—always tearing down the old to make way for something newer and bigger and taller—seemed to have skipped over this small section of the West Side. The elaborate details on these nineteenth-century buildings made him feel at home, as if he were back in Paris.

In the early evening shadows, the Phoenix Foundation took on an almost mystical appearance. As if all the reincarnation investigation that went on inside—examinations into the synchronicity and parallels of lives lived and lost and found again, and the complicated philosophical, religious and scientific issues raised because of them—had given the building a rich patina.

Even though his sister had known Dr. Malachai Samuels, the foundation's codirector, since she was a teenager and Robbie had been the one to introduce Malachai to Griffin North, he'd never been here before. Now, with a thrill of excitement, he climbed up the six stone steps, each one bringing him closer to deciphering what he'd found in Paris among his father's papers.

When Robbie had started searching for the formulas for Rouge and

Noir that his sister had asked for, he'd been horrified at the mess he'd discovered. The disease that had confused his father's mind seemed to have manifested as physical chaos in the workshop. Every cabinet and drawer had been emptied onto the floor. Every book on every shelf had been removed. Stacked in piles. All the oils and essences and absolutes had been left open to evaporate. Hundreds of thousands of euros' worth of supplies, ruined. Slowly and methodically, Robbie had tried to sort through the detritus of—how many years? No one was quite sure how long his father had really been ill. Louis had always been eccentric; the line from there to dementia was a blurry one.

And then Robbie came across a cache of broken pottery scattered in the bottom of a carton. At first he thought the turquoise, coral and black designs on the glazed white background were abstract. But when he found two shards that fit together, he realized they were hieroglyphics. Bending over his puzzle, trying to fit more pieces together, he'd detected a very faint scent. Only a trace. But that trace was everything to him. He needed his sister to smell it. Jac had the most attuned nose of them all. When they were children, their father would test them on combinations of essences and absolutes on linen squares. Robbie was right only half the time. Jac never got one wrong. With study, he improved, but he'd never have the innate ability she did. Their father said that Robbie had the faith and Jac had the nose—and as long as they worked together, the House of L'Etoile would be safe for yet another generation. Except they weren't working together, and the house was in danger.

But at least, now, finally, he was in New York. And Robbie was sure the time was right for his Zen approach. For tranquil, spartan scents based on natural accords. Each orchestrated to evoke a sense of spirituality, of meditation, of connectiveness. Someone was going to fall in love with his new perfumes.

And maybe the time was also right for him to be the member of his family to discover a very old scent that could matter even more to the House of L'Etoile.

Standing in front of the large wooden door, Robbie inspected the bas-relief of a large bird rising out of a fire, a sword in its talons. There was a glyph on one of the pottery shards depicting a similar bird. Robbie inspected the mythical image. Tempted to pull the photographs out of his briefcase and compare the two phoenixes right away, he resisted and instead reached out and rang the doorbell.

A few seconds later, he heard a responding buzz and pulled open the door. On the other side, he found himself back in time. The décor was nineteenth century. A Tiffany chandelier cast soft green and blue reflections on the foyer's polished black-and-white marble floor. A potted palm with elongated, leafy fronds sat beside a carved giltwood table.

"Can I help you?" A receptionist beckoned him forward.

"I have a meeting with Griffin North."

"Yes—Mr. L'Etoile. He'll be out in a minute."

While he waited, Robbie admired more of the décor. He'd guessed the ornate moldings that capped the high ceilings and framed the autumnal colored Art Nouveau wallpaper were originals—though in America you could never be sure. His family's *maison* in Paris dated back to the mid-eighteenth century. One shouldn't tear down the past to make way for the future. That's how lessons were lost. The art of keeping a civilization alive, like the art of making perfume, was in the blending.

"Robbie. It's so good to see you," Griffin said, striding to greet him.

The two men embraced, French style, kissing each other on both cheeks.

The first summer that Jac and Griffin were together, he'd come with her to their grandmother's house in Grasse. Robbie, who was thirteen at the time, had been in awe of the nineteen-year-old American who knew so much about the archaeological history of the area. The three of them hiked to dozens of ancient Roman sites, exploring the ruins and remnants of the past. Through the legends that Griffin recounted about the twelfth- and thirteenth-century Cathars who'd lived in those hills until being exterminated during the Inquisition, the younger boy had first discovered the idea of reincarnation. This, in time, would lead him to Buddhism and change his life.

Robbie inspected his friend. The hair that fell in waves across Griffin's face was still thick but shot through with silver, and there were laugh lines in the corners of his mouth, but the explorer's gray-blue eyes were as inquisitive as ever.

The Lama Yeshe, with whom Robbie studied Buddhism, had once said that self-confidence is not a feeling of superiority but of independence. Griffin had always seemed intelligent without being condescending and self-confident without being arrogant.

Robbie knew it was because nothing had come easily for his friend. When Griffin was a high school junior, his father, an inveterate gambler, disappeared for the last time. All he left behind were bills and a second mortgage his wife's job couldn't cover. Griffin worked his way through college and then grad school to become an archaeologist. His grief hardened into determination, his loneliness into energy. Every discovery, every new idea separated him further from his father's fate.

"It's been way too long," Griffin said. He led his friend down a hallway lit by stained-glass wall sconces. "At least six years, I think."

"Nine years. You need to visit Paris more often."

"There's no doubt about that. I work too much."

"Too much brain at the expense of the soul?"

Robbie worried that was his sister's problem, too. When he looked at his fellow students of *zazen,* or sitting meditation, and the lamas he knew, they seemed to be able to acknowledge the world's deficiencies and sufferings but still hold on to their younger selves' sense of delight. Fatigue didn't affect you quite the same way when you lived mindfully.

"I'm dealing with much more practical problems. Private school costs a fortune. Not to mention divorce lawyers."

"Divorce?" Robbie put his arm out and stopped Griffin. They were standing in a pool of warm light, and he could see sadness in his friend's eyes. "So then it *is* your soul. I'm so sorry. Are you sure?"

"No, as a matter of fact, we're not. We got pretty deep into it legally, but we were both too upset about our daughter and what it was doing to her, so we decided to give it a few months more before signing the papers. There's no acrimony. There's just stasis. While I'm here, I'm living downstairs in the studio apartment we used to rent out."

"When do you go back to the dig in Egypt?"

"Not till the fall."

Since getting his degree, Griffin had been working at a dig 186 kilometers west of Alexandria, searching for Cleopatra's and Marc Antony's tombs. He'd also published a book, and he taught at New York University each fall. Because of the separation, he'd decided to delay his return to Egypt and for the next few months was working at the Phoenix Foundation's library, researching the origins of reincarnation theory in ancient Greece.

While Egyptians believed in the afterlife, they didn't accept that the dead returned to earth. And yet hieroglyphics found at the site outside of Alexandria suggested the Greeks' notion of soul transmigration had taken hold in Egypt during the Ptolemaic period. Griffin was trying to chart how the philosophy might have developed and affected Egyptian religious practices.

"So for now, you and Therese are closer by not being as close?"

Robbie's question made Griffin frown. "Well, aren't you the prescient psychologist."

"I hope you find the right solution." Robbie had no advice to offer. His own relationships were anything but conventional. His partners—both men and women—always started out as, and settled back into, friendships. He never left anyone. Even if his passion burned out, his love never did. Nurturing those he cared about, he always kept them close.

Only one liaison—with a woman he'd met on a retreat—haunted him. The only lover he'd lost.

Griffin stopped in front of a door on the right. "Come in."

Robbie took in the overcrowded room. Every corner, shelf and tabletop gleamed with gold and silver, bronze and copper, soft lights and shining crystals.

"What is this, Ali Baba's cave?"

"Close. This is the Talmage Cabinet of Curiosities. My favorite room in the institute. Trevor Talmage founded the Phoenix Club in 1847 along with Henry David Thoreau, Walt Whitman, Frederick Law Olmsted and other well-known transcendentalists. His original mission—the search for knowledge and enlightenment—led to his starting this collection. I've appropriated it as my office while I'm working here." He gestured to a desk that was covered with stacks of books and a laptop.

"The library is huge but subterranean and too sterile for me, so I bring as much of my research up here as I can," Griffin said. "Let me show you some of the highlights."

The room was paneled in walnut veneer, like the library in his own home in Paris. Exquisitely crafted glass cabinets lined the walls. Robbie glanced into one vitrine that held silver and gold chalices. Each was in the shape of a human face studded with all-too-realistic glass eyes. Another case housed a gilded birdcage with a bronze tree, complete with turquoise, onyx, malachite and amethyst birds perched on jade leaves. So true to life, it seemed at any minute they might take flight. A third was crammed with human and monkey skulls, bird and rodent skeletons, preserved lizards and snakes. A fourth held nothing but eggs: from the smallest sky-blue robin eggs to giant ostrich and emu eggs.

"I've become fascinated with these *wunderkammers*," Griffin said. "Cabinets of curiosities first came into fashion in the seventeenth century, when people were obsessed with the theme of the inevitability of death and the impermanence of life. Collecting was rebellion. Objects like these proved permanence. Two hundred years later, reincarnationists like Talmage and the other members of the Phoenix Club saw them as examples of the endless and repeating cycle of life and death." Griffin pointed to a cabinet in the corner of the room. "Come look."

When he got closer, Robbie recognized that it was made of amber, a hardened resin that had oozed from the bark of trees millions of years ago. A highly coveted material, it glowed like a slow-burning fire.

"It's magical," Griffin said. One by one, he opened the small, perfectly crafted drawers revealing a priceless collection of amber pieces, insects and amphibians held hostage for all time. They seemed still alive—just about to move—from the smallest bug to a large spider poised as if waiting for an insect to fall into its web.

"Now for the pièce de résistance," Griffin said as he opened the bottom drawer. Each of the dozen compartments, lined in chocolate velvet, had a depression in its center. Nestled within every hollow except the last was a crystal flacon decorated with an amber-and-silver top. Each contained a lake of viscous liquid. Perfume thickened by more than a hundred years.

"Can I smell?"

"Go ahead."

Robbie lifted out the first, unscrewed it and sniffed. The scent was basic and primordial. Rich with frankincense—he sniffed again—and borage, storax and myrrh.

For a moment, he couldn't catch his breath. The scent was almost agonizing. "What do you know about these?"

"They were an experiment funded by the founders of the Phoenix Club, who were on a constant search for fabled lost memory tools. One was supposed to be a fragrance that helped you enter a deep meditative state."

"So you could remember your past lives?"

"That was their hope, yes."

"Like our family legend."

"What?" Griffin asked.

"Don't you remember? One of my ancestors supposedly found an Egyptian 'soul-mate' perfume in Egypt. And a book of formulas—"

"From Cleopatra's fragrance factory. Yes, I remember now. Your grandmother told me about it."

"She loved the legend." Robbie stopped to inhale the next sample. "You know these are all slightly different formulations of the same scent?"

"Is that meaningful?" Griffin asked.

"I don't have any idea."

"Are you getting bombarded by memories?"

"Not from a past life, but these are all familiar scents to me—essentials that go back as far as recorded fragrance history in ancient Greece, Egypt and India. All of them remain major popular ingredients today." Robbie inspected the flacon, turning it in his hand, peering closely at the engraved markings. "Do you know where these bottles came from?"

"According to Malachai, the Phoenix Club commissioned a French perfumer to work on the formula in the 1800s."

"The designs certainly fit French perfume bottles of that era." Robbie removed the one he was holding up to the light. Turning it slowly, he examined the facets until he finally found something. Then he checked the next flacon. And the one after that.

"No one could convince me this is mere coincidence," he said as he handed one to Griffin, pointing to an area near the bottom. "Do you see that?"

"Those scratches? Wait." Griffin pulled his reading glasses down off the top of his head, put them on and peered closer. "I see it but can't make it out. Let me get a stronger—"

"No, I know what it is. It's a maker's mark—hard to read unless you're already familiar with it. Back then perfumers had different flacons made by glassmakers. A customer would pick out the one they preferred and have it filled with the fragrance they chose." Robbie touched the silver-and-amber top.

"You recognize the mark, don't you?" Griffin asked.

"I certainly do. It's an *L* and *E* inside of a crescent moon. The numbers underneath are the date: 1831. It's my family mark."

"The House of L'Etoile? Your family's firm? That's impossible!" Griffin shook his head and laughed. "And to think there are people who doubt synchronicity and the collective unconscious."

"You're going to be even more astonished after you see what I brought to show you." Robbie opened his briefcase, pulled out the file of photos of the pottery shards he'd found in his father's mess, and handed them to Griffin.

After examining them, Griffin handed the photos back to Robbie. "It looks like late-period Egyptian, but to be sure, I'd really need to see the actual objects. Pieces of pottery aren't worth much, though. Only a few thousand dollars. Maybe ten, depending on what the inscription says." Griffin knew about the House of L'Etoile's financial problems. "I'm sorry."

Robbie shook his head. "*Pas de probleme.* I didn't imagine these were worth enough to solve the crisis we are having. I told a friend of mine who is a curator at Christie's about them, and she said pretty much what you said. If they were genuine, they'd be an interesting artifact, but pottery shards are not very valuable."

"Then why do you want me to look at them?"

"I want you to help me translate them."

"They're probably just inscribed with a prayer for the dead."

"I'd like to make sure."

"Why's that?"

"I found them in the workshop. And I'm sure they have something do with that soul-mate scent I mentioned."

"In which case they could have some connection to the fragrance in these crystal bottles? Do you actually think you've found some sort of ancient memory tool, Robbie?"

"Even though I believe that everything, no matter how trivial it is, is connected to everything else and that there are no coincidences in life . . . something like this . . . it seems impossible, doesn't it?"

Seven

Warned not to be late, Tom Huang hurried across the street while scanning the long block for number eighteen. The teahouse was in the section of Paris they called *Quartier Chinois,* but little about the area was as appealing as the appellation. Unlike the narrow streets and charming ambiance of old Paris, the thirteenth arrondissement's Chinatown was overpopulated and overcrowded with skyscrapers and supermarkets. There were none of the chic cafés, charming florists, iconic boutiques and authentic bakeries that made so much of the city attractive. This wasn't Huang's Paris, and whenever he visited here, he felt oppressed. Especially during the day, when every ugly nuance of the blocks of buildings stood out in high detail.

At least now, at night, the blazing neon signs advertising everything from McDonald's to traditional French fare offered some visual excitement that matched his mood. A clandestine meeting with the head of the Chinese underworld in Paris was not, even for Huang, a regular occurrence. But yesterday, after getting word through his spies that a curator at Christie's had inspected fragments of an object purported to be a reincarnation memory aid, Huang had to act.

He finally found the restaurant squeezed in between a bank and a laundry. The small, shabby place was just one room, crammed with yellowed Formica tabletops and cracked red leather seats. The floor was a checkerboard of linoleum, the black and white tiles stained and faded. Despite the late hour, more than half the tables were filled with groups of Chinese men, drinking tea and talking—not French but a cacophony of different Chinese dialects. Hundreds of pieces of calligraphy—black characters with occasional touches of red—hung on the walls, and the glass covering them was smudged with years of restaurant grease.

Despite the visible signs of neglect, Huang felt reassured by the familiar incense of seeping tea, brewed flowers and spices and roasted rice and toasted barley. Huang circumnavigated the tables to the far-right corner, where a wizened man, bald and slightly hunched over, sat with his back to the wall. He was ordinary looking, wearing ordinary clothes. Yet this was the man who oversaw a network of tens of thousands of members, a sworn brotherhood engaged in a wide range of criminal activity specializing in smuggling, VAT fraud, drug trafficking, and more.

Huang paused as the waiter set down a glazed teapot. He'd been instructed to act as if he and the man were already acquainted, so he nodded his head, said hello, pulled out a chair, and sat down. On the table in front of him were thirteen white porcelain teacups arranged in a rectangle with one cup in the middle.

The ritual Huang was about to engage in was over three thousand years old and had been abandoned by most *Hak Sh'e Wui* bosses, but the head of this local black society—only Caucasians called them Triads— still engaged in the old customs. The ancient ceremony had been a way to test an unknown visitor and ascertain if he was a member of the secret society or not. It made sense in the days when there was no internet, telephone, or even a dependable mail system, but now it was just another of Gu Zhen's idiosyncrasies.

Huang reached for the lone cup in the middle—in the Triad's language telling the boss he was one of them, literally an insider.

Gu Zhen poured tea for himself and then for his guest. Huang watched, riveted by Zhen's deliberately slow, teasing movement as he put the teapot back down. If he placed the spout facing Huang, it would mean the meeting was over, that he'd considered his request, didn't trust him or was upset with him and wouldn't give Huang his help or his blessing.

The spout was facing away from him. This meant his next step was to drain his cup and set it back on the table bottom up to send a signal that he wanted to discuss something. He did so.

Gu Zhen nodded. "I can help you," he whispered in a low rasp. "But it will be expensive. We prefer not to deal outside of our regular businesses."

"Money's not an object. Our government doesn't want this toy to get into the wrong hands."

The old man raised his gray eyebrows. "Toy?" He said the word as if he tasted it and then took a sip of his tea.

Huang had been warned that it was in his best interest to respect the elder, engage in the tea drinking ceremony, and not exhibit any sign of impatience if he wanted to get the help he sorely needed to accomplish this mission. So here he remained, sipping tea from a small, stained porcelain cup, twenty minutes, eight kilometers and a world away from his elegant office in the Ministry for Foreign Affairs of the People's Republic of China on Avenue George V.

"So what can you tell me about this toy, as you call it?" Gu Zhen asked.

"It's supposed to be some kind of ancient tool to help people remember their past lives."

"Which you think is a joke?"

"What I think isn't important. The way we're fighting this war, we're not making headway. We have a situation with no end in sight. Buddhists are not giving up. The world is still on the side of the exiled Tibetans, even if most governments are afraid of us. We don't want this unrest. We don't want any more monks becoming martyrs by setting themselves on fire. The last thing we need is a rumor that there is a way to finally prove reincarnation." Huang had heard of other portals that supposedly helped people connect with past lives. An ancient flute in Vienna. A cache of stones in Rome. The Chinese had been unable to get their hands on any of them. But according to information that came from his undercover connection in the Buddhist community, this one was here in Paris.

"If it were to get into the hands of the religious zealots, it would give them fuel. They broke the law two weeks ago. They claimed they found a reincarnated lama in Lhasa. Something expressly forbidden." Huang spat out the words. "Every time they stage another so-called *peaceful* protest, they know we're going to step in. Then the fighting starts all over again, and more monks martyr themselves. That brings the media. And it turns into an international circus. The Tibetans know that. That wolf in monk's robes knows it. Two hundred people were killed in the last two weeks. And we all have the blood on our hands."

"Who has this tool?" Gu Zhen asked. "And do you care what happens to him?"

Eight

"In the middle of the nineteenth century one of my ancestors—along with some other members of the Phoenix Club—funded a project. Its goal was to identify a scent to help people remember their past lives," Dr. Malachai Samuels said. Then, with a flourish, he handed Jac a deeply faceted crystal flacon, empty save for a quarter inch of viscous amber perfume.

As she took it, sunlight coming through the French doors leading to the courtyard set it aglow. Fiery sparks leapt onto the ceiling. Rainbows of refracted light danced.

When she was a little girl and her mother wanted to work on her poetry and the nanny was off or busy with Robbie, Audrey would sometimes take Jac down to the workshop.

Sometimes the doors to the garden were open. "The breeze clears out all my mistakes," her father always said. And it did. On those days, Jac wouldn't smell any perfume at all—just grass and cypress, along with whatever was in bloom: roses or hyacinth or peonies.

Louis would put cushions on the floor for her and then give Jac the carton filled with crystal bottles that had lost their stoppers and stoppers that had lost their bottles.

It was one of her favorite games.

Jac would position the glass and draw on the ceiling with the reflections.

"My light painter," her father would say with delight and applaud her efforts.

That was one of the good memories of being with him, there in his workshop on the days when the sun and the breeze kept the strangers and their shadows away.

"Open it," Malachai said, bringing her back to the present. "Smell it. I want to know what you think."

The heavy silver cap studded with pieces of amber unscrewed easily. Jac bent her head and sniffed the mixture. The scent was ordinary. Frankincense and myrrh. Storax. It smelled like it looked—flat, lacking in luminosity and life.

"Do you know exactly how old this is?" she asked.

"According to the correspondence I found, it dates back to the 1830s."

"And do you know who created it?"

"The Phoenix Club commissioned a perfume workshop in France to create the scent . . ."

She looked away from the bottle and back up at him. She guessed what he was about to tell her.

"The perfumer was the House of L'Etoile?"

He nodded.

"Robbie said I'd be surprised."

"I hope delightfully so."

"What an amazing coincidence." As soon as she said it, she knew he was going to correct her.

"Synchronicity is not a coincidence," said Malachai. "It is the governing dynamic that underlies all human experience throughout history. Concurrent events that seem to be coincidental often later turn out to be related."

Jac waited for the lecture to conclude. "Is there a maker's mark?" she asked.

Malachai proffered a magnifying glass. "It's down here." He pointed. "Until last week, I always thought that was the jeweler's mark. Which I know now is why my research never generated results. It hadn't occurred to me that the perfumer would have stamped it. Or that I'd have such a strong connection to the family of perfumers all these centuries later."

He smiled, which for him meant his mouth moved the right way, but his eyes never reflected any of the emotions associated with smiling. You never sensed his pleasure or humor or kindness. He wore expressions like masks. But rather than make her feel uncomfortable, this made Jac feel safer and more grounded when she was around him.

It wasn't his heart but his brain that had helped bring her back from the precipice of insanity sixteen years before.

Jac's illness had reached its fevered pitch after her mother died. Nothing the battalion of doctors prescribed helped banish the delusions. The pills exhausted her and numbed her mind. The frightening machine that blasted her with electricity left her nauseated and confused. After six miserable months of all the accepted treatments, her grandmother stepped in and flew Jac to Zurich to the controversial Blixer Rath clinic.

This "last resort," as her father had called it, was run by two disciples of Carl Jung who believed that curing whatever psychological disease Jac suffered had to begin with healing of the soul. Like his mentor, Rath believed that the psyche required mythic and spiritual exploration, along with low-dose medications only if completely necessary.

The traditional medical community was openly hostile to this holistic, soul-centered approach. During her nine months in the clinic, Jac took no drugs. Instead, she was exposed to in-depth analytic therapy designed to strengthen her own healing abilities. In order to understand the symbolism of her dreams and drawings done after deep meditative sessions—in order to translate her symptoms and recognize any possible synchronistic events in her life that might have a deeper meaning—Jac had to learn the universal language of the soul, as Jung called mythology. And the man who taught her that language and spoke it with her was Dr. Malachai Samuels.

On leave from his practice at the Phoenix Foundation, Malachai was at Blixer Rath as a Jungian therapist, not a reincarnationist. He never talked to any of his patients about possible past-life episodes. Only years later, reading a magazine article about Malachai, Jac realized he'd been at the clinic investigating his theory that a high percentage of schizophrenics were misdiagnosed and suffering from past-life memory crises.

"Can you tell the date from the mark?" Malachai asked. He peered over her shoulder while she examined the engraving.

"No. I don't know as much about the history of these things as I should."

Malachai shrugged. "That's entirely all right. I didn't ask you here to talk about the past, Jac. I want you to help me find it."

The combination of the intensity of his gaze and his mellifluous voice was mesmerizing. He commanded her full attention. And offered back his own. She'd never known him to be distracted when he was talking to her. That was one of her first memories of him at Blixer Rath. She arrived there a frightened, malnourished teenager, scared of the shadows that haunted her awake and asleep. She couldn't meet his eyes for more than a few seconds at a time. But when she did, he was always there, present, in her moment. He never once had looked away from her when they conversed. Not then. Not now.

In her therapy sessions in Zurich, and whenever she visited in the intervening years, she thought of him as a wizard who managed to suspend time. Here in his library, with its rare wood paneling, rich oriental carpet, and Tiffany glass lamps, it might be New York City a hundred years ago. It wasn't just his surroundings. Malachai dressed and spoke formally, in a classic style that was neither dated nor modern. Today's navy suit, carefully knotted silk tie and the monogram on his crisp white shirt suggested the wardrobe of a gentleman of an earlier time.

"Jac, let me build a perfume workshop for you here at the foundation. State of the art. Your show is on hiatus for the summer, isn't it? Work here and create the fragrance your ancestors commenced working on but never finished. If you succeed, I'll be able to pay you enough to secure the future of the House of L'Etoile."

"Robbie told you about our financial problems?"

Jac's grandmother had taught her never to discuss money outside of the family—not even with someone who mattered to her as much as Malachai—and it embarrassed her to do so now. She wished her brother's email had contained more details about his meeting with the doctor.

"Yes, but I'd already read about it in the papers."

Jac returned her attention to the crystal flask she was still holding and once more sniffed at the odd fragrance. She was astonished. Not by Malachai's offer itself but by the faith he'd exhibited by making it.

"You'd go to all that expense to explore a fantasy?"

"You know as well as anyone that I don't believe reincarnation is a fantasy."

In the years since Blixer Rath, she had learned a lot about Malachai's foundation and knew that he worked with thousands of children who remembered their past incarnations. He and his aunt, the other codirector, had documented the children's journeys and presented remarkable proof of the lives they discovered in their regressions.

"Yes, but you operate as trained psychologists seriously searching for psychic DNA. Your investigations are carried out under strict and rigorous circumstances. You've fought to keep your work free of populist faddism. How does that track with something as fantastic as a perfume to help people remember their past lives?"

"Reincarnation is a fact," replied Malachai. "A fact of life. Of death. And just as I know reincarnation is real, I know there are real tools that can aid in recovering past-life memories. I told you, didn't I, that I was present when one of them caused a mass regression? Hundreds of people, all hypnotized at the same time, experiencing past-life memories. An astonishing moment. As close as we've ever gotten to proving reincarnation."

"When you were shot? Yes, but you didn't tell me—"

"I'm sure they exist," he interrupted. "Aids. Tools, Jac . . ."

She'd never heard him so wistful. "Some of them are lost," he continued, "some destroyed . . . But there are others still waiting to be discovered . . . They might not have been used since ancient days, but they exist. I know they do."

His dark eyes gleamed. His lips parted. There was something akin to sexual longing on the therapist's face.

He lusts after this information.

Jac crossed her arms over her chest. She'd known Malachai a long time. He was always in control. Unemotional. Reserved. Never this intense.

But, then, his life had become more intense in the past few years. Twice he'd been a suspect in different criminal cases involving stolen ancient artifacts, and he'd been referred to as a person of interest in a third. Because of Malachai, the Phoenix Foundation had been in the news more in the past few years than in the past few decades combined. Were these artifacts the memory tools he was talking about?

"You and your aunt have gained so much respect over the years from the scientific community for how careful you are with your research," said Jac. "If you seriously pursue a perfume because you think it will help people remember their past lives, you'll be putting the institute's reputation at risk. And yours."

He leaned back in his chair, and the expression on his face relaxed. He was once again the esteemed therapist in his well-appointed office. Confident, erudite and charismatic.

"In ancient times, priests burned incense because they believed souls traveled to the afterlife on the swirls of smoke. Mystics sniffed incense to enter into altered states so they could visit alternative dimensions. Certain cultures use scented oils to open the third eye so they can experience psychic perception otherwise unavailable to us."

"I know the different ways fragrance has been used."

"Then surely you can understand why I believe fragrance might aid us in accessing our past lives."

"Even if I wanted to, I can't help you. I'm not a perfumer, Malachai. I'm a mythologist. Why not offer Robbie the job? He believes in the things you do."

"Robbie said that as good as he is, his nose is mediocre compared to yours. That you'll be able to take this"—he held up the crystal flacon—"and intuitively know how to build out the fragrance from this base."

Once, a lifetime ago it seemed, she'd wanted to be a perfumer. But that idea had died with her mother. Jac had an aversion to the idea of ever sitting down at a perfumer's organ again.

Her grandfather had always said that she was the culmination of centuries of great perfumers—that she, not her father and not her brother, was destined to be one of the great noses. Robbie believed it too and sometimes admonished her that that she wasn't doing the work she was born to do. He wondered why she'd turned her back on becoming the artist she was capable of being.

"My brother's wrong about me, about my ability."

"He seemed very certain," Malachai said, and then added an aside: "I'm glad the two of you have remained so close. You have, haven't you?"

She thought she heard something mournful in his voice. Or maybe it was her own projection because she and Robbie had been at odds these past few months, and she missed their easy camaraderie. Jac felt the pain of letting Robbie down. She hadn't been able to conceive of a plan to solve the House of L'Etoile's financial crisis without irrevocably disrupting the company.

Malachai was watching her. Waiting for a response.

"Yes, we're still close."

Sadness lurked in Malachai's typically inscrutable brown eyes. What about this conversation was affecting him so much that he was letting his guard down? He'd never shown her this side of him. She'd never seen him in any kind of emotional distress. What was it? She knew he was unmarried and without children, but did he have a sibling? Was he estranged from a brother or sister? Or, worse, did he have a sibling who was ill or had died?

For someone who'd been so crucial in her life for so long, Malachai had kept Jac woefully ignorant about his personal life. He'd paid attention to and kept up with her career, much the way she imagined a proud father might. But like many fathers, he shared little about himself other than news of his work.

Malachai reached into his jacket pocket, pulled out a deck of playing cards, and began to shuffle. Jac found the slapping sound familiar and annoying.

"I'm not nervous," Jac said.

She knew firsthand that when he worked with young patients, he used tricks to relax them.

He laughed. "Of course not, dear. Just a habit." He held the deck out to her. "But please, indulge me."

Jac took a card, noting the elaborately colored fleur-de-lis pattern and fine gilt edges. He had a huge collection. All antiques.

"These are beautiful."

"From the court of Marie Antoinette. I think the most beautiful cards I have in my collection are from France."

Jac shivered. It came from deep inside her, emanated out to the tips of her fingers, and raised the hair on the nape of her neck. She looked around for a reason for the sudden chill. The two windows on either side of Malachai's desk were open.

"Are you cold?" he asked. His lips were lifted in a curious smile, as if he knew something about how she was feeling that she didn't.

She shook her head. "It must have been the breeze."

"Of course," he said, but he sounded as if he didn't believe her. "Would you like me to close the windows?"

"No, it's fine." She glanced into the small courtyard with its informal garden. The cherry, crabapple and dogwood trees were in bloom, and she enjoyed their faint, flowery scent. Her home in Paris featured a much larger courtyard that had functioned as a magical playground for her and her brother, an herb garden for the cook, and a natural laboratory for generations of perfumers who grew many of their own exotics.

"You still have no curiosity about whether or not you've had any past-life memories?" Malachai asked, leaning slightly forward, acknowledging the intimacy of the question.

"Still none." Her answer came quickly. Even a little coldly. This was one area where she felt he sometimes overstepped his bounds. She hoped he wasn't going to push her again. Jac wasn't interested in the debate. She had enough of it with Robbie, who was a great believer. Nothing about the subject interested her.

"So if I were to find one of these memory tools, you wouldn't be curious to test it out?"

"I respect you and what you do," she said evenly. "I know the children who come to you are terribly unhappy and that you help them, and I'm proud that you can do that. Isn't that enough? Do you need more than that from me?"

"Can I tempt you with the mythology of the memory tools?"

She wanted to object, but he'd mentioned the one subject that she couldn't resist.

"It is believed that four to six thousand years ago, in the Indus Valley, mystics created meditation tools to help people go into deep states of relaxation during which they would have access to past-life memories." Malachai's voice lulled her, as it had so long ago, and she settled into the story.

"There were twelve tools—twelve being a mystical number that we see repeated all through various religions and in nature. Twelve objects to help pull memories through the membrane of time. I think, and other experts agree, that it's quite possible two of these tools have been found in the past few years. The first was a cache of precious stones, and the second was an ancient flute made of human bone. Depending on what newspaper you read, what happened to those tools differs, but one thing I can assure you: both have been lost to research, and there's nothing we can learn from either of them for now. It's a travesty."

"How were they lost?"

"Red tape. Ridiculous protocols. Accidents. Fate. Despite the fact that I spend my time helping people look back, I don't believe in doing that in situations like this. What is past is past. I'm not going to lose any more chances to find the tools." He paused and searched her face as if he were looking for something. When he resumed speaking, his voice had taken on more gravitas. "Over the past one hundred and fifty years, members of this society have heard about the tools, or met people who knew about them, or in some cases may have seen them or even owned them." Malachai spread his arms wide, as if embracing the entire foundation. "One of the tools was a fragrance. And the stories I've heard about it are curiously similar to the family legend you told me about years ago."

"Which you believe is a serious piece of synchronicity."

"Which I *know* is. Nothing is an accident or a coincidence, according to past-life theories that go back though history, through the centuries, circling through cultures. If we were in the East, being skeptical about these moments that seem to be part of a bigger plan would be as unusual as questioning the wetness of water."

Jac knew better than to argue. She'd done it before. Malachai would start naming all the geniuses who'd believed in reincarnation over the centuries, starting with Pythagoras and moving up to Benjamin Franklin, Henry Ford and Carl Jung.

"If you could discover a scent that works like a memory tool, it would be worth a fortune."

He'd never seemed to care about money before, and she was surprised that he mentioned it. But then, so many aspects of today's conversation were unexpected.

As if anticipating her question, Malachai said, "The money doesn't matter to me. It would be yours. Enough for you to ensure the future of the House of L'Etoile. All I want is the memory tool."

"To help the children?" Jac was certain there was more to his need. She wanted to know what it was.

"Of course." He frowned. "Do you doubt that? I've spent my life trying to help them."

She'd never suspected him of doing anything untoward; never doubted he had any but the most moral and principled motives. What was it about this conversation that suggested otherwise?

Jac lifted the flask to the light. An inch of rainbow appeared on Malachai's white shirt cuff. She moved the glass container, and the rainbow leapt onto the wall.

"Was there anything in the letters about this formulation? Do you know what they based this scent on?" she asked.

"The letters I found are between two members of the society: one in New York and another who lived in France. The Frenchman wrote about a perfumer he'd met in Paris who had a remnant of an ancient scent that he believed was a portal to past lives. The foundation funded his efforts to create a new scent based on that remnant."

Jac nodded. "Back then that would have required a lot of guesswork and a fair amount of luck. If it was an ancient Egyptian scent, it would have been seriously diluted by the nineteenth century. Essences lose their potency over time. And quite a few ancient sources were extinct by the nineteenth century. Even if you smelled them, you wouldn't have been able to name them or find them."

Malachai was staring at her.

"What?"

"I never told you it was an ancient Egyptian scent."

Somewhere in the building, a telephone rang and a door closed. Jac had been so intent on their conversation, she'd forgotten there were other people here. She shook her head, got back to the facts.

"Even if I wanted to help you, Malachai, the mess in this bottle isn't even a starting point. It's a group of four or five ordinary essences."

"But they *are* a starting point," he insisted. "The perfumer was working from some formula, Jac. I have a case with eleven versions of this same base."

"You didn't tell me that. Eleven versions of this scent. And why eleven? That's an odd number."

"There's room for twelve in the case."

"One broke?"

"Or maybe one held a memory tool and someone took it."

She shook her head. "It's a myth. You're the one who taught me that myths are a culture's collective dream. Small stories about individuals that, out of the thousands told, were the ones that clicked with the most people because of the patterns in our collective unconscious. As the stories are handed down, they change, grow, become more extravagant and magical. Like stalactites in a cave that start out as one drop of water."

"Robbie and Griffin both warned me that you'd be hard to convince. I told them they were wrong; that you're more open minded. I suppose I was wrong."

Jac put her hands on the chair's carved lion's-head arms. Her fingertips pressed into the grooves. "Griffin?" She tried to keep her voice even, to make it sound like a normal, off-the-cuff question.

"Griffin North. Your brother's friend. I thought from the way he spoke about you that you two knew each other."

Hearing Griffin's name out of context confused her. "Yes, I do know him. *Knew* him. I haven't seen him in a long time. You know him?"

"Robbie introduced us a few months ago. Griffin wanted to do some research in our archives for a book he's writing. Robbie came to visit him here about two weeks ago. It was just a marvelous piece of synchronicity that Griffin showed Robbie the case of perfume flasks. I'd forgotten about them a long time ago."

"I didn't know Robbie saw Griffin when he was in New York."

It was difficult for Jac to keep up a pretense at conversation. Griffin worked here? Was he here now? Had that been his phone ringing? Had he closed the door she'd heard shut before?

She'd come across the book he'd written when it first came out. Stood in the store and read the flap copy and his bio. So she knew he lived in New York and Egypt, worked on an important dig near Alexandria, was married and had a child. But those were very public things.

The color of the walls in the office where he worked, the street he walked down to go home at the end of the day, the view from his window when he looked up from his research—those were details to which she wasn't privy. She resented being given information about him without wanting it. At the same time, she was jealous of Robbie and Malachai. Of the room in this building that absorbed Griffin's breath and the chair that held his body. Jac knew better than to indulge in the delicious pain of remembering him. Of wondering who he'd married. How old his son or daughter was.

Griffin had hurt her. Left her. People who left you once—even just once—were not ever to be trusted again.

"I'm sorry." She stood up. It had nothing to do with Griffin working here. It was preposterous even to imagine there was a fragrance that could help you remember past lives. She'd been telling Robbie that since they were children. And if there was, she was not about to start playing at being a perfumer after all these years.

Malachai stood too and came around his desk to escort her out. She didn't believe in any god, but she started a fervent prayer that she wouldn't run into Griffin.

"So nothing I've said makes you even a little bit curious," he asked.

She laughed. "I don't have the luxury of being curious."

"What if I could promise you the three million you need to pay off the banks? Would you accept my offer then?"

"Are you offering that?"

"Would it make a difference?"

"Even if I was capable of doing it, I don't have the time it would take.

I need to raise the money now." The desperation in her voice matched the desperation in his eyes.

"Will you at least promise me you'll consider it? Think of what it would be like to prove a myth like this."

"I'm the perennial skeptic. That's what you used to call me. Now you're asking me to believe on faith in something that's a dream."

"What if you're wrong, Jac? What if it's not a dream?"

Nine

Griffin had never seen such expensive *poupées,* as the French called them, and he knew his wife would object. But Therese wasn't here. And the image of his daughter opening the box and seeing this Parisienne doll was impossible to resist. At six years old, Elsie had blond hair like her mother and gray-blue eyes like his. She was a serious child who played piano dazzlingly well. Probably prodigy material, though he and Therese had agreed not to pursue the stressful virtuoso path. He'd lost enough of his own childhood to know how important having one was.

All the more reason that his heart ached so for his girl; he worried about how the possible divorce would affect her. Of course, he couldn't protect her completely, but he didn't have to be the one to bring the darkness into her life, either. If he and Therese broke up, he wouldn't be abandoning Elsie the way his own father had abandoned him, but the result wouldn't be all that different.

There was a small brochure by the cash register—the history of the store presented in five languages. Maison des Poupées had been on that corner for more than a hundred years. There seemed more respect in Europe for rituals and institutions. New wasn't revered quite as much here as it was back at home.

Home.

Well, that almost worked, Griffin thought to himself ruefully. He'd managed to push his thoughts to the transitory nature of the universe but still wound up right back with his little girl nonetheless.

He'd been a reluctant father. And it hadn't taken years of therapy to understand why. But on top of his apprehension about repeating his father's mistakes, Griffin had been worried. Therese didn't want to move, and he was committed to spending at least five months a year in Egypt. His time out of the country put a strain on their marriage. How much worse would that strain be with a child in the equation? Therese had persevered. And in time won.

From his first days as a parent, Griffin had been surprised at the intensity of his feelings for Elsie. He'd told Therese that it was like he was walking around with his heart outside of his body.

The shop girl emerged from the back room carrying a large gift box. "Voila, Monsieur North," she said, handing him the elaborately wrapped parcel.

He arranged to have it delivered to his hotel, the Montalembert, later that afternoon, and then walked the three narrow blocks to Rue des Saints-Pères, where, nestled between two antique stores, was L'Etoile Parfums.

During the summers he'd spent with Robbie and Jac in France, their grandmother had entertained him with stories about the family history going back to prerevolutionary Paris and Jean-Louis, the glove maker who learned about fragrance in order to scent the leather he sold from this very building. Opening the front door, Griffin listened to the fanciful bell that announced him. Could it be the very same bell that had tolled during Jean-Louis's life?

Lucille, the manager, looked up from the magazine she was reading to say good morning. She stood out—starkly modern in a monochromatic black shift, black high heels, and a black scarf—in the eighteenth-century store. All the walls were paneled in mottled antique mirror. The ceiling, too, was mirrored. The corners were decorated with pink-tinged fat angels and flowers in a mélange of pastels, painted in the style of Fragonard. The four small Louis XIV desks scattered around the room were originals, as were the smattering of chairs with avocado-green velvet seats and the glass and rosewood cabinets filled with antique perfume paraphernalia. Oversize bottles of each of the house's forty fragrances—factice bottles, Robbie had called them—lined mirrored shelves, with the signature fragrances front and center. Blanc, Verte, Rouge, and Noir had all been created between 1919 and 1922, and were still considered among the top ten scents of the entire industry, alongside such classics as Chanel No. 5, Shalimar, and Mitsouko.

Lucille told Griffin that Robbie was waiting for him and pushed open one of the mirrored panels that lined the room. Griffin walked through the false door and hurried down the secret corridor that connected the store to the workshop. It was narrow, dark, and undecorated; poor in contrast to the two areas it connected.

He knocked.

"Entrer."

Griffin pushed open the door.

Even after spending the past four days working with Robbie, Griffin marveled at the centuries-old workshop. It was like stepping inside a kaleidoscope of light and scent. Thousands of bottles of sparkling liquids in all shades of yellow, amber, green and brown glittered and shimmered in the morning sun.

A set of French doors opened onto a lush and almost overgrown courtyard. It was a lovely scene until you looked closely and realized that there was paint chipping by the door frame and the blooming flowers and verdant trees outside were in serious need of a gardener.

Robbie sat at his desk, reading his computer screen, tapping his foot restlessly, a frown creasing his forehead.

"What's wrong?" Griffin asked.

Even in the face of the crisis confronting him, Robbie had remained tranquil, handling his problems with an equanimity that Griffin found not only admirable but also almost implausible. This was the first time he'd seen his friend genuinely nervous.

"I got back the chemical analysis of the pottery shards."

"Were they able to identify any of the ingredients?"

"Yes." Robbie gestured to the screen. "They found trace amounts of at least six essences impregnated in the clay. Of those, only three are identifiable, and they're the three I'd already guessed."

"Why can't they identify the others?"

"They don't have any matching chemical fingerprints in their database. The ingredients could have corrupted over time and be unrecognizable now. Or there could have been a metal liner of some sort between the clay and the wax that changed the chemical deposits and contaminated the analysis. Or the ingredients are extinct."

"Damn." Like Robbie, Griffin had been hoping for a different outcome. Pulling over a chair, he sat down on the opposite side of the large partners desk, his own temporary workspace while he was in Paris.

Robbie had said that since 1780, every director of the House of L'Etoile had run the business from this desk. Griffin was impressed by that kind of continuity. He found solace in history. What any single man lost in one lifetime was inconsequential when observed through the lens of time. Perspective mattered to Griffin. He relied on it. It kept him centered when nothing else could.

"Don't worry," Robbie said as he stood. The optimism in his voice suggested that his mood had already begun to lift. "Regardless of what their GC-MS machine says, we'll find out what those ingredients are." He walked across the room and stopped in front of an ornately framed still life of roses and irises in a china vase. Robbie swung the painting open like a medicine cabinet, revealing an old-fashioned wall safe. He turned the dial first to the right, then the left, then back to the right.

Last Friday when he'd sent the pottery fragment to the lab, he'd explained that a GC-MS—or a gas chromatography–mass spectrometry machine—was typically used for drug detection, environmental analysis and explosive investigations. Usually fragrance companies employed the highly complex instrument to study the competition's scents. In just days, the machine could break down a rival's formula that had taken months to create.

Robbie withdrew a black-velvet-lined jeweler's tray from the safe, closed the metal door, swung the painting back into place, and gingerly walked back across the room, depositing it in front of Griffin.

Like a precious gem, each pottery shard was laid out with ample space around it.

"The answer has to be in the part of the inscription you haven't yet translated," Robbie said.

"Anything is possible."

Griffin opened his briefcase and removed his notebook, glasses and a black lacquer fountain pen. He had a laptop and a cell phone complete with video capability, but at this stage of the work, he preferred black ink flowing onto the pristine white pages of a black-bound unlined Moleskine notebook—the same kind he'd been buying for years. Without a father's rituals to emulate, Griffin had invented some of his own.

Both men studied the white glazed clay pieces, which ranged in size from splinters to one and a half inches long, all decorated with turquoise and coral designs and black hieroglyphics.

Since he'd been in Paris, Griffin had managed to fit more than half the shards together and definitively date the broken pot to the Ptolemaic period, from approximately 323 to 30 BCE. He'd translated twenty-eight Egyptian words and discovered a story he couldn't find any reference to in any online database. There were still some libraries he needed to visit, but he doubted he'd find more specific citations.

The narrative recounted a story of two lovers, each buried holding a pot of fragrance to take into the afterlife. Once the lovers reincarnated into their next lives, the fragrance would help them find each other again and so be reconnected throughout the ages.

While the afterlife was absolutely part of the Egyptian religion, opinions differed about its acceptance of reincarnation theory.

The pharaoh Amenemhat I's name meant "He who repeats births." The pharaoh Senusert I's was "He whose births live." And in the Nineteenth Dynasty, the spiritual name (or ka-name) of Setekhy I was "Repeater of births." But most comparative religion experts believed that those appellations referred to a soul being reborn in the next world— the afterlife—not in this world again.

Griffin knew that certain sections of the Egyptian *Book of the Dead* could be translated to suit a reincarnation bias, but he'd never seen any definitive evidence that the ancients expected to be reborn again as men on earth. His own theory, though, was that there was a strong belief in reincarnation in the final years of the last great dynasty.

Egypt's first Ptolemaic ruler hailed from Greece, and for the next three hundred years, all the kings and queens who came after him, including Cleopatra, not only spoke their native language but also studied Greek history and philosophy. This indicated they would have been exposed to and familiar with the teachings of Pythagoras, a great proponent of reincarnation.

Following that logic, it was more than possible that the concept of a soul being born again in a new body had gained popularity. This pottery might be tangible proof of that.

Griffin was certain that if he found proof, his theory would command the academic community's attention. But would attention be enough to wipe his reputation clean?

A year before, Griffin had published a book tracing texts in the Old Testament to references in the Egyptian *Book of the Dead*. It had stirred controversy and sold better than the dry tomes his father-in-law, the noted Egyptologist Thomas Woods, and many of his colleagues published. Griffin enjoyed the notice the book received until Woods's publisher accused him of plagiarism.

Until the allegation was made, Griffin hadn't realized that the attributions he'd included in his manuscript had been left out of the printed book. Neither the proofreader, the copy editor, nor Griffin had caught the error. Somehow in the editing process they'd been deleted.

Despite producing the manuscript and the allegations being dropped, the damage was done. And it was hell. Griffin had been through an accusation of plagiarism before, in graduate school. It had almost destroyed his chances for his degree and had cost him the woman he'd loved.

And now he had to live through it again.

He could have gotten through it intact if he hadn't seen the doubt in his wife's eyes; the same doubt he'd seen in Jac's eyes so many years before.

He told Therese he wanted a separation.

For the rest of the morning, Griffin struggled to piece together the next shard and then the next. With three new ones in position, he scrutinized the glyphs for their meaning, testing each word against the previous one, rejecting some choices, finding alternative interpretations, testing again.

While he worked, Griffin became aware of scents swirling around him, merging, melding together in fragrances.

"What are you mixing up? It's starting to smell like an old tomb in here."

"I'll take that as a compliment," Robbie said and gestured toward a dozen glass bottles on the tabletop. Each was filled with a few inches of liquid—each a different shade of amber, from a pale yellow to a deep rich mahogany. Sunlight pouring through the doors sent colored flecks of light dancing. The visual interplay as intriguing as the mixture of musky scents.

"I'm trying to amass all the essences and absolutes that we know ancient Egyptians used and that are still available. I want to be prepared when you find that list of ingredients—"

"*If,*" Griffin interrupted.

"*When,*" Robbie corrected emphatically.

Robbie's enthusiasm was as contagious as ever. Griffin remembered him as a thirteen-year-old boy rooting through the ancient ruins in the Languedoc, in the south of France. They'd been exploring the remains of a castle since early that hot, sunny August morning. Suddenly Robbie let out a whoop and jumped up into the air. For a split second, the young boy hung there: arms outstretched, silhouetted against the sun; frozen in an exultant pose.

Robbie had found a beat-up silver clasp engraved with a dove and was sure it was a Cathar relic. He was so excited and certain that Griffin hadn't been surprised when an expert later confirmed its provenance and dated the artifact to the early thirteenth century.

At a little before one in the afternoon, Griffin's cell phone rang. Checking the caller ID, he saw it was Malachai Samuels. He took the call.

"Your sister turned down his offer," Griffin told Robbie after he hung up.

"I'm disappointed but not surprised. Since our mother died, no one has gotten her back into a workshop. I thought that maybe an ancient myth about reincarnation would at least tempt her."

"Malachai's very disappointed. He asked me about the chemical analysis. That didn't improve his mood. Nonetheless, after I told him where I was with the translation, he upped his offer for the pot shards."

Robbie acted as if he hadn't heard. "It's time for a café au crème, yes?"

"Robbie? Malachai is damn serious about buying the pottery. Will you at least let me tell you what he offered?"

"I can't sell it."

"You don't even want to hear the amount?"

Robbie laughed. "Why, is he offering you a commission?"

"I should be insulted," Griffin replied sharply and then said: "Two hundred and fifty thousand dollars."

"I can't sell it," Robbie repeated as he opened the door.

He was gone for a few minutes, and when he came back, he hovered over Griffin's shoulder, looking down at the enigma on the velvet tray.

"There are so many ways to read the same symbols," Griffin said. "You think you're going in the right direction, and then you find the next piece of the puzzle, and suddenly everything reads different. Listen to this: 'And then through all time, his soul and hers were able to find each other again and again . . .'"

"Can I read it? Everything you've translated so far?"

Griffin handed him the notebook.

While Robbie read, Griffin stood on the threshold of the French doors and looked out into the garden.

Bound by fifteen-foot-tall stone walls, the L'Etoile house on one side and the workshop on the other, the courtyard was invisible from the street. Designed in the late 1700s, the deep and dense *petit parc* was planted with dozens of ancient trees and Egyptian-style topiaries and decorated with statuaries. In its center was a cypress hedge maze. On Saturday Robbie had recited the parc's history while he and Griffin walked on glossy black-and-white-pebbled paths through the labyrinth to its heart, a little oasis with a stone bench, flanked by statues of sphinxes and a tall, authentic, limestone obelisk.

There was a knock on the door.

"Entrer!" Robbie called out.

Lucille entered the room with a tray.

Only in Paris, Griffin thought, watching as she set down a cup in front of each of them. The repast had been sent by the neighborhood café complete with china cups, glasses of water, napkins, and spoons. Croissants at breakfast and sandwiches or pastries in the afternoon.

Robbie took his coffee over to the perfumer's organ and sat down. It was a wondrous apparatus patterned after the musical instrument of the same name. Eight feet long and six feet tall, it was made of poplar wood and took up a full quarter of the room. On the console, first, second and third tiers—instead of keyboards—held rows and rows of small glass vials of different essences. Over three hundred of them.

"How much do you know about the organ's provenance?" Griffin asked.

Robbie ran his fingers lovingly over the shelf's rim. "I don't know who the cabinetmaker was, but according to my grandfather, it's as old as the shop."

"So it predates the French Revolution?"

Robbie nodded and sipped his coffee. "For centuries, perfumers have been practicing their craft at laboratories like this one." He put down the cup, picked up a disposable plastic pipette, opened a small bottle, squeezed the bulb and then dripped several droplets of a tawny liquid into a clean glass vial. "Even though many modern labs have stopped using these organs, for me there's no better way to work. Perfume is about the past . . . about memories. . . . It's about dreams." He spread his arms. "All the generations of perfumers in my family have used these same bottles, sat in this same chair."

"Now the youngest member of the House of L'Etoile is keeping the oldest method of orchestrating a perfume alive," Griffin said.

"Traditions matter, don't they? Give us grounding. And without knowing what he was doing, my father has put it all at risk."

Griffin nodded. He knew how his friend felt and put his hand on Robbie's shoulder. "Consider Malachai's offer. Despite the lab results, he's willing to pay you three times the amount the auction house estimated."

"It's a generous sum, but even if it were enough to offset the debt, now that I know what's written on the pot, I'd have to think twice. I've made up my mind about what I'm doing with the shards."

"Yes?"

"Once you're done with the translation, I'm going to give the pottery to the Dalai Lama."

"The Dalai Lama? Are you nuts? What will he do with a box of broken pot shards?"

"A lot more than Malachai will by putting them on display in one of those lovely cabinets of his. I've been thinking about nothing but this for the last two days—ever since you made the first real breakthrough in the translation. If there once was an actual fragrance that helped people remember their past lives, there could be one again. The fact of that will be enormously inspiring to the Tibetans and invaluable to their cause. It could help raise awareness and bring even more attention to the crisis they're facing."

"It's an inscription on a piece of pottery, Robbie," said Griffin. "We don't know that any such unguent ever existed. The pot could have been filled with an ordinary fragrance, and the legend could have been an ancient version of a modern-day sales pitch."

"Or maybe there really was a fragrance that triggered past-life memories. You sound like my sister. Why is it my karma to be surrounded by cynics?" He shook his head. "His Holiness will be in Paris next weekend. I'm trying to set up a meeting with him through a lama I study with at the Buddhist center."

"That's it? You're committed to giving this treasure away? There's nothing I can say to talk you out of it?"

"Why would you try? It can do His Holiness more good than it will ever do me."

"Even if it could pay off part of the company's debt?"

"Malachai's offer would cover only a small percentage of what we owe. We'd still be facing the bank's deadlines. My only choice is to give in to my sister's solution. The entire amount will be paid"—he snapped his fingers—"with one drop of the guillotine's blade."

"But the pottery has historical significance."

"And nothing will interfere with your establishing it. You have almost a week left. You'll be able to translate it by then as well as verify your work."

"It's not about me or my work," Griffin argued.

Or was it? Wasn't that what he was really worried about? What if he couldn't finish the translation in time? Sure, he could take photographs, but working from two dimensions wasn't the same. There was a connection when you could hold and touch and turn the object.

"It's been in your family for centuries." Griffin couldn't give up that easily. "It's one thing to be unselfish. But to the point of self-destruction?"

"Ah, but there, my friend, you're wrong. Attempting heroism is a very selfish act. Proof of how much more enlightenment I've yet to achieve."

Robbie added two drops of russet liquid and then three of amber to the vial. "Don't you see? Even a small bit of reincarnation evidence might help the Dalai Lama keep the Tibetan culture and belief system alive in the face of Chinese atheism. Their entire way of life and their culture is at stake and in danger of becoming obsolete. There has even been talk of His Holiness appointing a successor instead of relying on the reincarnation method." Finally, he swirled the concoction. "Come smell this."

Griffin inhaled the glass tube.

"Name a place," said Robbie. "The first place you think of."

"Church."

"Similar, yes. You're smelling frankincense, myrrh, and the essences of several other exotic woods. These are the oldest ingredients we know of. For over six thousand years, ancient priests in India and then in Egypt and China have been using these elements to make incense. Fragrance was holy before it was cosmetic. People believed the soul traveled on smoke up to the heavens—up to the gods."

"We haven't found evidence of reincarnation, Robbie," said Griffin. "We've discovered only a myth written on the side of a pot."

"So far that's all we've found. But we have six days before the Dalai Lama arrives. Six days for me to arrange a meeting and for you to find out what the rest of those missing ingredients are—and maybe have a past-life adventure of our own."

Ten

François Lee stood in the building's vestibule and waited to be buzzed up. The beauty of Valentine's renting in this high-rise was that the traffic never ceased, even at odd hours of the day and night. No one watching the building's entrance would pay attention to three men arriving individually within forty minutes of each other.

He tapped out a rhythm on his watch with his fingernail. The smell of onions and garlic reminded him that he was hungry. He hoped she'd have some food; he'd skipped lunch, and now his stomach was growling. Valentine was supposed to keep the kitchen stocked but rarely remembered. She tried to, but she resented her domestic duties, and he didn't blame her. She'd been working for the Triad for almost ten years and wanted to move up, have more responsibility, be out in the field more. But she was a woman, and the organization was typically misogynistic. He'd warned her when Valentine first told him that she wanted to join, but she was stubborn and sure she'd make them change. That she'd be the exception.

"Look at what I've already done," she'd say and laugh. "You never thought I'd get this far, did you?"

Not at first, no. Certainly not on that freezing cold February night twelve years before.

François had finished up his last set at Le Jazz Hot in the Quartier Chinois at two in the morning. By the time he left the club, the street was empty. Or so he thought, until he tripped over the prostrate form curled up in the shelter of the doorway.

She was a skinny Chinese girl with long, stringy black hair. Despite the winter temperature, she wasn't wearing a coat. Just a stained red and orange sleeveless silk cocktail dress with black patent leather high-heeled boots. Her arms were bare, and the track marks told him every-thing else he needed to know. Bending down, getting closer, he peered into her face. Blue lips. Skin pale and lackluster. Too pale.

When he shook her, she was nonresponsive. There was nothing on the ground beside her. No bag. No jacket. There were no pockets on her dress, and he couldn't find any identification. What to do? It was late. Cold. He was tired. But she was alone. Helpless. If he just kept walking, she might not make it.

François picked her up and carried her to his little car. She was as light as a child, and her skin was far too clammy.

At the hospital emergency room, a nurse and orderly took her from him, settled her on a gurney, asked him if he knew what was wrong with her, and when he said no, rushed her away.

A few minutes later, an administrative nurse sat down with him and shot a battery of questions at him.

What was her medical history? She appeared to be suffering from a drug overdose; was he sure he didn't know what she had taken? What was her name? What was his name? What was their relationship?

François figured the truth wouldn't do either of them any good. The authorities would never believe that he'd simply been unable to walk by and leave her there. They'd suspect him of being her dealer. Or, worse, her pimp.

"I'm her uncle," he said. "My brother has been frantic. They live in Cherbourg. She ran away from home a few days ago, and I guess she came to the club looking for me, to help her . . . but she didn't quite make it inside."

"What is her name?" the nurse asked again.

François didn't know, so he gave the girl a name—the first one that came to mind. Inspired by the last song he'd played that night: "My Funny Valentine."

"Last name?" the nurse asked him.

He gave his own.

For the next eight hours, he sat in the waiting room, dozing on and off while they saved Valentine Lee's life.

There were enough prostitutes on the street—he'd never felt the need to play the saint and rescue one. Why this one? Why did he care about what happened to her?

They finally let him see her the next afternoon. Her hair was soaking wet, and her sallow skin was slicked with perspiration. In the throes of withdrawal, her whole body shook. She was so skinny the pale blue hospital gown billowed around her. A little, lost girl.

The hopeless expression in her eyes brought tears to his.

Even though Valentine didn't acknowledge him, the nurse encouraged François to stay. "It's good for her to have company and know that someone cares about her," she said.

But he was a stranger. It couldn't possibly help the girl for him to be there for her. And yet he stayed and sat by her side while she twitched and vomited and shook and moaned. He stayed all the next day while she went through the worst of the withdrawal symptoms.

After that, he visited Valentine regularly, showing up early every morning and not leaving till he went to Le Jazz Hot. The doctor gave him a full report once a day, filling François in on the antianxiety drugs and antidepressants they were giving her and on her progress. "Don't expect too much too quickly," he warned.

Whenever François entered her room, she turned away. When he talked to her, she pressed her lips together and refused to speak. The nurse told him it was part of the detox process. He shouldn't take it personally or be insulted.

When he arrived on the fifth morning of her stay, the doctor told François that Valentine was ready to be released if he was prepared to take her home.

Take her home? He hadn't thought that far. He couldn't take her home.

He walked into her room and found her sitting on the edge of the bed. Showered and dressed. Painfully thin. A sullen expression on her face. Dry-eyed now, but he noticed the tearstains on her cheeks.

"They won't let you leave unless someone takes responsibility for you," François said. "Do you have someone I can call who can come get you?"

She didn't answer.

The dress she'd been wearing when he brought her in—the red and orange silk shift with little red bows on each shoulder strap—looked shabby in the overly bright hospital room. Her tall patent-leather boots with their worn-down high heels looked cheap.

"Do you have anyplace to go?"

No answer.

"Do you have a pimp? Were you living with him? Was he the one giving you the smack?"

She didn't answer this time either, but he saw a pale blue vein in her forehead twitch.

"I can give you a place to stay for a while."

She shrugged.

"Do you want a place to stay?"

Finally, she turned to face him. The fierceness in her eyes startled him. "You want me to fuck you for a place to sleep? Is that it?" she mouthed off in a raspy, raw hiss of words. "I won't do that again. Ever. I'll figure out some way to take care of myself, but not that."

"I'm not asking you to fuck me." He laughed. "Darling, I'm as gay as they come."

Her eyebrows arched. "What's the catch, then? What do I have to do?"

"You don't have to do anything. Except clean up after yourself."

Surprise replaced the suspicion. "Why do you want to help me?" Her voice suddenly sounded very young.

He didn't have an answer. He didn't know. For a few seconds, they just sat there. Valentine, on the edge of the hospital bed, her feet not even reaching the ground; François, in a fake leather chair that had cracks in the armrests. Outside in the hallway, the steady din of hospital personnel going about their work filled in the silence.

"I was a pretty different kid from my brothers and sisters," François said. "No one related to me . . . except the dog. She was supposed to belong to everyone, but she was really my dog. Even slept with me. Before I went to bed, I'd let her out to do her business. She'd root around for a while, but I always waited for her, and she always came back. Until one night. I stayed out till morning looking for her. And then refused to go to school so I could keep looking. I kept thinking about how helpless she was. How vulnerable.

"When I still hadn't found her by the end of the second night, I started to pray she'd been taken by someone. I didn't care if she'd been stolen. As long as she wasn't lying somewhere alone . . . hurt . . ."

Valentine's black eyes grew even blacker.

François realized how that might have sounded. "I hope you're not insulted. I only meant that worrying about her was—"

"I'll come with you."

Valentine's mother was a prostitute and a drug addict whose pimp had seen potential in the woman's young daughter. It hadn't taken much to hook the kid on horse and get her out on the street hooking.

But it took a lot to get Valentine to trust François and believe that he didn't have some deviant ulterior motive.

As much progress as he made, he didn't really get anywhere with her those first few weeks until she discovered he wasn't just a jazz musician. François was a martial arts expert and a high-ranking member of the Chinese mafia.

She begged him to train her, and she turned out to be an apt pupil. Her passion for the art of self-defense grew as she improved and then became devoted to the point of obsession. She had been victimized for so long, the high of independence was as addictive to her as the drugs had been.

Once she mastered the physical arts, she asked to learn about the organized crime family to which François belonged.

Being part of a triad was a noble calling, he explained. Dating back to 1000 BCE, peasants formed secret societies to protect themselves from the evil lords and leaders. Even Chinese monks committed to fighting injustice were involved in founding the triads. Over time, the groups helped topple corrupt emperors and take down dishonest politicians.

For someone who'd had no ritual or moral training, the strict Confucian code of ethics, the mystique, and the highly symbolic ceremonies appealed to Valentine. She was determined to become a full-fledged member of the Paris Triad even though there were only a handful of other women members at that level.

Valentine had never been part of a family before. Her loyalty was absolute. During her induction ceremony, when she pledged her fealty and recited the thirty-six two-hundred-year-old initiation oaths, her voice never wavered:

"I shall not disclose the secrets of the Family, not even to my parents, brothers, sisters or husband. I shall never disclose the secrets for money. I shall die by a swarm of swords if I do so."

An excellent student, she was soon a valued member of François's team. But recently her frustration had grown. There were too many restrictions on what a woman could do. There were thousands of members in the Paris branch of China's black society alone, but not one woman above her in rank.

François checked his watch again. What was Valentine doing? Had he gotten the time wrong? He pulled out his cell phone and checked the text.

"She'll be ready for you at two fifteen this afternoon. Bring cash."

It was always a similar message suggesting an assignation of a very different kind. If the phone ever was taken from him, if the police ever had reason to examine it, they'd think he was a man with a fairly active libido who favored prostitutes over more cumbersome relationships; he rarely made more than two appointments a week.

The front door opened, and a young woman entered the building. Blond hair, low-cut white blouse, tight black skirt. She eyed him openly, starting at his black lizard boots, gazing up the length of his jeans, taking in the worn leather jacket and staring at his hands—he had the long, nimble fingers of a pianist, which women often found attractive.

She opened the door with her key just as the buzzer rang, letting François enter. She smiled and held the door for him in invitation. They were both here for the same thing: they were going to fuck someone for money.

Eleven

"It's been at least ten minutes since you last asked me if I've translated any new phrases," Griffin said.

It was late afternoon, and they had been working straight through since they'd stopped for lunch at one o'clock. Robbie was researching ancient Egyptian fragrances online, and Griffin was trying to fit additional shards together and complete more of the puzzle.

"I don't want to be a complete pest."

Griffin laughed.

"And I assume when you have more, you'll tell me."

"I have more."

"Yes?" He was up and over at Griffin's side of the desk in seconds.

"A new phrase. One I think you're looking for." Griffin read: "'And then through all time, his soul and hers were able to find each other again and again whenever the lotus bloomed.'"

Robbie repeated the last four words, "*Whenever the lotus bloomed.* The lab didn't confirm any traces of Blue Lily but that doesn't mean it wasn't there. In all my reading that flower has been named over and over as a very popular ingredient in ancient times."

The more excited he was, the more pronounced Robbie's accent became, and Griffin had to struggle to follow what he was saying.

"Are you saying the *Blue* Lily?"

"Yes," Robbie nodded. "The Blue Lily. It's still in use. Also called the Blue Lotus or even the Egyptian Lotus." Robbie picked up Griffin's magnifying glass and peered down at the mosaic of broken bits of pottery. "If this ingredient is listed here, maybe the rest are. We're going to solve this, you see? We are."

Once again he was that thirteen-year-old leaping up into the air.

"Maybe we are." Even Griffin was starting to believe.

Outside, the wind picked up and rattled the French doors. Robbie walked over and shut them. Then he returned to the desk and again bent over the pottery.

"Blue Lily, hmmm . . . let's see." He breathed in deeply once . . . then twice. He smiled. "It might be my imagination, but I think I can smell it."

Griffin bent over and inhaled, then shook his head. "The only thing I've been able to smell since I started working on this project is clay. I guess I must not have a very sensitive nose."

"I don't inherently have one. Mine is all training. Jac is the one with the magical gift." Robbie inhaled again and this time remained hunched over the fragments for a few seconds. When he straightened up, Griffin noticed that he rubbed his forehead.

"Something wrong?"

"This happened the other day. If I sniff these shards for too long, I get lightheaded. Almost as if I'm going to faint."

"You know Blue Lily is a hallucinogen, right?" Griffin asked. "Except it couldn't still be potent after all this time."

"No, it couldn't be," Robbie said, but he didn't sound convinced. "Other than as an ingredient in fragrances, I don't know much about its history. Was it a fairly common flower?"

"Popular and plentiful, yes. You'll find it carved on the tops of columns and in tomb paintings, and there are records of it being used in rituals and rites. But I wouldn't call it common. It's the Egyptians' most sacred plant. A symbol of death and rebirth. Osiris was said to be reincarnated as a blue water lily."

Robbie's eyes widened.

"Yes, another coincidence for you," Griffin said.

"If you insist on calling them coincidences."

"What would you call them?"

"Signs. Amazing, life-affirming signs."

As people grow up and age, few hold on to the delight and wonder they had as children. But Robbie had. He was unusual that way. Griffin wondered if Jac was as unchanged as her brother.

"Tell me what else you know about the symbolism of the lotus," Robbie asked.

"According to ancient legends, the world was dark and chaos ruled until the morning the Blue Lily rose up from the depths of the river. When the flower opened, a young god was sitting in its golden center. The divine light he emitted illuminated the world, and the sweet scent he gave off filled the air and banished universal darkness. The Egyptians believed that when the flower opened anew each morning, it chased away the chaos that reigned during the night."

"Hence it being a symbol for renewal. How did they use it as a hallucinogen?" Robbie asked.

"Mostly by drinking it. There's an ancient recipe that called for nineteen flowers to be soaked in wine. The wine was then used in religious rituals and recreationally at parties. A lot of the time, you see lilies in tomb paintings of sexual scenes. Tutankhamen's body was covered with them."

"Any idea of the effects of the hallucinogenic properties?"

"You sort of drift into a state of euphoric tranquility. A few of us brewed some up when we were in grad school."

Robbie's eyebrows arched.

"We got curious. There were references to it everywhere. This flower is so important, it's in the Egyptian *Book of the Dead*." Griffin recited from memory: "'I am the cosmic water lily that rose shining from Nun's black primordial waters, and my mother is Nut, the night sky. O you who made me, I have arrived, I am the great ruler of Yesterday, the power of command is in my hand.'"

Outside, heavy gray clouds blew across the sky. Robbie turned on the desk lamp as the early evening turned prematurely dark and cast the workshop in deep shadow.

"How can something that ancient give me a headache and yet not be picked up by the lab?" he asked.

"Makes no sense."

"You feel fine, right?"

Griffin nodded. "No headache. And certainly none of the feelings I remember from drinking it."

A sudden flash of lightning lit up the courtyard beyond. The electric zigzag mesmerized both men, who watched as a second flash hit.

"What the hell? Did you see that?" Griffin pointed to a spot in the garden.

"The ghost?" Robbie asked.

"Well, I doubt it was a ghost, but there's a man out there."

"No one can enter the courtyard except through these doors here or from the house. What you saw is the shadow of a very old tree to the right of that hedge. Jac and I used to call it *the ghost*. In certain light, it looks like a man." Robbie opened the door to the windswept courtyard. "Come, I'll show you."

Just as he stepped outside, another bolt of lightning hit, and rain started to pour down. In the odd light, it looked as if Robbie were being splashed with liquid silver. Ducking back inside, he brushed himself off, then reached for a bottle of Pessac-Léognan. "I'm going to open some wine. You'll have some, yes?"

"Yes."

Robbie uncorked the Bordeaux. "Sometimes in the dark we imagine things that aren't there. And sometimes deep concentration can bring them to life."

"Manifest them?"

Robbie nodded as he handed Griffin a goblet of the supple red. "There are Tibetan monks who can create creatures—*tulpas*, they're called. Have you heard of them?"

"I have. Supposedly, highly evolved monks can give form to thought by meditating."

"You don't sound as if you believe it," Robbie said.

"I don't. Do you?"

"I do."

"Somehow that doesn't surprise me," Griffin said.

"What *do* you believe in, my friend?"

Griffin laughed. "Not much, I'm afraid. If I have a religion, I suppose it's history."

"History isn't a belief system. Are you quite serious? Despite all the religions you've studied, you don't believe in anything?"

"Joseph Campbell said—" Griffin stopped. "You know who Campbell is, right?"

"Yes, of course, the mythologist. Jac's been quoting him for years."

It was the second time in the last half hour that Robbie had mentioned his sister. Griffin wanted to ask about her but refrained. What good would knowing do? It would just raise the specter of the past. "It's not surprising that Jac quotes him." Even saying her name aloud, moving his mouth to make the sounds, felt awkward. "He's something of a guru to anyone who studies mythology."

"You probably don't approve of having a guru, do you?" Robbie asked.

"Let's say I'm skeptical about them, too."

"Let's say you are." They both laughed. Then Robbie became serious again. "There are wonders out there, my friend. But cynicism blankets them in invisibility. You and my sister . . . seeped in the world of magic and mystery but closing yourself off to it. Turning it into something one-dimensional to study and catalog."

Griffin had watched Jac's television show but couldn't glean who she'd become from the image on his screen except to notice that she was lovely. Still lovely. Her hair was as long as it had always been, and he was glad she'd never cut it. Rich, dark hair that cascaded down her swanlike neck in waves. He remembered how heavy her hair was and how it felt when he wove his fingers in it and pulled her to him and kissed her. He remembered her thick lashes that fringed her wide, almost lime green eyes and the frightened expression he'd see there sometimes. A look that made him ache and promise her he'd keep her safe. But he hadn't done that, had he?

Sipping his wine, Griffin glanced down at the jigsaw of pot shards. It was one thing to discuss and dissect the ancient past—but not his past. "So Campbell wrote that if you substitute 'goodness' for 'god' in every story, myth, religious text, homily, or treatise, then you'd really have the perfect religion to live by. If I had to pick something to believe in, trying to be good would do."

Another lightning flash lit up the sky, followed by a crack of symphonic thunder that rattled the glass. The rain beat harder on the doors. The lights in the workshop flickered once, twice, and then died.

Robbie lit several votive candles and positioned them around the room. Long, sinister shadows danced in the light. "These are infused with one of my new scents. You'll have to tell me how you like it."

"You're asking someone with such an insensitive nose?" Griffin pulled a candle even closer to the pottery and peered down at the broken bits. There was still so much left to do. It had been a relief to escape from all the problems in New York. But he couldn't stay away forever. He had to get this translation finished and go home. Closing his notebook, he took off his glasses, and rubbed the bridge of his nose. "That's it for me. I can't do much of anything in this light. Let me call the hotel and see if they have power. If they do, come have dinner. There's not much you can do here in the dark either."

"The lights won't stay off for long," replied Robbie. "Besides, I have an appointment with that journalist in an hour. It's good they're interviewing me about my new line. A little press will go far in helping me find some outlets other than our own little store."

The hotel did have power. So Griffin confirmed his plans to come back the next morning, as usual, at about ten, then borrowed an umbrella and left.

As he walked down the street, he remembered about Elsie's doll and that it would be waiting at his hotel. How delighted she'd be. At the end of Rue des Saints-Pères, the streetlight wasn't working, and it was difficult to see through the pelting rain. He peered out. No lights. No oncoming cars. He stepped off the curb, the wine and the idea of his daughter's pleasure adding a lightness to his step. He neither heard nor saw the car careening around the corner until the instant of impact.

Twelve

Malachai wanted to hurry, but walking fast might draw too much attention. If it had been raining, he'd have had an excuse. But it was a warm day, and most of the strollers in Central Park were taking their time: walking dogs, pushing baby carriages, or just admiring the blooming apple and cherry trees. The lush pink and white blossoms perfumed the air. If not for Jac L'Etoile, Malachai wasn't sure he would have noticed. Until two weeks ago, he rarely thought about scent. Now he was preoccupied with it.

West of the Dairy, Malachai entered the Chess and Checkers House. It was cooler inside the red- and white-brick building, and he smelled a fruity pipe tobacco that wasn't altogether unpleasant. Two men were playing at the first table on the right. To their left was a clean-cut man in his midthirties wearing chinos and a blue button-down shirt. On his table, along with the chess pieces, were the pipe, unlit, and an open book. As he approached, Malachai saw illustrations of chessboards on its pages.

"Finally studying Petrov's Immortal?" Malachai asked.

Reed Winston looked up. "Very imaginative game, you're right." Almost good-looking, he had a square jaw and strong features, but his eyes were too small and he showed too much gum when he smiled—which he did too often. Especially when he was delivering less than good news.

"Perhaps one of the most imaginative ever played. And exciting."

"Should I reset the board?" Winston asked.

"No, I don't have enough time for a game. I was delayed at the office and do apologize. But I have time for coffee. Would you join me?"

While Winston picked up the ivory pieces and returned them to the chess box, Malachai engaged him in a conversation about the famous 1844 game between Russian chess master Alexander Dmitrievich Petrov and F. Alexander Hoffmann. They were still talking chess as they left the building. Only when they were out on the open path did Malachai broach the subject that was the reason for the clandestine meeting.

Malachai had his office swept for bugs every week. But there was little he could do about directional mikes, which the FBI had used on him and the foundation in the past. Over the last few years, Malachai had been questioned about several robberies. Even taken into custody. Although never formally charged with any wrongdoing, he was always one of the FBI's prime suspects in any crime involving memory tools. And even though there was no overt sign or obvious reason for the bureau to be currently paying attention, he preferred to conduct certain conversations outdoors.

"What kind of connections do you have in Paris?" Malachai asked.

"Good connections."

A toddler broke free from his mother's hand and stepped out in front of the two men. In seconds his mother was on top of him, apologizing for getting in their way.

Malachai smiled at her and told her not to worry. He didn't respond to Winston until they were out of the woman's earshot.

"I would prefer *excellent* connections."

"I'll do my best."

"This time I'll need some guarantees."

While he didn't take part in criminal activity himself, Malachai had found himself on the wrong side of the law several times in the last few years. He wasn't the only one pursuing the fabled memory tools, and more than once he'd had no choice but to engage people to do some rather dirty work for him. Unfortunately, none of those efforts had proved successful.

"We've had too many accidents, Winston. Missed far too many

prime opportunities. If anything untoward happens this time, you can be sure we won't be working together in the future."

"We had a terrific team—"

Malachai put his hand on the younger man's shoulder. To anyone watching, they appeared to be father and son or uncle and nephew. "I'm not asking you to defend your work. Just giving you some advice. All right?"

"Yes, fine," Winston said. This time without one of his trademark smiles.

"Pictures of the object will be delivered to your abode tomorrow along with a name and an address."

"'Abode.' Ha. If you saw my apartment, that's the last thing you'd call it."

They had reached a wisteria arbor. About ten feet long, it was overburdened with green, leafy vines and lush, lavender blossoms. As beautiful as the foundation's Tiffany stained-glass windows of wisteria were, the actual flowers were far lovelier. Malachai lifted his head toward the low-hanging flowers and breathed in the scent. He didn't recall ever smelling it before. In his recent reading, he'd learned there are flowers whose scents can't be extracted. Chemists reproduced the scents with synthetics that came close but rarely matched nature's handiwork. When he got back to his office, he was going to call Jac and find out if wisteria was one of those.

"Have you ever smelled wisteria?" Malachai asked Winston.

"Smelled it? Not that I'm aware of." He looked confused, then sniffed the air. "You know . . ." He inhaled again. "I think I *have* smelled it before. It reminds me of my grandmother's house; this must have been that big vine that grew along the front porch."

"Scents stir the memory. You can stumble on one fragrance and suddenly remember an entire day of your childhood—and it will be as real and as vivid as if it happened just hours before." Malachai didn't usually digress. "It's a subject I've been studying."

"Because it has to do with what you want me to find?"

"Yes."

"And when I find it, you want it taken?"

"No. We're just watching for the moment. Not touching."

The ex-Interpol agent arched his eyebrows. "That's what you want me to organize?"

"Yes. We are going to go slower and be more careful this time. I can't afford another misstep. And the people involved are friends of mine."

"Play it safe?"

Malachai nodded. Any memory tools that had survived this long could be anywhere. He knew it. And the FBI knew it. The objects could be hidden in plain sight, buried in a ruin, on display in a museum, or sitting in an antique store or in some grandmother's curio cabinet. To date the search had taken years and cost a fortune. Not just in money, but in lives. It was anyone's guess how much longer it might take. All Malachai wanted was one tool: intact and functional. That's all.

Except that was like saying "all" you wanted was to pull down a star from the heavens.

So far finding a tool had proved an impossible dream. But Malachai couldn't let go. He had devoted his life to the study of reincarnation and had grand plans to reorient human belief in past, present and future lives. He wanted to give the gift of hope to the world.

But that wasn't his only motivation. Or the reason he was in a hurry. His father was still extremely healthy for an octogenarian, but how many more years would he remain compos mentis? Malachai had to find out about his own past lives soon. If what he guessed was true, he wanted to shove it in the old man's face. He wanted to hear his father's reaction and savor his father's pain when he realized what he'd thrown aside so casually.

Three times he had come close to owning a tool. Three times he had failed. There couldn't be a fourth.

"We've been walking for too long," he observed to Winston. "But before I go, I think I'd like you to get a beat on Agent Lucian Glass. Make sure he's not paying any attention to me, can you? If we get any indication he is, I'm going to want to rethink our strategy."

And then without saying good-bye or giving the ex-agent any indication he was leaving, Malachai turned around and proceeded to walk back around the lake in the direction he had come. He stopped only once, under the wisteria pergola, to inhale yet again the purple blossoms' sweet fragrance.

Thirteen

Robbie was pleasantly surprised when the reporter arrived exactly on time despite the rain.

"I'm Charles Fauche," he said, oblivious to the fact that his umbrella was leaving a pool of water on the eighteenth-century parquet floors.

"Yes, yes, I'm Robbie L'Etoile. Come in. Let me take that from you." He snatched the umbrella and deposited it in a Meissen stand. "Can I get you something warm to drink? Coffee? Tea?" he asked as he led the middle-aged man through the storefront and down the corridor.

"Tea would be great."

"I'm impressed with your fortitude. It's a heavy storm," Robbie said as he opened the workshop door and led Fauche inside.

"I was already out. I'm on a tight deadline. I hope you hadn't made other plans?"

"No," Robbie said. "I'm really excited about the magazine's interest in my line."

The last time he'd been in the press was eight years ago, when he moved to the south of France. It had been news that a sixth-generation L'Etoile had started a niche fragrance company in Grasse. Now they wanted to know how he was progressing.

"Have a seat." Robbie offered the journalist one of the upholstered chairs in the corner of the room. "Let me just get the tea started." He turned on the electric kettle and then filled a wire basket with a generous helping of fragrant tea leaves.

"This is Sûr le Nil. A blend of green tea, some spices from Egypt and citrus. Are you a connoisseur?"

Fauche shook his head. "I'm usually just grateful that it's hot. But it sounds good."

The kettle started singing.

Robbie shut it off and ritualistically poured in a small amount of water to warm the pot. Swirling it, he made sure the leaves were wet and then filled it. He put the pot on a tray already set with two cups and linen napkins.

"Here you are," he said as he placed the tray on the low front table in front of the reporter.

"Can you tell me a little about the inspiration for your new perfumes?" Fauche asked, beginning the interview without any warm-up.

"I'm a Buddhist," Robbie said.

"Yes?" The reporter raised his eyebrows.

"And my beliefs have greatly influenced this line. I used the idea of yin and yang and created pairings of scents to enhance our spiritual and sensual natures."

"Interesting." Fauche scribbled some words in a notebook.

Brand new, Robbie noticed.

The tea had steeped long enough. Robbie poured the steaming liquid.

As he handed a cup to Fauche, his fingers brushed the reporter's worn leather jacket by accident. It was soaked through. Why hadn't he taken it off?

"Perhaps you'd like to smell the scents." Robbie walked over to the organ and picked up a small bottle marked *44*. He sprayed a burst of the scent on a white card and then offered it to Fauche, who took it, lifted it to his nose and breathed in deeply.

"Interesting," the reporter said.

Robbie repeated the action with vial *62* and watched as again Fauche put the card up to his nose and inhaled.

"This one is very interesting, too," he said.

"All the scents have international names that need no translation. Those are two halves of the whole I call Kismet. You can wear each separately or combine them." Robbie sprayed another card with both scents and watched with surprise as, for the third time, the journalist failed to wait for some of the alcohol to evaporate, or to wave the card and smell the fragrance in the air.

Why had a prestigious international fragrance magazine sent someone so jejune to interview him?

The third card slipped from Fauche's fingers and dropped to the floor.

Robbie watched the reporter as he leaned over to retrieve the sample. He was wearing expensive lizard-skin boots, soaked through from the rain like the jacket. When he straightened up, his jacket was pushed back at an odd angle. Quickly he pulled it closed.

What is he hiding? Robbie wondered.

"Maybe I could mix up a version of a new scent right now. You could write about the experience of smelling it as I formulate it. I'll use six ancient essences and absolutes: almond, juniper . . ." Robbie pulled out one bottle after another and dripped a few drops of each liquid into a glass vial, all the while watching Fauche from the corner of his eye.

A reporter who specializes in scent is sitting in the workshop of the House of L'Etoile and is totally uninterested in watching me work a formula. He's not writing a word down?

Fauche had gotten up and was walking around the workshop, inspecting the items on the shelves and on tabletops as if looking for something specific. An invited guest wouldn't do that. Not even one who was a nosy reporter.

Standing in front of his worktable, Robbie turned on the Bunsen burner. "I have to heat two of these essences together." As he talked, he calculated. Precision was required. Too little, and the fumes wouldn't be potent enough to have any effect—too much, and they could be fatal—but he had to be prepared. Something was very wrong.

The burner was glowing. The solution was ready. Robbie would give the reporter the benefit of the doubt and allow him one chance to explain who he was and what he was really doing there. If the answer didn't make sense, then he'd do what he had to do to protect himself.

"Mr. Fauche?"

"Yes."

"You haven't asked me many questions."

"I've been busy taking notes."

"Are you really here to interview me about my new line? Or is there perhaps another story you're after?"

The tense smile the reporter offered almost put Robbie at ease. "Yes, actually, there is something else."

"What is it?"

"There's a rumor about an Egyptian relic that you found."

"How did you hear about that?"

"A reporter never reveals his sources." Fauche looked pleased with himself for coming up with the cliché.

Griffin wouldn't have told anyone. Robbie tried to think. How would the word have gotten out? He'd talked to the Rinpoche about giving the gift to the Dalai Lama, but surely the monk hadn't revealed that to the press. Who else? Ah, yes: it had to be the curator at Christie's auction house who he'd asked for an estimate when he'd first found the pot shards. So that's all this was. The interest in his new fragrance line was just an excuse to get in the door and get an exclusive about the Egyptian find. Robbie relaxed.

"Could I see the jar?" Fauche asked.

"I'm sorry, but no. It's in pieces, and they haven't all been cataloged yet. I wish you'd been honest with me about the story you were after. You came out on a very wet night for nothing."

"I must insist you reconsider." Fauche's jaw clenched with barely contained rage. His hand moved to his pocket.

It was all the warning Robbie needed.

"No, no, there's no reason to get upset," he said. "If it matters that much, I'll gladly fetch it." Robbie turned his back on Fauche and slid the beaker over the flame. In the French doors' reflection, he watched the man who certainly wasn't a reporter pull out a gun.

"Hurry up, L'Etoile. Show me the damn pottery."

"I just have to get the key to the safe," Robbie stalled and pretended to look through a small drawer, moving pens and paper clips and droppers around as the liquid in the beaker began to smoke.

"Ah, here it is," he exclaimed, turning abruptly.

The man who called himself Fauche relaxed momentarily, expecting to see the key. When he saw Robbie was empty handed, he started to protest, but his words stuck in his throat. He couldn't catch his breath. He gasped. And then gasped again.

Fourteen

NEW YORK CITY

TUESDAY, MAY 24, 4:00 A.M.

Preferring uninterrupted quiet, Jac worked through the night, as she often did when she was editing an episode of her TV show. Before watching her final cut, she needed to clear her head, so she leaned on the windowsill and breathed in the cool air. Through the spaces between buildings, she could see the Hudson River, and for a few minutes, she followed a tugboat until it disappeared behind a warehouse.

"The Minotaur" was going to be her best episode yet. Her treasure hunt for the myth's genesis had been difficult and even dangerous, and her conclusions were controversial. When the show aired in the fall, the evidence she and her team had discovered about the kernel of truth that sparked the myth should itself spark a serious debate with scholars, mythologists and archaeologists.

According to ancient legend, King Minos of Crete constructed an impressive maze to imprison the repulsive product of his wife's affair with a beautiful white bull that came from the sea. The offspring was the Minotaur—which had the body of a man but the head and tail of a bull—a creature with a monstrous appetite for human flesh.

The Minotaur caused so much terror and destruction that the architect Daedalus was brought to Crete to build an intricate labyrinth to contain it. Trapped, the beast lived in the maze. Every nine years, seven young men and seven young women from Athens were brought to the labyrinth for it to feed upon.

The revolting sacrifices were devastating. The loss of life left scars. Engendered fear.

Finally, Theseus, the son of King Aegeus, declared he would slay the beast and end the cycle of destruction. He volunteered to be one of the victims.

When Theseus arrived on the island, Minos's daughter, Ariadne, fell in love with him. The idea she might lose him was intolerable. She gave him a sword and spool of red fleece so that he could kill the bull and then find his way out of the maze. And then marry her.

Face to face with the monster, Theseus attacked him and killed him. The Minotaur slain, its blood spilled, Theseus returned to Ariadne and took her with him to Athens.

Was there a real basis for the story? Had there been a monster or a madman imprisoned in a maze?

Archaeologists had long believed the ruins of Knossos Palace in modern-day Heraklion in Greece bore a resemblance to the fabled labyrinth. And even though no actual evidence was ever found to support the theory, the city benefited financially from the tourists who came to see the palace and its environs for themselves.

But Jac had learned of a quarry twenty miles away in the village of Gortyn where a team of archaeologists was excavating two and a half miles of tunnels and caves. Was it possible that was the site for King Minos's labyrinth? She took her production team to Greece to find out.

Working with the Gortyn archaeologists, they explored the intertwining passages that twisted and tangled into one another. While filming in one of the dead-end chambers, the cameraman's lights illuminated a faint outline of an archway in what had appeared to be a solid stone wall.

On camera, the archaeological team excavated the area and found a sealed-up entranceway to a hidden cavity. Jac's director of photography filmed its opening, capturing the first light in thousands of years shining in on the jewel-like hollow.

The wall was decorated with red figure paintings on a black

background, all framed with glowing gilt funeral wreaths. These amazingly fresh paintings of groupings of men and of women covered every inch of space. Some appeared to be planned for; others were squeezed in as if the artist had run out of room.

Jac counted. There were fourteen to a group. Seven men and seven women. Each time.

What appeared to be a stone altar sat in the center of the chamber. Six feet long and three feet high. Highly decorated and carved with—were those eye sockets staring at the interlopers? The cameraman shone his light on the ceremonial table. And a terrifying and—to Jac—marvelous fact was revealed.

The altar wasn't made of stone at all but of human bones. Hundreds of femurs, tibias, fibulas, ulnas, radiuses and pelvic girdles had been fitted together intricately to form the rectangle.

Jac was sure, without knowing how she could be certain, that she was standing in the Minotaur's lair and that testing would prove the bones were from approximately 1300 BCE—the same era as the mythical bull.

When the lab reports came in, she was the only one not astonished to learn that the human remains and paintings were dated approximately 1300 BCE.

She shivered now, remembering the feeling she'd had while reviewing the paperwork. Her instincts had been right.

Now it was time to go back to work.

Jac crossed her spare, white office, sat down at her desk and hit the Play button. The opening shot was of the entrance to the caves. She turned down the volume. It was always smart to watch an edit once without sound and just focus on the cuts.

Ten minutes into the episode, her phone rang. No one except her brother ever called this early. If Robbie was excited about something, he was more than capable of forgetting the time difference.

"Out of area," intoned the phone's mechanical voice. The machine never recognized overseas calls; it had to be Robbie. So she answered it.

Despite the interruption, she was always glad to talk to him, even if they wound up in another argument. But all of that would soon be over. The sale of the two perfumes was all set to go through. Robbie just needed to sign the papers, and then the House of L'Etoile could pay off its debt, and they could go back to being simpatico siblings.

"Hi, Robbie."

"*C'est* Mademoiselle L'Etoile?" the male voice asked. It clearly wasn't Robbie.

"Yes, who's calling?"

There was a beep and static. "Hello?" the voice repeated.

"Yes, I'm here. Who's calling?"

"This is Inspector Marcher. I'm calling from Paris. I'm sorry to disturb you. I know it's very early."

"What is it, Inspector?"

"When was the last time you spoke to your brother?" The urgency in his tone cut through her fatigue.

"My brother?" Her heart lurched. When Jac had heard it was the police, she'd assumed this would have to do with her father. "Robbie?"

"Yes, mademoiselle."

"He was here about two weeks ago, and—"

"Have you talked to him since then? On the phone?"

"Has something happened to him?"

"Have you heard from him since then?"

"Yes, of course."

"When was the last time?"

"Yesterday. He emailed me in the morning. Doesn't Lucille know where he is? She's the woman who—"

"Yes, I know who she is. So you haven't heard from him since then?"

"No. What is this about? Isn't he at the office? Sometimes he goes off on spiritual retreats on the spur of the moment. Maybe he's—"

The inspector interrupted again. "No. He's not at a retreat. And he's not at home. He had several appointments this morning that he didn't cancel."

Jac reached for her bag. If something had happened to Robbie, she had to get home, pack, get on a plane, get to Paris.

"What is this about, Inspector?"

"We have reason to believe your brother is missing, mademoiselle."

Fifteen

Breakfast at Chez Voltaire had become part of Griffin's morning routine. At lunch and at dinner, the restaurant catered to a well-heeled
crowd, but for its simple *petit dejeuner,* only the basics were offered and
only locals stopped in.

Maybe it was because of the close call with the car the night before,
but Griffin was hyperaware of everything that morning. How buttery
the croissants tasted. How the homemade jam smelled of just-picked
strawberries. And as he lingered over a second perfect *café au crème,* he
tried not to relive what had happened. But he kept seeing the car nick
the lamppost and skid. Hearing the sound of tires on wet pavement. The
rain was in his eyes. Barely able to see, he jumped behind the stop sign.
Tripped. Fell onto the cobblestones. Scraped the palms of his hands.
Ripped his trousers.

He paid the bill. Walked outside. Breathed in the morning. Paris
awoke with the same flair and elegance with which she did everything
else, he thought. It was something that he wished he could take home
with him.

There it was again—home. At the core of all his thoughts. The
knowledge that this was only a respite. Waiting for him in New
York were failures he had to face, sadnesses he had to own. What

the possibility of divorce had already done to Therese—and what its reality would do to Elsie—made his heart ache. But why put it off? Eventually he disappointed people. He always had. Why should this be any different?

Strolling along the banks of the Seine, watching a tourist boat float by, he tried to convince himself that everything would be all right. By the time he reached the corner of Rue des Saints-Pères, he almost believed it. Then he saw the police cars.

What was going on?

"La rue ici est ferme," the policeman said when Griffin reached the barricade.

"Mais j'ai un rendezvous avec Monsieur L'Etoile," Griffin answered in his best high school French.

"With Monsieur L'Etoile?" the policeman asked, switching to English. "This morning?"

"Yes, this morning. Now."

"You will wait, yes? I will find someone."

The policeman returned, saying that the inspector wanted to speak with him, and ushered Griffin inside the store. Lucille was already there, seated at one of the antique tables. Her eyes were red, and she clutched a rumpled handkerchief so tightly in her hand her knuckles were bone white.

"What's wrong?" Griffin asked. "What's happened here?"

"The store wasn't locked when I arrived." She looked around the boutique. "But nothing seemed out of place." As if reenacting what she'd gone through earlier, she turned and stared at the glass shelves lined with bottles of liquids. "I thought Monsieur L'Etoile had left the door open for me and then had been called to the workshop. It's happened before. So I did all the things I normally do. With no idea. I don't go back to the workshop. I never do. Monsieur L'Etoile always comes to say good morning at nine thirty when I order us both coffee. He doesn't enter though the front." She pointed to the street entrance. "He comes from the house to the workshop to here."

As she spoke, officials and police officers came and went, silent and serious. Some murmured to one another or talked on the phone.

Others took photographs, dusted for fingerprints, picked fibers out of the rug.

"When Monsieur L'Etoile didn't arrive, I waited. I don't like to disturb him even though he says he doesn't mind. He's so thoughtful—" She broke off and closed her eyes.

"A call came that he was expecting, and so I buzzed him on the intercom. When he didn't answer, I went back and knocked on the door. I never go in if he doesn't answer, but he'd told me the day before how important this call was. I knocked again . . . I don't know, maybe I shouldn't have gone in . . . should have left it for the police . . . now I won't ever forget. It will be in my eyes forever."

"Please Lucille, tell me what happened to Robbie."

Lucille shook her head. "I don't know. He wasn't there. And he's not at home. And he doesn't have his cell phone with him. It's on his desk."

"But surely all this"—he gestured to the police activity—"can't be about him just not being here?"

"There was a man—on the floor." She was talking in a staccato rhythm as if she could only get the words out a few at a time.

"I didn't know what to do. He looked like he was sick. I touched him—" Again she broke off. Griffin saw her body shudder. "He was cold. The man was . . . he was . . . I didn't even have to check . . . I knew . . . he was dead." She was crying now, with full-out sobs. Griffin pulled his chair up so that he could put his arm around her and hold her, this woman he barely knew, who was scared and alone and reliving a nightmare that would surely plague her for the rest of her life.

"You called the police then?"

"Yes. And they came right away. But still Monsieur L'Etoile is nowhere."

"He has to be somewhere, Lucille. Was it possible the front door wasn't left open but forced? Was there a break-in? Was anything stolen?"

Before she could answer, a man interrupted. "Are you Monsieur North?" He was fairly short: five foot seven and slim. His navy suit fit him well, and his white shirt looked fresh. His black hair was slicked back, and he wore stylish wire-rimmed glasses. Where his right eyebrow should have been was a ragged white scar, like a crack in an otherwise fine piece of glazed pottery.

"I'm Inspector Pierre Marcher; I would like to ask you some questions." When he spoke, the area around his right eye didn't animate at all. His English was almost perfect.

"Of course."

"If you wouldn't mind leaving us, Mademoiselle Lucille?"

"Pas de probleme," she said as she got up and the inspector took her seat. Pulling a miniature tape recorder out of his pocket, he placed it on the table between them. "It is all right to record our conversation? I find it easier than taking notes."

Griffin nodded.

"Can you tell me why you are in Paris?"

After he explained the reason for his trip, Marcher asked where he was staying.

"At the Montalembert Hotel. A few blocks from here."

"Very nice hotel. Can you tell me what you did yesterday?"

"I worked here all day on the pottery and left at about seven and returned to my hotel."

"So you left in the middle of a blackout—in the storm?"

Griffin noted the incredulous tone. "The hotel is only a few blocks away," he repeated. As he explained, he flashed on the image of the car coming around the corner too fast, seemingly out of nowhere.

"What is it, Monsieur North?"

Griffin told him.

"The car did not hit you?"

"Just missed me."

"Do you remember anything about it?"

"It was a dark sedan."

"Anything other than that it was a dark sedan? Anything from the license plate? The make of the car?"

Griffin shook his head. "No, it was raining too hard. The car was moving too fast."

"Have there been any other incidents like that while you have been in Paris?"

"Accidents? Close calls?"

"Whatever you choose to call them."

"No. Nothing. My stay has been uneventful until now."

Marcher looked thoughtful for a moment, as if he needed to process that. "Last night when you left here, Monsieur L'Etoile didn't leave with you? It was dark, was it not? There was no electricity."

"No, there wasn't, but he'd lit a bunch of candles."

"Did he go back to the house when you left?"

"I don't know. When I left, he was still in the workshop. Robbie said he had an appointment with a journalist."

"Did the journalist arrive before you left?"

"No."

"No one was with Monsieur L'Etoile when you left?"

"No one."

"On his desk," Marcher said, "we found a jeweler's tray. Do you know anything about that?"

"Yes. That's where Robbie keeps the pottery shards we were working on."

"And they were in the tray the last time you saw them?"

"Yes, of course. They're ancient. Fragile. I'm trying to fit them together so we can read the legend on the side of the pottery—but I don't take them out of the tray."

The inspector had not broken eye contact with Griffin once. His voice had been even-keeled and curious. Not accusatory. But Griffin knew he was being interrogated and that something was coming. He just didn't know what.

"So you'd be surprised to know the tray is empty?"

Griffin was stunned. "Empty?"

"You are certain Monsieur L'Etoile would not have taken them out of the tray and put them away somewhere else at the end of the day?"

"No, he's kept them in the tray the whole time I've been working on them. At night he locked the tray up in a wall safe. But I don't know what he did last night. I left before he did."

"So when you left, Monsieur L'Etoile was alone. When we arrived about fourteen hours later, we found a dead man on the floor, the tray on the desk, its contents missing, and your friend nowhere to be seen. Would you mind if we searched your hotel room?"

"You actually think that I had something to with this? Would I have come back here of my own volition if I had?"

"Not likely, no. Unless . . ." He paused as he thought it out. His left eye blinked, his right didn't. "Unless that's exactly why you have come back. Because it would make you an unlikely suspect."

Sixteen

A dour-faced official took a pair of jeans out of Xie's suitcase, unfolded them, and methodically fished inside each pocket.

Xie, who stood with Cali on the other side of a plastic partition, averted his gaze. Even though he had known there were sometimes spot exit inspections in China and that his bag contained no contraband, he was nervous. Why had they singled him out? Had Chung guessed that Xie had ulterior motives for wanting to make this trip and put out an alert?

"After this checkpoint, we'll have to separate," Cali said and pointed toward the next security area.

Xie thought her hand looked like a flower in a breeze.

"We'll say good-bye, and then you'll be on your way."

Her chatter was a welcome distraction from the guard, who was making him more and more anxious with every item of clothing he removed from the bag.

"Have you ever been so far away before?" Cali asked.

"No. I've never been out of China." It surprised him how easy it was to lie sometimes, even to someone he cared so much about. "Last year I went to Hefei to see Professor Wu receive the Lanting Award." It was for excellence in calligraphy. The most prestigious award in all of China.

The guard took a gray sweater out of the bag and shook it. Xie tried not to stare.

"A two-and-a-half-hour bus ride isn't what I mean," Cali said. "This time you're leaving China. Flying on a plane. Seeing foreign lands. Eating food you won't recognize." Thinking about the trip, her eyes shone.

"You should have been chosen too," Xie said. "Your work is as good as anyone's who was picked. Better than most."

"But I'm too outspoken. I'm almost subversive." She laughed. "I'm not upset that my work wasn't picked. I'm upset that you're getting out and I'm not. I want to see all the art you're going to see." Despite the partition, she lowered her voice to a whisper. "And I want to talk to the people you're going to meet. Tell them what's going on here. Really going on."

"I know," he said.

The guard unrolled a pair of black socks and searched inside each.

"I'll tell them."

Her dark brown eyes flickered with anger. "No, you won't," she said. "You're not going to take any chances. I know you. You're going to be careful. Please, Xie. Don't be careful. We need to tell people how bad the censorship is here. How they are trying to control us."

It had taken Xie two years before he'd trusted Cali enough to confide in her that he had a secret. When he finally told her what it was, he'd still told her only half of it. "I want to become a Buddhist monk." That's all he'd said. He didn't know how to form any of the other words, didn't know how to make entire sentences out of the story locked up inside of him about being identified as a lama, the years at the monastery, the fire and his kidnapping.

She'd been confused at his desire to live such an austere lifestyle and got angry with him when he couldn't articulate why becoming a monk mattered to him. Instead, she'd argued, he should join her and her friends, young radicals who wanted to change China, to be part of the new generation who opened doors.

But he wanted to go in the other direction, back to a meditative world of seclusion that had all but disappeared.

Even though Cali didn't understand, she willingly agreed to help him. Using her knowledge of how to hack through China's internet policing, she sent encrypted emails to monasteries in other parts of the world on his behalf. Believing he was asking for spiritual guidance, she never guessed what Xie was actually saying in those messages or what he was trying to set up.

And now here they were. Cali wanted to change the world, but he was the one going off to try to accomplish it. Frustrated that he couldn't tell her that their goals were the same and that this trip was part of the effort, at least he could comfort her. "You'll have your chance," he said. "Next year. Second-year grad students always have the best shot anyway. Next year."

The guard was examining Xie's running shoes now. First the left, then the right. Even taking out the innersoles. Sweat dripped down Xie's back. Was this just a delaying tactic until a higher official arrived to take him into custody? No, they wouldn't handle it this way. There would be no pretense. If they suspected him, they would just arrest him. Wouldn't they?

"You have to remember every single thing you see." Cali had moved from one of her passions to another. Now the art was making her forlorn. "All those paintings and all that sculpture . . ."

But the paintings and the sculpture didn't matter. London wasn't important. Neither was Rome. It was Paris where the opportunity lay. It was Paris he had to get to, no matter how many obstacles he encountered between here and there. It would be in Paris where he'd make a political statement that would at last make Cali proud of him.

As long as he got out of China. As long as his government didn't find out what he was planning. As long as he didn't do anything to raise suspicion with any of the students traveling with him who belonged to the Ministry of Public Security.

The government had spies infiltrating every aspect of society—ordinary citizens, active in the job or organization or university they were monitoring so they always fit in. But trained to observe those around them and report unusual activity.

Xie suspected the PRC students on this trip would be extra vigilant. There would be eyes watching him wherever he went. Taking note of everything he did. If he wasn't conscientious, it would be easy to become anxious and self-conscious.

That's what the PRC wanted. Citizens aware and afraid. Citizens controlled.

He was going to have to fight against it. Say his mantra. Constantly refocus his mind. Concentrate on what was next, on the importance of his mission.

If the PRC found out—if they discovered that a lifetime of "reeducation" hadn't worked—he'd never get another chance. If the authorities discovered that he remembered his abduction, the murder of his teachers, and—above all, that he knew he was the Panchen Lama they all feared surfacing—then he'd never succeed in being reunited with the Dalai Lama.

The itinerary included excursions to Rome, London and Paris, but it wasn't the great museums in each city that Xie thought about. When he let his mind fly, it was to one very small museum situated in the middle of a garden. No matter how many other people were around him and how crowded or noisy the gallery was, that's where everything would change. For the rest of his life, there would forever be the time before that visit and the time after it.

Unless the PRC noticed him and found him out. If that happened, then he'd never leave France alive.

"I wish you could put me in that suitcase," Cali said despondently.

"And then what would I do with my clothes?"

"You can buy new clothes when you get to London."

"And how would you get through customs?"

"Please. No one opens bags at customs in London."

Her earnestness made him laugh, and that made her laugh.

"So it's a deal?" she asked. "Once he's finished repacking your bag, I'll climb in?"

As he had a hundred times before, Xie wished he had a different destiny. One that allowed him to take this girl up in his arms, make love to her, to join her cause and be satisfied with that life. Instead he was bound to something he believed was his karmic duty. A path he was obliged to follow no matter what the cost.

"Mr. Ping?" The official spoke through a microphone. "I am going to need to see your tickets now."

Xie pushed them through the slit in the partition and watched the man read the documents. With a sinking feeling in the pit of his stomach, he watched the official frown. Beside him, he felt Cali take his hand.

Seventeen

Traveling all night and constant worrying had exhausted her. Jac closed her eyes, but the taxi was no more conducive to sleep than the plane had been. The closer they got to the city, the more her anxiety escalated. Jac hadn't been back home to Paris since she'd left sixteen years before. Her grandmother lived in the south, in Grasse, along with the rest of her French family. Aunts, uncles, cousins. Even Robbie had moved there. Everyone except her father. And she'd had enough of him. Before his illness and since.

Robbie.

Where was Robbie?

Even as children, they'd been emotional opposites. Somehow she found melancholy at the edge of things in which he delighted. But they shared so much. Cared so much. Despite their age difference, they'd been each other's best friend. She was young for her age; he was old for his. Together alone in the mansion, they invented worlds to conquer and games that kept them busy during the long, dreary periods when their father was preoccupied with work and their mother was lost in her unhappiness.

One game they invented, The Game of Impossible Fragrances, had become an obsession. Sitting at the child-size perfumer's organ their father had built for them in the playroom, they cooked up fragrances to use as words. An entire vocabulary of scents they could use as their secret language. There were juices for laughter, fear, happiness, anger, hunger and loss.

Looking out the window, Jac noticed more and more familiar sights. By the time the driver reached the sixth arrondissement, she could hear her own heartbeat.

They turned down Rue des Saints-Pères. A police car was parked crazily—half on the sidewalk, half off. Two gendarmes stood outside the boutique's entrance. She'd anticipated the scene, but its reality was chilling.

Even though the police were expecting her, first one officer and then the other examined her passport. Finally, Jac was allowed to open the front door with her own keys. It had been over sixteen years since she'd used them.

Holding her breath, Jac crossed the threshold. Looked around. Everything in her life had changed since she'd last been here, but nothing seemed different. The same antique mirrors reflected her face back at her—so tired, with deep circles under her eyes. The familiar mélange of the house's classic scents greeted her. She looked up. The charming, lighthearted Fragonard-style cherubs in the ceiling mural welcomed her. This morning their cheerfulness was an affront to the seriousness of the situation.

The sound of her footsteps echoed in the crystalline showroom. She stooped at the counter. Ran her fingers over the cool glass top. Her father had sold perfumes here. And his father before him, and on and on, going all the way back to the first L'Etoile, who'd opened this store in 1770. Like all early perfumers, he'd been a glove maker who used scent in order to imbue the kidskins with a more pleasant aroma. When he saw how well his efforts pleased his clients, he added other scented products to his wares: candles, pomades, soaps, sachets, powders, skin oils and creams.

Robbie loved all those old stories. Knew every ancestor by date and which fragrances he had created.

Robbie.

No matter how long Jac postponed the inevitable, she couldn't avoid it. If there were clues to where he was and to what happened, she wasn't going to find them in the showroom. How foolish she'd been to think that she'd never have to confront the workshop again.

With a trembling hand, Jac pushed on a mirrored panel behind the counter. The secret door opened. The corridor lay before her. Dark and uninviting. She stepped into the void.

The heavy wood-paneled door at the end of the hallway was closed. She put her hand on the knob but didn't twist it open. Not yet. If she ever lost her mind anywhere, Jac thought, it would be here.

The old sadness settled on her shoulders as she stepped inside. Looking around for some evidence of what had transpired, she was aware only of the familiar, ghostly fragrance. Spices, flowers, woods, rain, earth—a million extracts and distillations—combined to create this room's own particular and unique odor. Sometimes she woke up from dreams, her cheeks wet with tears and that smell in her nostrils.

Jac rarely cried except in those dreams. Even as a child, when she felt the sting of tears, she blinked them back. Her mother was just the opposite. Jac often found her sitting at her desk in her turret office, her head bowed over her papers, tears sliding down her face.

"Please don't cry," Jac would whisper. Seeing Audrey so sad made the little girl's stomach cramp. Reaching up, she'd stroke her mother's cheek dry. The child comforting the mother. The opposite of how it should be.

"Stop crying, please."

"It's not bad to cry, sweetheart. You can't be scared of feeling." What contradictory advice that had turned out to be—coming from a woman who ultimately surrendered to her own feelings. Became their victim.

Suddenly Jac couldn't catch her breath. The cacophony of scents in the workshop was even more overwhelming than she'd remembered.

It had been so many years since Jac had suffered an episode, she'd believed she was cured. But here, for the first time since she was fifteen years old, she felt the never-forgotten shivers run up and down her arms. Painful pinpricks of cold. The smells around her intensified. The light dimmed. Shadows descended. Her thoughts threatened to wave away.

No. Not now. Not now.

At the clinic, Malachai had taught her an exercise using her own innate abilities to help control the visions. Her "sanity commandments," she called them. Now, effortlessly, she remembered and followed the string of instructions:

Open a window. A door. Get fresh air. Take long, concentrated breaths. Stop your mind from spiraling by giving it a task. Identify the scents in the air.

Without being conscious of having left the workshop, Jac found herself standing outside in the courtyard. Breathing in the cool morning garden air. Grass. Roses. Lilacs. Hyacinth. She almost smiled at all the deep-purple hyacinths planted along the pathways.

Jac kept breathing. Walked past boxwood pyramids and into the labyrinth.

Now she was home. Here. Hidden by the two-hundred-year-old cypresses pruned into impenetrable walls so tall that a man couldn't see over them. This complicated puzzle of warrens and dead ends. Anyone who didn't know how to navigate the maze was lost. But Jac and her brother knew the route by heart. At least, they had as children.

At the maze's center, two stone sphinxes waited for her. In a fit of laughter, she and Robbie had named them Pain and Chocolat—after their favorite breakfast croissant.

Between them a stone bench. In front of the bench, a stone obelisk covered with hieroglyphics. Jac sat down in its shadow.

No one in the house liked coming inside the maze. So to escape an angry parent or nanny, this green room was her hiding place. Here she was safe from everyone but Robbie.

And she never minded when he came to keep her company.

Where was he?

Jac felt panic threatening. That wouldn't help. She needed to stay focused; try to find some answers. She inhaled the sharp, clean smell. Forced her mind to return to the state of the workroom. It was chaos. Even if there were clues to what had happened there two nights ago, who'd be able to sift through the mess to find them?

Robbie had described the confusion and clutter he'd inherited, but she hadn't understood how horrific it was. "A visual metaphor for the state of the family business," Robbie had warned her. "For the state of our father's mind."

He'd said Louis had become a hoarder in the past few years. Kept every piece of notepaper, every bill, every piece of mail, every bottle and box. The visible evidence spilled from cabinets and shelves. Robbie complained that every time he opened a drawer, he confronted yet another set of problems.

"Mademoiselle L'Etoile?" The male voice was muffled by the thick hedges.

"Yes," she called. "It's a small labyrinth but easy to get lost in. Stay where you are; I'll find you."

After making her way back through the twisting green corridors, Jac found a well-dressed, middle-aged man frowning at the maze.

"I realized right away I wasn't going to make it through." He extended his hand. "I'm Inspector Pierre Marcher."

There was something oddly familiar about him; something in his face that she recognized. "Have we met?" she asked.

"Yes, we have," he said. "Long ago."

She couldn't place him. "I'm sorry, I don't—"

"I've been assigned to this district for the past twenty years."

Now Jac nodded, understanding his shorthand.

"So you were here that day?"

"Yes, and I spoke with you," he said gently. "You were so young. It was a terrible shame you had to be the one to find her."

Audrey had killed herself in her husband's workshop, expecting he'd be the one to discover her body. It was the weekend. Robbie was at their grandmother's. Jac was staying with a friend and her family in the country. But the other girl had gotten sick, so they'd returned early and dropped off Jac. The house had been empty. Jac saw the lights on in the workshop and went to see if her father was there.

Jac's grandmother had been the one to crawl under the organ. She'd unwrapped the girl's arms from her dead mother's legs. Pulled her head up from her mother's unmoving lap. Jac was soaking wet with tears and the spilled tincture from a hundred broken bottles. Bloody ribbons of flesh hung off her fingers. Angry red scratches encircled her wrists and arms like piles of bracelets.

Because Jac had been the one to find her mother's body, the inspector had to ask her some questions. But it had taken hours for him to get answers. In her confused state, she couldn't make sense of what she'd seen.

There had been a screaming crowd in the workshop with her. An angry mob. They'd been the ones to break the glass and smash the bottles. To get away from them, Jac had hidden under the perfumer's organ at her mother's feet. What if the intruders found her? They'd killed Audrey. Would they kill her too? Why did they want to destroy the workshop? Why were they dirty? Why were they dressed in such old, ragged clothes? And why did they smell so bad? Not even the bottles of scent they broke disguised their stench.

No. She didn't know how long she'd been there. No, she hadn't made the mess. No, she didn't know what was real or imagined. Not anymore. And maybe never again.

Marcher pulled out a pack of cigarettes. "Do you mind," he asked, "as long as we're outside?"

Even though she didn't smoke anymore, she asked him for one. He shook the pack toward her, and she extracted the cigarette that slid forward. She put it between her lips, and he lit a match, extending it. The mixture of tobacco and sulfur was a delicious distraction.

Jac sensed that the inspector's quiet demeanor represented almost an apology, an acknowledgment of the regret that came with having witnessed the tragedy of her early life.

Even one puff of the strong cigarette was too much. Jac threw it on the pebbled path and ground it out with her heel, noticing the yin-yang pattern in black and white pebbles circling the obelisk. She'd forgotten about that too. All that Eastern influence. "Let's go back," she said, and as they walked, she questioned him.

"Have you found out anything at all to suggest where my brother may be?"

"We haven't, no."

"And what of the man who you found here; do you know who he is?"

"We're having a bit of a hard time with him too."

"What do you mean?"

"In your brother's diary, there's a notation of a meeting with Charles Fauche, a reporter with the *International Journal of Fragrance*. And while there is indeed a man with that name who's affiliated with the journal, he's currently in Italy on an assignment and has been for the last five days."

"So you have no idea who you found here?"

"That's correct. We know only that whoever he is, he doesn't have a criminal record. His fingerprints aren't on file with us or Interpol."

They'd reached the workshop. The French doors were still opened.

"Inspector, do you have Robbie's diary?"

"Yes, I do."

Marcher gestured for Jac to go inside first. He followed her and shut the doors behind him. Jac reopened them. She didn't want to smell all those warring scents.

"Could I have it back?" she asked.

"It's evidence."

"Take down any information you need. Xerox it if need be, but I'd like to have my brother's—" she broke off, confused. "Evidence?"

"Yes."

"Robbie's missing. I thought you were looking for Robbie because you think he might be in danger."

"Yes. And because he is also at this point in time a person of interest in this case."

"I don't understand. On the phone, you said that Charles Fauche—or whoever he is—died of natural causes. That he'd had an asthma attack."

"That's right. He did. Brought on by what he breathed."

"But that can't be Robbie's fault. The man knowingly came to a perfume workshop."

"It appears your brother was burning a toxic chemical in here that brought on the attack."

"My brother is a perfumer. He works with all kinds of toxic chemicals. Surely you can't—"

Marcher bowed his head in deference to what she was saying, but his words belied the action. "We don't know anything, mademoiselle. Not yet. But you might be able to help us learn more. Could you look around at what's on the table here and tell me what kind of perfume your brother was working on that would have required him to burn benzyl chloride?"

"Inspector, someone came here to see Robbie. Someone who wasn't who he said he was. Now my brother is missing—for all we know, he was kidnapped. How can you jump to the conclusion that he committed murder?"

"Mademoiselle, I am not jumping to any conclusion. Far from it. What I am doing is considering all possibilities. One man is dead. Another is missing. Objects from the workshop appear to have been taken. Whether they have been stolen or not isn't clear. We don't yet know anything, but let me assure you, I intend to find out everything."

Eighteen

After the detective left, Jac sat down at her brother's desk and began to look systematically though his papers. What else was there to do? She had to try to find out what Robbie had been doing. Whom he'd been seeing. What he'd gotten involved with. The police had probably gone through his things already, but maybe there was a clue to what had happened that they wouldn't have recognized.

Her brother had to be all right. He had to be somewhere near.

The phone rang. She jumped. Stared at it as if it were a creature, coiled and waiting to spring. It rang again. There was an answering machine. And Marcher had told her his team was monitoring all calls. She didn't need to answer. Except what if it was Robbie? What if he'd been hurt or injured, had been staying with a friend and was finally well enough to call?

"Bonjour?"

There was no reply.

"Robbie?"

A breath. Then a beat of silence. Then a click. Damn. She never should have said his name. What if he had been reaching out to her? What if he was in trouble and calling for help? He might not want the police to know about it. Might have assumed they'd be listening.

Once she'd identified him, he couldn't have answered even if he'd been desperate to.

No, that was crazy thinking. Robbie didn't even know she was here in Paris. Whoever had called was expecting to get Robbie, heard her, was confused, and hung up.

She stared at the phone, willing it to ring again. For whoever had called to call back. Silence mocked her magical thinking.

Turning her attention back to her task, Jac opened the desk's top drawer and was rifling through its contents when a gust of wind blew in through the opened garden doors. Bills, envelopes, letters and notes flew around the room.

After shutting the doors, Jac set to picking up the new mess. Some of the papers had wedged in between the bottles on the perfumer's organ. She stood on the opposite side of the room from the self-contained antique laboratory and stared at it. Not quite ready to go near it.

When she was a child, the organ was off-limits to her and her brother; the precious essences stored there were too expensive. Forbidden, the organ took on larger-than-life proportions. It was wizardry. And temptation.

Sometimes she would sit far across the room and watch the light play on the small glass bottles. The reflections danced on the walls and ceiling—even on her arms when she held them out. Beautiful for the moment. Until the clouds moved and the organ settled back into shadows. A phantom in the corner of the room. The monster of scent. Giving up ugly and strange and beautiful and powerful smells.

Some of the oils were now so old that Jac doubted her brother could even use them. Some must be nothing but sediment. Others, she knew, were so rare that once he finished them, he could replace them only with synthetics.

The perfume industry was changing. Only the talent required to create a truly worthy perfume was the same. Melding dozens of individual notes into a truly sensuous, memorable bouquet would always require a sorcerer of scent.

Going back over two hundred years, her ancestors had sat there mixing up elixirs from the ingredients in these antique bottles. Now they stood, hundreds of glass tombstones in an alchemical museum, waiting for their wizard to come give them life. Could Robbie be that magician?

She was too old to be afraid anymore. Jac crossed the room and sat down at the organ. The essences here were no different from the ones any perfumer used. But no matter how many labs she'd been in, none smelled the way this room did. She breathed it in: the perfume she hadn't smelled since her mother had died. Jac folded her arms on the wooden shelf. Rested her head. Shut her eyes.

As a child, Robbie had named it the Fragrance of Comfort. As an adult, he'd tried to recreate it. She said he was crazy and argued that it was anything but comforting. Dark and provocative, it was, for her, the perfume of time long gone. Of regret. Of longing. Maybe even of madness.

It was no surprise that the smell was more intense now that she was on top of it. Overwhelming. Intoxicating.

A headiness that was almost euphoric filled her and threw her off balance. Grabbing the edge of the organ, she held on as the swell took her. With her eyes closed, she saw a blaze of orange-blue light. Then a swath of opalescent darkness. Then a verdant, marshy, churning green.

The kaleidoscope of images swirled, fracturing before she could identify them. Each thread of scent had a color, and she saw them mingling; saw the chemical bonds forming, sending olfactory shivers up and down her spine. It was more than an aroma or an odor. Much more. The scent was a drug of dreams. A vivid magic carpet ride. Suddenly she was sailing over icy mountains of clouds and oceans of forests, lush and beautiful beyond her dreams. Seeing fragments of faces; eyes that spoke to her, lips that watched her.

The images came faster now, breaking apart over her, spilling like mosaics at her feet. Turquoise and lapis lazuli. Gold. Silver. The scents whispered to her. Teasing her. Then a damp cold enveloped her, locking her inside a prison of emotion: heartbreak, sadness, relief. Still spinning, she held on and forced the procession of pictures in her head to slow down so she could see them. All unfamiliar, places she'd never seen, never visited. A riverbank, a stone enclosure, a courtyard with palms. Sound, too. Birds. So many birds. A woman crying. A man whispering comforting words to her there by the river. Fragments of language. French? No, not French. And a million smells. Some familiar, some as foreign as the language the man and the woman were speaking. He was dark skinned, wearing a wrapper around his waist. At first Jac couldn't see the woman.

Then she realized: *she* was the woman. Her thighs were covered with a thin linen robe; her feet encased in jeweled sandals. The man was somehow familiar. Not his face, but his smell. It was spiced, exotic amber that wrapped around her and drew her in. Close. Warm. Wanted. Whole. Finally. She belonged here. With him.

Then the fear hit. A wrenching fear of impending separation. What was wrong? What was happening?

Jac tried to open her eyes but couldn't. And then she was spinning again. The man and the woman were gone. The river was gone. There was no perfume at all. Dark night sky breaking into slivers of glass. Shattering.

And then she was in a new place.

The air was heavy with burning incense. The terror was gone. Here, inside the church, with her parents and her sister, here she was safe. Here, only peace.

Nineteen

Saint-Germain-des-Prés, with its gilded copper and gold mosaic basilica and marble columns, was the oldest church in Paris and the one place where Marie-Genevieve Moreau always felt at peace. But today she felt as restless as her little sister, who was playing with the hem of her dress even though their mother had twice pulled the child's hands away.

The site of the church had been a temple to the Egyptian goddess Isis hundreds of years earlier, and that was one of the reasons she looked forward to coming here. Not because she felt closer to God here, but to Giles. And when the priest swung the shining silver censer and she breathed in the dense smell of the incense, she felt her lover's presence even more palpably.

Giles L'Etoile had left for Egypt a year ago. His father and brothers had been excited about the youngest son exploring ancient perfuming methods and materials perhaps unknown to them. Egypt's history was full of perfume secrets: the timeless methods of extracting the essences of scent from flowers and woods; the processes of expression, *enfleurage,* maceration and stream distillation from the land that had invented many of them. If Egyptian processes and techniques were superior, then L'Etoile Parfums would have an edge over the competition. And there was much competition in Paris in the last decade of the century.

Only Marie-Genevieve had been afraid for Giles.

She didn't remember a time when she hadn't known him or loved him. Her father, a tanner, supplied the elder L'Etoile with the leather he needed to make the fine scented gloves he sold in his store. The two children had been inseparable since childhood—almost, Marie-Genevieve's mother used to say, as if one was the right glove and one was the left.

There had never been any question they would marry. Marie-Genevieve had thought that would happen when she turned eighteen, but Giles had decided to take the trip to Egypt first. He wanted to see something of the world beyond the street that he'd been born on, he told her. The comment stung, though she knew he hadn't meant to be cruel. She just couldn't imagine that there was anything beyond this street—and particularly his arms and his warmth and the smell of his neck where his soft brown hair met his skin—worth leaving for.

"I'm scared," she'd finally admitted in a whisper the night before he set off.

He laughed. "You think I'm going to meet some exotic Egyptian princess who will keep me there?"

"No . . ."

"Then what?"

She didn't want to tell him about the terrible dream she'd been having over and over.

Giles down deep in a tomb when a sandstorm struck. In agonizing slow motion, she saw the grit whorl around him, getting in his eyes, his mouth, filling up his throat, and finally suffocating him.

"What is it, Marie?"

"I'm afraid you're not going to come home."

"But how can that be? What could make me stay there with you waiting for me here?" He kissed her in the secret way they had. They were careful. She was a smart girl and scared of having a baby too soon. Not for any of the religious reasons, not because it was a sin, but because she didn't want to share Giles yet.

Now she knelt at the altar, pressed her hands together and lifted her face up to the crucifix of the savior Jesus Christ and waited patiently for the priest to give her the body and blood of He who had risen. She closed her eyes and imagined Giles there naked before her, not Jesus. Imagined that it was her lover's body and blood that were going to be given to her. And then she felt the familiar hysteria rising in her.

Why did she imagine such blasphemous things? Yes, the incense always reminded her of Giles, but to imagine that the priest was holding wafers made of Giles's flesh and offering a gold cup that held his blood?

She went to confession and tried to admit these travesties but never managed—she was always too embarrassed to speak of them. Instead she'd tell the priest about her other failings.

"I worry so much about Giles that I make a mess of my embroidery, and then Maman gets upset and yells at me because she can't sell it if it's not perfect."

"You have to trust in the Virgin Mary," the priest would intone through the iron grill. "And when you feel the fears coming upon you, you must pray, Marie-Genevieve. Pray with all your heart."

And that's what Marie-Genevieve was doing while she waited patiently for her portion of the holy host. Behind her, as the parishioners who had already received communion returned to their seats, she heard their feet scraping against the stone floor, the rustle of their dresses, the clinking of their rosaries, the soft murmur of their prayers all filling the church with a familiar sound: the sound of faith. Faith that she tried so hard to have.

"*Mon Dieu, non, non, mon Dieu!*" A woman's cry that was rough and raw, that had escaped rather than been uttered. Extraordinary in the church during a service.

Marie-Genevieve looked to see what was wrong, turning her back on the priest as he approached.

Giles's mother was standing in the aisle next to Jean-Louis L'Etoile, who was holding up his wife. Marie-Genevieve focused on his horrified face. His expression that said all the things his wife's voice had suggested. It was as if he were suddenly one of the stone statues in the side chapels, not Giles's father any longer.

Beside them was a bedraggled man, in dirty, worn clothes, who looked like he had not slept or washed for days. Had he brought this bad news? From far away? How far? From weeks at sea? From Egypt?

Marie-Genevieve tried to run toward them, but her mother held her back.

"No. You must wait until they come to us."

But Marie-Genevieve didn't care about convention. She pulled out of her mother's grasp and ran toward Giles's parents just as his brothers joined the group.

The priest had stopped the mass.

The church was silent.

Everyone was watching.

As if his wife were a rag doll, Jean-Louis L'Etoile handed her over to his eldest son and went to Marie-Genevieve. When he took her hands, his were freezing cold, and she pulled back. From his touch, she knew she didn't want to hear what he had to say. Maybe if she didn't hear it, it wouldn't be true. Maybe if she never heard the words, she could go on waiting for Giles to come home, go on being his betrothed, go on living on the memory of what he had looked like, and smelled like, and how gentle he had been with her and how the two of them were like the two hands of one pair of fine French gloves.

"It's our Giles . . ." Jean-Louis began in a broken voice.

And she felt her legs give way beneath her.

Twenty

"Dead?" Valentine repeated, staring at William in disbelief. He'd said more than that, but she wasn't sure she'd heard anything else. "François can't be dead." As sometimes happened, she'd slipped out of French and into the Chinese dialect her mother had used with her when she was a child.

"But he is," William said. Even though it was a warm morning, he was shivering. His arms were crossed over his chest, hugging himself. "My contact emailed me a copy of the police report. And the death certificate."

"It's a mistake. Someone else's."

"There's a photo, Valentine. A photo taken of François. In the morgue—"

She screamed over his words. "Shut up! Just shut up! It's not true!"

William reached out for her. Took her in his arms. Put his head on her shoulder. She felt his tears through her thin T-shirt.

Gagging, she pushed him away and rushed to the bathroom. Leaned over the bowl. Retched.

When she'd finished throwing up, she slipped to the floor and lay down on the cold tile.

It was impossible. It was all a mistake.

William had called her at midnight when François hadn't returned home. She'd told him not to worry. Things happened on a job. François never gave up. He was probably chasing the perfumer through Paris.

At two in the morning, William called again. And again at dawn. Each time she told him to calm down. To wait.

Tuesday had been the longest day she could remember. No matter how many times William broke, she held strong.

"You know the rules," she told him, echoing what François had taught her. "Without confirmation, no assumptions."

William came into the bathroom without knocking. Helped her to her feet. Wet a washcloth with cold water. Gently washed her face. He squeezed out an inch of toothpaste and handed her the brush. "It will make you feel better," he told her and left her alone.

When Valentine came out of the bathroom, he was sitting at the dining room table staring at an empty vase. Valentine sat opposite him, pulled an ashtray and her cigarettes closer. Shook one out of the pack and lit it. Took a long, deep drag.

"You said asthma?" she asked.

He nodded.

"I'd have known if François had asthma. He would have said." She looked down at the burning ember between her fingers. "I smoked in front of him."

"I'm going to make tea." William got up.

"Tea?" Her laughter sounded hysterical in her own ears. François always made tea, too. Was never without a cup, especially in a crisis. Crisis equaled tea in so many cultures. As if heat could heal. Who started this nonsense: the Indians, the Chinese, the British? Macerated dried leaves wouldn't solve anything.

In the kitchen, William started the ritual. Every sound—the water running, the cabinet squeaking open, the china cups clinking on the countertop—grated on her nerves. She needed to try calming down; to practice one of the meditation techniques that François had taught her when he'd first taken her in.

"Why would he let me smoke in front of him?" she called out. "Why wouldn't he tell me he had asthma?"

"He didn't want anyone to know."

"Not even me? I don't believe it."

William came out of the kitchen, holding a tray, shaking his head. She thought she detected a little smile of satisfaction on his lips. William was always slightly jealous of her relationship with his lover. She'd even wondered if he'd joined the Triad just to keep an eye on François. He'd never seemed to care about the cause, the brotherhood, or the thousand-year-old traditions. She and François had been the true soldiers. Comrades in arms. And now she was left with the wrong partner.

"He wanted to appear invincible," William said.

"He was invincible," she whispered.

"Will you come to the hospital with me this afternoon?" he asked quietly.

"Where?"

"To the hospital. We can't leave his body unclaimed. We have to honor him."

She looked at him as if he were insane. "How can we claim his body? Who do we say we are?" She realized that she was yelling and raised her hand in apology.

"You took an oath," William said.

Since the nineteenth century, all members had taken the same thirty-six oaths. She'd memorized them and still knew them by heart.

I shall assist my sworn brothers to bury their parents and brothers by offering financial or physical assistance. I shall suffer death by five thunderbolts if I do not keep this oath.

William was right: she had to help him. "But not yet," she said. "François would tell us this job comes first." Trying to keep her voice from cracking, Valentine clenched her fists. She'd killed someone once with her hands wrapped around the man's neck as François stood nearby, giving her instructions on how and where to press.

She tried to summon him.

What should I do? With you gone, who do I ask for help?

François had trained her for this contingency.

"No one of us is as important as the society," he'd asserted. "If one of us is caught, even killed, the rest of the team continues."

He'd given Valentine marching orders and made her memorize them like she'd memorized her oaths.

"If a plan fails, create a new plan. Don't forget that if you need to, you can go on without me. You're ready." He'd smiled proudly. "You're ready. Do you understand?"

Valentine crushed the cigarette out. Drank the strong black tea that François favored. That she always found so bitter.

"I need to call in the rest of the team," she said. "Reorganize. We need to get someone outside the House of L'Etoile with directional microphones and find out what's going on."

"Shouldn't we contact Beijing first?"

"It's too late in the game for that. They might send in someone new to oversee us. We'll lose our momentum. *We* need to take charge."

"So you're appointing yourself incense master?" William asked, referencing another of the oaths they'd all taken.

I shall be killed by five thunderbolts if I make any unauthorized promotions myself.

"No. Of course not. Beijing can name anyone they want to fill the official position. We need to finish the job François started."

He was looking at her as if she were a stranger. "You're ready to go back to work? We have to mourn him, Valentine."

"There's no time now. The Dalai Lama will be in Paris on Saturday. We have four days to make sure the Egyptian pottery doesn't wind up in his possession."

Now she placed her hands on William's shoulders and looked into his red eyes. "I promise, we'll mourn him properly when this is over. For now we honor him best by finishing the work he died for."

François had been worried about this job from the beginning. But not for himself. For her.

"It's one thing when the enemy is unknown," he'd warned her just two days ago. "When your victim is a stranger. But this could be the most difficult test you've ever faced. You're going to have to steel your soul, Valentine."

There had been just two men who'd mattered to her.

François Lee, who'd saved her life and had been the only father she'd ever known.

And Robbie L'Etoile, who'd opened her heart and been the only lover she'd ever taken.

Now in avenging one's death, she might have to kill the other.

Twenty-one

Jac gripped the edge of the perfumer's organ and tried to stand. Her body trembled. The room glowed, as if there were light escaping from the perfume bottles, as if they were alive. Backing up, she took a first tentative step and then a second. Finally, she was on the opposite side of the room, her back up against the door, ready to escape.

The organ was just a workstation again.

Her eyes swept over the inanimate objects, making certain nothing moved, nothing waved or shimmered; that all was once again normal. That was how she could be sure she'd returned to her own mind—that the awful episode was over.

According to the black-onyx-and-alabaster clock, very little time had passed. Five or six minutes, no more.

It had been so many years since she'd felt the known world slip away and had found herself—or some version of herself—alive and terrified in another place and time. But the experience of a psychotic episode is not something you forget. This one had lasted longer and been more detailed than any she'd endured as a child. Compared to this, those had been cracks. This was a gaping hole.

Jac could not allow this to happen. Not now. Not with Robbie missing. Not with the police coming in and out of here. Not again. Not while she was alone. She slid down and sat in a crumpled mess on the floor. She pounded on the floor with her fists.

When she was younger, the hallucinations had been elusive and incoherent, and when she came out of them, she rarely remembered details. But she could recall everything from this incident. None of the images had dissipated or dissolved. She could see the church in all its detail and hear the people and smell the incense, all with an intense clarity. She remembered exactly what that sad woman had been thinking, exactly what she'd seen . . .

Wait. She had a name. Her lover had a name, too.

Jac had never before conjured a hallucination about people whose names she knew. But she'd cast a L'Etoile ancestor in this one.

A brutal knock on the door reverberated through her body. She jumped and faced the door like an executioner was on the other side.

"Who's there?" she called out.

It was one of the gendarmes stationed outside.

She opened the door.

"The inspector dropped this off and asked me to give it to you."

The policeman held out a slim black leather book. On the cover, Jac saw the initials—R.L.E.—and something inside her chest constricted. When she reached out to take it, she noticed her hands were trembling.

She murmured thanks.

"Are you all right? Can I get you something? Call someone?"

"No." She smiled. "I'm fine. Thank you for this."

Once he was gone, Jac once again opened the French doors, let in the fresh air, and sat down at the desk. For the next forty-five minutes, she rifled though her brother's datebook, absorbed by the distraction. She stopped on the entry for a date two weeks ago: the anniversary of their mother's death. The day Robbie had flown to New York. He'd been with her at the cemetery and then said he had an appointment. He'd never mentioned who he was meeting. She hadn't asked.

But here it was. A name she'd never expected to see here. Why had her brother met with Griffin North in New York? She paged ahead. More appointments with Griffin. Why was he here in Paris? Why had Griffin been seeing Robbie every day for almost all of last week?

A scent memory swept over her.

She'd smelled Griffin North before she'd even met him, attracted to his aroma before she knew his name or heard his voice. He was standing behind her at a party. For a moment, she didn't turn. Didn't try to find him. She just breathed.

Later Jac discovered the cologne he'd been wearing had been created in the 1930s by an American fragrance house. And it had been discontinued in the early 1960s, before Griffin was even born. He was the first and last man she'd ever met who had worn that fragrance. When she'd asked him how he even knew about it, Griffin told her he'd found it in a beach house his grandparents had rented one summer. It was the single item the owners had left behind in the bathroom. "The only thing I've ever stolen," he once told Jac.

Griffin didn't have much of a nose for fragrance. But what really appealed to him was the mysterious story. Why had it, alone, been left behind? Orphaned?

Jac thought the scent promised stories, too, but based on its essences. Its ingredients were as old as the Bible: bergamot, lemon, honey, ylang ylang, vetiver, civet and musk. Rich florals and animalic accords that blended together to create a particular scent that for her would always be associated with Griffin. With their time together. With wonder. With falling in love. With a cessation of loneliness. And then with anger and grief.

Long after they'd broken up, she still scanned tables at flea markets and auctions on eBay, buying up even half-empty bottles. In the recesses of the armoire in her bedroom, she had a cache of eight bottles. Even in sealed packaging, even in the dark, cologne evaporated. Like moments in your life. Time fades the details.

No culture had been more proficient at creating long-lasting perfumes than the ancient Egyptians. It was said their fragrances improved with time.

Wait.

Egypt?

The woman in the hallucination was thinking about Egypt too.

Jac struggled to remember why.

Her lover had been killed there.

Now, in her mind, that strange woman's pain echoed and merged with her own. Except Jac's lover hadn't been killed. He'd left her. But hadn't it been a death of sorts?

She'd been innocent about relationships the way you can be only the first time. Before you understand that the underside of love is so rough that just the slightest contact with it rips your skin to shreds, makes you bleed, causes a kind of pain that goes so deep you can't see beyond it.

Jac had just finished graduate school in California. Griffin had completed his PhD at Yale University and had landed a highly coveted job on a prestigious Egyptian dig. The team of archaeologists, sponsored by the Smithsonian museum, was using magnetic sensors to locate and map key pharaonic sites around the areas of Portus Magnus of Alexandria, Canopus, and Heraklion. Griffin was their first new hire in over a year.

Before he flew off, they were going to spend a week together in New York.

It was a warm summer evening, and dusk was settling over the lake, casting long shadows. They were so deep in Central Park the hum of insects and birdsong had replaced city traffic. While they drank cold white wine dockside at the boathouse, rowers skimmed the water, lazily dipping their oars, barely disturbing swans and mallards. The bucolic scene was enhanced by the dozens of butterflies flitting around a large patch of wildflowers growing just to the right of the deck.

Jac, who'd written her thesis on the symbolism of butterflies in mythology, had been surprised to see so many different families and subfamilies in the midst of Manhattan. She pointed out a silvery gray Spring Azure—almost the hue of mother-of-pearl. And an iridescent-blue Pipevine Swallowtail.

Griffin didn't respond. He drained his wineglass in one gulp, looked away from Jac, and, in a voice so low she had to lean forward to hear him, told her that he didn't expect her to wait for him to come back from Egypt.

"Wait for what?" she'd asked, not understanding.

"For me. For us."

The blue-black butterfly was so close she could count the seven round orange spots on its hind wings. They never touched, she'd read, but were spaced so that they remained separate.

"Why not?" The words felt like cardboard in her mouth. It sounded to her as if she were spitting them out instead of saying them.

"You expect too much from me and for me. I'll never measure up to how you see me."

She heard the words. Understood each in the abstract but couldn't piece them together to make sense of them as a whole.

He must have sensed her confusion. "Your great expectations for me make me feel small. I know I'm always going to disappoint you. It's not how I want to live." He sounded defeated.

"Is this about your dissertation?"

She'd been waiting to read it for months. He'd kept putting her off. Telling her he didn't want to show it to her until it was complete. She'd accepted that. Jac knew the topic was giving him problems, that the research was proving elusive, and that he was up against a deadline. When Griffin stopped complaining, she'd assumed he'd worked it out.

Then this morning, while he was still sleeping and she was straightening up the hotel room, she saw his thesis protruding from his knapsack.

She opened it to the first page.

"I, Griffin North, declare that 'Greek Influence on the Representation of the Butterfly in Ptolemaic Egyptian Art: Tracing Horus to Eros and Cupid and Back Again' is my own work and . . ."

Beside her, a butterfly was feeding on a pink-and-yellow lantana flower. She watched as another joined it. This one was black with red median bands and white spots. She'd forgotten its name. Suddenly remembering became critical.

"I, Griffin North, declare that 'Greek Influence on the Representation of the Butterfly in Ptolemaic Egyptian Art: Tracing Horus to Eros and Cupid and Back Again' is my own work and that all the sources that I have used or quoted have been indicated and acknowledged by means of complete references."

Except that he hadn't. Griffin had lifted entire paragraphs—a few times, whole pages—of what she'd written without citing her own thesis at all.

She tried to talk herself out of being upset. His work wasn't identical to hers. She hadn't written about Greek influences on late-kingdom Egypt. But he'd used all her research about the symbolism of the butterfly in Greek mythology to tie the insect to Eros and Cupid. Griffin had used her analysis to make his case that paintings of butterflies in late-period tombs were a result of the Ptolemies' Greek heritage.

If he'd asked, Jac would have gladly given Griffin her paper. Without a PhD, he'd be unable to secure a position in the field. And that's where his passion lay. Not in the halls of academia but in the desert with sand under his fingernails. Grad school was tough on anyone, but for him it had been brutal. The professor he'd assisted knew that Griffin needed the job and that there were no other assistantships open, and so the man took advantage of him, dumping a massive amount of responsibility on him.

Sitting on the floor, Jac had read through the whole dissertation, skimming some sections while giving others careful attention. It wasn't what he had done but that he'd done it without telling her.

And when he woke up, she confronted him.

He'd barely explained. Just accused her of looking though his things without asking.

"If anyone finds out they'll withdraw your degree. Accuse you of plagiarism," she said.

"No one could find out unless you tell them. Are you planning on doing that?" He was shouting.

She was suddenly staring at a stranger. "How could you even ask me that?"

Griffin had stormed into the bathroom, taken a shower, dressed, and gone out, all without saying another word to her. Left her to feel guilty for what she'd done. She'd been astounded by his effort at manipulation. He'd never done anything like that to her before.

At four o'clock he called and asked her to meet him at the boathouse.

Jac had expected him to be contrite and apologize. She knew she was going to forgive him. But leave her rather than deal with what he'd done?

The following morning, she got herself out of bed and to the airport. She went to her grandmother's house in the south of France; the only safe place she could think of. Every day that first week, she expected Griffin to call or email. Every night she'd climb into bed and cry, devastated. She'd get to sleep only by telling herself that she'd hear from him the next day. For sure.

Every morning, she woke up angry with herself for being needy. For still wanting a man who was so weak that he wouldn't even fight for her. She'd get out of bed resolute. If he called, she wouldn't talk to him. If he emailed, she'd delete it.

And then she'd wait.

By the end of August, Jac's emotional reserve had dried up, and she returned to New York with only half her heart.

After that summer, whenever Jac needed to remind herself that she'd once made a grave error opening up and trusting someone, she had a ritual.

She'd remove one of the bottles of his cologne from her armoire. Shut off the lights, pull the blinds. Sit on the edge of the bed. Holding her breath, she'd wet her fingertips with some of the precious liquid, dab it across her collarbone and both sides of her throat, then down one arm and up the other. Finally, she'd bring her hands up to her face and inhale, allowing the full impact of the scent to hit her.

The powerful musk embraced and enveloped her, lulled her into believing that she was still with Griffin—that she'd once more found the soul she was truly connected to.

Then she'd open her eyes and look around at the bedroom with its beautiful damask curtains, engravings of ancient roses on the wall, and the dozens of glittering bottles of L'Etoile perfumes on the vanity. In the mirror, she wouldn't see herself as much as the emptiness in the space beside her where, but for an instant, she'd imagined Griffin to be.

And then, because the whole exercise was a punishment, so that she'd never again forget how foolish it was to believe in dreams, she'd allow herself to remember more. The first time they'd been together in her bedroom in her aunt's house. Dusk was turning to night. After they'd made love, he'd told her the story about the two halves of Plato's whole.

"We're those halves . . ." he'd said.

"Âmes soeurs." She'd translated the phrase into French.

"You were too vulnerable when you met him," Jac's grandmother had told her, trying to console her. "You were too impressionable and too much a loner. Too young. He got too deep under your skin. You're going to have to make an effort to get over him. But you will. Do you hear me? You will, in time."

Jac had made the effort. She turned Griffin into a lesson learned. Used him as a map of terrain to avoid.

But no matter how happy she was in subsequent serious relationships, her deep connection to Griffin haunted her.

And now he was here in Paris. Why? There was a phone number beside his name in Robbie's agenda. Jac hesitated. Call him after ten years? Hear his voice again? How could she let any of that matter? Their connection to each other was long, long gone. Evaporated. Robbie was missing. That was her only concern now—not her past.

She dialed the number.

"Hello?"

The sound of his voice froze her own. A vertiginous wave of feeling broke over her, and she struggled to pull herself back to the surface; to say something, to find her voice over the roar of the imaginary, turbulent ocean. It had been so many years since she'd last talked to Griffin. Suddenly, she rememberd watching his back as he walked away from her that last time.

"Griffin," she said, "it's Jac."

She heard a sharp intake of breath and was satisfied by it. At least there had been that.

Twenty-two

The wind had slowed to a breeze, and the cyclists, two couples from London who often traveled together, were enjoying a respite and some lunch by the shore of the river. The past three days spent exploring the forty-kilometer-long estuary, sprinkled with islands and edged by marshes, had proved to be everything the travel agent had promised: a haven for bird watching, perfect for fishing, and when they wanted to get off their bikes, there was more than enough to see and do in the ancient cities nearby. Sylvie had a degree in French history and entertained them all with her anecdotes that were always spiced with salacious or gruesome details. Her husband, Bob, joked that she was a walking repository for the dark side of history.

"During the French Revolution," she was saying now, "there was a victory here for the Jacobites in 1793 that was very important, but what the area was most famous for was the hundreds of thousands of Republican marriages that took place here."

"Why do I get the feeling that's not something as simple as a Bush marrying a Cheney?" Olivia said.

They all laughed, and Sylvie continued. "It was a term that referred to a Jacobite method of execution. The antireligious revolutionaries stripped men and women—most were priests and nuns—and, standing them back to back, tied their wrists together, took them in a boat onto the river and then baptized the union by throwing them into the water, where they eventually drowned."

They looked at the churning current that was pulling north, heading out to the sea, as she finished. "They didn't call it the Reign of Terror for nothing." Reaching forward, Sylvie dipped her fingers in the water as if cleansing them after telling the story. The sunlight glinted on a rock that had—she looked closer. Was that a credit card sticking out from under it? She reached down. It wasn't a rock. It was a soggy wallet.

"What have you got?" Bob asked as he came up beside her.

"Someone must be pretty upset," she said as she showed him.

"When we go back to town, we should drop it off with the police."

"There's more than that to show the police," John called from a few feet away. "Look at this." He held up a black loafer.

"That shoe doesn't necessarily have anything to do with the wallet," his wife, Olivia, said. "You're always seeing something suspicious."

Bob inspected the wallet. "Is there a label in the shoe?"

"Yes. J. M. Weston."

"I'm betting these things belong to the same man, then."

"But anyone could buy Weston shoes. We're in France," Olivia said.

Sylvie argued her case for her husband. "Expensive shoes, expensive wallet," she pointed out. "Washed up on the shore of the Loire four feet away from each other."

"Is his name in the wallet?" John asked. "There seem to be initials inside the shoe, under the tongue. How rich do you have to be to have your friggin' initials inside your shoes?"

"Rich enough to live in one of the most exclusive areas in Paris," Bob said. "Are the initials R.L.E.?"

John raised his eyebrows and looked from one face to the other. "So it's the same bloke," he said finally. "I think we'd better find a bobby."

Twenty-three

Jac saw him before he saw her as he came through the café doors. His easy gait was the same; she remembered how gracefully he moved despite his height. Griffin's mouth was set in a serious straight line, and his gray-blue eyes were the color of a troubled sea. But when he noticed her, he smiled—that same strange, satisfying smile she remembered that lifted a little higher on the right side. His hair was shot through with some silver, but still thick, and waves of it fell on his forehead. He tilted his head just a fraction to the left, and his eyebrows raised almost imperceptibly. With that one look, he managed to convey the depth of his concern for her, and she remembered what it had felt like to think that they'd belonged together.

In the past few hours, when she'd allowed herself to imagine this moment, Jac hadn't pictured him wrapping his arms around her before they'd even spoken. Yet now he took her in his arms without hesitation and held her tight.

She breathed his smell. Impossibly, still the same.

"I'm so sorry," he said as he let her go. "We'll find him. I know we will."

They sat down. Despite the jet lag and the shock of Robbie's disappearance and the police having discovered an unidentified dead man in the workshop, something inside of her lifted. It was *Griffin* opposite her, holding on to her with his eyes. How could he still pull at her like this? As if no time had passed, when a lifetime had. When he'd left her, she was so lost and so angry that she'd never wanted to see him again. Now here he was, and she needed his help.

The waiter arrived, and they ordered coffee.

"I'm sorry," Griffin said again.

"Why are you apologizing? Was there something you might have done to prevent what happened?"

He shrugged. "No. Probably not. But I was there. I'd just left." His eyes didn't leave her.

"How long have you been in Paris?" Jac asked.

"A few days." He put his hands on the table.

The years of working with stone and sand had taken their toll, and she wondered how rough the tips of his fingers would feel on her skin.

"On business?"

"Of a sort. When Robbie found out my wife and I separated, he asked me to come help him with something."

"You and Robbie remained friends? He's never mentioned you."

"We keep in touch. I've kept tabs on you, though." Another smile. This one slightly sad.

"What were you helping him with?"

"He'd found something and wanted me to figure out what it was."

"Stop being cryptic. You're always so stingy with details." Remembering this about him and how it used to frustrate her, she half smiled. Then her worry took over again. "What did he need help with?"

"He didn't tell you?"

She paused, thinking back to the last time she'd seen her brother and their conversation in their mother's crypt. "I think he tried to, but we were arguing."

"He told me that."

"Really?"

"We've been together twelve, fourteen hours a day since Thursday. There's been a lot of conversation."

"Then you know what kind of shape the House of L'Etoile is in?"

The waiter brought the coffees, and she drank hers too quickly and burned her tongue. The sting was a welcome relief from the roiling emotions.

"He was hoping his find would pay off a chunk of those loans."

"What are we talking about? What did he find? Can't you just tell me, for Chrissakes?"

"When Robbie took over from your father, the workshop was a mess. You've seen it?"

She nodded.

"He said it was as if your father had started looking for his memory and took the entire place apart trying to find it. In one of the piles, he found a small box filled with pottery shards. He did some research and found out they were ancient Egyptian. At that point, Robbie came to see me in New York, and I agreed to help. I've been able to determine the object was once a round pot from the Ptolemaic Dynasty that was filled with a waxy substance, like a pomade. Its bowl is decorated with hieroglyphics that tell a story of lovers who use its perfume to remember their past lives and find their *ba*, their—" He'd used the Egyptian word.

"Soul mates," she finished for him, remembering the story her father had told her and Robbie. The ancient book of formulas and the fragrance found in Egypt over two hundred years ago. The lost L'Etoile treasure.

"Your family's legend, Jac, it's real. Robbie found proof of it."

"Proof of what, though?" She ran her finger around the rim of her coffee cup, feeling the smooth, round edge. "Cracked pottery could be manufactured. Fakes were a big business even in the nineteenth century. A story like that would sell more perfume. There's no scent that triggers—"

She broke off. Remembered what had just happened to her in the workshop.

Some therapists theorized that certain odors could trigger psychotic episodes. The scientists at Blixer Rath had conducted tests with her, but hadn't found an olfactory response.

Griffin looked at her with fresh concern. He'd always read her so closely and reacted so quickly to her changing moods or thoughts. That he could still do this surprised her.

"What is it? Jac?"

When they were together one night, she and Griffin had sat in bed in the dark and told each other their secrets. His about his father. Hers about finding her mother. And the episodes. But she didn't want to discuss her private demons with him now. Not after all these years.

"There's no book of formulas."

"Cleopatra had a perfume factory, Jac. It's real. Mark Anthony built it for her. They've found it in the desert at the south end of the Dead Sea. Thirty kilometers from Ein Gedi. Ancient perfumes were found there."

"There's no soul-mate scent," she said. "It's all the stuff of fantasy. That's what perfume is: magic and imagery. My ancestors made it all up to enhance the aura of the House of L'Etoile."

Griffin's eyes darkened. She'd forgotten that—how when the light shifted, they could lose their blue hue and turn to cold, impenetrable steel. "It wasn't all made up," he said intently. "The pot shards are authentic. And the chemical analysis of the clay shows it was impregnated with ancient oils."

"Then Robbie should have been able to reconstruct the scent and prove what it can and can't do. He has access to all the same oils and essences the Egyptians used."

"Apparently there are some unidentifiable ingredients, Jac. The lab couldn't isolate them, and Robbie can't sniff them out. The inscription on the pottery lists the ingredients. That's what we were working on."

And as Griffin continued to explain, despite her conviction that any such fragrance was only a fantasy and that there was nothing logical about what he was suggesting, she found herself wondering again. What was that thread of scent she'd always smelled in the workshop? That unidentifiable odor that neither her brother nor her father could smell but that she *could*? And did it have something to do with her attacks?

Twenty-four

Malachai walked up the broad steps to the New York Public Library. It was an unusually warm morning. Even though it had been a short walk from the taxi up the stairs, once inside, he welcomed the cool and dark oasis.

And it welcomed him.

Over the years, coming here to study obscure treatises that touched on past-life theory, he'd learned the library's grand spaces and secret recesses. It was a living entity that shared itself willingly and appreciated those who appreciated it. A romantic notion, Malachai knew. But one he enjoyed.

Across the lobby, he stopped for a moment at the stairway to prepare himself for the effort. An accident two years before during a concert in Vienna had left him with a slight but ever constant pain in his hip that climbing worsened.

He glanced upward. The high ceiling transfixed him. Lifted his soul. Made him draw in his breath and filled him with reverence. The library was a house of worship to the spirit of creativity and the pursuit of knowledge.

Reed Winston sat at a long table in the main reading room, a half-dozen books spread out before him. He didn't turn when Malachai passed him. And he didn't acknowledge his boss's presence when Malachai sat down across the table from him eight minutes later.

Malachai opened the book he'd requested from the stacks: *The Letters of D. H. Lawrence.* Rifling through it, he searched for a particular page. When he found it, he removed a small leather-bound book from his pocket and took notes.

For the next thirty minutes, the two men sat at the same scratched wooden table, sharing the same green glass lamp. To anyone watching, it appeared that they were unaware of each other. At eleven, Malachai returned his book to the front desk and left.

He reached the corner of Fifth Avenue and Fortieth Street as the light turned red.

"I think you left this in the library."

Malachai turned.

Winston, out of breath, held out Malachai's leather notebook.

"So I did. Thank you."

Winston shook his head. "That's okay."

If Winston hadn't followed him, Malachai would have understood the ex-agent was concerned they were being watched.

The light turned green. The two men crossed the street together. On the other side, they began to talk in earnest as they walked toward Madison Avenue.

"What on earth happened in France?" Malachai asked. "You assured me you had the right people in place. That nothing was going to go wrong. That we were, above all, not going to lose sight of our goal."

"They are the right people."

"But Robbie L'Etoile's disappeared?"

"Yes. It seems impossible, but that's what my contact reported."

"Is he getting that from the police?"

"Yes. L'Etoile is missing. And he's the prime suspect in their murder case."

"And the victim is still unidentified?"

Winston nodded.

"What about his sister?"

"Under surveillance."

"By who?"

"The best we have."

Malachai looked at Winston.

"There was nothing that could have been done to prevent this," Winston argued, even though Malachai hadn't said a word. "There was no way to anticipate what happened."

"You and the men you hire are paid to anticipate everything."

"Yes. But it's not possible."

Despite his frustration, Malachai knew the ex-agent was right. There were things you couldn't anticipate. Like suddenly becoming aware of smelling the world around you when you were fifty-eight years old.

"There is no way that this is going to slip through my fingers." Malachai was talking about a piece of pottery. He was picturing a woman.

"I understand."

"It's going to require a trip to Paris," Malachai said.

"I can go tonight."

"Not you. I'm going." He didn't like leaving his practice on short notice. The children he helped were sacrosanct. But if the pottery shards were a memory tool, and if they were missing, that took precedence. He could arrange for another therapist to take over his cases for a few days. He couldn't trust anyone else to go to France.

"I'll be flying out tomorrow. Fire whoever you had working for you over there. Find me someone who doesn't know the meaning of the word *impossible*. In French. Or in English."

Twenty-five

When Jac and Griffin arrived back at the workshop—so he could show her photographs and read her his translation of the story on the pot— Inspector Marcher was waiting.

"I've received a call from the police in the Loire Valley," he said without preamble.

"Yes?" Jac asked. She hadn't realized how much tension she'd expressed with the single word until she felt Griffin gently take her arm.

"Your brother's wallet and his shoes were found by the shore of the river," the inspector informed her in an even, unemotional voice, as if he were describing the weather.

Jac had been standing; now she found the first place to sit and crumpled into the chair in front of the perfumer's organ. "What does that mean, exactly?"

"Nothing definitive. Someone might have stolen these things from him and thrown them in the river."

"Stolen his shoes?" Trying to ward off the rising panic, Jac took a deep breath. Then another. And despite the fact that they were discussing the disappearance of her only brother, Jac's attention was averted by her sudden awareness that she was again inhaling the same mysterious scent that had so transported her earlier in the day. A scent that hovered in a cloud around the organ. That faint wave of dizziness she'd experienced before returned.

"Why would someone have stolen his shoes?"

"We don't know what happened yet. That's why we are actively engaged in doing a search of the whole area," the inspector explained.

Jac was looking at the tiny glass bottles gleaming in the afternoon sunlight. There was no dust anywhere. Robbie kept everything here so clean.

"His wallet and shoes? Are you certain they are his?"

"I'm sorry, but I am sure."

Some of the labels on these bottles had been handwritten by her grandfather. Others by her father. Robbie must have written some of them too. He'd been working here for the last three months. Surely he had brought in some new synthetics. But she couldn't find a single label with her brother's handwriting. There was no proof of his existence in the place where he'd last been.

"Are you saying that you think he's drowned?" She took another deep, deep breath. The air was getting stuffy again. "He can't be. My brother is a very good swimmer."

Griffin came up behind her and put his hands on her shoulders. For an instant, it felt as if he were the only thing keeping her from floating up and disappearing into the scent cloud.

"The river is famous in that area for its strong currents. I'm hoping he's nearby, perhaps only slightly hurt. If he's there, we'll find him. We have teams searching from above the point where we found his items all the way down to where the Loire opens to the sea."

Jac rubbed her eyes. One summer, their grandmother had taken Robbie and Jac to stay in a cousin's chateau in the Loire Valley near Nantes. Despite the beautiful countryside and the ambling river, Jac had been unusually restless. Physically uncomfortable. During their first night there, she suffered terrible nightmares. Woke up with Robbie shaking her. "It's only a dream," he reassured her. "Only a dream." That night he sat with her, talking, keeping her distracted until the sun rose. At breakfast, he convinced their grandmother they should leave earlier than scheduled. "Something about this place and Jac didn't like each other," he'd said at the time.

"Where in the valley?" Jac asked now. "Where exactly were his things found?"

"In Nantes."

Jac understood what Marcher said, but it was too confusing. Nantes? It was such a peculiar coincidence.

She needed to let in the fresh air. She stood and started toward the French doors. But before she got to them, the scent drug started to pull her away.

The last thing she remembered, from a distance, was Griffin's voice.

"Jac, are you—"

Twenty-six

Marie-Genevieve Moreau stood in the bright sunlight and felt the sweat run down her neck. Despite the beauty of the shore and the river, the scene was hellish. Hieronymus Bosch's twisted, turned-inside-out hell. That was where she was. That was what she was living.

"You, next." The soldier with the wart on his nose pulled her roughly toward him. His counterpart, a short man with a brilliant red scar on his chin who stunk of rotting teeth, tore her habit off of her, as she knew he would. As he'd done to the other victims before her.

After the wool of her habit was ripped free, he yanked loose her underthings. Naked, she covered her breasts, but that left the triangle between her legs bare. She didn't have enough hands. She tried turning her back, but they wouldn't have that.

"Not while we're enjoying the sight of you so much, Sister," the stinking one laughed as he yanked her upright. The other stepped close, groping her breasts with his filthy hands.

"I hope you weren't thinking you were going to meet your maker still a virgin." He laughed, pushing her to the ground and unbuttoning his trousers. "Have much of this in the convent?"

Marie-Genevieve forced her mind to escape as he lowered himself on top of her. At least this monster would not be taking her virginity. No. She'd shared that willingly with someone who hadn't abused it.

Her attacker was clumsy and nasty. His stench made her gag, but he finished blessedly quickly. Once he was off her, she tried to prepare herself mentally for his counterpart's assault. But there was no second attack.

She was lifted up off the ground and then felt smooth cold skin, just as naked as hers, pressed up against her back. From her calves to her buttocks to her shoulders. But this man wasn't pushing or groping. He was praying. Marie-Genevieve, who hadn't entered the convent because of her love of God but because of her love of one man, listened to the soft words.

"Pray with me, my child," the priest said as the soldier pushed the two of them even closer together. "Our Father, who art in heaven . . ."

If she could let go, the way she sometimes did during mass at the convent, and not hear the words but move with the sounds, she could lull herself into a state of almost sleeping while standing. Of dreaming somehow outside of her body. She didn't know what to call it and had been afraid to tell any of the other sisters. Not sure if this *mind escape* she was capable of was a great gift or something heretical.

The soldier with the stinking breath wound a length of coarse rope around her wrists, binding her to the man behind her. So the rumors were true. They were bringing priests and nuns down to the river. Tying them up. Torturing them. Killing them.

"Get moving," the soldier said as he pushed her. "Time to take a boat ride, down there." He pointed to the riverbank.

It was a struggle to walk in tandem, but she and the priest managed without falling.

"What is your name, Sister?" the priest asked her.

She started to answer, but the soldier smacked her face. "Keep moving!" he barked. "No conversation."

Around her the air was filled with crying and shouts—and yet, coming through the other noises were the persistent reassuring sounds of prayers and birdsong.

Her executioners—she had no doubt now that's who they were—pushed her and the priest into a small boat. He got the worst of it, falling on his face, yelling out in pain, while she only hit the side of her head.

With a grunt from one and a laugh from the other, the soldiers pushed the boat out into the river. The current was strong here and the little skiff moved rapidly. For a few minutes, Marie-Genevieve was hopeful. Maybe they'd figure out a way to untie each other. Maybe the boat would go aground. Then she noticed the water seeping into the wooden vessel.

When Giles's death had been reported from Egypt, her father had arranged an alternate marriage for her. Marie-Genevieve begged him not to thrust her into a union so fast. Give her time to grieve; to get used to the idea. But Albert Moreau was a businessman; if the son of the man who bought the finest skins from his tannery was no longer able to marry his daughter, he would marry her off to the manufacturer who bought his second-finest skins.

The shoemaker was a recent widower. No, he wasn't young and good-looking like Giles, but Albert told his daughter none of that mattered.

"You don't have the luxury of falling in love again. The right marriage and a marriage of the heart—the best of all worlds. But it is not to be. You're not any younger, and I don't want you to wait and risk the widower finding someone else. Besides, he has ties to the revolutionaries. If this unrest erupts into the war that we expect is coming, he will be able to aid us all."

When Marie-Genevieve could not be consoled, her mother helped her run away to the convent of Our Lady of the Sacred Heart.

Now as she sat in the boat in the river, unable to do anything to stop the leak, she watched the water rising and considered the irony of what she'd done. Given the revolutionaries' greed and lust to destroy the Church and everything connected to it, the safety of the church proved no safety at all.

The water rose around them, and still the priest prayed. She was submerged up to her knees. Then her shoulders. Then her chin. She thought of Giles and how he'd once dipped his handkerchief in water to wipe away the tracks of her tears. It was the day he'd told her he was going to Egypt to learn about ancient scents so he could enhance the perfumed gloves and soaps and candles and pomades and make the House of L'Etoile the talk of Paris. He had been excited by the adventure, but she'd been afraid for him to go; had a premonition that he was not going to come back.

But now she was going to meet him again. This cold, cold water was taking her to him. It was closing over her and washing away the stain of the stinking soldier and the touch of his greedy fingers. Giles was waiting. She knew he was. He'd promised her, before he left, they'd be together always. They belonged together, he'd said. They were *âmes soeurs*.

Twenty-seven

Plagued with fears about her brother, confused by her hallucinations—the most recent transpiring while Inspector Marcher there—and thrown off balance by Griffin's sudden presence, Jac didn't even try to sleep that night. She went through the motions of undressing and getting into her childhood bed, but she didn't fight the hours of wakeful worry that followed.

Terrible scenarios of what might have befallen Robbie plagued her. Was her brother all right? Had he really been in Nantes? He must have been, or else how would his shoes and wallet have been found there? And why, of everywhere, in that place where she'd been so uncomfortable years ago? And how could just hearing the city's name trigger such a horrible hallucination?

Over and over, she relived what had been happening to her in the workshop. Trying to make sense of why her illness had returned with two episodes now, after so many years. It made her so anxious to think the plague had returned; that she would go back to living split apart, nervously waiting for the next break. Waiting for the awful first symptoms. Carrying the dread with her.

This last hallucination had seemed to last at least an hour, but when she broke from its grip, Griffin still had his hands on her shoulders.

This had been worse than any episodes she'd suffered as a child, and she came out of it in a panic.

"You're still here?" she asked him, momentarily disoriented.

"I never left," he answered.

His presence was more reassuring than she was comfortable with. How could they have been apart for so long and slip back into this kind of intimacy so quickly?

"Are you all right, Jac? For at least a minute, you didn't seem to hear a word the inspector or I said."

A minute? That was all? What to tell him? Until she understood what was happening, she decided to keep it to herself. She especially didn't want to talk about it with Marcher there.

Thursday morning, Jac was showered and dressed and back in the studio by eight o'clock. Overnight the room's scent had built up to a disturbing intensity. Despite the morning chill, she flung open the French doors, welcoming in the fresh air. She wanted coffee and remembered that her father always kept an electric kettle and French press here. But where? Everywhere she looked were boxes of papers and paraphernalia. If this was how the workshop looked after months of Robbie's trying to clean it up, how had it looked before? She finally found the coffee accouterments tucked away in a corner of a shelf with a tin of ground beans that smelled fresh enough. The same brand her father had always favored.

Usually she thought very little about her father, but it was impossible to put him out of her mind here. His personality before the disorder descended was evident in a hundred ways, from his collection of spy novels shelved two and three deep, to the dozens of framed photographs of his second wife, Bernadette, and her two children. Behind them, Jac and Robbie were equally represented in ornate frames. Ten snapshots. One even had their mother in it. Jac pulled it out, placed it up front. Wiped the dust off the glass. Then gently touched her mother's cheek.

The picture had been taken so long ago. A lovely, dark-haired woman sitting under a big red umbrella on the beach in Antibes with a sweet smile on her lips. The baby in her lap was Robbie. Jac, a three-year-old with a mop of the same dark hair, was standing beside her mother, leaning over, whispering in her ear.

Jac didn't remember the trip. Or the day. Couldn't pull up that moment.

She poured herself a cup of coffee and looked back at the photo. Where were memories stored? Why could she conjure imagined moments from lives of people long dead but not dredge up actual instances of her very own life?

When the inspector arrived at nine, Jac was feeling the jittery addition of too much caffeine to her anxiety over Robbie.

She and Marcher sat on opposite sides of a Louis XIV desk that had been in the family since it was made. Her father had auctioned off the truly valuable antiques trying to stave off financial disaster over the years. What was left—a few pieces like this desk—were in such poor shape that they weren't worth selling.

"Can you tell me a little about the argument you and your brother were having?" Marcher asked. "We know the two of you weren't getting along. That your plans for the company didn't match his."

"How do you know about that?" Jac looked over at Griffin.

She'd been surprised he'd phoned early that morning. Even more surprised at how glad she'd been to hear his voice. When she told him that Marcher wanted to talk to her again, he volunteered to come over. She had been too exhausted and upset to argue.

Now he shook his head in answer to the question she hadn't voiced.

No, he wouldn't have told Marcher something like that. So how had he found out?

Jac's eyes rested on the photos she'd just been looking at. Ahh, she thought. Marcher must have talked to Bernadette. The witch, who once upon a time had been her father's lovely assistant, bringing them presents of chocolates and fresh madeleines. Then Bernadette had stumbled upon evidence of Jac's mother's affair and exposed her. Audrey's indiscretion would have ended eventually, and perhaps her parents would have stayed together had Bernadette not presented proof of the transgression to Jac's father. Instead she started a spiral that ended in Audrey's suicide.

"And what did the current Madame L'Etoile have to say about my brother and me?"

The inspector glanced down at his notepad for a moment. Jac liked him a little more for having the decency to look away.

"I'm not at liberty to discuss that, mademoiselle. Can you help me understand this feud between you and your brother?"

"Feud? What century are you living in? It's an ongoing business discussion about how we are going to solve our financial problem."

"That reached the point where the two of you rarely saw each other."

"I live in New York and travel all the time. Robbie lives in Paris. We both have jobs. How often could we see each other? And besides, what does any of this have to do with what's going on? With where he is? With what happened here?"

"About the feud?" the inspector prompted.

"Fine," she said, realizing he wasn't going to give. "I've found a buyer for the rights to two of our signature perfumes. The purchase price will bring in enough cash to pay off our debt, allow us to restructure our loans, and infuse the company with the capital we need."

"Your brother didn't like the idea?"

"Doesn't. He doesn't like the idea. He has some misguided belief that our signature scents are our lifeblood. That if we sell even two we will be defaming the house."

"But you need his vote to make the sale?"

"Yes, we own the company equally."

"Except you'd own the company completely in the event of your brother's death, wouldn't you?"

A sound escaped from Jac's throat. Like the cry of an animal caught in a trap.

Griffin stood up. "Inspector, I think that's enough."

Marcher ignored Griffin. "We're going to have to ask you not to leave the country, mademoiselle."

"Why is that?"

"I'm afraid you're a person of interest in your brother's disappearance and possible death."

"That's absolutely ludicrous." Jac put her hands on the desk and stood up abruptly, accidentally knocking over a small perfume bottle sitting precariously close to the edge. The vial fell and shattered.

An intense scent enveloped her, so powerful that she barely noticed as the inspector excused himself and left. Jac hadn't smelled it for years but recognized it instantly. This was one of the scents from The Game of Impossible Fragrances. In the scent vocabulary that made up her and Robbie's secret language, this was Fragrance of Loyalty, Jac's favorite. Adding notes of bergamot to a rich earthy base of oakmoss, she'd come up with a chypre—a type of warm, woody scent, first made famous by the legendary perfumer François Coty in 1917. Jac's Fragrance of Loyalty was neither feminine nor masculine, and could be worn by either brother or sister. And that was as it should be, she'd said, so they both could use it to signal when something was wrong and they needed help. Usually that meant they were in trouble with their mother or father and wanted saving. She wound up putting it on far more often than Robbie did.

Jac didn't even know he'd kept any of those fragrances. Why had this one been sitting on the edge of the desk?

"Did Robbie tell you about this perfume?" Jac asked Griffin as she picked up the broken pieces of glass after Marcher left.

"No."

"You're certain?"

"Yes. Why? What is it?"

"I don't think it was here yesterday. If it had been, I'm sure I would have noticed it or smelled it. I've sat at this desk a dozen times since I arrived in Paris. And the bottle—our father stopped using them years ago. He gave the ones he had left to us to play with."

"I don't understand. What does a broken bottle of perfume have to do with anything?"

"What if Robbie is alive? What if he was here last night? He could have left me this bottle as a message. Maybe the shoes and the wallet were a message, too. Robbie could have left them by the river hoping they'd be found and I'd be told. It can't be a coincidence that they showed up somewhere Robbie and I had been before. A place that scared me so much he convinced my grandmother to cut our visit short and get me away from there."

Twenty-eight

It was misting when Griffin came out of the Porte Dorée metro station. The afternoon sun had disappeared behind a bank of clouds and the entrance to the Bois de Vincennes was shrouded in fog. Through the vapor, he saw glints of gold, but it wasn't until he was right beneath her that he could make out the towering sculpture of Athena shining like a warning beacon through the haze. The fountain at her feet spilled down into a long reflecting pool that mirrored the gray sky, and the royal palm trees that flanked the fountain stood like masts in the miasma.

On a weekend, he imagined, this park would be crowded, but now, in the rain, there were long stretches where he didn't see a soul.

Suddenly a large black dog burst out of the mist, racing right toward him, followed by a pack. Within seconds, sniffing dogs surrounded Griffin, inhaling his scent and snarling.

Griffin knew he could take on one dog but not a pack, so he stood still and silent, readying himself for a possible attack. After a few long seconds, however, the alpha male seemed to lose interest. He turned away and took off, with the rest of his pack following. Once the dogs were gone, Griffin realized his heart was racing.

If he'd known how big the park was—how long it would take to get here or how deserted it would be—he'd have suggested an alternate meeting place. But the lama hadn't explained much on the phone, just that he was a friend of Robbie's and wanted to set up a meeting.

And to please be discreet.

Griffin had wanted to ask the lama how he'd found him. But the lama had hung up too quickly. It wasn't a secret that Griffin was in Paris working on the Egyptian artifact. A few nights before, Robbie had invited the curator from Christie's to dinner with Griffin. The archaeological community was fairly small. Maybe Robbie had shared what the curator had said with the lama

By the shore of the Lac Daumensil, Griffin finally found the temple he'd been told to look for and walked around to the entrance. Inside he was confronted by a gleaming Buddha at least twenty-five feet tall. The icon was so dazzling, its stature was so commanding, that Griffin didn't even notice the Buddhist nun, wearing saffron robes, who sat at the sculpture's feet.

"Mr. North, thank you for being so prompt," she said, startling Griffin. "I'm Ani Lodra." She extended her hand.

"I was expecting to meet the lama. Is he here?"

"No, he offers his apologies. He's been detained and asked me to conduct the meeting."

Griffin nodded.

"Time is of the essence." The small, wiry woman with a shaved head gestured to a cushion next to her own. "Will you have a seat, please?"

Incense permeated the air, and votive candles flickered in their red glass holders.

"I feel as if I've left France and crossed over into India," Griffin said as he sat down.

"Yes, it's very much like home. It's nice for those of us when traveling to come here for a respite and to meditate."

"You're from India?" Her features didn't fit. She was slight, with yellow skin and slightly oblique brown eyes.

She nodded. "Most who followed His Holiness into exile live now in McLeod Ganj, India. There are over one hundred thousand of us there."

"You hardly seem old enough to have fled Tibet in 1959," Griffin said with surprise. The nun looked to be about twenty-eight or thirty.

"My parents were followers. I was born there. My envelope is twenty-eight years old."

Griffin had met other Buddhists who considered their bodies to be hosts for reincarnated souls. *Envelope*: there was something intriguing about how this woman phrased it.

"Let me explain why we've dragged you to the middle of this park. We assume you must be as concerned as we are about Mr. L'Etoile."

"I am, of course."

"His Holiness has been looking forward to meeting with Mr. L'Etoile when he visits next week," said the nun. "So when we read the news that he was missing, we became concerned. Were you able to see the ancient artifact before Mr. L'Etoile disappeared?"

So Robbie really had been keeping the lama updated. "Yes, I've been working on it for several days."

"And were you able to finish your translation?"

"Not completely. There are still phrases I hadn't pieced together and nuances I hadn't worked out."

"But what you did translate suggests the fragrance in the pot was a memory aid to help one remember a past life?"

"It mentions specifically finding a romantic interest in a past life, yes. A soul mate."

"That's interesting but not that surprising. There is much attention to soul mates in reincarnation literature."

At the sound of a kettle whistling, the nun stood. "Excuse me. I prepared some tea." Walking around to the side of the statue, she took the kettle off an electric burner and arranged a tray.

"In a temple?"

"There is a Buddhist tea ceremony, *Chan-tea*, that dates all the way back to the Western Jin Dynasty, where the tradition began at the Tanzhe Temple to help enlighten and reveal the truth." She poured the steaming liquid. "Monks there picked and dried the leaves, then brewed the tea, which they discovered helped during long meditations."

Griffin sipped the hot, fragrant beverage. "It's very good."

"Yes, it is. But I miss the buttered tea my mother used to make," the nun said as she lowered her own cup.

Griffin nodded. "I've had yak butter tea."

"It is superior. In the same way that butter candles have a softer and warmer light than these," she said wistfully.

"Tibet is a wonderful country."

"It was. It could be again. It's being destroyed by the political situation. Which is a travesty."

"I agree," Griffin said, sensing they were getting to the heart of the reason for this meeting.

"Mr. North, we have only two days before His Holiness arrives in Paris. This memory tool is something that he would very much like to share with his followers. If there is any chance of finding it—of finding Mr. L'Etoile—we'd like to offer our services."

"The police are doing everything they can to find Robbie."

"The police?" the nun's voice was surprisingly cynical. "Red tape will stop them from working with the speed necessary to accomplish this goal in time. We want to help you and Mr. L'Etoile's sister to find him."

Earlier today, after Inspector Marcher had left, Jac had asked Griffin to help her search for Robbie. She was certain that he was alive and trying to contact her. The phone call the first night she arrived in Paris, when she could hear someone breathing but no one answered. Robbie's shoes and wallet being found in the Loire Valley. The Fragrance of Loyalty that hadn't been there the day before. She was convinced Robbie was sending her messages: "I'm alive. Find me. Help me."

But how could the lama or this nun have known what Jac and Robbie were planning?

"We must get to Mr. L'Etoile before the Chinese government does. They are actively doing whatever they can to discredit His Holiness by regulating reincarnation to ensure that no more lamas are found outside of their provinces. It's not that they believe in reincarnation; rather they are determined no one outside of their control claims to rule Tibet."

"I see."

"The world sympathizes with us exiles but doesn't act on their kind words. What Mr. L'Etoile found could be a powerful weapon in the struggle. Even if there is nothing left but a legend, words have influence. If we can even suggest there might be a way to ascertain who is a true incarnation and who isn't, we can cast enough doubt on the Chinese government's actions in Tibet since taking control of the government to energize our cause."

"We're talking about a myth written on broken pot shards."

"What are myths?" the nun asked.

"Stories."

"True stories?"

"No. They are emotional, spiritual and ethical maps laid out for people to follow."

The nun shook her head as if the answer disappointed her.

"What makes you think Robbie is alive and that his sister is looking for him?" he asked. "How do you know what her plans are?"

"Do you know what tulpas are?"

"I do," Griffin replied. It was curious: just that week, Robbie had mentioned tulpas: forms created by the thoughts of highly evolved monks.

"Do you think they are true beings?"

"No."

"When my father was a boy, in the mountains in Tibet, winters were always brutal. But one year was especially bad, and my grandfather became very ill. My grandmother tried all the remedies she knew of, but to no avail. The snow made it impossible to go for help, and the family was in despair. On the third day of my grandfather's illness, it seemed as if the storm was going to outlast him. The fever was eating him alive. Late that night, there was a knock at the door. My grandmother opened it to find a monk. He was very short and thin and had a big smile. Despite the terrible weather, he was dressed similarly to how I'm dressed now and didn't appear to be at all uncomfortable. He was barefoot."

The nun stopped to sip her tea.

Over the years Griffin had met a few natural-born storytellers, people who, once they started to spin a tale, managed with a steady gaze and an expressive voice to pull you in and keep you transfixed. This woman was one.

"The visiting monk sat down by my grandfather's bedside and stayed there throughout the night. He sent the rest of the family off to their mats and even made my grandmother go to sleep. She fought him, but the truth was, she was exhausted and needed the rest.

"Mr. North, you are a smart man. So you can guess why I'm telling you this story. The next morning, my grandfather was improved. Though it would take over a week for him to regain his strength, he was no longer fevered, and his life was no longer in danger.

"The monk wouldn't take anything from the family but a cup of buttered tea. Then he walked off, out into the storm. His job, he told them, was done.

"Six months later, my family set off to visit my great-uncle in his monastery. When they arrived, one of the first things my great-uncle asked was how my grandfather was feeling after his illness. My grandfather asked how his brother had known about that. 'I dreamed it,' my great-uncle said. 'So powerful is the bond between us.' My grandfather and his brothers were amazed," the nun told Griffin. "They knew about the power of dreams, but this was the first time they'd seen proof."

As she continued telling the story, the nun refilled their teacups.

"My grandfather, who had no trouble accepting that his brother had dreamed about his illness, asked if he could meet the monk he'd sent, so he could thank him. My great-uncle reminded him that it had been the dead of winter. There would not have been any way for someone to cross the mountains. The monk who had come to visit had been a tulpa. Created through prayer and meditation. Tulpas. Created when a highly disciplined disciple gives palpable being to a visualization through sheer willpower."

"And are you one? Can you create these thought forms?"

"Sadly, I am not yet that learned. But my teacher is. Tai Yonten Rinpoche is from one of the oldest lineages of all reincarnated lamas."

"And you're saying that your teacher created a tulpa who has kept you informed as to our plans?"

"Yes."

"Or maybe it wasn't a bad guess that the sister of a man who's missing would go in search of him." Griffin drained his cup. "How do you propose to help? Having the tulpa find Robbie and lead us to him?"

"It's your choice to believe whatever you see fit. But the Western way of thinking is narrow and constricting. You seem to be a cynic."

"I'm not a cynic—I'm a researcher. I put my faith in stones and ruins. Record them and analyze them and make sense of them."

"And turn them into the dust under our feet instead of the shine of the stars."

"Lovely image." He hadn't meant to be sarcastic, but as his wife was fond of saying, it was his natural default position when he felt out of control.

The woman's eyes locked on Griffin's, her expression inscrutable. "We believe that your friend is alive and is in trouble with the police, and is probably trying not to be arrested before he meets with His Holiness, as intended, to give him the pottery."

Griffin was taken aback. "You're saying that Robbie was given an appointment to meet with the Dalai Lama?"

"That's correct. He was waiting for us to confirm it and give him instructions on where that meeting would take place. We didn't get to him in time. We know—and so assume he must too—that there are Chinese nationalists who do not want that meeting to take place. Even if you, or Mr. L'Etoile's sister, find him on your own, it's me he wants to talk to. I am the map to that meeting."

Twenty-nine

Jac was sitting in her old bedroom in front of the windows, looking down at the courtyard garden, trying to think like Robbie and imagine where he'd go and what he'd do if he were in trouble. When her cell phone rang and she saw it was Alice Delmar, she answered it.

"I'm sorry to hear about your Robbie," Alice offered in her crisp British accent.

Jac nodded, then realized she couldn't see her and thanked her.

"Any news?" Alice asked.

"No, none."

There was a moment of transatlantic silence. Jac pictured the kind woman on the other end of the phone sitting in her office overlooking Central Park. Alice and her husband, who owned a large cosmetics company, were old friends of Jac's father's. They'd treated her like family, inviting her to their house on holidays. She'd have given anything to be back there with Alice, sitting over dinner in Sant Ambroeus, sipping wine, listening to her complain about overpriced ingredients and perfume sales that had dipped 14 percent in the last year.

"Is there anything I can do? Get on a plane and come and be there with you?" The suggestion was like an embrace, offering momentary solace.

"No, please don't. The police are doing everything they can."

"But it's not enough, is it? Your brother is still missing."

"That's true. But there's nothing I need now. Not right now, honestly."

"I hear something in your voice. What aren't you telling me? Is it about the loan? If the damn French bankers are breathing down your neck, we can arrange something."

Alice ran the company's fragrance division. She'd been the one to come up with the idea of buying Rouge and Noir in order to solve the House of L'Etoile's financial crisis.

"Thank you, but we're fine for a little while longer." Jac was staring down at the garden. The topiary that was usually shaped into pristine pyramids hadn't been trimmed in a long time. The shapes were losing some of their form.

"Then what is it?"

"The police think I'm involved in my brother's disappearance because he was getting in the way of the sale and that I—" she couldn't finish.

"That's preposterous," Alice's voice blustered. "*You?* He's your family. You adore him."

Jac pressed her forehead against the glass, comforted by its cool smoothness and neutrality. The absence of scent was a relief.

Outside, the wind picked up, the leaves in the trees danced for her, and the sun hit the seven-foot obelisk in the maze's center. The object supposedly dated back to Egypt at the time of the pharaohs. In yet another family legend, Giles L'Etoile had brought the limestone needle back from Egypt along with the rest of the treasure. Jac knew it was just as likely a nineteenth-century copy. No one had ever bothered to find out. Her family preferred to believe the fantasies that were the cornerstone of the House of L'Etoile. She knew the shaft's tip was white like the rest of it, but from the window, its top looked like it had been capped with something black.

After finishing the call with Alice, Jac went out to the garden. Walking down the allée created by the centuries-old cypress hedges, she breathed in the refreshing perfume; the spicy, clean scent. She'd traversed this labyrinthine pathway hundreds of times when she was a child. Its smell was as intrinsic a part of its design as the pebbled pathway.

At the maze's heart, she looked up. So it wasn't a shadow or a trick of light. The triangular tip of the column was darkened. Standing up on the stone bench, she reached out. Just managed to touch the tip. Her fingers came away black. She smelled them. It was dirt. Probably from the garden. Why would someone have smeared dirt around the needle's top?

Jac sat down on the bench. It had been misting, and her hair was already curling around her face. The air felt suddenly chilly, as if this new mystery had affected the very atmosphere. She wished she'd brought a sweater, but she wasn't going back now. She had to figure out what was happening.

Why was there dirt on the obelisk? Jac looked at the ground for some kind of clue. And that's when she noticed. The black and white pebbles forming the ancient ying-yang symbol had been disturbed. Their separate fields were mixed together. The teardrop shapes bled into each other.

Someone had *done* this. Deliberately. She stared at the stones as if they had the answer. Clouds rolled across the sun, showing the garden in darkness. Then the sun peeked out again. Something on the ground glinted. Metal? She looked closer. A patch of pebbles were brushed aside, exposing—what was it?

Dropping to her knees, Jac swept away the stones, revealing more and more of what lay beneath them. A large, circular plate came to light. At first she wasn't sure what it was, then realized: a manhole cover. And it wasn't fitted tightly into its ring but gapped as if someone had slid it back in a hurry.

After escaping down the shaft?

Jac leaned down and sniffed the space between the metal plate and the edge of the hole. The cool air smelled of vinegar and decay and maybe something woodsy, too. Yes. She could identify the same scent that had filled the workshop a few hours before, when she'd broken the bottle of the Fragrance of Loyalty.

Thirty

Xie sat on the edge of his bed in his hotel room in Kensington and stared at the telephone. It seemed such a simple act. All he had to do was pick up the receiver and make the call. But he remained immobile, his hands useless by his sides.

Was this an emergency?

The thin bedspread wicked up the sweat on his palms. Ten more seconds passed. Twenty. Soon he'd run out of time. All the students were going to a reception at the Victoria and Albert Museum. He needed to be downstairs in ten minutes. If he wasn't, someone would come looking for him. He couldn't let them find him like this, nervous and bathed in perspiration.

Xie crossed the room in six steps, threw the lock, and opened the window. Noise from the busy street below wafted in with a warm breeze. The traffic sounds were less ominous than the silence. When it was too quiet, he could hear his own heart.

Since he'd left China, meditating had failed him. Anxiety was his constant companion. He'd waited so many years to take this trip. Made so many preparations. Took so many chances hiding messages in his calligraphy. Put Cali's and his teacher's lives in jeopardy.

Now he was behaving like a frightened child. He'd been told not to make contact unless it was an emergency. Was it?

An hour ago, he'd caught his roommate looking through his draw-ers. Ru Shan had claimed he'd gotten mixed up.

Xie looked down at the phone as if it were a sleeping dragon he was afraid to wake. What if the call was traced? What if his government was monitoring all calls the students made? Could they do that here in London? What if Xie's roommate came in while he was talking?

Ru could be waiting outside the room now, ready to follow if Xie went anywhere not on the itinerary. It wasn't allowed, of course. The students were forbidden to leave the hotel except as a chaperoned group. But most of them had been sneaking out late at night. So far no one had gotten into trouble.

Xie hadn't wanted to go with them. Despite his curiosity about being in a foreign city and tasting some of its forbidden fruits, he didn't want to take any risks. Wanted to save his escapes for the grand one. Except he'd been concerned that if he stayed in when everyone else snuck out, that alone would appear suspicious. So he'd gone to the bars with his fellow students. Despite his anxiety, he'd been fascinated by Western culture.

How Cali would have enjoyed the scene. The lively students, the freedom, the lack of surveillance. The absence of military police.

But he and his fellow artists could only observe such liberty. It wasn't theirs to share. Their government couldn't even send a group of artists to Europe without moles. Was Ru spying? Beijing offered students special treatment for turning in their classmates. What had they tempted him with?

Without Cali and her wizardry with a laptop, Xie was incapable of checking out the Tsinghua University student's background. He missed Cali in other ways too. Missed her bravado and passion.

There was a knock on the door.

Xie had missed his opportunity. He cursed his hesitation. Cali would have laughed at him and called him a coward. And she would have been right.

"Yes?"

"Xie, it's Lan. I was just heading downstairs. Are you ready?"

He shouldn't have answered. He wasn't being clever or smart about any of this. His nerves were interfering with his thinking.

He opened the door. "Come in. I'm almost ready—I'll just be a moment."

The young woman from Peking University was not only the finest calligrapher of them all but also the shyest. Lan gave Xie a half smile as she walked in, her eyes cast down.

They'd sat next to each other on the plane. When he'd realized how quiet she was, he'd gone out of his way to respect Lan's timidity and also put her at ease. Since then, she'd made an effort to pair up with him at every opportunity: on the ride from the airport to the hotel, during meals and on group walks.

In the bathroom, he splashed his face with cold water, then lingered a few seconds to stare in the mirror. He could see the fear in his eyes.

Om mani padme hum.

Four times, he intoned his mantra and then brushed his hair, tugged his shirt cuffs, grabbed his jacket off the hook on the back of the door and shrugged it on.

Downstairs they joined the group of a dozen students already boarding the waiting bus.

The entrance to the Victoria and Albert Museum's nineteenth-century marble splendor also incorporated contemporary design. Beside him, Lan stepped into the high-ceilinged lobby and looked around at the orange, yellow, and red flags emblazoned with the names of current exhibitions.

"I never dreamed my work would ever be seen anywhere like this. Did you?"

It hit Xie then. The fact of this trip. Not the covert reason but the obvious one: his artwork had been chosen. He was capable of creating paintings that were worthy of an honor like this. There was no telling what the rest of the trip would bring, but he knew that he owed it to his teachers and himself to at least stop and be aware of this moment. The swirls of ink on paper, the concentration it took to make the brush dance, not stumble, the years of study and sacrifice. It wasn't only about reclaiming his individuality and helping His Holiness—it had its own value. The message on the paper. The peaceful poetry of the art form.

No matter what else happened, that was important, too.

Swept up with the other students, he followed the guides into the Chinese sculpture galleries. Here tall windows faced a garden with an oval pool. Buttery gold light reflected off the water and back into the hall.

Their calligraphy hung on fine fabric partitions that had been positioned around the room. With Lan by his side, Xie walked in and out of the pathways created by the dividers—their very placement artistry in itself. It was a village of Chinese art—on the walls and on the panels—created centuries apart but all sharing the same spare, simple power.

Yes, there would be hours ahead to worry and plan. Days ahead to try quelling his apprehension and accomplish his goal. Tonight was for the work. It spoke to him. His job—to listen. To honor in the way he knew best. The way the Tibetan monks who'd been burned to death in the monastery had taught him when he was just a child.

With mindfulness.

Professor Wu corralled Xie and Lan and ushered them toward the rear of the galleries. "There will be time to look at the work. You need to thank our hosts first."

The bar was set up with bowls of nuts, little sandwiches, wine, and soft drinks. To its right was the receiving line where the Chinese ambassador to Britain and other officials from the embassy stood with museum officials, greeting the students and guests.

When it was his turn to shake the hands of his countrymen, Xie bowed deeply and spoke in the soft, monosyllabic style he'd assumed since childhood. None of the dignitaries seemed any more interested in him than in any of the other students. That was a relief. Interest suggested attention. And drawing attention was to be avoided.

So it pained him when Ru approached him and in a belligerent tone that was clearly the result of drinking too much wine in too short a period, verbally attacked him.

"You think you are superior to all of us," Ru intoned, pointing at Xie with his glass. "You think your work is better." Wine sloshed over the rim, and red droplets fell on the white marble floor. "You are no better than anyone else. Your strokes are no finer. Your lines are no clearer."

Emphasizing his point, Ru drew an imaginary line in the air with his glass. The wine splashed onto Xie's face and into his eyes.

Tears of red burgundy stained his cheeks and his shirt.

Ru stared, pleased with himself for a moment—and then terrified as he realized he'd created a scene on this very important night.

Before either of them could speak, a tiny, elderly woman approached Xie and thrust a paper cocktail napkin at him. "Oh, this won't do," she murmured. While he dabbed at his face, she took him by the arm and steered him away.

Although Asian, she spoke with a perfect British accent. "Let me show you to the lavatory, where you can clean up as best you can."

They were headed for the main doors. "I'm so sorry this happened." She wore a bright red suit with lipstick to match. Her grip on his arm was surprisingly tight. "What a shame. On this night of all nights." If he'd wanted to escape, he would have had to pry her hand loose.

As they exited the room, the noise level dropped. "You know your paintings are indeed better than the other students'."

"I'm humbled."

"I've been studying them for the last two days."

"I'm glad they please you."

"You have a subtle style."

"Are you a curator at the museum?" Xie asked.

"Yes. Calligraphy is my specialty."

"Are you from China?"

"I was from Tibet."

Xie felt a shiver start at the base of his neck and travel down his spine.

"And I have studied your work very carefully," she continued as she led him down a quiet hallway devoid of any museumgoers. "I saw many things."

"I hope you liked what you saw."

"You have imbued your work with very understated themes. Easy to miss. Important to find."

Xie hadn't expected actual contact before Paris. He hadn't allowed himself to hope he'd get help.

"Here we are," she said, stopping in front of a door. "You can make your way back to the gallery after you are done here?"

"Yes. Thank you. Thank you so much."

"All right, then. Now be careful, Xie Ping."

He nodded.

"There are many people who want your work to succeed," she whispered. "They will be watching out for you on your journey. Don't look for them. They'll find you. You're very brave."

"Thank you," he repeated and bowed.

When he looked up, she'd already turned away.

Opening the bathroom door, Xie stepped inside and walked toward the sink. He didn't see the man come up behind him until he was right on top of him. A flash in the mirror. A large hand covered his mouth. Xie tried to shout, but the stranger's flesh absorbed the sound.

Thirty-one

The sunset reflected on the Seine. Yellows gave way to dusky pinks, which faded to lavender; all the colors splashing on the surface of the water as if an Impressionist painter were using the evening as a canvas.

"I'm not sure this is a good idea," Jac said.

"Walking across the bridge?" Griffin asked.

"Going out to dinner." She'd forgotten how he always played with what she said that way. "What if there's a break in the search?"

He put his hand on her arm, stopping her.

"Marcher has your cell phone number and mine."

She felt the pressure of his fingertips through her jacket. The instant heat of his hands melted something inside of her. She resented it and moved her arm.

"And Robbie wouldn't forgive me if I let you go hungry," Griffin said.

Jac wondered if he remembered those Sunday night bag dinners, or if the reference to their past was unconscious. Jac thought of the ribbon, frayed and worn, back in New York inside of her jewelry box. She couldn't tell him. The admission would suggest a level of emotional involvement that she didn't feel. She'd kept the ribbon to remind her not to be weak, not because she still cared about him.

Griffin leaned on the parapet looking toward Notre Dame Cathedral. Jac looked the other way, toward the Grand Palais. The setting sun glinted off its glass roof. The Victorian building looked like it was on fire.

Around them, other pedestrians crossed the Carrousel on their way from the Left-Bank to the Right-Bank or vice versa. Jac and Griffin weren't the only ones who'd stopped on the footpath to look out over the cityscape. To their left, an elderly couple stood close together, pointing out the sights and taking pictures. To their right, a man and a woman embraced passionately. Jac looked away. Toward the river.

"Are you with anyone?" Griffin asked, speaking softly.

She hadn't expected such a personal question. She wasn't sure what she wanted him to know.

"I was until a few months ago," she said, still looking out over the river.

"Did you end it or did he?"

"Strange question."

"Is it? Sorry."

She shrugged. Bit her lip. "I put him in a position to end it."

"What does that mean?"

"He wanted me to move in with him. When I wouldn't. . . . You know, I don't think I want to talk about it after all."

Griffin reached out, put his hand on her shoulder, and turned her so that they were facing each other.

"If you want to tell me, I'll listen."

Jac shrugged again. "It's getting cold," she said, pulling her jacket tighter around her. "We should go."

In silence, they reached the end of the bridge. Waited for the light. Then walked under the large stone archway into the Louvre museum complex. Crossing the Coeur de Napoléon, Griffin stopped in front of I. M. Pei's glass pyramid.

Around them, hundreds of people milled about, some taking pictures, others lolling by the fountain. The square had an almost fairground levity. Very few were studying the architecture with Griffin's intensity.

The last rays of the sun shined in Jac's eyes. She blinked. Around her, the scene waved. For a second, she saw a horse-drawn carriage. Liveried servants opening the doors. A woman in a gold brocade gown and fanciful wig descending. She smelled floral perfume and the odor of unwashed skin.

"There's evidence that the pyramid shape draws microwave signals out of the air and converts them into electrical energy."

"What did you say?" Jac asked. She hadn't heard a word.

"There's evidence that the pyramid shape draws microwave signals out of the air and converts them into electrical energy. That's why they say even a newly constructed pyramid acts as a fulcrum for magic."

"Surely you don't believe in magic now. You haven't changed *that* much, have you?"

"No one's more skeptical than I am. But I've spent the night in a pyramid, and I experienced something I can't explain."

She shook her head. "I am. I'm more cynical than you are."

"You didn't use to be. When we were . . ." He didn't finish what he was going to say. Started again. "What happened to you, Jac?"

She almost said, "*You* did," but held back. "What happens to everyone? Only Robbie is still innocent. Still as happy as he ever was." She choked back a sob. Jac didn't want Griffin to comfort her. She knew how easy it would be to be seduced by his concern. He was so damn good at caring.

Le Café Marly was tucked under the stone archway in the Richelieu wing. Even though there were usually a few tourists here because of its proximity to the museum, the restaurant catered to Parisians.

"Robbie told me this is one of his favorites," Griffin said as they walked in. "Chic without being pretentious. Easy without being ordinary."

The maître d' showed them to a table in a corner of one of the inside rooms. Griffin ordered wine and some cheese to start.

This section of the ancient palace had been renovated to accommodate a modern restaurant, while retaining its majesty and grandeur. Ornate gilt moldings framed the high ceiling. The four-hundred-year-old marble floors were uneven with wear. The deep chairs were upholstered in rich red velvet.

"I want you to try to relax," he said. "Take a few sips of your wine." He slathered some of the soft, runny cheese on a piece of crusty baguette and handed it to her. "And eat this."

"Orders?"

"Suggestions. You're under a lot of stress. I'm just trying to help. When was the last time you ate?"

Jac resented that he'd remembered this about her and took a small bite of the bread, more to stop herself from commenting on what he'd said. She was hardly hungry.

"It doesn't feel right to be in a restaurant while—"

Griffin interrupted. "We need to eat, and we might as well do it someplace where the food and the wine are good. And where no one is watching the door."

"What do you mean?"

"Marcher has someone following you."

"Protecting me or watching me?" Instinctively, she turned around. She hadn't noticed before, but the room was eerily empty. All the other guests were on the terrace, enticed by the view.

"Protecting you, I hope. But I'm not positive. That's why I insisted we go out—so I could talk to you. I'm not sure if it's safe in the house, the store, or the workshop."

"Safe?"

"They could be listening, too."

"How do you know all this?"

"I saw a man follow us here. Noticed him on the bridge. And then in the reflection on the pyramid. That's why I think he's protection. It was too easy to spot him. He's not trying to be invisible."

It was suddenly oppressively hot in the room. Jac wanted to get up. To run. She couldn't just sit there while Robbie was missing. She'd been crazy to think she could manage it.

As if he sensed what she was thinking, Griffin covered her hand with his, and the slight pressure was enough to tether her to her seat.

"It's okay. I promise."

With his other hand, he lifted his glass and raised it toward her.

"To Robbie," he said, softly, kindly.

Jac felt tears prick her eyes but blinked them back.

She put the glass to her lips. Out of habit, before she drank, she sniffed the bouquet. All the subtle smells came together in a smooth wave of scents: cherry, violet, and roses along with leather and oak. She sipped. The taste danced in her mouth. It seemed indecent to notice the subtleties of the wine while Robbie was out there somewhere. In danger.

"What happened to your hands?" Griffin asked.

There were angry scratches across her knuckles where blood had dried in thread-thin lines. Cuts from when she'd tried to pry off the manhole cover at the center of the labyrinth. She rubbed at them, but only made them redder.

"Jac?" His voice was laced with worry.

"Even though the room is empty, could they be listening?"

He shook his head. "I don't think so."

She leaned across the table toward him, not realizing how seductive the movement was until she saw its impact reflected in his eyes.

"I think I know where Robbie is," she said in a quiet rush of words.

"Did he contact you?"

"No. But he left another sign. I think I know where he is. But I can't get there by myself." She held her hands out as evidence. "I tried."

"Were you going to tell me?"

Jac frowned. "I am telling you."

"Only because I asked about your hands."

She'd been foolish to think they could ignore the past—just move around it—without acknowledging it or giving it its due. "Let's get this over with. Okay? I'm not the one who left, Griffin."

His expression told her that he hadn't expected her to broach this subject. For a moment, he was quiet. Drank some of his wine. Reorganized his utensils. "No, you weren't."

"Then why are you angry at me?"

"I'm not."

She raised her eyebrows.

"You wouldn't have been happy with me," he said in a low voice.

"You decided that. Not me."

"I knew it."

"You thought you knew." She drank more wine.

"All these years . . . we really haven't forgotten about each other, have we?" He'd asked a question. It sounded like a confession.

Jac thought about whether or not to answer. About how to answer. Her feelings were buried so deep, and were so private, talking about them seemed almost obscene.

Griffin leaned in. She could smell him. The scent of punishment.

"They don't sell that cologne anymore. Haven't in years. You're still wearing it?"

"I've never found another cologne I liked, so your brother offered to have the formula analyzed and then recreate it for me. He replenishes my supply whenever I run out."

Jac's laugh sounded slightly hysterical even to her. While she had been buying up memories—half-empty bottles of the fragrance at flea markets—Robbie was in touch with Griffin, mixing up fresh bottles of the cologne for him.

"Whatever it is, tell me."

She lifted her hands. Tried to say something coherent. The air fell through her fingers. Jac couldn't order her thoughts or make sense of what she was thinking. She shook her head.

Griffin scooted his chair a quarter of the way around the table, moved his wine glass beside hers. And then leaned in, as if he were going to tell her a secret.

Then his mouth was on hers, and suddenly she wasn't just smelling him and tasting the wine but remembering what she'd thought she'd forgotten about how they were together. About the way he held her when he kissed her, with his hands on either side of her face. About the pressure of his lips moving on hers. Them together, the two-ness of them, was woven into the fabric of who she was. This memory was so deep, she felt that if she pulled the string of it and followed it, she'd wind up—where? The feeling of his palms on her cheeks, of his breath inside of her, of his hair brushing her face. It felt familiar in another way too. This was what Marie-Genevieve had been remembering while she was drowning. This was what the Egyptian princess on the edge of the river had been remembering when her lover told her he was going to be killed.

Killed? Drowning?

Jac pushed Griffin away so hard that he fell back against his chair. At first the look on his face was shock, then it moved to curiosity.

"You look scared, Jac. I didn't mean to—"

She shook her head. "It's not about me. It's Robbie."

"No. Something happened to you just now. I saw it on your face. What is it?"

"Forget about me!" She was almost shouting. "All that matters now is my brother."

The dinner arrived. They were both silent as the waiter placed the chicken paillard in front of her, a *croque monsieur* in front of Griffin.

For the next few minutes, they ate and drank without saying much, then Jac put down her fork and knife. She'd consumed only a little of her food.

"Can't you eat any more?"

She shook her head.

"When my daughter won't eat, I bribe her."

"I'm not your daughter, and there's nothing you have you could bribe me with." Jac had meant it to sound light. Instead it came out bitter.

She pushed away her plate.

"Will you come with me and try and find Robbie now?"

"Yes," he answered without hesitation.

As they left the restaurant, neither of them noticed the pale woman sitting by herself in the corner of the terrace listening to headphones while she sipped a glass of white wine and nibbled on foie gras and French bread. But once they'd walked outside, Valentine Lee threw a handful of euros on the table and followed.

Like the Champs-Élysées, the Louvre's courtyards were always crowded. It was easy enough to get lost among them and avoid the plainclothes policeman who was also watching Jac and Griffin.

Valentine wove in between the steady stream of people crisscrossing the wide-open space. Keeping her prey in her sight, she sauntered around a group of teenagers hanging out in front of the pyramid, smoking, texting and talking on cell phones. Twice, she avoided being photographed by tourists taking shots of the scenery.

She hadn't taken out her earbuds. A woman listening to an iPod was an ordinary sight. But there wasn't any music coming through. The directional on her belt was picking up traffic and ambient noises. She couldn't hear Jac and Griffin's conversation any longer, but she'd heard them throughout dinner.

Where were they going now? Where did Jac think Robbie L'Etoile was hiding? She'd never mentioned a location.

As Valentine crossed the Pont, she kept a safe distance between her and the couple she was following. When the light turned red at the end of the bridge, she stopped, pulled out a camera, and snapped pictures of the Seine.

Paris was dark now. The city's lights shimmered off the river's surface. A tourist boat drifted under the bridge, and from its deck, strains of Django Reinhardt wafted up.

The sound of the familiar music wrapped itself around her and squeezed her tight. Valentine was helpless to fight back. A wave of emotion broke over her. The sound was François. It was his rhythm. It was his beat. He moved to this music. Lived it. Breathed it. Played it. Reinhardt had been François's idol. The loss she'd refused to deal with came at her now. Greater than she was prepared for. Part of her welcomed the grief. It had been wrong to keep moving when she heard François was dead. He was as close to a father as she'd ever had. She should have stopped. Just sat and cried. Wept. Mourned for him. Let the pain of losing François take her over. Now, standing on the bridge, the strains of the music drifting downriver, she couldn't pretend she was all right.

No one around her seemed to notice the woman weeping as she looked out at the City of Lights. There was no better disguise, it turned out, than tears. It was the first lesson she'd learned without François by her side in over twelve years.

Thirty-two

Jac stepped out onto the terrace and reached for the light switch.

"Wait." Griffin stopped her. "Let's see if there's enough ambient light."

"None of the surrounding buildings can see down into the maze."

"The maze? Is that where you think Robbie is?"

She nodded. "I'll show you."

Griffin looked up and craned his neck. "Are you sure no one can look down on us? What about there?" He pointed.

"That's part of our building. These trees were planted so that no one can see the labyrinth except us. One day if a skyscraper goes up nearby, perhaps, but not yet."

"It's still better if you don't turn on the lights. Even if they can't see us directly, there might be some kind of glow. You don't want them to know you're out here at night."

"I'm just taking a walk in my own garden," she argued. "How suspicious could that be?"

"Let's try it without the lights."

As stubborn as Jac was, he was worse. She bristled. How, after so long, could they reprise their roles so easily? The good and the bad. The comforting and the annoying. Over the years, Jac had assumed the grooves they'd worn in each other's psyches would have smoothed out.

But they hadn't. In little more than twenty-four hours, she and Griffin had slipped back to the way they had a decade ago.

It was a moonless night. Opaque black. But Jac knew the twists and turns in the warren of lanes by heart and led the way without a misstep. She could have done it blindfolded—by smell. There were roses and jasmine planted in the center, and the stronger their scent, the closer she knew she was.

Arriving at the maze's heart, she dropped to her knees and with the palms of her hands moved the black and white pebbles away, revealing the metal disc she'd discovered earlier that afternoon.

There had been no flashlights in the *parfumerie*. Or if there were, she didn't know where to find one. Griffin always carried a penlight in his briefcase, but that was back in his hotel room. A supply of scented candles from the shop was the best they could manage. Fat, expensive votives that were imbued with the signature fragrances of the House of L'Etoile.

Griffin squatted beside her, struck a match. Once the candle came to life, he shone it on the manhole cover.

"This is a couple of hundred years old." He ran his fingers over the metal numbers.

1808.

"How could I have missed that this afternoon?" she said, annoyed with herself.

"You weren't looking for it. You were looking for Robbie."

What had been impossible for Jac to do alone, she and Griffin did in their first effort. They lifted the plate and moved it aside revealing a three-foot-wide hole in the ground.

"What's down there?" he asked.

Trying to ignore her growing panic, Jac kneeled down and peered over the edge. The scent that wafted up contained dirt and dust. Slightly rotting wood and moldy stone.

Griffin lowered the candle into the hole. The small flame only illuminated the metal rim and a few feet of stonework. Beyond that, all Jac saw was an infinite darkness that offered no clues.

"Can you smell the loyalty perfume?" he asked.

"No, not anymore."

Defeated before they even began.

Griffin lifted up the candle but the speed of his action was enough to blow out the flame. Now the garden was as black as the inside of the hole.

"Don't worry. We'll find him."

Jac couldn't see Griffin's face. Just heard his voice. It was like a cool wind. Coming from a distance. Washing over her. The familiar voice that made her shiver with its familiarity and pull her sweater tighter around her shoulders. As if she could protect herself from him.

Griffin struck another match. The wick sputtered to life. He lowered the candle slowly, so that this time the flame didn't blow out.

The light illuminated only another foot of the stone tunnel. Jac still couldn't see the bottom. Her heart was beating so fast she could hear it. Panic curled around her and teased her, threatening to paralyze her.

"Are you all right?" Griffin asked. "This must be hell for you."

She nodded. For one moment, her fear was replaced by surprise that he'd remembered this, too.

Jac had a fear of edges. It was a peculiar phobia. Rare, too, according to the therapists she'd discussed it with in Switzerland. Heights didn't bother her at all. Her apartment in New York City was on the twenty-seventh floor. But she couldn't stand on the edge of a train platform without feeling her heart speed up. What if she tripped, or slipped, or—even worse—became paralyzed on an edge, unable to move?

She knew how it started, but identifying its genesis did little to eradicate its grip on her. She and an eight-year-old Robbie had been playing hide-and-seek. He'd climbed out the attic window onto the roof. She'd looked up there and, seeing the window open, climbed out after him. The roof was large, and the many chimneys and eaves were excellent hiding places. Jac was prowling around looking for him. Suddenly she heard voices. Walked to the edge. Looked down. Her parents were below, standing in the street, arguing. They fought hard and often, and it always bothered Jac. She couldn't bear either of them being unhappy.

This altercation was especially nasty and loud. She was so absorbed in their insults and threats that she didn't hear Robbie come up behind her. He said her name, startling her. She turned too fast and her left foot slid over the edge. She was falling. Robbie grabbed Jac, held on, and pulled her up across the tiles—scratching her as he dragged her, but saving her from what would have surely been broken bones or worse.

Breathe. The trick to everything. Breathe, she told herself.

If Robbie is down there, you have to help him.

She knew how to calm down. Inhaling, she focused on deciphering the scents in the air. Earth. Rotting wood. Stone dust and mold. Crisp, clean resins from the cypress hedges that made up the maze. The night-blooming jasmine planted in the garden along with the early roses. And grass. Together all the scents created a loamy dark *Oud*. A mysterious and bewildering earthy perfume that suggested forests heavy with foliage. So thick only shafts of sunlight penetrated. So dense a child could wander forever and never find her way out.

Nowhere in the scent was a hint of what she was searching for.

Was her brother here or not? Had he been giving her clues? If not, then why was the tip of the obelisk smeared with dirt? Why had the pebbles been awry? Was it just a cat creating havoc?

"Robbie?" she called out, then strained to listen.

An echo of her own voice mocked her simplistic effort.

As if he might be there just waiting for her, she thought to herself.

"Robbie?" She tried again, despite knowing better.

Nothing.

"What *is* down there?" She whispered as much to the night as to Griffin. She sounded scared and was suddenly ashamed.

Griffin opened his fingers and let the candle drop. For a few seconds it enlightened more stonework. Then, like a shooting star, it tumbled downward, extinguishing itself through its own velocity.

Jac was shaking. Shivering as badly as if she were out in a snowstorm without any protection. She knew her physical symptoms were due to the phobia, but she couldn't stop them. She turned to Griffin and was about to say something, when he put up his hand to stop her.

When the candle hit bottom, the sound was faint, far away.

"Why did you do that?"

"I wanted to see how long it took to fall. Figure out the depth by feet per second."

"How long did it take?"

"Almost thirty seconds to hit bottom."

"How deep is that?"

"Over a hundred feet."

Griffin lit a second candle, leaned as far over the rim as was safe, and lowered the light.

"It's just a rock wall covered with moss and lichen."

"No, look," he said.

She inched closer. Her heart accelerated. Jac couldn't tell where he was pointing. "Where?"

"See that indentation?" He pointed.

Two feet down was a depression.

She shook her head. "What is it?"

"Steps, Jac."

He leaned down a little bit farther. "See. There's another one. They're carved into the stone. And probably descend all the way to the bottom."

"We have to go down there. Look for him."

"I know, but not yet."

"Why not?"

"We're not prepped." He pointed to her shoes, her clothes. "We need sneakers, helmets with lights. We need rope and a first aid kit in case Robbie is hurt."

She tried to argue, but his experience trumped her impatience.

"Not till we're outfitted. If we get hurt, we won't be able to help Robbie."

"Even if I knew where to go to get that kind of equipment, there's not going to be anything open tonight."

"I'm sorry, but we'll have to wait till tomorrow. We have no way to see where we're going. No way of tracking our path. We don't know where that goes. We could get lost."

Sweat was dripping down Jac's back despite the cool air. She was frightened, but that didn't matter. Robbie had left a message for her. He was all that she had. She'd fought worse demons than this. Visions and nightmares had once threatened her sanity. They'd put her in the hospital. Given her electric shock. Drugged her. She could tolerate a tunnel.

Even though she'd just agreed with Griffin that they should wait, she couldn't do it. Getting down on her knees, she backed up toward the opening.

His fingers wrapped around her wrists. His grip was so tight, pain shot up her arm. He pulled her away from the hole.

"You're hurting me," she gasped.

He let go. "You're crazy, you know that?" His face was twisted in anger. "Why didn't you listen to me?"

Her heart was pounding, and she couldn't catch her breath. Sitting on the damp earth, she leaned against the hedge. Her arms ached from being pulled away. She blinked back tears. The very last thing she was going to do was cry in front of Griffin.

"If Robbie escaped and is down there—he's as safe there as anywhere. No one could possibly know where he is. He'll survive another night. We'll go down tomorrow."

She nodded, not trusting her voice.

"I promise," he added.

The combination of fear, frustration and sadness mixed in with the memory those two words elicited proved too much. The first hot tear slid down her cheek. She turned away from him. A second tear.

She felt his hand on her shoulder.

"Let me help you. I pulled you pretty hard. I was worried you might fall."

Ignoring his hand, she stood up, wiped her hands off on the back of her jeans, and started for the house.

Thirty-three

Whenever he came to Paris, Malachai stayed in the same suite at L'Hotel. He felt at home in the ornate apartment. The gold-and-red brocade curtains that matched the bedspread harkened back to the era of kings and queens. The crystal chandelier always sparkled. The fine French linens were always ironed.

He opened the window and looked out over the rooftops and the bell tower of the church of Saint-Germain. The view hadn't changed in hundreds of years. The tower was one of the oldest in the city and dated back to the tenth century. Malachai checked his watch. Fifteen minutes after nine. Then he popped the cork on the bottle of Krug that was on ice and waiting for him—a welcome-back note from the hotel propped up against the silver bucket—and poured himself a glass. Champagne in hand, he opened the doors to the small balcony and walked outside just as the church bells began to peal. Leaning on the balustrade, he soaked in the music, the same ethereal chimes that parishioners had been hearing since the Middle Ages and throughout the revolution. Malachai sipped the creamy sparkling wine, shut his eyes and tried to imagine he'd stepped back in time. His imagination wasn't up to the task. Oh, how envious he was of the children he worked with, who were able to travel back and forth through the ages.

He, too, wanted to truly see and taste and hear the past. Be in the past. Walk the streets and interact with the people. Discover the secrets that were otherwise so elusive.

The bells' reverberation disappeared. Street noises wafted up. A pigeon cooed. Malachai sat on an iron chair and pulled out one of his two cell phones—one to make calls, one to receive them. It was safer that way. Harder to trace.

As lovely as the room was, the balcony was his primary reason for renting the extravagant suite. He could talk freely here and not concern himself about bugs. And that enabled him to travel under his own name, which he preferred. While an alias ensured anonymity, it didn't engender the attention and service he received when he checked into hotels as himself.

He punched in Winston's cell.

"I've arrived," he told the ex-agent.

"Good. How was the trip?"

"Uneventful. So tell me, is everything okay at the office?"

"Yes. Everything is status quo."

Before Malachai had left America, Winston had reported there was no new information in the case. The pottery shards that had disappeared with Robbie L'Etoile were of little importance, historically or monetarily. Their estimated value was $5,000 or less. The French police had listed them with Interpol. But since they didn't know they might be memory tools, they hadn't logged them as such. No one had waved the flags that would have placed Malachai under surveillance. Every time he left the country, passport control alerted the FBI Art Crime Team in New York City that he was traveling abroad. But his relationship with the L'Etoile family allowed him to be here with impunity. He'd treated the sister of the man who was missing. He was here to make sure she handled the stress of his disappearance without having a psychological setback.

"Any news on your nephew?" Malachai asked, using their cipher for Lucian Glass. The ACT detective, who had handled the last two memory tool cases, had jeopardized not only Malachai's relationship with his family but also his reputation with the Phoenix Foundation.

"My nephew's busy. He's got less time for me than ever. A new job and a new girlfriend. I can't compete."

Malachai smiled. It was always a relief to know Glass wasn't on his back. At least not yet.

"Good for him."

After the phone call, the therapist returned to the sitting room and settled down at the antique desk. He had two hours before he was to meet Winston's colleague.

Using his Montblanc and the elegant hotel stationery, Malachai wrote a note to Jac telling her he was here and offering any help she could use.

The tone wasn't right. He ripped up the effort. Dropped the scraps of paper into the brass trash basket.

They'd met when she was a gangly teenager and he'd been one of Jac's therapists. While the gap in their ages hadn't changed, it didn't have the same significance as it had all those years ago. She was an accomplished woman now. But still alone, scared and in need.

He read over his second effort. Much better. Folding it, he slipped the letter into an envelope. He called down to the front desk and asked if the bellman would be willing to travel a short distance early the next morning to make a delivery.

The concierge didn't hesitate. "*Bien sûr*, Doctor Samuels."

Everything for a price. Well, almost everything. He'd offered Robbie L'Etoile more for the shards than he'd get from anyone else in the world. And the perfumer needed the money. Desperately. Yet he'd rejected the offer.

Why? What was he going to do with them? Did Jac know? Well, Malachai was in Paris now. He had arranged with his bank in New York to take out a loan against his half of the Phoenix Foundation building to get L'Etoile to sell him the pottery. *If* he was still alive. *If* he still had the shards.

Malachai checked his watch. He had a reservation at the restaurant downstairs. Sealing the letter, he put it in the pocket of his Savile Row suit.

Yes, it was a much better idea to write her a note than to phone. Surely the telephones at the House of L'Etoile were bugged. Malachai didn't need to announce his arrival to the police like that. The FBI would let them know he was here soon enough. Besides, there was Jac to consider. By having the letter delivered, he would spare her the anxiety she must be going through each time the phone rang as she waited to hear news of her brother.

He never connected to patients personally. So why was he thinking about her like this? Almost with emotion.

Walking from his room toward the elevator, Malachai tried to understand. As honest about his faults as his attributes, he was well aware he was an excellent therapist for the same reason he wasn't a decent friend or lover. Empathy wasn't his strength. He listened objectively to those who came to him for help. Navigated through their complicated emotional waters without ever drowning in them himself. Years of his own analysis had exposed his narcissistic tendencies—the psychological condition that protected him from feeling for anyone else.

The elevator doors opened. Malachai joined the man and woman inside. He stepped to the left and faced front. The couple was reflected in the highly polished brass panel. They leaned close to each other, their bodies touching along their arms. They were holding hands.

Averting his eyes, Malachai looked at his own reflection. Fifty-eight years old and still chasing the same dream. Never married, he had neither children nor many long-term relationships. His aunt, codirector of the Phoenix Foundation, had a grown son, and Malachai took his relationship with the now-fatherless man seriously. But a cousin wasn't the same as his own progeny.

The doors opened. The couple walked out. Suddenly feeling tired, Malachai stepped out into the dramatic Belle Époque lobby. Took in the exquisite sun motif in the marble floor. The six-story-high Grecian frieze. The plush fabrics and opulent seats. The lush, low lights. L'Hotel was a romantic spot. He supposed he'd always known that, but he'd never felt out of place there. Until tonight.

Thirty-four

They went back in the same way they'd come: not through the workshop but via the French doors in the living room of the residence. Navy silk jacquard curtains with white stars and moons and gold suns draped windows that looked out onto the courtyard. Created in the early nineteen hundreds for her great-grandparents, the motif was repeated all over the room. There were gold stars painted on the night-sky-blue ceiling. Astrological signs woven into the gold carpet. The furniture was a mix of pieces from different eras arranged artfully. Classic but comfortable.

Before Jac had a chance to say anything, Griffin asked her where the bar was.

"I don't know how well stocked it still is. Robbie drinks only wine." Jac pressed a mirrored panel. It revolved in, and a sparkling cabinet with crystal glasses and marvelous antique decanters swung out.

"Everything in this house is hidden behind something else," he said. He poured two glasses of brandy and handed one of the tumblers to Jac. "Drink it, Jac. It's shock therapy."

"I'm fine."

"I'm sure you are. Drink it anyway."

She sipped the amber liquor. It burned going down. She'd never acquired a taste for Cognac, even as aged as this one.

"Is there a stereo hidden behind one of these mirrors, too?" he asked.

She pointed to the matching panel on the other side of the bar. "You want to listen to music?"

He shook his head. Put his finger to his lips. She remembered what he'd told her in the restaurant. If the police were watching, there was a good chance they were listening, too.

Griffin pressed on the upper-right-hand corner of the mirror and a full stereo swung out. He hit the eject button, saw the tray was full, then pushed the tray back and hit play.

He kept his eyes on the console, waiting for the first strains of music. Saint-Saëns's *Danse Macabre* filled the room.

Jac recognized the piece. "Great choice," her voice thick with sarcasm. She sat on the couch, drink in hand.

He pulled over a chair, faced her. Talked softly. "I know how much you want to find him. But you have to trust me. We have to do this the right way."

"I can't bear to think he's down there. Alone. Scared."

He drank some of his brandy. "We have to wait, we have no choice."

"You don't understand." It came out more sharply than she intended.

Griffin put down his drink on the coffee table between them and stood. "If you'd rather, I can go back to the hotel."

She wanted to tell him yes, that it would be much better if he left. Instead she shook her head. Rubbed her wrists and said, "No. I'm sorry."

"Maybe I'm not as worried as you are . . ." His voice was low and kind, and she felt as if he'd put his arm around her even though he hadn't touched her. "But I want to find Robbie too. Please stop fighting me. I'm not the enemy here."

She shut her eyes.

"Do you know anything at all about that tunnel?" he asked.

"It was another one of those crazy legends that my family seemed to collect the way other people collect china dogs. Have you ever heard of the *Carrières de Paris*?" She realized she'd used the French and corrected herself, referring to them in English. "The quarries of Paris?"

"Yes," Griffin said. "The city is built on mines, some of which date back as far as the thirteenth century, right? The stones that built Paris came from those quarries, leaving a network of empty tunnels and caves that became the catacombs. Most archaeologists know about them."

"Exhuming the dead from overcrowded aboveground cemeteries that were causing health problems started in 1777," Jac continued, "just as the revolution was gaining momentum and the government's greed for accumulating land was growing. The House of L'Etoile was already founded by then. My grandfather used to tease us that our ancestors weren't above us in heaven but beneath us in the cellar. 'A city sitting on an abyss,' he'd call it. When I was little and didn't get what I wanted, sometimes I'd stamp my foot and—"

"Why am I not surprised?"

Jac ignored Griffin's comment and continued. "Grand-père Charles would warn me to be careful. 'If you stomp too hard, you'll make a hole in the earth and fall though. And then you'll have to make friends with those bones.'"

She still missed her grandfather, who'd died while she'd been living in America. Everyone she cared about in her family was gone except for Robbie.

"I didn't believe him," she continued. "I wanted to know how he knew people were buried there. When I was old enough, he told me that he and his brother were part of the resistance movement during World War II, and they used the tunnels and galleries beneath Paris to help Allied soldiers and airmen escape." Jac got up and walked over to the glass doors leading to the courtyard. Her grandfather had planted those bushes, imported heirloom roses from all over France and England. He'd cultivated hybrids as he strove to create scents other houses couldn't copy.

A fine rain was falling in a shimmering mist. She opened the door and breathed in the semisweet nighttime scents and green cool air. "Grand-père said he had his own private entrance to the tunnels. That it was more secret than most because of where it was and how it was hidden. Robbie used to pester him to take us down."

"Did he?"

"No."

Griffin got up to refill his glass. She'd never imagined she'd see him here. But he belonged in a way. Wasn't this room a repository for memories? Antiques and artifacts dating from eighteenth-century L'Etoiles sat on tabletops and on shelves. Silver perfume chatelaines amassed by a great-great-grandmother. A large assortment of Limoges snuffboxes that had been collected over generations.

Jac's grandmother had a penchant for enameled jeweled frames. Crystals set in scrolls. Ruffles edged with marcasites. Openwork gold studded with pearls. Dozens sparkled all over the room. Once there had been Fabergé borders around the likenesses of long-dead family members, but those had long been sold.

On the mantel was a gold clock decorated with symbols of the earth, moon, sun, and stars of the zodiac. It not only told the hour and the day but also the times of sunset, sunrise, moonset and moonrise.

It had been broken when Jac spotted it in a corner booth at the flea market early one Saturday morning. Her grandmother had bought it over Jac's mother's protestations that it was going to be impossible to fix.

Grand-mère had patted Audrey's hand in that way she had. "It's a beautiful piece," she said. "We'll find a way."

Robbie's collection of malachite, quartz, lapis lazuli, and jade obelisks flanked the clock. On the other side, a Lalique bowl was filled with green, blue and milky-white sea glass that Jac had collected with her mother the summers they'd spent in the south of France. There was nothing here that didn't have memories attached.

"Is it possible your grandfather took Robbie down into the catacombs and not you?"

"Of course. After I left—when I was in America—my grandfather lived for another six years and was very healthy until the end."

"When was the maze in the courtyard constructed?"

"The exact date? I don't know, but those are architectural drawings of the house and the courtyard." She pointed to a series of six framed etchings. "They date back to 1816, and the maze is in the second to the end."

"So it's possible that the manhole in the center of the maze is the entrance to the underground tunnels that your grandfather used to tell you about. And that he showed it to Robbie?"

"Yes. Don't you think?" She was excited by the idea. If her brother was down there, he might be safe after all. "If there's a city of the dead underneath our house, it's exactly the kind of mystery Robbie would gravitate to."

Griffin stared into his glass. "When I was younger," he said, "I wanted to grow up to be the kind of man whose friends and lovers had secrets."

"Did you?"

He nodded. "I discovered we all have secrets. You know most of mine."

"I did, but . . ." She didn't complete the thought.

After a minute, he said, "We need to go online. Do you have a computer with you?"

Jac fetched her laptop from the desk in the corner. "The house is wireless. Robbie saw to that. What are you looking for?" she asked as she handed it to him.

"Maps first. There are always maps. We need to figure out what's down there and how to prepare for it. The more we know going in, the more likely we are to meet with success."

For the next hour, they sat side by side on the couch. Said little. Read a lot. Most of the information was in English as well as in French, so Jac didn't have to translate much.

The city beneath the city had first supplied Paris with all the limestone it needed for its grand mansions, wide boulevards and bridges. The hollowed-out earth and tunnels then became home to the bones of more than six million dead crowding cemeteries that couldn't contain them anymore. Over the years, the catacombs had been utilized as makeshift resistance bunkers during the war, galleries for avant-garde artists, prisons and escape routes. All but a mile of them had been officially shut down—that mile was now a tourist destination. But the laws didn't prevent determined cataphiles from continuing to go underground for all sorts of reasons.

"It's illegal to explore the tunnels," Jac said as she skimmed another article. "I don't even want to read these stories about people who have gotten lost and never came out. There are one hundred and ninety miles of underground passages. Uncharted, and, for the most part, unmarked and dangerous."

"I've crawled through pyramids. I know how to take care of us."

"And find him? In all those tunnels?"

"He found a way to get you to the tunnel. He'll find a way to lead you to him."

According to the Greeks, the fates—three minor goddesses—appeared seven nights after a child's birth. Their job: to determine the trajectory of the baby's life. Clotho spun the thread of life that Lachesis measured and that Atropos cut after deciding how old the child would be and how death would occur.

And yet, even with the goddesses making the decisions, man had the freedom to influence and alter his fate. Jac believed everything in mythology was a metaphor. She didn't believe in fate. But as she stared at Griffin, she wondered about the odd coincidence that he would be in Paris now. Griffin. An expert in exactly the kind of mission necessary to find her brother.

"There are no coincidences," she could hear her brother saying. Someone else had said it to her recently too. She struggled to remember. Then it came to her. Malachai Samuels.

She glanced back at the computer. "It says most of the tunnels are over a hundred feet down. That's what you said. When you dropped the candle. That the chute went down a hundred feet?"

"From the sound the candle made when I dropped it, absolutely."

"That's about five to seven flights of stairs, depending on how far apart they are, right?"

He nodded.

"Seven stories is twice the size of this building."

"You don't have to go if you're uncomfortable. Let me do it. I've gone down deeper—it doesn't bother me at all."

"It's Robbie. I'll manage."

"There are tricks to not panicking. One is, don't anticipate what's ahead of you. Not being able to see ahead of you—not knowing where the end is—can be the worst part."

"I'm not afraid of heights; I don't imagine I'll be afraid of depths."

"Or the dark?"

"No. I like the dark. It's comforting."

Griffin laughed. "Well, then, you'll be happy. It's going to be dark.

There's no natural light that far down. This article says that in the early nineteen hundreds, the catacombs were used to grow mushrooms."

They made a list of what they'd need to buy in the morning.

Jac checked the clock on the mantel. It was ten. "The stores won't be open for another twelve hours."

Griffin followed her glance. "You should try to go to sleep."

"I won't be able to."

"You're not going to be any good to Robbie if you're exhausted." Griffin crossed the room and placed his glass on the bar. "I don't think you should be alone in the house. I'll camp out on the couch."

"I'm not afraid to be alone."

"No. I'm sure you're not." He almost sounded aggrieved. "But I'm afraid for you, and I'll be able to sleep better knowing you're not here by yourself."

"I'm not in danger, Griffin."

He just nodded.

"You think I am?"

"I just don't want to take chances."

Jac looked at him. Held his eyes. Once she had imagined so many stories, all with him in them. Once she had thought that they would be together. Once she had believed in him the way she now understood no one should ever believe in anyone. Yes, she'd had great expectations for him. For him and for Robbie—and for herself, too. It might have seemed like too much pressure. Maybe she'd been wrong to want so much for him and to think that accomplishments defined a person. But he'd accomplished it all, hadn't he?

"Why are you shaking your head?" he asked.

"Was I?"

"Like you were having an argument with someone."

"You're doing what you always wanted to, aren't you?" she asked.

"For the most part, yes."

"What I thought you'd do." She smiled.

"You knew exactly who I wanted to be."

"Then what was the problem, Griffin?"

"I couldn't bear the thought of failing."

"Failing?"

"Failing and being a disappointment."

"To who? Me? Or you? Which one of us?"

He didn't say anything for a moment. Then: "I thought you. Now I'm not sure."

He came back to the couch and sat beside her. He put his hand on her shoulder and turned her toward him. "You ask impossible questions, you know that? Things people don't ask. Frank. Forward. You haven't changed." He laughed. But it wasn't joyful. "You want to go so far in. To know so much. Too much. You're so damn curious."

"Not me. I stopped being curious a long time ago."

"Liar," he said. And then he pulled her toward him and kissed her.

Jac felt more questions swirling in her head, demanding she not ignore them, insisting she take them seriously and focus on them. But the pressure of his lips was too distracting. She was tired. And, yes, scared. If she didn't think, if she rested here inside his embrace for a little while, it would be all right. Wouldn't it?

Griffin's smell swirled around her. If she let herself, she could get lost in that smell. If she could forget what had happened between them— no, not forget, but let it go for now. Just for a little while. It had been so long since she'd felt this urgent pull. And she wanted to give in to it.

Except not with Griffin.

With anyone but him.

It had taken her so long to bring herself back from the brink where he'd left her. Was she strong enough to now take what she wanted without unraveling afterward? A mixture of want and fury pounded in her veins. Her fingers dug deep into his arms. Pulling him toward her, she hoped she was hurting him. Wanted the pressure to cause him pain, but from the way he leaned deeper into her, she wasn't sure. Then his fingers were pressing into her flesh. There would be marks left on her skin tomorrow. Black-and-blue imprints of his touch. Long ago he'd gone away and had left invisible bruises that had never quite healed. But these would. These were only surface blemishes.

Her body was betraying her. For years Jac had stood up to the

memories of this man. Kept them from tempting her. And now? Now
she was giving herself up to every single sensation he elicited from her.

Damn. Her body had not forgotten. Not his smell and not his taste.
Not the way his hair curled at the base of his neck. Not the warmth of
his skin. Not the way he enveloped her whole body in his embrace so
that the rest of the world fell away and they were alone living out the
minutes on the rims of their lips. Her craving to be next to him without
clothes between them embarrassed her. This want was more primal and
urgent than any she'd ever experienced. Ever even guessed at. Suddenly
needing to feel him on her was more crucial than breathing. Her fingers moved to his shirt buttons.

Griffin didn't stop her or help her. He allowed her to undress him.
Watched her. She felt as if she was admitting something in each movement that he needed to know, wanted to know.

Jac whispered, "Do you remember what we were like?"

He didn't answer.

She wanted him to talk. To center her. If she could get him to speak
about who they had been, maybe it would prevent her from creating a
new story with him. It was one thing to relive the past, but she didn't
want to open up a new path to the future. Not with this man to whom
she'd given too much before—and who had squandered her gift.

"Is this what we were like before?" she asked again.

He kissed her until she was quiet.

She pulled off his shirt and unbuttoned her own. Unfastened her
brassiere. Pressed her chest to his. Felt the cool air on her back and the
hot skin against her breasts.

"Do you remember us?"

Griffin moved his lips down her neck and across her chest, and he
left kisses on her skin like messages written in a language she could no
longer decipher. He was telling her skin secrets. Her body understood.
Her mind didn't.

She wanted to use him so she could stop worrying about her brother
for a while. It wouldn't be wrong to use Griffin. He'd hurt her. He owed
her this.

His lips were on her shoulder—he'd found the spot he'd been the first to find when she was seventeen years old. Lightly gnawing on it, he sent fiery shivers down her back.

Everything was a soft, inviting darkness. Not the cold black of the tunnel leading down into the earth where Robbie was waiting. This was a blood-lust darkness. If she could shine a light on it, she was sure it would be flush with deep maroon and suffused with the scent of roses and cinnamon and musk.

No one she'd been with other than Griffin had urged her body to give off that particular aroma. It was as if he excited some secret part of her self that opened and bloomed under his fingers and tongue and teeth and lips and cock.

Naked now, the two of them moved from the living room up to her bedroom and lay on her childhood bed, the powder-blue chenille bedspread soft under her. His body rough on top of her.

They'd always been aware of the need to be quiet. In college and grad school, they'd each had roommates in crowded, small quarters. When she'd taken him to her grandmother's house in Grasse, they'd had to worry about making too much noise while the rest of the house slept. During the day, Griffin led her and Robbie on expeditions to archaeological sites, looking for remnants of the Romans and the Cathars. Breaking for lunch, they'd sit in the shade, hiding from the strong Provence sun. They'd eat honey that smelled of lavender smeared on baguettes filled with goat cheese and drink fruity rosé wine. When Robbie would take off to hunt for more shards of ages long gone, they'd lie on the grass and explore each other's bodies, hurrying a little, so they'd be done before he got back.

Now they didn't have to be cautious. The house was empty except for the ghosts of L'Etoiles who had lived here for almost three hundred years. Jac couldn't imagine they would be shocked by anything she and Griffin were doing. They'd certainly seen and done worse over the years.

Suddenly an image flowered in her mind: a woman and a man making love here, in this house, in this room, almost as if they were superimposed over her. Their smells were all different. Sour and pungent. Musty sweat, face powder, and candle wax. Scents Jac didn't remember her father mixing. Combinations she and Robbie never played with. Old-fashioned, from another time.

The woman—was it the woman from Jac's hallucinations?—was crying. Holding onto the man, she wept on his shoulder. Her tears soaked his skin. Even as he pushed inside of her and filled her up in a way that she, too, had forgotten was possible—in the same way that Jac had forgotten that only Griffin could fill her, the man in the shadows whispered that he was sorry. That he was so sorry. That he never meant to cause her pain.

Or was it Griffin saying that as he thrust up inside of her? Jac couldn't separate the picture and the smells and the words.

She heard screaming somewhere in the distance and then the wrenching sound of wood splintering and heavy footsteps and another smell—overwhelming everything else now—the smell of fear. Seeping under the door, through the cracks in the window, wafting up. A gun blasted. Panic shot through her with more force than the man's thrusting. Fear that this time would be the last time. Reunited, were they about to lose each other again?

"Not now that I finally found out you're alive," Marie-Genevieve sobbed. Or was it Jac? Was she crying? Her tears? Someone else's? Someone else's words? She was feeling Griffin inside of her. It was Griffin, wasn't it? Not Giles.

She was lost again as new waves of sensation swept over her. Bouquets of scent enveloped her. Roses. Cinnamon. Musk. She tasted her own salty tears and the sweet taste of his lips. There was no space between their bodies. No way of knowing where one of them started and the other stopped. His touch and his smells were a drug. They had once meant all this and more to each other. They had created a world out of each other's bodies and yet had walked away from it. He had. He had left this. Let this go. Let her go. Let go of this magic that was more alchemical than any fragrance any perfumer had ever concocted. This was the scent of secrets, and as long as you could smell it, you would live forever.

Jac thrust her hips up. She met his movements with her own, her bones grinding into his. Their flesh smacking against each other. His face was hidden in her neck. His mouth on her shoulder now, again.

That spot. Electricity shivered through her. His fingers dug deep into her skin. She was surrounding him, but he was all around her. There was no memory, and yet it was all memory.

"Are you crying?" he whispered.

Jac wasn't sure. She didn't want to know. Was this another psychotic break? What else could it be? This strange half dream. Hauntingly beautiful. Bitter green with sadness. Another time. Long ago. A woman and a man in this room. Love lost. Love found. Making love. Sorrow swelling as they faced some kind of tremendous terror.

She shuddered. Griffin mistook it for passion. He arched up again inside of her. And she was lost again. It was even darker and smoother. The smells were evening out into one commingled sighing scent, hotter, lusher. She was traveling the maze. He was at the center. Held out his arms. They moved in unison—practiced lovers who might have been dancing this way together for hundreds of years.

There would never be any more sadness. Never any more longing, because they would never again separate. This act sealed their fates. They were two woeful halves coming together. Forming a whole that left no room for air, for fire, for scent or stink, for water, for breath. They were together. Without thought or wisdom or words. They were together. As they had always been, forever, Jac thought in one moment of clarity as she was overwhelmed by the gift of oblivion that only such a deep and painful explosion could render.

Thirty-five

On the opposite side of Rue des Saints-Pères, inside the courtyard of the nineteenth-century apartment complex, a chestnut tree cast the navy-blue Smart car in shadows. William had secured the parking space from the concierge. Three hundred euros in exchange for the numeric code that residents used to open the heavy wooden gates. Only two families had cars, so there were three unused spaces.

Despite the privacy the tree afforded, Valentine kept the lights off and the windows rolled up. The electronic listening device had been modified so its switches didn't illuminate. Her headphones were state of the art. Even when William was in the car with her, he couldn't hear what she was listening to. She had been trained to take every precaution.

The whole time she'd been sitting there, no one had come or gone. Everyone seemed to be in for the night.

Valentine shifted in her seat. Arched her back. Stretched her legs. She ran ten hours a week. Practiced martial arts another five. Her diet was macrobiotic laced with vitamins. Under François's tutelage, she'd turned her body into an instrument. One that no one could take from her. Her only vice was cigarettes. And she allowed herself only eight a day.

Four hours in the car was nothing. Her longest stint had been nine hours. But that had been a success. So far, tonight had been anything but.

Valentine had followed Griffin North and Jac L'Etoile back to the mansion after their dinner at Café Marly. For a few minutes, she'd heard them clearly, then nothing. After an hour, a few sentences, then Griffin put on the stereo. After that, she'd heard only intermittent pieces of conversation. Nothing valuable. At least on the surface. Maybe later, when she could play it back, there'd be some clues.

It was hot and cramped inside the vehicle, but Valentine was trained not to let that distract her. She just listened. Because the subjects spoke only English, it was taking more concentration than usual. And proving more frustrating. Valentine was missing nuances of any of the conversation she did hear.

She'd understood the sound of their lovemaking, though. And for some reason, it had embarrassed her. It had been four years since she'd been with a man. And he had been the only man she'd been with since François had picked her up off the street and taken her to the hospital.

The knock on the window startled her. Instinctively, she put her hand on her knife. Like soldiers in the People's Armed Police in China, she was trained in many killing techniques: shooting, knifing, hand-to-hand combat. Like François, she preferred knives to guns. The butterfly knife she wore on the belt around her waist had been his gift to her on her indoctrination into the Triad. Dragons were beautifully engraved on the blade. Leather strips, softened by years of use, wound around the steel tang.

In ancient times, these knives were favored by monks, who wore them under their robes. They sharpened only the tips so they could use them in self-defense without causing death.

The blade of Valentine's knife was sharpened all the way to the hilt.

When she saw that it was William, her grip relaxed. She unlocked the doors.

Once inside, he offered her one of the two cardboard cups of steaming tea. She thanked him. It had been a long night, and the drink was welcome. She opened the tea, and the windows fogged.

"Has there been a lot going on?" he asked.

In between sips, she filled him in. It was strange to be with William without François there. Awkward to be two instead of three. She wondered if she should have brought in a third. There were four other members of the team. She could add any one of them.

"Where do they think Robbie L'Etoile is?" William asked. "Have they said?"

He was jittery and had circles under his eyes.

"No, they didn't. But for a while I think they left and went to find him."

"I checked with our men on the way here; no has left the house since they came back from dinner."

"They left. They must have used another entrance."

"We have both entrances covered. I know how to set up surveillance."

"Well, they left."

"There isn't any other way out," William said. "I'm certain."

"That's impossible. From their conversation, it was clear they went somewhere to look for him. You have to find it."

"François wouldn't argue with me. Valentine, I told you. I know how to do my job."

The stress. The sadness. The loss. She knew how he felt. "I miss him too."

"What does that mean?" William asked.

"It's hard to do your job right when you're preoccupied. Emotion gets in the way. But no one is going to accept missing him as an excuse for slipping up."

"How dare you. I didn't slip up."

"Then where did they go?"

"You have no idea of how I feel. What do you know about loving someone? A little street whore. If François hadn't saved you—you'd be dead by now. He told me you're damaged emotionally. That you're a sociopath who—"

Valentine threw what was left of the tea into William's face. He coughed. Sputtered.

"You're out of your mind, you know that?" he growled.

Valentine pulled her cigarettes out of her backpack. Shook one out. Lit it. "It's late. Why don't you go home, William? Cry in your pillow. I'm fine on my own. I'm not going to let your emotional reactions impede the success of this mission."

William wiped off the rest of the tea. "If there is an exit," he said finally, firmly, "I'll find it."

"We're wasting time. Let's take the perfumer's sister. L'Etoile will come out. He'll do anything he has to, to save her."

"How do you know that?" William asked.

"Isn't that what family does? Or don't I know about how families respond to situations, either?"

"Even if that was the right solution, we'll never get to his sister. The police are watching her twenty-four hours a day."

"Since when is that a problem?" Valentine looked at him. He was facing forward. His profile was toward her. The prominent nose. Receding chin. A little extra flesh where the years were catching up to him. François had been lean. Kept himself hungry. "You sound like a coward." She inhaled. Drew the smoke into her lungs.

"Fuck you." He banged his fist on the dashboard. "You go too far."

"People who don't like to wait are waiting." She exhaled. "The longer the pottery is out there, the better chance there is of its getting into the wrong hands. Our bosses will hold us responsible for our failures."

Smoke had filled the car. Blue smoke. The color of François's music.

Thirty-six

In the past hour, Xie had recognized a Beatles ballad and a Green Day song but nothing else. He had no idea what the DJ was playing now. Western music made its way to China, but it took awhile for it to get there. Whatever was blasting must be new. Xie was grateful for the music's deafening level. It meant he didn't have to engage in small talk. He could just sit back, sip his beer, and work at appearing relaxed. The cold ale was superior to Yanjing beer. A second bottle would help calm him. But he forced himself to go slow. Be disciplined. He could allow himself only this one bottle.

He couldn't take any chances.

Xie had managed to avoid sneaking out with any of the students for the past two nights, but this wasn't a clandestine jaunt. This excursion had been arranged by the embassy. The son of the Chinese ambassador was hosting the artists for a night on the town. They'd had dinner in a typical pub and now were enjoying a private club.

Well, most of them were enjoying it. Xie was preoccupied. The five-ounce electronic device in his inside jacket pocket weighed on his mind. He might as well be carrying a loaded gun. The cell phone was contraband. No other student had one. If found, the phone would—to use one of the slang expressions Cali had learned from watching old American movies on the internet—be a dead giveaway.

But Xie was as afraid to get rid of it as he was to hold on to it.

He chugged his beer as a Rolling Stones song blared out of the speakers. Xie knew this one. "I can't get no . . . satisfaction . . ."

Did airport security check cell phones? Did you have to put the phone on the tray with your keys and change? It was yet another question he should have thought to ask. But Xie had been so scared when the stranger in the bathroom had clamped his hand over Xie's mouth, warned him to be quiet, and dragged him into a stall.

"I'm on your side," the stranger said as he slapped a phone into Xie's hand. "In case there is an emergency, the phone is preprogrammed so you can get help fast. Look in the contacts, depending on where you are, just hit London. Paris. Or Rome."

"I'm not—"

"No time to talk. Hide the phone. Be careful. There are people like me all along the way. To help you. Now, wash your hands and try to get some of that red wine out of your shirt so it looks like you were here for a reason."

And then the man walked out of the stall and left Xie there.

Even now, in a room packed wall to wall with people and smoke and music and liquor, Xie felt as if the phone sucked all the air out of the space. It could save his life. He knew that. But it could also be the thing that got him killed before he ever got to Paris. If his roommate was spying on him and found the phone . . . If airport security found it and someone from the school noticed . . .

"You look so serious," Lan said as she sidled up to him. Usually so quiet, her flirtatiousness was out of character. But then so were her three beers.

"I'm just watching. Listening."

Lan moved a few inches closer. He could smell her hair. It reminded him of a fruit, but he couldn't place it.

Strains of another Beatles song, "Here Comes the Sun," flowed out of the speakers. Xie knew this one too. And he liked it. Cali would want to know if the consulate asked the club to play some older tunes to make the students comfortable or if this was a typical mix. He was surprised by how her inquisitiveness had become second nature to him. He kept imagining how she'd react to what he was seeing, and all the questions she'd ask. This was the first time in the past two years they'd been separated for any length of time. He'd spent years without having a close friend—and only now, on the eve of losing her, did he understand how much he'd come to care about her.

Even though he knew, without doubt, that he was on the path he was meant to follow, he was going to miss his friend.

"I think I'd like to dance," Lan said shyly.

He could smell the beer on her breath.

"With you," she said even more softly. "I've never danced with anyone before."

He didn't mind dancing, but she was half drunk. What if she got too close to him and felt the phone? What if he slipped or bent over, and it fell out of his pocket? But what possible reason could he give for not dancing with her? What if he said no and she made a scene? Sober, she was a quiet sensitive girl, but half drunk?

No matter what he chose to do, it could be the wrong choice. So he would do what he had always done. Take the path of least resistance. Avoid attracting attention. Acquiesce.

Following Lan out onto the dance floor, Xie felt Ru Shan's eyes on him. Was it his imagination, or was Shan always looking at him? The calligrapher was one of the best there were; a prodigy who had been singled out when he was only twelve for his work. Xie had admired his work long before this trip. And told him so when he'd been assigned to share a hotel room with him. Shan had nodded, took the compliment, didn't react to it. Cali was always asking Xie to describe things to her in far more detail than he was naturally inclined to deliver. Xie could hear her asking him about Shan. Slim. Short. Lithe. His hands were full of grace, even when he opened a door or held a glass. Small eyes blazing with intelligence. And he liked to talk. Not about art— which would have pleased Xie—but instead about women in the most pornographic ways.

"They told me you're quiet," Shan complained when Xie didn't contribute much to the scatological one-sided conversation about the British girl Shan had picked up in the hotel bar the first night.

"Who told you I was quiet?" Xie wanted to ask. Had Shan slipped? Or had he just meant the other students on the trip who knew him from school? But Xie couldn't ask. Couldn't do anything with his suspicions but be plagued by them.

Once Xie and Lan started dancing, he maneuvered so that she was facing Shan.

Lan leaned closer into him. He was vaguely aware of thighs and breasts pressing into him. But it was the phone he was most conscious of. Her head was right up against it, pressing it into his chest.

She looked up at him. Her eyes were half closed.

"You're a nice dancer," she said, smiling. "At least I think you are. Since I've never danced before." And she giggled.

"Thank you," he said and turned, hoping if he kept moving, he'd keep her distracted. Could she feel the plastic rectangle? And if she did, would she question him about it? What would he say?

Looking up, Xie saw Shan had danced his partner around too, so he was once again facing Xie. Just a coincidence. Or was his roommate watching him?

Xie didn't know.

Thirty-seven

It was a ritual of sorts. His first night in Paris, Malachai always visited the Bar Hemingway at the Ritz Hotel. On his eighteenth birthday, his father had brought him here to introduce him to his first drink and his first cigar. It was one of the very few good memories Malachai had of the distant figure who was always finding fault with his youngest son. That night his father somehow resisted invoking the name of the sainted other son who had died too early. Until it was time to leave. "Your brother would have appreciated it here."

Tonight the bar wasn't as crowded as usual. The recession, Malachai thought as he sauntered into the wood-paneled room. It was small and cozy with the feel of a genteel club. Copies of Hemingway's novels sat on shelves. Press clippings and photographs of Papa, as the author was called, hung on the wall. A shrine of sorts, not just to the man but also to his love of a good drink. Colin Field, the head bartender, who'd been here for more than two decades, was famous for his offerings—one being a cocktail made with rare cognac that actually cost more than most people pay for an entire meal at a three-star restaurant.

Malachai slid onto one of the black leather stools and greeted Field.

"Dr. Samuels, it's a pleasure to see you again."

"You, too, Colin."

"What can I get you?"

"I started out with Krug at my hotel," Malachai said. "So I'll leave it to you."

Minutes later the bartender placed a flute in front of Malachai, who raised it to his lips and sipped the concoction.

"Grapefruit juice, champagne, and . . . I'm stumped."

Field smiled. "A splash of gin." He gave Malachai a small plate of olives, nuts, and potato chips.

"What brings you to Paris? Business or pleasure?"

Over the years, Malachai had learned that Field was exceptionally well read; in addition to keeping track of his clients' drink preferences, he kept up with them in the press.

"A client."

"A child?"

"A little girl with strange memories."

"Past-life memories?" Field asked.

"She doesn't think so . . . but I do."

"I thought about you a couple of weeks ago. I read about that Chinese ban on reincarnation. What did you make of that?"

"It's an absurd law. Political posturing. A power grab." Malachai ate a few nuts. "What's happening to Tibet and its traditions is a tragedy that only gets worse."

Malachai finished his drink, paid Field, and left. Walking through the long corridor filled with glass vitrines, he examined the displays of costly antiques, china, and fashion accessories. There were silk ties and gold cuff links. State-of-the-art phones. Top-of-the-line watches and pens. Women's jewelry, scarves, lingerie and gloves.

He stopped in front of a display of gold and what he assumed were white-gold or platinum women's bracelets. Some plain. Others diamond encrusted. There was one on the bottom shelf. Blackened gold links. No stones. Just big links—almost two inches wide. He was seeing it on Jac, accenting her delicate wrist.

Passing through the lobby, he smelled something he hadn't noticed before. He stopped. Sniffed. It was spicy and warm. Welcoming. Ha.

She was right. The more you thought about scent, the more you developed a language for it.

"Are you burning incense?" Malachai asked the doorman.

"Non, monsieur. It's the hotel signature scent. It's called Ambre. It is for sale in the gallery during the day."

Malachai thanked him and strode outside.

"*Un taxi?*" another doorman asked.

"I believe a car was supposed to meet me . . ." As if on cue, a black Mercedes sedan with darkened windows pulled up.

The doorman leaned in, asked the driver who he was picking up, and then turned back to Malachai. "Dr. Samuels?"

Only after they'd left the Place Vendôme and the driver turned right on the Rue de Rivoli did either of the two men speak.

"Thank you for being so prompt, Leo." He looked into the rearview mirror. The driver met his eyes. He was wearing a black uniform, white shirt, and black chauffeur's cap, with thick wavy dark hair curling out the back. He had on glasses and appeared to be in his early thirties, but it was hard to tell.

"No problem, sir," Leo answered in an Italian accent.

"Winston gives you high marks. You worked with him at Interpol?"

"I did."

"How long have you been on your own?"

"A few years."

Leo wasn't chatty. That was fine with Malachai. He didn't require conversation. Just results.

"Have you been able to gather any new information?"

"Yes. A bit more than we reported to Winston this morning."

Malachai was hoping they'd been able to locate Robbie. "About L'Etoile?"

"No. The police still don't have a lead on where he might be and are—"

"What's the news?" Malachai interrupted.

"They've identified the man who was found dead in the perfume store on Rue des Saints-Pères. He wasn't a reporter; he was a jazz musician. A well-respected one."

"Masquerading as a reporter? Why?"

"It's beginning to look like he had another career, too."

Malachai understood. "Who was he working for?"

"The local Chinese Mafia."

How curious that earlier that evening, Colin Field had just brought up that newspaper story about the Chinese government outlawing reincarnation without obtaining a license.

"That's very bad news for us," Malachai said, more to himself than to the operative. "That means they know what L'Etoile found. I would imagine now they will spare no expense to get it."

Thirty-eight

The bellman from L'Hotel delivered Malachai Samuels's letter to the residence at L'Etoile Parfums the next morning just as Jac and Griffin were leaving. She took the envelope, opened it and glanced at the letter. As she maneuvered Robbie's Citröen out of the courtyard and onto Rue des Saints-Pères, she told Griffin what it said.

"He believes that the pottery is real; that the fragrance is real," she said. "He's a brilliant scientist, but . . . we're such a sad, desperate species, aren't we?"

"That we search for something to believe in?"

She nodded. "Mythology is what we call someone else's religion."

"Ah, your old friend Joseph Campbell."

She laughed, but instead of joy it was with defeat.

"Hope dies last," Griffin said. Now the defeat was his.

It was an overcast morning, slightly too cool for the end of May. Melancholy. But melancholy fit Paris. The city wore gray skies with the insouciance of a French woman in high couture. Jac rolled down her window. The air smelled of the river a block away, early morning traffic, the buckets of roses in front of the corner florist, and the fresh bread from the baker down the street.

Like different instruments all contributing to a symphony, the strains created a unique odor that was unlike that of any other city—or even this city at any other time of day.

"There's a dark-blue car following us. It's been with us since we left," Griffin said.

"The police?"

"Could they be this bad at surveillance? Don't worry. We have over an hour to get to a store that's five minutes from here, right? We'll lose them."

At the next corner, the car continued on after Jac made a left.

"Okay, he's gone," Griffin told Jac. "And I don't see anyone else on our tail. At least not yet. Circle this block. Nice and slow."

"You sound pretty knowledgeable about evasion tactics."

"Everything I know is from movies on plane trips and books I read when I'm on a dig. I always mean to read the kind of novels that get reviewed in the *New York Times,* but I can't help it; I'm drawn to high-octane thrillers. If my favorite authors do decent research, we should be okay. If they don't . . . well . . ."

"That's not the most reassuring thing you've told me."

"No, I wouldn't imagine it is. "

They drove for another five minutes in silence and then he said, "There could have been more than one car. Someone might have called for another vehicle to pick us up at another point, but I don't see anyone on our tail."

"On our tail. Very dramatic."

"I'm all you've got. Go easy on me. Okay?"

She nodded. "Griffin?"

Out of the corner of her eye, she saw him turn.

"Do you think Robbie's okay?"

"Yes. He's resourceful. He's clever. But more than that, he believes in what he's doing. If anyone can survive on sheer will, it's Robbie."

After another few blocks, he suggested they stop and have breakfast. "We have at least an hour before the stores open. Find someplace where we can sit and watch the street from the window."

Jac took a left, then a right, and stopped in front of a café.

They got a table by the window with a view of the wide boulevard.

They ordered cafés au lait and croissants. Didn't talk much while they drank the coffee and picked at the buttery pastries. Even though neither of them brought up what had happened the night before, Jac felt it was being discussed in the silence. She didn't know if the encounter had been about her and Griffin or an escape from the awful situation. She'd need to sort it out. But after Robbie was back. And safe.

"I have about two hundred euros," Griffin said. "It should be enough for the supplies. But if it's not, do you have cash?"

"I have a credit card."

"We shouldn't put anything on cards. They're traceable."

"Once we get all these supplies, how are we going to get them back into the house without alerting the police that anything suspicious is going on?" she asked.

Griffin took a sip of his coffee. "Did Malachai give you his number in that note?"

Jac fished the letter out of her pocketbook and handed it to him.

Griffin took out his cell phone and punched in the reincarnationist's number. "Malachai, it's Griffin. I'm with Jac. We need you to help us."

An hour and a half later, Jac pulled up in front of the House of L'Etoile and opened the gates to the courtyard. Anyone watching saw her park the car and then saw three people emerge.

Jac. Griffin. And Malachai Samuels, carrying a suitcase. A visitor coming to stay.

He'd taken a taxi from his hotel and met them at the sporting goods store, where they'd filled his empty suitcase with their purchases.

Once inside, Griffin turned on the stereo, then took the suitcase to the kitchen. "Give me a few minutes," he said. "I have to call Elsie. I'm her wake-up call."

"You do that every morning?" Jac asked.

"No matter where I am," Griffin answered and headed out to the living room.

"He's a good man," Malachai said. "Robbie's lucky to have him as a friend."

Jac nodded. Didn't trust herself to say anything. Griffin's dedication to his daughter had moved her.

Jac opened the bag and with Malachai's help emptied the spelunking equipment on the table.

"Thank you," Jac said. "You were a great decoy."

"My pleasure. That's what I came here for. To help any way I could."

She picked up a helmet and, using the kitchen scissors, cut off the price tag. "It's a long way to come. From what Griffin's been telling me, I don't think there's anything you can do to get Robbie to sell you the pottery."

"I've raised over a quarter million dollars."

She shook her head. "Robbie might have poisoned someone. Killed him. Money's not going to get him to change his mind." She shook her head again. "This is all so crazy. Ever since we were kids, he took chances that he shouldn't have for his ideals. He almost got killed when he went to Tibet in the middle of an uprising to see if he could help the monks save their relics. But this time . . ."

"He has strong beliefs."

"In things that can't matter. In shards of pottery that are part of a made-up fairy tale. Myths are metaphors."

"The pottery isn't a myth. It's real. Reincarnation is real," Malachai said.

He was ready to fight. Jac wasn't.

"It's not worth dying for," she said.

"Anything worth living for is worth dying for." There was a longing in Malachai's voice that made Jac hesitate before responding.

"You sound like him."

"We share a lot of the same beliefs."

"I never thought of you as a romantic."

"That doesn't surprise me. I got to know you far better than you got to know me."

"I didn't get to know you at all."

"Jac, I desperately want to know what the pot shards say and have there be a fragrance that helps people remember their past lives. But I didn't come just to acquire a memory tool. I'm here because I'm worried about you. I wanted to be here if you needed help, too. I had a brother once . . ." His voice drifted off for a few seconds. "I want to help you find your brother." He put his hand on her wrist.

Bruised from where Griffin had pulled her up out of the hole the night before, she tried not to flinch.

He looked down at the spot he'd touched.

"I hurt myself. It's nothing."

As Griffin came back into the room, he snapped his phone off and put it in his pocket. Jac saw a slight frown crease Malachai's wide forehead.

"How's Elsie?" she asked.

"Bereft. One of her goldfish died overnight. I had to promise two more to replace it. And an underwater castle."

Before Jac could respond, the house phone rang. Rushing, she picked it up before the second ring.

It was Inspector Marcher.

Jac's heart sped up, and she held her breath.

"Do you have news?"

"No. But would it be possible for me to drop by and speak with you?" Marcher asked.

Jac walked out of the kitchen and into the pantry to take the call in private. "Can't we talk now, over the phone?"

"It will take only a few minutes."

The smells in the white-tiled room brought back long-forgotten memories. She used to love to cook with her grandmother, who always gave Jac the job of gathering the ingredients. The stored dry goods gave off a warm odor. A corner of her heart hurt.

"Have you made any progress?"

"Nothing substantive, mademoiselle."

One shelf held a dozen black packages of Mariage Frères Chinese and Japanese green teas. Her brother's favorites. She ran her finger over the gold writing, spelling out evocative names. Aiguilles de Jade. Bouddha Bleu. Dragon de Feu.

"Then what is there to talk about?"

"I know this is difficult," Marcher started.

"I don't want your empathy; I want to know what you are doing to find my brother."

Jac leaned against the door and shut her eyes. She never would have guessed it would be Robbie's collection of tea that would make his disappearance the most real to her.

"Mademoiselle L'Etoile, I need to talk to you. Just for a moment?"

"Why are you having me followed?"

"We're protecting you. Not following you. That's exactly what I wanted to discuss with you."

"Protecting me from whom?"

"I'm afraid I can't say."

"Or won't say?"

"I'm not at liberty at this point—"

"It's my *brother*." Her voice echoed in the small pantry.

"I am well aware of that. And I'm sorry I can't be more helpful. Believe me—if we had any confirmed information about his whereabouts or well-being, you'd know."

"Have you at least been able to identify the man who died here?"

"Nothing definitive."

"You think you know who he was?"

"We're working on a lead."

"What the hell does that mean? A lead? Do you know who it is or not? Someone died in our boutique."

"Jac?" Griffin was outside.

She opened the door.

"You okay?"

She nodded.

"We have something, but we're having a hard time verifying it," Marcher said.

She didn't care if she was being rude. Or if she sounded hysterical. "My brother has been missing since Monday night. It's Friday. *Friday.* I want to know what you know."

"I understand this is frustrating, Mademoiselle—"

Jac took a breath. Stared up at the ceiling and the ordinary light fixture. How long had it been there? Forty years? Sixty? A hundred years?

It was amazing how some things lasted. Never changed. Others did so quickly. So fast.

"When I know anything that I can tell you, I will. In the meantime, the reason I wanted to talk to you was to ask you to please accept our protection and not go out of your way to avoid us like you and Mr. North did this morning."

"What kind of danger am I in?"

Instead of making her afraid, Marcher's warning angered her. She was out of patience.

"We don't know what incited the original incident. If it was personal . . . a lover's quarrel . . . a business deal gone bad . . . then no, you're not."

She was tired of listening to Marcher.

"But if the intruder was after the pottery shards your brother and Griffin North were working on," Marcher continued, "then yes, you could be. Very serious danger. As long as your brother is missing, the whereabouts of the pottery are unknown. Whoever wants it might think you know where it is. Or that Robbie hid it on the premises and that if you are incentivized you could help them—or be forced to help them—find the treasure."

Jac shivered. He'd done it: managed to scare her. Damn him. She wasn't going to let him distract her. All that mattered now was finding Robbie.

Thirty-nine

Jac hadn't looked down yet. Waiting for her were miles of inky black tunnels running beneath Paris. World War II bunkers. Chapels dedicated to Satan. The bones of more than six million of her countrymen exhumed from their previous resting places. Fragile galleries mined to the point that sometimes they still collapsed in on themselves. And hopefully, somewhere in the ominous twists and threatening turns: her brother.

But her terror lived on the edge of the tunnel opening. It wasn't sharp or ragged. There was no threat of ripping her skin or tearing her clothes. But once she put one foot over that edge, she would be in danger of falling into the abyss. Darkness and damp. Unending space. The unknown.

"The steps are fairly wide," Griffin called up to her. He'd descended first, and was about ten feet down, waiting for her.

Malachai had remained behind. An accident two years ago made climbing impossible, and, besides, they needed someone to be ready in case of an emergency. Cell phones wouldn't work so far deep in the earth, but the two-way radio system Griffin had bought at the store might.

"Just take it slow, Jac. I'm right here."

Jac breathed in deeply, inhaling the dry, dead smells. Finally, she peered down. Her helmet illuminated the narrow stone tunnel much better than the single candle had done the night before. Yet now that she could see where she was going, the reality of what was ahead seemed no less daunting.

Griffin was perched on the steps, looking up, encouraging her. Beyond him: darkness. "I've got your back," he said. "Just take the first step."

"How far down are you?" she asked.

"I've counted about forty steps so far. One at a time. Go slow. You'll be fine."

Maybe. Maybe not. Each and every step was an edge. An extended and exaggerated phobic situation had the potential to become a full-blown crisis. She'd spent a year in therapy learning the landscape of her own mind. And how to navigate its most treacherous terrain. Jac had learned how to control her fears and panics. Knew all the tricks. But would they work?

Inhale. Smell the scents. Dissect the odors in the air.

Chalk.

One step.

Dirt.

Another step.

After she'd conquered the first dozen steps, Griffin resumed his climb.

"I've hit bottom," Griffin shouted up. His voice echoed and sounded hollow. Almost inhuman.

Jac shivered. Looked down. His lantern illuminated a circular area that didn't look much bigger than an elevator. She didn't have a good sense of distance and was surprised how far away he seemed.

"How many steps is it?"

"Seventy-five."

How many had she done? She hadn't been counting. Seventy-five seemed impossible.

"You're already forty steps down," he called out as if reading her mind.

Thirty-five.

Clay.

Thirty-four.

Dust.

"And it's pretty muddy down here. Be careful when you step off," Griffin said when she got to eight.

Wet with sweat, shaking, her heart banging, Jac stepped onto the ground and looked around. The area was five feet across. Everywhere was rock—rough-hewn blocks of gray limestone.

The first thing she did after calming down was to inhale. Closing her eyes, she analyzed the odors, seeking the Fragrance of Loyalty.

Not a trace.

"I think we go through there." Griffin pointed to a narrow opening. Jac peered at it. The crevice was only two feet wide and ragged.

"It looks more like a fissure. Are you sure?"

"There aren't any other exits but up. Let me go first."

Three seconds later, he called out, "It's all right. Just be careful. The rock face is rough."

She followed him through the crack. On the other side was a tunnel, too narrow for them to walk abreast. So Griffin led and Jac followed. Several times they had to twist around and walk with their backs to the wall. Still, rocks on the facing wall grazed their noses.

The silence was absolute and overpowering. Other than hearing Griffin breathing and their footsteps, there was no sound. Jac wasn't sure she'd ever been anywhere as quiet. But it wasn't peaceful. The world above them might have come to a standstill and ended, and they wouldn't know.

After about a hundred yards, they reached two ancient rock steps leading up to a small landing where the ceiling suddenly soared to at least ten feet high. Then another two steps leading down to a continuation of the last tunnel. This one as narrow as the last, but filled with water that looked as if it would reach the middle of her calf. Higher than her boots.

"You game?" Griffin asked.

The water was cold. Her boots squished in the mud. Her jeans wicked up the water and after only a few feet, Jac's pants were wet to just below the knee. At the end was an archway. Griffin shined his helmet light on the lintel, illuminating handwriting on the wall.

Faded. Hand lettered. It looked as if it had been there for at least fifty years.

"What does it say?" he asked.

As she translated, she read out loud. "The right path is often the most difficult."

"I wonder if Robbie could have written that and doctored it to look old. Is it his handwriting?"

"No . . . but . . ." She pictured the bottles of essences in the workshop. "It could be my grandfather's."

"So far there haven't been any offshoots—we're on a direct path from the inside of your family maze. So if your grandfather did bring Robbie down here, this is the route they took. You okay to keep going?"

"I'm fine."

"Was your grandfather ever decorated?"

"Decorated?"

"After the war, did the French government honor him?"

"If they did, I never heard about it. He didn't talk much about his wartime experiences. Other than a few stories he told us about hiding people in these tunnels."

"So you didn't realize he was a hero?"

There was a subtext to Griffin's question, but she didn't understand it.

"My grandmother used to tell us that he was. But he didn't like her to mention it. Why?"

"You're always looking for heroes. I wondered if you knew you grew up with one."

For a moment, she had a glimmer of understanding: this was something important, but now wasn't the time to try to figure it out. Ahead of them was an incline. Five steps leading up into a tunnel with a ceiling so low they were forced to crawl on their hands and knees. Luckily they had gloves, or the floor would have ripped the flesh from their palms. After eight feet, the tunnel ended—not with steps but with a stone chute.

"Where does it go?" Jac heard the quaver in her voice.

"There's no way to know."

"We can't go down there."

"There's no other option."

For the first time since Marcher had called her in New York, Jac cursed Robbie.

"Let me go first," Griffin said as he climbed into the hole.

"I thought that was a foregone conclusion."

"It's a little tunnel . . ." His voice was getting fainter as he crawled in deeper. "And then a slide."

Jac heard a splash.

"Are you all right?" she called.

His voice came from somewhere far away. It was the first time they'd been this far apart since coming underground.

"It's water up to my thighs. But perfectly clear. Very cold. Fresh. There must be springs under here."

Jac wanted to stop. To tell Griffin that she couldn't do this. This newest challenge was testing her sanity.

"It's a two-foot slide, then a drop of about three feet. I'm standing right here at the bottom."

Jac climbed inside. Looked at the edge of the opening: eighteen inches. This was as close as she could get. She was going to have to work at this one. She took a deep breath. Inhaled the stale, damp air. Focused on the smells. Mold. Stone dust. Dirt.

She was almost at the edge of the opening.

Crawled another inch. Took another breath. Another inch. She imagined Robbie in here two days ago. What had he been doing for the forty-eight hours? Worked his way through these tunnels and somehow gotten to Nantes? Concocted the elaborate ruse with his shoes and wallet and then made his way back? All to make the police believe he was dead? All to protect the pottery shards? Or was she wrong? Maybe an animal had disturbed the pebbles. Gotten dirt on the needle. Maybe it was wishful thinking that the dirt smelled like the Fragrance of Loyalty. She'd been wrong about it all. Convinced Griffin.

"Forget it! Let's go back!" she called out. "Robbie's not here."

"You can do it, Jac. I'm right here waiting for you. I've never known anyone more determined that you. What was it you used to say: 'What's the worst that can happen?' Right?"

She was a little girl. On the beach in Cannes with her grandmother and Robbie. The turquoise water shimmered and invited her in, but when it lapped her toes, it was too cold. Robbie was already in—swimming and howling with pleasure. Her grandmother watched Jac.

"Just run in. Don't stop to think about it. Plunge fast. The pain of it will be over in a moment, and then your body temperature will adjust. You have to be brave, *ma chérie*," her grandmother said. "It's only cold water—what's the worst that can happen?"

Be brave, ma chérie, Jac said to herself. *What's the worst that can happen?*

Jac propelled herself down the smooth stone chute. As she landed, her right ankle went out from under her, and she tripped.

Griffin reached out and helped her catch her balance.

"You okay?"

She nodded, not wanting him to hear the fear in her voice.

He put his hand up to her face, brushed away some dark curls that had escaped her barrette. "Really, are you okay? You're doing great. Like you've been doing it for years. Your brother knows how to take care of himself. You both do, Jac. You're survivors."

Ten yards into this tunnel was a set of five steps leading up to a dry landing. From there Jac and Griffin looked into a stone cathedral, majestically carved from the quarry itself. The vaulted ceiling soared up almost twenty feet. Where windows would be were hollowed-out openings looking into more stone.

Black stenciled letters on the wall spelled out: *Rue de Sèvres 1811*.

The night before, she had read an article on the internet explaining that the underground was marked with street signs to designate the areas above. Not just so the workers didn't get lost but also so they were able to orient themselves. It prevented panic, the writer said. And seeing one now, Jac understood why. It was oddly reassuring. Even though she couldn't burrow up a hundred feet through rock, knowing where she was had a calming effect.

On the wall to her right was more graffiti: men's names written in white paint and dated 1789 through 1799. On the left wall was more, with dates that continued into the early 1800s. There was a mural of a devil being followed by a mass of people in black robes. A chalk drawing of a guillotine. There were symbols and sayings in an old-fashioned typeface that appeared to have been created with the smoke from a lantern or candle. Other phrases were painted more recently with green and blue Day-Glo paint.

And three archways.

Finally they had arrived at a crossroads.

Jac walked over to each and sniffed the air. Took it deep into her. Tried to find some remnant of her fragrance. But there was nothing.

"Robbie had to have left us some kind of clue," Griffin said. He examined the areas around the openings. There was nothing on the one on the left or the right. But words were etched into the lintel of the middle archway. Not something Robbie could have done—this had taken time and looked as if it had been there for hundreds of years:

Arête! De l'autre bord de la vie est la mort.

Jac translated: "'Beware. On the other edge of life is death.' Knowing my brother," she theorized, "we can go this way. I can hear him laughing at how perfect the clue would be."

"Look." Griffin pointed to one of the columns supporting the middle arch.

In dark charcoal was the drawing of a crescent moon with a star inside of it.

Without hesitating, they walked through that archway and entered the next chamber.

The walls were uneven. Made of rocks. Yellowed. Wet.

Beside her she heard Griffin gasp.

She was about to ask him what he'd seen when she realized it for herself.

Everything she was looking at was made of bones. Bone walls. Shelves of bones. Brackets of bones. Altars of bones. Bone beams and arches. Even crosses made of bones. Not bleached white and purified, but decayed with dirt. Damp. Hundreds of bones. No. Thousands of bones. Skulls. Femurs. Pelvis bones. Bones stacked one on top of the other in perfect symmetry. Rounded ends out. Creating designs. Architectural details.

They'd entered the consecrated cemetery. The repository for the over-crowded cemeteries aboveground. They were now in the city of the dead.

"It's so strange, isn't it?" Jac remarked as she walked around the room, mesmerized. "They're not people. Not at first. Are they? It's just all a design."

Interspersed with the bones were cracked tombstones. Most were from the seventeen hundreds. The detritus of aboveground cemeteries had been deposited here with the calcified remains they'd once identified.

"I've spent so much time in tombs . . . but there's one thing I never get used to. So many silenced people whose names we will never know," Griffin said.

"When I was little," said Jac, "I used to go with my grandmother when she went to tend to her family's cemetery plots. She brought bouquets of fresh flowers or wintergreen to her parents once a month. And a single stem to a baby she'd had that lived for only a week. One day I realized there were no tombstones from before 1860. She explained all the bodies buried before that had been emptied into the catacombs." Jac faced the long dead, the rows and rows of bones. The more she looked, the more she saw. A bullet hole in one of the skulls. A large crack in another. A smashed cranium. "Emptied them here."

Somewhere in the distance, water dripped. Slowly. Methodically.

Jac imagined she heard the name of the woman from her hallucination in their rhythm: Ma-rie—Ma-rie—Ma-rie.

And then another noise.

Jac couldn't be sure which direction it came from. It seemed as if it was above them. Or around them.

She looked at Griffin. She started to ask him what it was—but he put his finger to his lips.

There it was again. Louder this time. It was more than pebbles spilling. It sounded like bones falling. Or rocks collapsing.

Forty

Valentine didn't hurry. William was on duty in the car. She was on a break. Trying to walk off the emotional cacophony playing in her head.

She stopped in a small grocery store. Bought two apples and two bananas. A liter of bottled water. And cigarettes—her indulgence.

Back on the street, she listened to the street noises and snatches of conversation. Tried to notice the rest of the world going by; to pretend, for a few minutes, that she wasn't wound up and anxious. Wasn't worried about failure. Didn't miss François. That she believed she could take on this herculean task of running the mission herself. A mission that had become personal.

In the reflections in the store windows she passed, Valentine checked to see if anyone was following her. She didn't expect there to be. But she always watched.

A few people inside glanced back idly at her. Some with mild curiosity. They didn't see her. Not really. It was her look that caught their eyes. Diverted them from noticing her identifying features.

The uniform, cultivated over the years, was calculated to be just slutty enough so that the people who looked twice didn't see past the outfit: shoulder-length, thick black hair. Bangs. Oversize black sunglasses that hid half her face. At night she substituted an oversize pair of tinted

glasses even though she had 20/20 vision. Skintight blue jeans. Leather
boots up to her knees. A white or black T-shirt. Never a bra, so there
was typically a suggestion of nipples. Depending on the weather, either
one of two old worn leather jackets: a fawn-colored blazer she'd appropriated from François's closet years before, with double pockets inside
and out; or a thrift-shop black bomber with a dozen pockets. She always
had to have her hands free. Around her waist, she wore a belt. Halfway
back, her knife hung off it. Invisible under the jacket, she felt it. And
there was a gun tucked into the right boot.

She punched in the code and went through the door. William was
where she'd left him. Sitting inside the parked car.

"Anything happen while I was gone?" she asked.

"Music. Kitchen noises. Dead fucking nothing."

Earlier that morning, Valentine and William had followed the
Citröen to the café. While Griffin and Jac were eating, Valentine had
managed to attach a GPS device to the underside of their car. It had
been routine, simple: she went to a bakery and bought some croissants,
then walked down the street where they'd parked the Citröen. Just as
she passed the car, she pretended to trip, dropping the bag. While she
bent over to pick it up, she reached out and voila—it was done.

But the damn device had only helped them track the car to a parking
lot used by a complex of stores. Too many stores. There had been no way
to tell which one they'd gone into or what they'd bought.

No way to watch all the doorways and create a diversion and abduct
Jac L'Etoile. They were going to have to find another opportunity.

Back on Rue des Saints-Pères, she and William had watched them
get out of the car. Griffin carrying a suitcase. The two of them accompanied by another man. From the scraps of conversation they were able to
hear with the directional mike in the following half hour they were able
to pick up his name—Malachai—and a few words suggesting Jac and
Griffin were going to make another effort to find Robbie. But no one
had left the house or the boutique.

On every job, there were always stops and starts. But there were usually breakthroughs. If they didn't come, you made them happen. So far
there had been only stops.

She pointed to the laptop he had opened.

"Any luck getting information about the guy?" she asked him.

"Loads. Yeah. Malachai Samuels. He's a past-life therapist from New York City."

"Someone else who's after the damn pottery," Valentine said. "So do you think he's still there alone?"

"Yeah. It's too quiet for there to be three people there. Even if they were all just sitting around."

"Where did they go, William? Where do they think L'Etoile is?"

He handed Valentine the computer. "I got this, too. You're not going to like it much."

Was it her imagination, or did he sound slightly pleased?

She looked down. It was a blueprint. It took her only a few seconds to recognize the mansion across the street. There were two exits. The door to the shop. The door to the house. A courtyard in between. A wall around the courtyard.

"No exits other than the two we have under surveillance," William said.

She bit into the shiny red apple. "Well, they aren't being helicoptered out." The fruit tasted mealy. She threw it on the floor with the rest of the mess that had been accumulating. Rubbed her eyes. "We have to create some kind of diversion. Force her out of the house. And take her."

"The police aren't going to let her out of their sight."

She was so sick of William. Of his negativity. Of his high-pitched, whiny voice. Of his habit of clearing his throat before he spoke. Of his red-rimmed eyes.

The wrong partner had lived. She wanted François back. She tried to think. What would her mentor tell her to do?

A melody might be set, but you could change the key. The tempo. You could always riff.

The hair against the back of her neck was making her hot. The collar of her T-shirt was damp.

Riff.

forty-one

Through a crack in a wall, Jac and Griffin watched a group of four women and two men, all wearing dark robes, pass through a narrow corridor. Their faces were in shadows, hidden by their hoods.

Jac tried not to move. Not to breathe. Afraid to alert the strangers to her presence. On the internet, she'd read about the artists and musicians, drug users, and adventurers who visited the catacombs. Among the cataphiles were satanic groups who, for centuries, had been using the stone galleries to hold ceremonies.

Is that who these people were? What if they knew they'd been seen? What if they discovered her and Griffin? Were they dangerous? What if they'd already found Robbie? Would they have hurt him?

The group moved slowly. Their progress through the tunnel seemed endless.

Finally the corridor was empty again. Footsteps no longer echoed in the rock cavern. Jac started to step forward. Griffin reached out and held her back, his hand on her shoulder.

"Let's just make sure they are gone," he whispered.

Five minutes later, certain enough time had passed, Griffin nodded. "Okay. Let's get going."

The path ahead was wide but arduous. Jac and Griffin crawled side by side through the pebbles as the passageway twisted and turned. Finally, they reached an opening.

As she dropped down into the next room, Jac sensed something here was different. But before she had time to look around, before she even saw him, she heard his voice echoing in the small rock chamber.

"I knew it!" Robbie laughed as he ran to her. "You always were such a wonderful puzzle solver."

Jac threw her arms around her brother. They'd followed a faint clue into an impossible place and found him! He held onto her just as tightly.

Robbie smelled of the underground. Of the same mold and dust and death smell that she'd been inhaling for the last hour. Slightly vinegary. Definitely unpleasant. But that hardly mattered. The path to reaching her brother had been treacherous. She and Griffin had dislodged rock and bones, but they were here.

When she pulled back, she saw dried blood on his cheek. His shirt was filthy and ripped. "Are you hurt?"

He shook his head. "Why?"

"You're scratched. On your face."

"I suppose I brushed against some rock. In the beginning, I was moving so fast."

"But you're all right?" She couldn't take her eyes off him. She wanted to put her fingers on his wrist and feel his pulse. To be certain. She'd been so afraid of what might have happened, of what might have been.

"It's all right." He put his arm around her. "I'm all right, Jac."

She rested her head on his shoulder. Closed her eyes for a minute.

"You can stop worrying about me now." He rubbed her back. "I didn't want to scare you, but it was impossible to get a message to you any sooner or any other way."

She smiled. He was always so good at reading her.

"Did you know who the man in the studio was? Robbie, he's dead. You know that he's dead?"

"He wasn't supposed to die. But he had a gun. He was going to kill me if I didn't give him the pottery. I burned just enough to knock him out." His voice was trembling.

Griffin pulled a bottle of water out of his knapsack and handed it to him.

"Have some. There's time to go over everything that happened."

Gratefully, Robbie unscrewed the cap and gulped down half the bottle.

"How did you know about this place?" Jac asked.

"Come, there's a table and chairs in the next chamber—we can all sit down. I can explain everything. And you can tell me what's going on. It's unsettling being a hunted man."

"A table? Chairs?" Griffin asked.

"Come see. There are beds down here, too. Ways to cook food. An entire universe if you know where to look."

Sure enough, there was a stone slab in the next room and makeshift benches made from tombstones piled on top of each other. At first Jac didn't want to sit. These were sacred stones. Memorials. But after Griffin and Robbie did, she sat as close to her brother as she could. And while they talked she kept reaching out to touch him. To finger the rip on his sleeve, to stroke his arm.

"Have you been down here since Monday night?" Griffin asked.

"More or less. I came down here first. Then took a train to the Loire Valley."

"At first I thought you were—that you'd drowned."

He put his hand on his sister's arm and leaned toward her. "I'm sorry," he said again. "I couldn't think of any other way. I needed to make them think that so they'd direct their attention somewhere else."

"And pick a place that would itself serve as a message?" she asked.

He nodded. "Do the police think that I'm dead?"

"They aren't sure. Marcher—he's the detective in charge of the case—isn't convinced. How did you find this place? Did Grand-père show you?"

Robbie nodded and pulled out a wadded-up paper from his pocket. Unfolding it, he laid it on the tabletop and smoothed it out.

He was always so careful with things.

The map was an unwieldy two-foot square, creased, worn, and stained. "We started coming down here after you moved to America. He gave me the map and let me guide him, so I'd learn how to navigate. He said everyone needed to have a safe place.

"We explored for hours. He hadn't been down since the war and would tell me stories about the resistance as we retraced his steps."

"He climbed down the tunnel? He was in his seventies!" Jac was astonished.

"I know. He was incredibly agile."

"What an amazing adventure you had with him," Griffin said. Jac recognized the ache in her ex-lover's voice. Griffin was bitter about his own family. He'd lost his grandparents when he was young and barely knew his father.

Robbie nodded. "I had no idea how important it would be for me to know my way down here. When I was a teenager, I got friendly with a group of cataphiles—musicians who used one of the chambers as a theater and gave performances a few nights a month. There's a universe here. There's art. And history. The macabre. And the sacred. With a million hiding places. There used to be so many ways to get in and out. But the city has closed off most of the exits. It took me three tries before I found an exit other than through the maze." He pointed to a spot on the map that was in the fourteenth arrondissement. "I used this one."

"Do the police troll down here?" Griffin asked.

"Too much going on aboveground. Besides, the people down here are harmless. Rebellious artists and amateur explorers. Misfits and fringe groups. People who feel like they don't belong anywhere else."

Then I should feel at home here, Jac thought and told him about the hooded people they'd seen.

"Where are we?" Griffin asked pointing to the map.

Robbie put his finger on a spot. "Here."

"How easy is this place to find?" Griffin asked.

"Not easy." Robbie drew a line with his finger. "There are two ways in and out of this chamber." He gestured to one. "The way you came, and this way." He pointed. "This dead-ends at another one of those narrow fissures. It's possible to pass through it, but not without getting scratched up. And then, once you get through, you're in a kind of bone dump—thousands of them piled on top of each other. To get across the chamber, you have to climb over them. They move under you, shifting and crumbling." He stopped.

The memory of the excursion was obviously upsetting.

"And on the other side of that room?" Jac asked.

"A series of vaulted chambers that are fairly uninteresting, and then you reach another cave. I got through there on my belly. There are enough other passages down here. It's pretty unlikely anyone would randomly choose to go through those obstacles."

"But they could?" Jac asked. "If they were looking. If they had, say, a dog that had picked up your scent."

"They could." Robbie shook his head. "But that's far fetched."

"No, it's not. You're wanted by the police." She heard her own voice wavering between anger and hysteria.

"I didn't know what else to do. Fauche had a gun. He wasn't a journalist."

"And he would have killed you for the pottery shards," Griffin said softly to Robbie. "You did the right thing."

"Why would he have killed you for them?" pressed Jac. "And where are they?"

Robbie took off a deep-purple ribbon he wore around his neck. Hanging from it was a velvet pouch of the same royal color. It was packaging from the L'Etoile line. Used for the smaller bottles of perfume.

"So you have had them all along. Marcher asked if I knew where they were," Griffin said, as Robbie tore apart the bubble wrap and revealed the turquoise, white and coral pot shards.

Jac, who'd never seen them before, leaned over to inspect the items. In her search for the roots of myths, she'd handled thousands of precious objects. These were neither the most magnificent nor the most interesting.

"They're just ordinary pot shards," she said.

"Not ordinary," her brother argued.

"Oh, Robbie." She was tired from the stress of the last few days. Had barely slept. Or eaten. Had done little but worry. Jac was exhausted, and her brother's idealism frustrated her.

"This is crazy. These don't matter enough for you to put your life in danger. It's just a story. It's make-believe, for Chrissakes." She was angry at her brother for being such a romantic and having such grandiose dreams. But even as she vented her frustration, she became aware of something else happening on another level. Something about these pieces of clay that drew her to them. It was their scent.

Shutting her eyes, Jac concentrated on the foreign yet familiar aroma. This was the same scent she'd smelled so many times in the workshop. There it was mixed up with a hundred other threads. Here, isolated in this stone chamber, it was unfettered.

The scents in the old glass vials in Malachai's cabinet of curiosities all shared this dense amber base. This variation, however, was more complex.

"Can you smell it?" Robbie whispered.

She looked up. Nodded. "Can you?"

Robbie's face clouded. "No. Not really."

Jac turned to Griffin. "Can you?"

"No. All I can smell is the dust. But then again, your brother says I have an immature nose."

Jac smiled.

"If anyone can figure out what this scent is made of, it's you," Robbie said to her. "We know four of the ingredients, for sure. We need to know what the others are. Can you tell?"

"What difference will it make? It's some smell that one of our ancestors impregnated into the clay. It's a made-up story. You're chasing a dream."

"All perfume is a dream. What do you smell?" he persisted.

She shut her eyes and inhaled again, even more deeply. Took everything into her nostrils. Griffin's scent, her brother's stink. The ancient aroma she was drawing out of the clay. She separated them. "Frankincense. Blue Lily."

In the distance she could hear water dripping from a ceiling and the gentle *plop* it made as it splashed in the puddle. It was an even rhythm. One drop after another. Steady. Continuing. Water. Falling. Water. The drip of the water. An even, calming sound.

Forty-two

There was a fountain in the center room of his workshop, and Iset liked to lie there after she and Thoth made love. Smell the clouds of perfume. Listen to the splashing. Sometimes she fell asleep while he went back to work. He'd let her nap until it was almost time for him to perform the evening rituals. Then she'd clean herself off and hurry home. If she was missed, if her husband sent servants looking for her, if she was found and her infidelity was discovered, her husband could have her put to death. A nobleman had that privilege.

The sound of many footsteps approaching startled her wide awake.

"Who's here?" She looked anxiously at her lover. "Were you expecting anyone?"

Thoth shook his head. "Hurry to the storeroom. Wait there," he whispered.

Quickly, Iset got up, wrapped her linen gown around her naked body and ran to the far end of Thoth's laboratory. Opening the door, she slipped inside.

The assault of smells was overwhelming. This was where the royal perfumer kept all the oils and unguents he used to create the queen's scents.

Clearing a space on the stone bench, she moved several glass containers and sat. She felt her body trembling with fear. The footsteps were closer now. So many of them.

While she waited, she lifted the covers off the jars and smelled their contents. There was cinnamon, turpentine, and the essences of iris, lilies, roses, and bitter almonds. One alabaster jar held a perfume. Rich and rounded, with no single element overpowering the others. A complex, beautiful scent.

Suddenly, Iset was overcome with sadness. A sense of her own hopeless destiny. This passion was going to lead to pain. And it would be her fault. It always was, wasn't it? Even when she was a child, her mother used to tease her that if there was ever trouble, she knew Iset was at the heart of it.

People were entering the workshop. Thoth was greeting them. Iset couldn't focus—she was seeing a river. Barges swiftly traveling downstream. Strong, well-oiled men, rowing away from the center of Alexandria. Men standing guard. Women crying; children clinging to their legs.

Part of her mind was lost in the escape, while at the same time she was aware she was probably reacting to the unguent. Thoth had told her he had scents that caused hallucinations.

She had to regain her equilibrium; she needed to be alert if she was going to stay hidden. So, struggling against the fog, Iset tried to replace the covers and stoppers in the jars. One fell. Cracked.

The sound! Iset held her breath. Listened. There was still so much noise outside, she wondered if anyone had heard. Her stupor was fading. Clarity was returning.

Outside, the din settled down.

"Is the fragrance I created to help lull you to sleep working?" Iset heard Thoth ask one of his visitors.

"Yes, far better than wine. I wake up without any of the headaches that the fermented grapes give me."

Iset put her hand up to her mouth lest she make a sound. It was her queen's voice on the other side of the door. Why had Cleopatra come to see her perfumer herself?

"Do you have need for more?"

"Probably, you'll have to ask Charmaine." She named her attendant, who always traveled with her. "Have you created any new perfumes?"

"Yes, two. One that has a base of roses. Here . . ."

The queen was considered an intelligent woman, well educated and fair, but when it came to her perfumes, she demanded much of Thoth. Her love of fragrance was almost a compulsion. To please her, Mark Antony had built her this perfume factory and planted the surrounding land with the raw materials that would yield her favorite scents. Groves of rare persimmon trees. Balsam. Fields of lush, fragrant flowers.

Cleopatra had a vast array of scents. Many to honor the gods. Others to anoint the dead; to accompany them to the next world. There were unguents for her body, her hair, her bed linens and her clothes.

She had a collection of potions said to affect people in myriad ways. To encourage amorous activity. To soothe and calm a nervous disposition. To take away sadness and encourage joy. Thoth had told Iset he used the extract of Blue Lily as a base for these more complicated scents.

"Now," Cleopatra said. "All of you. Leave me alone with my priest."

There was a flurry of activity as the queen's retinue departed.

Why did Cleopatra need to be alone with Thoth?

"Tell me about your progress," she said after a few moments.

"It's going very slowly, my queen. I don't have any formulas to work with. Nothing like this has ever existed—"

"But you'll be able to create it—won't you? You said you would be able to."

"I am doing all that I can."

"Thoth, there has to be a way to remember the lives we've lived before. Caesar believed it, and so do I."

Iset was shocked. Everyone knew that the soul traveled to the afterlife on the swirls of smoke. Incense was a ladder to immortality. Was Cleopatra suggesting that the ladder worked both ways? That the soul could descend by the smoke as well? Egyptians didn't believe they came back to earth again.

"I need to find out what the past was in order to understand the future. To know who I was. Whom I was with. What I can learn will help me rule . . ." Her voice drifted off, then resumed more softly. "And allow me some peace. If I knew that Caesar and I had been together before, that we could be again . . ."

Thoth had once told Iset that only Greek philosophers believed the soul could be reborn again here on earth. But then, the queen's ancestors came from Greece, didn't they?

"If we return . . . If I return and those I've loved return, how will we know each other if you don't help me?"

Gossips claimed Cleopatra still mourned her Caesar. That Antony was a simpleton compared to the elder statesman. That the queen was making the best of her fate but had lost her heart to the first Roman she'd loved.

"If the gods allow it, my queen, I will devise a way to find the formula."

"The scent of souls, Thoth. I want it."

Iset wondered what the queen's face looked like when she spoke so intimately. Wondered if she had put her hand on Thoth's arm. If she wanted him, she'd take him. The queen had amorous appetites. But Thoth wouldn't respond. Would he?

Iset felt a pang of jealousy. The queen was talking so softly now, Iset had to strain to hear. She inched to the door. Trying not to make a sound.

"I don't want anyone to know what you are working on. This concoction could be a powerful tool. One I wouldn't want my enemies to have. Imagine if we all could look back to who we were before we were born in this life . . . see the many, many people we had been. Know our karma. Understand our fate. Imagine the knowledge we would have. What do you think it would be worth?"

"Worth killing for, my queen."

"But not if no one know of its existence."

"No one will."

"What about your workers? Your lover?"

Iset stopped moving. Held her breath. Had Cleopatra heard something specific? Did someone in the court know? Or was it a random assumption because most men had lovers?

"This is your factory. Your oils. Your spices. Your flowers. Your incense. Your unguents. I do not speak of what I work on with other priests. Your formulas are written on scrolls that are hidden from sight."

"Promise me you won't give up till you have the scent," she said as she sat down.

Thoth's response was a low murmur.

Iset finally reached the doorway. There was just enough room in the space around the frame to see out.

Thoth was on his knees in front of his queen, his head bowed before her. Her hand played with his hair. But she wasn't looking down at Thoth. Staring straight ahead, she seemed to be searching for something in the distance. In the past? The future? Suddenly Cleopatra stood. Her voice returned to its strident tone. "Please keep me informed of your progress."

Iset stood in the dark and listened as the queen's footsteps retreated. Thoth would come and get her when all was clear. Waiting, she thought about what she'd just heard. Why hadn't Thoth told her what he was working on? Why hadn't he shared this important assignment? If there was a fragrance that would reveal who you had been before, she wanted to smell it. What if she had been with Thoth in another life? Who had she been? Maybe she'd done something terrible? That would explain the feeling she had so often of tragedy mixed in with her passion when they were together.

"You can come out now." Her lover stood at the entrance to the cool room, his hands outstretched. She ran to him. He pulled her close and ran his hands down her naked arms. "Is this where we were before the interruption?"

"Is it possible?"

"What, my sweet?"

"The fragrance the queen talked of? A smell that would show you past lives?"

"I don't know."

"But you said you'd find it."

"I said if there was one I'd find it. If I could."

"I want to smell it."

"It will belong to the queen."

Iset pulled back. "You won't let me smell it?"

"Let's not worry about this now." He was nuzzling her neck. "I like it in here. Dark. Cool. A perfect place to—"

"Who is your loyalty to?"

"Iset . . ." He ran both hands down her back, cupped her buttocks. Pressed into her.

For the first time since she'd been with Thoth, his touch didn't move her. His lips on her neck didn't burn even a little.

"Answer me first."

"You present me with a terrible riddle. I can't betray my queen."

She tensed.

"But I can't betray you."

She breathed in her lover's skin. His own scent. Bergamot, lemon, honey, ylang-ylang and musk. It pleased her more than any other fragrance he made.

"I will keep your secret, Thoth. Don't I keep all of our secrets?"

Forty-three

The fog was wet and cold. Like a thick winter rain. Lost in it, Jac shivered. She was dizzy. Disoriented. Somewhere in the distance, she could hear voices. Maybe she could follow them and find her way out of these shadows. Struggling, she concentrated. Where were they?

"What did you do with the man's gun?" Griffin asked Robbie.

The stone vault came into focus around Jac. The water dripped methodically. The air was again suffused not with the scents of exotic oils and spices but with dry clay and dirt. How long had this hallucination lasted? It had seemed like twenty minutes. But based on recent episodes, probably less than a minute had passed.

"It's behind a rock in the first tunnel," Robbie answered Griffin.

It was difficult to concentrate on their conversation. Jac felt groggy, as if she were breaking through the surface of a deep sleep.

Yes, sleep. The doctors had trained her to remember dreams in order to analyze them and find the clues to her illness.

Last night she'd dreamt she was in the garden, caught in the maze. Someone inside was calling out to her. Not asking for help but offering it. Promising she'd understand everything if she just found the center. A man's voice or a woman's? She couldn't tell. Or didn't remember.

In reality, the maze was small; in the dream, it had grown to infinite proportions. She couldn't find her way.

But dreams could mean nothing, too. The maze had been her childhood hiding place. Her refuge and sanctuary. And her brother's. Of course she'd dream about it.

"Jac. Let me have those," Robbie said.

What did her brother want? He was pointing at her hand. She looked down. She was still holding the pot shards, cupped in her palm. Her brother took them.

"Do you have any idea who would go to such trouble to get those?" Griffin asked Robbie.

As her brother wrapped up the broken bits of baked clay, he nodded. "They aren't worth anything financially; someone must want them for what they're worth symbolically."

Griffin nodded. "Or . . . maybe someone wants to prevent them from being used as a symbol. Make certain you don't give them to the Dalai Lama."

"Why would anyone care if you gave the pottery to the Dalai Lama?" Jac asked.

"I hadn't thought of that," Robbie said to Griffin. "That's brilliant."

"I'm lost. Can you explain what you're talking about?" Jac asked the two of them.

"Despite everything they've done, the Chinese have failed to crush the Tibetan spirit," Robbie said. "Their newest effort is a law they've put into effect requiring people to register to reincarnate. Ridiculous, I know. But they've done it. It's a desperate ploy to discredit any child born in a holy area in Tibet—where we expect the true incarnate will come from—from being named a lama.

"If the Chinese retain power over who the lamas are, they can choose His Holiness's successor when he dies."

"But the shards? What do they have to do with anything?" Jac asked.

"Whoever has the pot shards will hold in his hand the possibility that there is proof of reincarnation."

He finished rolling up the pottery and replaced the packet in the pouch around his neck.

"And they'd go to all this trouble?" Jac asked. "The shards don't actually prove anything."

"No. But they suggest something crucial. The way the system goes, Jac, a Karmapa or a Panchen Lama is the only one who can recognize a Dalai Lama. The last three Panchens who have emerged from Tibet have disappeared. The search for reincarnations of high lamas has been completely corrupted by the Chinese. Their power base depends on it. Tibet's future is at stake, and this is one more piece of ammunition." He patted the pouch.

"And how far are you willing to go to deliver the ammunition?" she asked. "Someone is dead. You are living underground in a cemetery, Robbie. Can't you just throw those things down some hole and leave them with the bones? We can go to the police. You acted in self-defense—"

"Stop. Stop." Robbie put his arm around her. "I have to do this."

"Why?"

"Do you have a plan?" Griffin asked.

"I can't risk being taken into custody until I can get the shards to His Holiness. He'll be in Paris in two days, and—"

"You'd stay here till then?" Jac interrupted.

"Yes."

"It's too dangerous here," she insisted.

"This is the safest place for me in all of Paris. Do you know how complicated this labyrinth is? If anyone was coming who I wasn't expecting, I could disappear in minutes."

Jac didn't understand his spirituality or share it. But even here, a hundred feet underground in this giant graveyard, she sensed Robbie's deep belief and saw the equanimity it gave him. She used to envy his faith. Not now.

"There could be criminals down here. Crazy people. You're just not safe."

"I was safe up there?"

"Robbie, a Buddhist nun contacted me," Griffin said, interrupting. "I met with her. She said she's from the center and that they have been working on your request and that she can help you."

"The lama can get me a meeting?"

Griffin nodded. "She offered to help Jac and me find you. She even suggested that she had some mystical powers that could help us."

"You should have taken her up on her offer; you might have gotten to me sooner. She said she's part of the center here in Paris?" He was excited.

"Yes, and she wants to meet with you."

"Yes, fine. Bring her here."

"Here?" Jac asked. She shook her head. Stood up. She walked to the chamber's exit, put her hand on the lintel, felt the cold stone and looked into the space beyond it. She'd taken off her helmet, and there was no lamp lighting the way. All she saw before her was a dark walkway dropping off into black eternity. She inhaled dusty stone and fungus and imagined she'd smell this mineral and mold combination forever. Without realizing it, she was playing their old game. Jac turned back to her brother.

"If I had to create the Fragrance of Futility, I'd start here."

He went to her and put his arm around her. "It is going to be all right."

"No, Robbie. It's not. We're not children, and we can't pretend." She threw off his arm. "The world is falling down around us. Someone tried to rob you. Was willing to murder you. The police think you're a killer. Our deadline with the banks is up in less than two weeks. We have to sell Rouge and Noir. There are no ghosts. No reincarnated souls. You are in danger and I'm having those—" She stopped herself. Telling him wouldn't help. "You can't stay down here till Saturday."

He was staring at her, a look of wonderment in his eyes. "Something happened to you when you smelled the pottery, didn't it?" He had lapsed into French and was talking rapidly.

"What do you mean?"

"You have a much more sensitive nose than I do. Than anyone I know. What happened when you smelled the pottery shards, Jac?"

"Nothing. You're dreaming," she said. "Like Papa." Spat out the word like it was poison. "This isn't the time for dreams."

"What did you see?" Robbie insisted.

"You saw something?" Griffin asked.

She didn't look at either of them. Part of her wanted to confess, to whisper it, because to say it out loud would be giving too much credence to the vision. But she couldn't. It was only one small step from psychotic episodes to reincarnation memories if that's what you wanted to believe. Malachai had been at Blixer Rath studying just that. He'd probably told Robbie and Griffin. They'd want to investigate. It would fuel the fire already burning so strongly in all of them.

"I didn't see anything."

But what if there was a connection? She'd been free of the horrific episodes all these years, but they'd returned now that she'd returned to Paris and the boutique. What was the link? Not a psychic paranormal connection. Not a spiritual one. But it was possible the hallucinations were a reaction to a scent. Some ingredient present both in the shop and in the shards? She'd wondered about it on Wednesday. Now it seemed even more likely. There were known cases of mental affliction triggered by sensory overload—why not olfactory overload?

Griffin had started to unpack one of the knapsacks, laying out the supplies they'd purchased earlier that morning. A roll of toilet paper. A high-powered lamp. Batteries.

Unwilling to argue anymore, Jac lifted up her knapsack too. She pulled out a baguette. A round of cheese. A knife. Four apples. A sack of hard-boiled eggs. Energy bars. Water.

"An embarrassment of riches." Robbie laughed. "The only thing missing is wine."

Griffin laughed. "Actually, there is wine. Decanted, too." He pulled out a plastic bottle. "It's filled with a Bordeaux from your cellar, so I'm assuming it's good. Only drink it if you have a safe place to sleep it off."

"I'm not going back up. I'm going to stay down here with you," Jac suddenly announced. "It's not safe for you to be alone down here."

"That will be very helpful when the police notice that you are missing too." Robbie shook his head. "Absolutely not. The best way to help me is to go back up there and keep the police busy following you around. And if there's any way, try to find out who the curator at

Christie's told about the pottery. Because other than Griffin, no one else knew what I had."

"That's not true," Jac said.

Both men looked at her.

"Malachai Samuels knew. You told him, Robbie. Remember?"

Robbie nodded. "He thinks I found a memory tool. But you don't suspect him, do you? You've known him since you were a girl."

"He's eccentric, yes, but not dangerous. He's a doctor. Works with children."

"Except," Griffin said, "he's desperate to find proof of reincarnation. It's his life goal. He was there in Rome when the first set of memory tools were found and then stolen. He was in Vienna when a second tool—a flute made of a human bone—was discovered. Maybe it's not Malachai, but maybe someone is following him."

There was a sound. Distant.

"Shut off all the lights, fast," Robbie hissed.

In seconds they were all plunged into darkness.

"What do you—" Jac started to whisper.

"*Shhh!*" Robbie chided.

The footsteps were closer now. And Jac could hear voices.

"Shouldn't we leave?" she whispered again.

"No time," her brother said.

The low murmurs were clearly chanting. Not French. Or Latin. Not a language Jac had ever heard. Low pitched and steady, it sounded both melodious and otherworldly.

A scent wafted in with the sound: paraffin, sulfur and smoke.

Suddenly in the solid darkness of the chamber, a pinprick of light appeared in the west wall.

Robbie crept toward it. Jac and Griffin followed.

He put his eye up to the hole. It was barely big enough for a mouse to crawl through. He watched for a few seconds, then stepped back and let Jac look.

It was the same six people—four women and two men—Jac and Griffin had seen before. But this time they had reached their destination.

As she watched, they arranged themselves in a circle around a pentagram of candles. Their faces were in shadows, hidden by their black hoods. They swayed in time to the indecipherable chant.

Jac turned back to her brother. "What do we do?" she whispered.

"We wait," Robbie said and smiled ruefully.

Patience had never been Jac's strong suit.

forty-four

Jac and Griffin navigated a complicated passageway in silence. If time had passed slowly on their way into the catacombs, it was interminable on their way out. It was psychological. On the way in, she had been so anxious about finding her brother that she hadn't focused on the potential hazards as much as the end result. Now, even though she knew Robbie was alive, the danger he was in was more complicated than she could have imagined. And it wasn't over. They had to get through the next two days.

"My brother's idealistic goal could turn out to be a suicide mission."

"He has to do this."

"Regardless of the consequences?" she asked.

"Because of the consequences."

"And you're determined to help him."

"Aren't you?" Griffin asked.

"Someone tried to kill him. Isn't that more important than a legend written on the side of a pot?"

"Not to Robbie."

They didn't talk for the rest of the journey, and when they emerged in the garden, the glare of the afternoon sun hurt Jac's eyes. She stumbled.

"It's always tough to readjust to the light when you've been in the dark for so long," Griffin said as he caught her.

His fingers, sure on her arm, held her for a moment longer than necessary. She didn't pull away. For a few seconds, they stood in the fragrant boxwood puzzle. Jac's head ached and her throat was dry. Thinking about Robbie made it hard for her to breathe.

She'd been frightened when the police had called to say that Robbie was missing. But because the two of them were so connected, she was certain that if something were truly wrong, she would have sensed it. It had been about finding a logical solution before. Now reason didn't enter into it.

In the stories she read and researched and retold, fate and destiny set you on a path. It was in your power to choose to follow or step off. The tales that were told and retold through time and became archetypes were the ones where following the road, despite risk and fear, led to greatness. Great tragedy, or great victory. These were the tales that utilized metaphors most dramatically and offered the deepest insight into the human spirit.

There must have been other stories, though—those lost to us— where a man stepped off the path and nothing dramatic occurred. Life just went on. These stories weren't repeated. The people who had lived them hadn't experienced high drama. No lessons learned. Nothing terrific or terrible occurred.

It would be a relief if her life and Robbie's could be uneventful like that. If Robbie could just crawl out of the cave and let the police take over. Turn over the shards of pottery to a museum. Or to Malachai. Or just smash them into dust and go back to making pretty fragrances.

Malachai Samuels was in the living room. A concerto by Tomaso Giovanni Albinoni played on the stereo. As they entered, he put down his book.

"Did you find him?" he asked, rushing his words as if to get to the answer quicker.

Griffin nodded. "Yes, he's all right."

"Thank God."

"Did anything happen while we were gone?"

Malachai shook his head. "The phone rang a few times—nothing else. And both of you are all right?"

"All right?" Jac shook her head. "I'm scared. I don't know what's more terrifying—what's already happened or what's going to happen next."

"For you, Jac, what's going to happen next is always the greater threat," Griffin answered. "Your imagination is your own worst enemy."

"I don't have to work hard to imagine these threats," she said. "I could take Argus, with his hundred eyes all over his body. Cerberus, guardian of the underworld, with his three gigantic heads. The Minotaur, a man-eating monster. But this . . ." She felt sick. Felt the dust clogging her pores. "I'm going to take a shower." Jac nodded at Griffin. "He can fill you in," she said to Malachai. "Tell you all about my stubborn brother and the insane artifact he's willing to risk his life for."

As she left the room, she heard Malachai ask, "Does he have the shards with him, Griffin? Does Robbie still have the shards?"

Forty-five

The bald Asian woman in amber robes looked at the LED readout on her cell phone, recognized the number, and answered it.

It was an incongruous sight: a holy woman talking into a state-of-the-art piece of electronic equipment. The picture had nothing to do with simplicity or mindfulness.

"What's happening?" the man on the other end asked without any salutation.

"The archaeologist was just here. He's asked me for my help."

The temple was empty as far as she knew. There had been only one visitor so far that afternoon, and he had left ten minutes ago, but still she walked outside and hid in a thicket of locust trees so she could see anyone who might be approaching.

Each morning before she got out of bed and each night before she fell asleep, she meditated on ridding herself of anxiety. She couldn't be out of her self if she was not one with her self. At the retreat, she'd learned deep meditation, and it had proved a worthwhile gift. The lamas might be disappointed to learn how she chose to use it, but the old ways belonged to history.

The future had to be honored, not just the past.

"What did he say?" the man asked, his voice insistent, stern.

"Robbie L'Etoile is safe and is asking for assistance in setting up a meeting with His Holiness." She smiled. "He also gave me a list of items I'll need to get in order to make the trip."

"The trip?"

The sky was clear. Only a few puffs of clouds moved across the blue canvas. There were no birds flying, but she could hear them chirping just on the edge of her consciousness.

"In order to see L'Etoile. He didn't explain."

"What are they?"

The woman in the saffron robes listed the items.

"So he's underground," the caller observed.

"It seems so."

"We should discuss next steps."

The birds were unrelenting. So loud that she was distracted. Their song set her teeth on edge. Picking up a handful of pebbles and dirt, she threw it into the tree to the right. Then another handful into the tree to the left. There was a flurry of wings and a cessation of song. Quiet. She could concentrate again.

As they described the plan, she felt confident it would work.

"Conviction but not certainty," she could hear her mentor warn. "Pride interferes with the task at hand. Plays havoc with concentration. Dilutes effort."

It was one of the lessons he'd tried to teach her—one that she'd never quite conquered. To transform pride in her work into pride in *their* work. To be truly selfless. Ego would get in her way. It was a conundrum, because growth only fed her ego more.

"We're counting on you," her superior said. "What L'Etoile has is very important."

"I understand."

"It's critical it not fall into the wrong hands."

"Yes, yes." She knew this much but little beyond it. She had been taught to accept what she didn't know. "I'd like to know why this pottery matters."

There was a moment of silence on the line. She always asked too many questions. Her mentor used to warn her about that, too.

"This isn't about you understanding, it is about you obeying."

Her curiosity, like her pride, needed more work.

"You are certain you can do this?"

"I've accepted every difficult task asked of me. And accomplished them," she said, trying to keep her tone deferential but secure. Except she hadn't often worked on her own. Now the operation was about to enter into its second phase. It made her heart race. Years had led her to this point. Now she could finally prove her worth. Reach her potential.

The call over, she leaned her back against the lotus trunk. Felt its solid, unmoving mass. The wind rustled. A lama at the retreat had said every time the breeze blew, the leaves bowed in thanksgiving.

Returning to the temple, she glanced around. She needed to clean up, put everything in order. But first she did what any good Tibetan nun would do. Made a cup of tea and sat down to mediate. She needed to prepare herself for the journey ahead.

Forty-six

This was a different path from the one they'd taken earlier. Jac and Robbie had agreed at least on this: they didn't want anyone to know there was a passage to the underground city from within the mansion's garden. So Robbie had charted an alternate course using a manhole on a quiet street in the fourteenth arrondissement, an entranceway used by many cataphiles.

The trio of amateur spelunkers had just made their sixth turn into the sixth tunnel. The underground was damper than it had been this morning. Quieter, if that was even possible. The smells were more disturbing. Jac wasn't sure if the dampness exaggerated them or if she was becoming more sensitive to them.

Jac's anxiety level was also more acute. Was it having the nun with them? Or anticipating narrow passageways and flooded tunnels—edges she would have to conquer?

They started up a steep, narrow stairway made of rough-hewn rocks.

"This reminds me of the stories my parents told me about hiding in caves in the mountains of Tibet before they left during the 1959 exile," said Ani Lodro.

Jac noted that the petite nun was incredibly agile. That in itself wasn't surprising, but she was wearing amber robes under her jacket that were tucked into her knee-high boots.

When Jac had taken a TV crew into Tibet in search of the Shangri-la myth of a lost paradise in the shadow of a white crystal mountain, she'd met many holy men and women and found them peaceful and inspiring. That trip was one of the highlights of her career. She'd been so far away, in a place so devoid of modern invention, that she could almost convince herself that the myth she was chasing was real.

In that rarefied air where her lungs struggled, where the land stretched out in patterns that had not changed for hundreds of thousands of years, Jac had wondered if there were really was a Shangri-la. And whether, if she found it, she would ever leave.

The catacombs they were trekking through were similar to that holy place in some ways. The silence. The isolation. Out of range and out of all communication except with fellow travelers. And once again Jac was chasing a myth. This time her brother's. The effort was no less intense, but the sense of futility was greater. Robbie had fought her so hard about not selling their two most popular scents, and yet he was being so stubborn about the pottery. Malachai Samuels had upped his offer since coming to Paris. The amount he was willing to pay might be enough so that they'd have to sell only Rouge.

Instead Robbie was willing to risk his own life to give the Dalai Lama these fragments of a dream.

They turned into a new tunnel. The stones on either side were slicked with water. The lights from their helmets shone silver on the rough limestone.

"Can I ask you something, Ani?" Jac asked the holy woman.

"Of course."

"Is my brother right? Do you agree the Dalai Lama will have a use for this gift?"

"I'm only a courier. It's not for me to interpret." She spoke French, and Jac was sure it was her native tongue. Her head was shaved—the stubble black. Her features were Asian. More Chinese, Jac thought, than Tibetan. "Do you have doubts about the wisdom of your brother's wishes?"

"From what I know about the problems of your people, it will be like bringing a splinter of the cross to the Pope."

"That may be." The nun was behind her, so Jac couldn't see her face, but she sounded as if she were smiling. "But saviors are not always who we expect them to be. And power comes in unexpected ways."

The tunnel ended in a simple and elegant twelve-foot arch. Beyond it was a high-ceilinged chamber with a stone altar in the center.

According to the map, this was where Robbie should be waiting for them, but they found no sign of him.

"Did we make a mistake? Take a wrong turn?" Jac asked Griffin.

"We're in the right place. Look." He pointed to the cross of skulls above the archway and the stone plaque beneath them that read, *"Croyez que chaque jour est pour vous le dernier. Horace."*

"Robbie's notes said there'd be an inscription from Horace here. What does it say?" Griffin asked.

"Believe that every day that dawns is your last," Jac said, reading the ancient Roman poet's words.

"So true," the nun murmured.

"Do you think something's happened to Robbie?" Jac asked Griffin.

"No. I'd guess that he ran into other explorers. He wouldn't want to risk having anyone follow him here. He'd stop and wait. Be cautious."

"What should we do?" she asked.

It wasn't Griffin who answered, but the nun. "We wait." Her voice was resigned, suggesting she knew how to do it well.

A half hour later, when there was still no sign of her brother, Jac suggested they start looking for him.

"We can't. We have no idea where he is," Griffin said.

"He's down here. We know that," Jac said.

"There are over five hundred miles of tunnels. Hundreds of chambers, thousands of passageways. We could be ten feet away from each other and miss each other entirely."

"What if he's hurt? What if whoever is after him found him down here?"

"How? No one knows he's here but us," Griffin said.

Jac turned to the nun. "Who did you tell you were coming here?"

"I had to tell my superior, who is setting up the meeting. The head lama at the Buddhist center here in Paris. But we all want to help your brother, mademoiselle."

"Besides, Jac, I told only Ani to meet us at the boutique—I didn't tell her where we were bringing her."

"But you told her to wear rubber boots and bring a warm coat. In the spring. On a sunny day."

"Even if someone figured out where we were going from those clues, there's no way they could come down here and happen on Robbie. They'd still need this map."

Jac wanted to argue but knew he was right; it wasn't enough information.

"So then where is he?" she asked.

"He'll be here," Griffin said reassuringly.

"A half hour more and then promise me we can start looking for him. There might have been cave-in. Or what if the police were down here in search of illegal adventurers and found him?"

"Then Marcher would have called you."

"Not if Robbie didn't tell them who he was."

She looked over at the nun, who sat cross-legged on the dirt floor. Her eyes were closed. The expression on her face suggested she'd traveled deep into meditation.

Jac tried to take the nun's lead and relax. She sat down, back up against the rock. Griffin joined her and took her hand. In this place, in this moment, with the anxiety flowing through her veins, his touch electrified as much as it ever had. From the beginning, Griffin made her feel that she was moving closer and closer to an edge. Exhilarated and afraid.

After he'd left, she sometimes wondered at how serene she was without him. So why had she missed him? Why had she still yearned for the unsettling excitement?

The sense that, come what may, she was supposed to be with him. Only subsided. Like a sleeping bear, hibernating through the long, long winter.

"You're really not worried?" she asked Griffin after another five minutes.

"I'm concerned. I'd be crazy not to be. But I have faith in Robbie. And I don't think anything has happened to him."

Fifteen minutes later, when Robbie still hadn't arrived, Jac dipped her finger in some muddy water and drew a partial moon with a star inside its crescent on the archway.

"Write 16:30, return 17:30," Griffin said. "That way, if he gets here and we're not back yet, he won't go off in search of us."

"Where are we going to look?" the nun asked.

"We should try to go back to the chamber where we met him yesterday. Can you find that on the map?" Jac asked Griffin.

He studied the chart, then folded it up again. "This way," he nodded and set off.

The route twisted and turned but was a relatively easy one until they arrived at a chamber filled with four feet of bones—not artfully arranged, just thrown on top of each other. Discarded like junk.

In order to get to the exit on the other side of the cavern, they were going to have to walk across the bones.

"Is this the room Robbie told us about yesterday?" Jac asked Griffin.

"It appears so."

"I can't do it," Jac said. "I can't just walk across these people's bones like this."

"They aren't here," the nun said with equanimity. "You're just looking at the shells of people who have moved on."

"We can go back. Do you want to, Jac?" Griffin asked.

Jac closed her eyes. Thought about her brother. Shook her head. "No. Let's go."

He held out his hand, and she took it.

They started across the sea of calcium sticks and stones. Jac couldn't stand the sound of the shifting and grinding.

"You do this all the time, don't you?" Jac said to Griffin. "You go into tombs and ancient burial grounds and deal with the dead as nothing more than history's debris. How do you get so inured to it?"

"I've never seen a mummy or a skeleton or a fragment of anyone's remains without being conscious that this once was a person who had a family. A life, hopes, failures. If I lost that . . . I'd be some kind of monster."

They'd reached the chamber's exit. Six steps led down to another enclosure.

When the first light from Griffin's headlamp shone on the space, Jac gasped. Flying buttresses, columns, an altar, pews, everything constructed with bones. An astonishing work of art. A chapel to the dead, using the dead to create beauty. In alcoves where there would have been stained-glass windows in an aboveground church were mosaic narratives created with fragments of broken bones. Bones had even been used to create a replica of the rose window in Notre Dame.

But for all its beauty, the room stunk. The stench assaulted her. Nowhere else in the tunnels had Jac smelled anything this repulsive. She knew what it was, but she couldn't understand it. She couldn't be smelling decomposing flesh; these bones were centuries old.

Jac shone her light onto the wall and leaned in close. Carved into the rock was a legend, identifying the remains as having come from the cemetery of Saints Innocents. Beneath that were six columns listing hundreds of names. Reading down the list, Jac sensed what she was going to find before she found it. And yet when she saw the letters she was astonished.

L'Etoile.

Jac did the math. Her grandfather had been born in 1915. If his father had been in his twenties then, he'd have been born in the late 1880s. So her great-great-grandfather would have been born around 1860. And his father would have been born in the 1830s or 1840s. The sixth generation back would have been born in the 1820s. So the L'Etoile here went back seven or eight generations.

She touched the incised letters.

The air in front of her waved. Jac smelled frankincense and myrrh. She inhaled more deeply and detected lotus and almond. And something else, elusive and beyond her reach: the odd fragrance from Robbie's pottery.

She knew it. Recognized it.

Ghostlike creatures appeared to materialize out of the darkness. Marie-Genevieve as a young girl with Giles. Whispering to each other. He was saying he'd created the perfume for her as a parting gift.

Jac leaned in to smell it but instead smelled the river in Nantes where the Jacobite soldiers expected Marie-Genevieve to die by drowning.

"Jac? We should go."

The images dissolved.

Jac turned to Griffin. She wanted to tell him. Then she remembered the nun. She couldn't talk about it in front of a stranger.

Finally, five minutes later, they found Robbie in the chamber where they'd met him yesterday.

"What a relief," Jac said. She went to her brother and hugged him for a long moment. The last few hours had been nerve wracking.

"What took you so long?" he asked, almost mischievously.

"Did you run into trouble?" Griffin asked. "Is that why you changed the plan?"

Jac noticed the nun had hesitated and remained in the shadows.

"Just a group of chatty cataphiles I couldn't quite escape from. Sorry about keeping you."

They were in a circular enclosure. At the far end was a drop-off. Jac wasn't sure if their headlamps couldn't penetrate that far or if there was a void. The scent coming from there was damp. Somewhere in that blackness, water dripped on rock.

"Friends?" Jac asked.

"A bunch of artists who come down once a month to create new wall art," Robbie explained. "They invited me to see what they'd done and it took me forever to get away from them. So are you two alone? Didn't you bring—"

Griffin gestured to the shadows.

"Yes, Robbie. This is Ani Lodro. Ani, Robbie L'Etoile."

Robbie stepped forward. The nun remained where she was. Immobile. But her eyes were shining with a softness Jac hadn't seen before. By her side, Ani's right hand twitched as if it had started to reach out of its own accord and she'd held it back.

Robbie was staring. Wearing an incredulous expression.

"Is it you?" Robbie's voice was low. Intimate.

They knew each other?

"All your lovely hair?" Robbie reached out to touch what wasn't there. Then he caressed her shaved head. An intensely personal gesture.

"I'm a nun now." Ani's voice was so soft Jac almost couldn't hear her.

"What happened? I waited to hear from you, and when I didn't I contacted the retreat. They wouldn't give me any information."

Ani didn't say anything but lowered her head, unable to meet Robbie's gaze.

"What happened?" he asked again. "I searched and searched. For such a long time."

"I'm sorry . . . my training . . . my mentor felt my being with you had interfered. I had to honor him . . . I wanted to honor what we had also, but I couldn't find a path that allowed me to do both."

The nun's whisper held so much pain Jac turned so she wouldn't have to look at the expression on her face.

"And now you're here," Robbie said. Not as if he were astounded by the coincidence but rather as if he'd expected it.

Ani straightened her shoulders as if she were shaking off the blow of seeing him. In a normal speaking voice, with an almost impersonal tone, she said, "I have news for you. From His Holiness."

Now Robbie bowed his head slightly.

"He would be very pleased to accept your gift."

"That's wonderful news. Especially being brought by you."

After four days down here in hiding, he was a mess. His beard had grown in. Multiple scratches left thin lines of dried blood on his hands, cheeks and neck. And there were dark circles under his eyes. But a beatific peace suffused his face.

Jac was amazed by the transformation.

"When will I be able to see him? Where is the meeting going to take place?" Robbie asked.

Ani shook her head. "I've been instructed to take the gift to him." She held out her cupped hands.

Before Robbie could say anything, Griffin said: "That's not what you told me."

She turned. "We had first thought we would be able to arrange an actual meeting. But because of security measures, that's no longer going to be possible. I didn't know that when I talked to you, Professor North." She returned her gaze to Robbie. "I'll give your treasure to His Holiness myself. I'll be sure that he gets it."

Robbie shook his head. "I can't. I'm sorry."

The nun was surprised. "But you know me."

"It's been too long a journey. Too many centuries have protected it. I'm sorry. I can't give it to anyone but him."

"Robbie," Jac said. "Give it to her. Then it's safe and you can come out and go to the police and explain what happened. The worst of this will be over. The shards won't be your problem anymore."

"Einstein said that he wasn't so smart; he just stayed with problems longer." Robbie turned to Ani. "I'm sorry you had to come all this way, but I can't give the pottery to you. It would be putting you in danger that is mine to bear."

"Robbie," Jac said, exasperated. "This is crazy."

"Your sister's right. There's no way that you're going to be given access to His Holiness. I've been instructed to take the gift to him. Please, may I have it?"

Robbie shook his head.

"Please." The nun seemed to be begging.

"I really can't."

Ani reached out and grabbed his hands. "Please," she repeated.

"I just can't."

Jac heard the nun make a sound like an animal in pain. The she shoved Robbie with stunning force and swiftness. As he fell on the ground, Ani turned toward Jac. While Griffin reached out to Robbie, Ani grabbed Jac around the waist and pulled her away from the two men.

Jac was startled by the strength of this tiny woman. Effortlessly, she was dragging her to the end of the cavern, opposite where Robbie lay, Griffin next to him. Robbie's face was bleeding.

The operation had been executed so quickly and was so unexpected that neither Griffin nor Robbie realized what else had happened in the shadows.

"I am going to have to insist that you give me the pottery shards," Ani called out. "There's no other way to ensure the safety of your sister."

Forty-seven

As the two men looked into the shadows, their helmets illuminated the scene. Jac watched shock register on their faces as they understood she was in grave danger.

"Ani? What are you doing?" Robbie asked. "Let go of my sister!"

"I need you to give me the shards. Now."

"I thought I knew you."

Ani shrugged as if his comment didn't matter. But the woman's body trembled against Jac's back.

"This doesn't have to end in disaster. I have a gun and I have a rope. Which I use is your choice. Let's consider the most civilized scenario: I take the treasure, tie you all up, leave you here, and then once I've delivered the gift intended for His Holiness, I'll call the police and tell them where you are."

"There are three of us; one of you," Griffin said in a voice that was as sharp as a knife's edge.

"There may be two of you. But I have her. And I have the gun."

Jac felt the air waving around her again. The scent of antiquity. Of icons turning to dust with one slight touch. The smells of the Nile Delta. Palm fronds. Women heady with power. Men thick with lust. The smell was making her sick. There was no question. Her sanity was being stolen by the scent.

She breathed through her mouth. Focused on her brother. He was pressing his sleeve against the flow of blood and looking at Ani with an expression of such confusion it made Jac's heart hurt for him. She shifted her gaze to Griffin, who was breathing hard and trying to send her some silent message with his eyes.

Jac looked back at Robbie. "Give her the pottery. It's worthless," she told him.

"It's not. You know it's not. I saw your face, I saw—"

"Robbie!" Griffin shouted. Jac knew he was interrupting him to keep him from giving away information.

"Your time is about up," Ani said. "I guess you need some incentivizing."

Suddenly Jac felt the cold nose of Ani's gun pressed into her temple.

"A gun going off down here could set off an avalanche. We'd all get trapped. Even you," Griffin said to Ani.

"I've taken worse chances."

"If you hurt us, how will you find your way back?"

The nun laughed. It was low and guttural, and Jac felt it in a hot breath on the back of her neck.

"I marked our trail with infrared ink. I won't have any trouble getting out. Robbie, please give me the pottery."

Griffin turned to Robbie. "Do what she says. Put the pottery down. There on the floor. Then back up, away from it."

Robbie shook his head. "I know her. She won't hurt Jac. She's not capable of doing something like that."

Jac felt the woman shudder.

"We can't trust she's who you think she is." Griffin pointed to a spot on the ground. "Put the pottery down. There."

The nun's grip on Jac tightened. Jac stared at her brother. Robbie took a step forward and gingerly placed the silk pouch on the dirt floor.

"Get back now, out of her way," Griffin instructed.

Robbie stepped backward. As he did his face caught in Griffin's headlight, and Jac could see that her brother had tears on his cheeks. She wanted to go to him and hold him. Comfort him they way they had consoled each other as children. Instead she looked at Griffin. His eyes were on her again. But his attempt at silent communication was failing. Whatever he wanted was impossible for her to glean.

Ani moved. Inched toward the pouch, pulling Jac with her.

Griffin had been so specific about where Robbie should put the pouch. Scanning the ground, Jac tried to figure out why Griffin had chosen that spot. There had to be a reason. What did he know about the cavern that she didn't? What had he noticed that she'd missed?

As she neared, the pottery's scent grew in intensity. Reached out to her with its accents of smoke. A cloud of pungency. Even from a few feet away, even under these circumstances, she felt the pull of the strange and elusive ancient aroma. A river of sadness. A desert of promise. The decipherable spicy notes and undecipherable ones that worked on her mind beckoned. Determined to remain conscious and present, she pushed back. Refused to give in to the scent. Surprisingly, at least for a time, she remained on the other side of it.

Jac judged they were two and a half feet from the pouch. Once they reached it, Ani was going to have to bend over to get it. Or she was going to make Jac get it for her. Either way, the nun was going to have to loosen her grip. What should Jac do when she did? Grab the gun? What it if went off? An explosion down here, as Griffin had warned, could cause a cave-in.

Her brother was still hovering near the pouch, unable to leave.

"Robbie." Griffin's voice was softer as he tried to pull her brother away with his words. "Let it go. Just let it go."

Robbie seemed unable to leave the object.

In the midst of these terrifying moments, with Ani's arm wrapped tight around Jac, digging into her, with a black gun shoved into her temple, with a hundred things to be worried about, what Jac thought about was the miracle of her brother's belief. What must it be like to care about something so much, to believe so deeply—that even faced with this kind of danger, you still had trouble giving up? It was ironic. Her only conviction was a commitment to nonbelief. To seeing stories as being nothing but stories. To deconstructing them to metaphor and nothing else. She was a realist: man created faith to light up the darkness. To gain a foothold into the crater of nothingness.

The pouch was within reach now. Jac felt Ani hesitate. Was she figuring out how to get it?

Across the room, Griffin's eyes bored into Jac. What the hell was he trying to tell her to do? He tilted his head to one side. What was he saying?

She was only going to have one chance to—

Ani's grip loosened. Jac wrested free. Backed away as fast as she could.

Ani reached down.

Griffin leaned forward. Picked something up off the ground. In the dark, Jac couldn't see what it was. He raised his arm. Then a loud crack reverberated in the chamber.

Ani fell. Sprawled on the ground. Her gun skidding.

Griffin's weapon, a hollow-eyed, yellowed skull, rolled toward Jac.

Then Griffin was on top of Ani, pinning her down, grabbing her hands and pulling them behind her. His knee on her back.

The nun fought hard. Griffin fought harder. She bucked. He pushed her back down. Got her by the neck.

"Jac, grab the gun!" Griffin shouted.

She reached for it, groping in the dark.

"Robbie, get the—" He didn't have to finish. Robbie had already scooped up the silk pouch.

Ani fought wildly. He yanked her arms behind her. She kept struggling. He increased his pressure. She came out of her jacket. She bucked again. Tried to kick him. Griffin wrenched her arms farther behind her. The nun let out a piercing cry. In seconds, beads of sweat dotted the woman's upper lip and forehead. He'd hurt her badly. Maybe dislocated a shoulder.

"Jac, look through her robe. She said she brought rope with her to tie us up."

"Don't bother," a voice boomed out from the far side of the vaulted chamber. Angry. Strident. "She brought me with her, too. So let her go. And step away."

forty-eight

5:55 P.M.

Most of the students and chaperones were unpacking and relaxing after the plane ride. In an hour a bus would arrive to take them to a private opening reception with Chinese and French dignitaries at the Musée de l'Orangerie in the Tuileries gardens.

There was no way that Xie could relax in the small hotel room he shared with Ru Shan, so he suggested to Lan and the professor that they unpack later and instead see something of the city. Walk from the small hotel on the Île Saint-Louis to the museum. Professor Wu, who wanted to get in as much of Paris as he could, was happy to chaperone.

The three of them stood outside the hotel, getting their bearings. Up and down the street were small shops, windows artfully designed to show off their wares.

"It's all so lovely," Lan whispered as they walked by a florist's storefront. A dazzling array of roses, poppies and peonies spilled onto the sidewalk. Reds and oranges and pinks all fighting and complementing each other at the same time. Colors on fire.

Xie was too concerned to truly appreciate all of it. He had to struggle to pay attention to what Lan was saying.

"Everywhere you look, there's something to see." She pointed at the window of a candy shop. Yellow cookie and candy boxes were stacked on top of one another, creating an Eiffel Tower.

Xie had been exhausted by the time their plane landed. The stress of getting through security with the contraband phone had worn him out. And it had been wasted anxiety. There hadn't been any trouble. The cell phone remained safe in his pocket. And now he was safe in France.

Strolling along the quai, Lan stopped to watch a tourist boat cruise by, then led them across a small bridge to Ile de la Cité.

"Look how the river shimmers. How the clouds drift by the sun. Like a Monet," she said. "Or a Pissarro. Or Sisley."

Xie saw only the shade under the trees where people whose faces he couldn't make out looked like they could be lurking.

Paris was a living canvas, and the artist in him wanted to thrill to the sights that filled his eyes. But he was worried about these last two days. About all the things he didn't know. When was the meeting going to take place? What was he supposed to do?

This wasn't smart. He knew his emotions were going to drain him, create an aura around him that would attract negativity. For the time being, for the time he was on this walk, he couldn't think about what lay ahead. He had to be here, in this moment, in Paris.

There was a phrase he'd learned at the monastery when he was a little boy, presented to him like a puzzle along with the lessons in deep meditation:

The no-mind not-thinks no-thoughts about no-things.

He intoned it silently now as they walked toward Notre Dame, and felt his energy returning. The majestic Gothic cathedral was a prayer made out of stone, one that demanded attention. Offering succor and refuge. Hundreds of people milled about it. Groups of kids, smoking and skateboarding and texting and being free.

As the three of them passed by, the church's bells began to ring out. Deep, booming, tremendous, and splendid; the sound reverberating inside of Xie's body.

Xie stopped walking. Slowly he turned. Took in the ancient rooftops and windows, bridges, the pulsing river.

"Professor," Xie said.

The venerable calligrapher turned to him.

"Thank you for all of this."

"You earned all of this." He bowed his head slightly, and Xie saw there was a smile playing around his mouth.

Wu would be in danger if Xie failed. This amazing artist who had taken the teenage boy under his tutelage was risking his life to help him.

Lan, who'd noticed the exchange, shyly took Xie's hand for a moment. With her quiet eyes, she too smiled.

"Can you imagine what it would be like to be an artist and live here?" she asked.

Xie shook his head.

"What it would be like not to go back? To run away. Now. This minute. Just take off. Stay in France. Paint?" She was breathless with the idea.

"Dangerous thoughts, my dear," Wu said.

Before Xie had a chance to concur, something caught his eye.

Not far from them, standing to the right of a group of kids, Xie saw Ru Shan.

There was only one reason he'd be there, hovering in the background. He was following them.

forty-nine

The intruder wore goggles and a helmet with such a strong light that when he turned, it momentarily blinded Jac.

When she could see his face, it was smeared with dirt—either on purpose as a disguise or by virtue of the machinations he'd taken to get here—and his features were indecipherable. But Asian, Jac thought. Like Ani.

No one moved.

Griffin continued holding Ani down. From her expression, the pain was intense, yet she didn't utter a sound.

Robbie stood beside Jac, his arm around her protectively.

The intruder remained at the far entrance to the room.

"I told you to let her go," his voice boomed out across the expansive space.

Griffin didn't move.

"I've got a gun," the intruder said.

"Yes, you do. But so do we," Griffin said. "And if either of us shoots in here, we're going to cause a major collapse. Maybe more than one. We're in a series of fragile mines. A loud noise could cause a cave-in."

"You're bluffing."

"Try me."

A drop of sweat dripped down Jac's back.

The man came toward her and her brother. Ignoring her, he focused on Robbie. "I've been looking forward to meeting you face to face," he said, "so I could give you this." He spat. A thick wad of spittle landed on Robbie's cheek. "For what you did to—" He hesitated. Thought. "Fauche." Then he smacked Robbie on the side of the head with the gun.

Jac tried to hold Robbie as he fell, but he came at her at the wrong angle. He grazed his face on the rock wall, and his cut reopened. Blood welled almost instantly. It dripped down his neck, onto his collar. Disappeared into his jacket.

"Don't hurt him anymore," she said as she dropped to Robbie's side.

"Shut up. Or you'll get the same gift."

She cradled her brother's head. "Robbie?"

He answered with a groggy grunt. "I'm okay."

"Touch either of them again, and I'll take it out on your friend here," Griffin called out. He jerked Ani's arms tighter behind her back. She swallowed a scream.

"Hurt her all you want. I don't care about her. I'm here to collect the pottery."

"And you're willing to let her die to get it?"

The intruder ignored Griffin. He squatted beside Robbie. "So, *Monsieur le Parfum*, where is it?" His voice was gentle, almost soothing.

When Robbie didn't answer, the robber used the gun like a hammer and struck him.

"Stop!" Jac shouted, reaching for his arm. The intruder shoved her away. In doing so, he'd turned his back on Griffin, who let go of Ani and jumped him.

Ani screamed out a warning. "William!"

"Keep her down!" Griffin yelled to Jac.

The nun was struggling to her feet. Jac reached her in two strides. As strong as Ani might have been, her pain was debilitating. She tried to fight Jac, and almost won. But Jac managed to grab hold of her injured shoulder. For the first time, Ani wailed. Blinked back tears.

Jac threw herself on of top of the woman and held her down.

Immediately she was assaulted by Ani's smells. Such intimate odors.

Perspiration, skin, breath. Jac could identify black tea and juniper berries. Cotton and talc. A hint of salt. Something else.

The stench of a man coming at Marie-Genevieve. To rape her. To laugh at her. He was talking about how her God couldn't save her from this. That man. This woman. Their smells were identical.

No. Not now. Jac could not allow her mind to fracture. Not now.

She looked up, searched for Robbie. Her helmet illuminated the corner, where it looked like the ground opened up. He wasn't there. Then she caught sight of him crawling toward Griffin. Probably to help. But drunk with pain, Robbie was unsteady and moved slowly.

Griffin struggled with the intruder. The men's helmet beacons created an insane light show on the chamber walls as they rolled around on the floor in the bones and debris.

Then the intruder maneuvered his right arm loose. "Watch out," Jac shouted as the man raised his arm.

Griffin moved just in time. The gun missed him. Griffin held on tighter and pushed them into the next roll.

They were in the farthest corner of the crypt now. Hidden in the shadows.

Jac couldn't see what was happening. She heard a grunt. Was it Griffin? Then another.

A swipe of strong light zigzagged through the chamber.

The intruder was standing. Griffin was down. "That's enough of that. Where is the fucking pottery?"

Griffin looked across at Jac. "Okay Jac, give him the pouch."

She was about to say she didn't have it, but he knew that. What was he doing? What was he asking of her?

"Throw it over here. Let him have it. We don't have a choice anymore," Griffin ordered.

What was she supposed to do?

"To you?" she asked.

"Not to me, give it to him, Jac."

Griffin could mean only one thing. He wanted the man distracted. Jac grabbed the skull that Griffin had used before, which was lying next to Ani. Trying to aim, not at the intruder, but just beyond his reach, she threw it. Close enough so that he'd think he could catch it, but too far for that to be possible.

The dark object sailed across the room.

The intruder lifted his hands up. Realized it was higher than he'd anticipated. Reached.

And in that moment, Griffin pushed him toward the ledge.

It was such a simple thing. A push. One shove. The man wearing the goggles disappeared. Only the glow from his helmet remained. Shining up toward the vaulted ceiling.

There was a millisecond of silence. Then a splash of water. Then angry cursing.

Griffin leaned over the edge of the chasm. "Hope you didn't hurt yourself. That's at least a twenty-foot drop."

There was no response.

Griffin and Jac bound the nun's hands together with the rope Jac found in Ani's robes. Then they tended to Robbie, who had an egg-shaped bump on the side of his head but otherwise was all right again.

"Now. Let's deal with her," Griffin said to Jac.

"What are we going to do with her?"

"Help me get her up."

Once they had the nun on her feet, Griffin nodded toward the far end of the chamber.

Together they moved her across the room.

At the edge of the abyss, Jac leaned over. The man in the goggles stood in mud or water—Jac couldn't tell—up to his waist in one of the deep wells so prevalent in the catacombs.

"Okay," Griffin said to Ani. "Jump. It's water. Our goal isn't to hurt you. Just take you out of commission for a while."

She didn't move.

He nudged her closer to the edge.

"If you don't jump, I'm going to have to push you. And if I push you, I might mistakenly touch your shoulder."

Ani launched herself off the edge.

Seconds later there were two sounds: the splash of her landing and what Jac guessed was a swallowed scream.

"The two of you can keep each other company." Griffin grabbed his knapsack and returned to the edge of the well. He unzipped the flap and stuck his hand in. "Here's some water to keep you alive." He threw in one bottle and then another. "Once we've delivered our package, we'll let the police know where you are. In the meantime, enjoy yourselves. Especially you, Sister. It looks like a peaceful place to meditate."

Fifty

The L'Etoile living room never seemed so lovely to Jac as it did now. The old faded fabric and worn rugs, strains of Prokofiev, and the scent of sweet tea welcomed Jac home.

Malachai stood as they walked in.

"What happened? Are you both all right? Is Robbie all right?"

"My brother is fine." She shook her head, remembering the argument. Robbie had insisted he remain underground, assuring her that he knew a hundred hiding places. They planned to rendezvous in two hours, which would give Griffin time to get to the Buddhist center and see if he could arrange for the meeting Robbie was willing to risk his life to keep. "But he wouldn't come up."

As Griffin explained what had occurred in the catacombs, Jac sank down on the couch. Her hand brushed the book Malachai had been reading, and she looked down at it. One of the Moroccan-leather-bound books from her grandfather's library: *Tales of Magic in Ancient Egypt,* part of his extensive collection devoted to magic.

When she was growing up, they had a ritual. The first of every month, he'd handpick a new title for her to read and give it to her after dinner with great ceremony. As if it were yet one more step in an initiation into a secret society. Religiously, each evening after she'd done her schoolwork, she'd go down to the library and read a section with him.

Some of the books were very old, and she needed to be especially careful not to rip the pages. He'd noticed how cautious she was. "Yes, the books are rare, Jacinthe," he'd said—he and her father were the only ones to ever use her full name—"but the real value is the knowledge they hold."

She read sitting at a fine mahogany and brass partners desk, in the light cast by a Daum Nancy art glass lamp—rose flowers against a light-green background. Then she and her grandfather would sip hot chocolate from the family's antique Limoges china and discuss the passage.

Grand-père was very serious about the lore on those pages. Believed there was an important science buried with the Egyptians that needed to be rediscovered.

Her favorite book, the one she'd asked to read again, was about Djedi, the ancient Egyptian magician renowned for bringing the dead back to life. It had been written in 1920, when the world was obsessed with Egyptology and the great archaeologist Howard Carter's finds. The book was heavily annotated. She studied her grandfather's notes as well as the text. He'd marked every mention of an herb, oil, spice or flower—as if he might figure out the soothsayer's life-reversing formula himself.

Jac remembered something else: Grand-père's black calfskin notebook. It was filled not just with Djedi's possible magical formulas but also all kind of alchemical possibilities. Formulations from all of ancient history. There was a heavy glass inkwell on the desk. She could picture him filling his fountain pen with its coal-black ink. His hand crawling on the page, leaving spidery possibilities. Where *was* that notebook?

Griffin was still explaining what had happened in the underground maze.

"Are the woman and her accomplice dead?" Malachai asked.

"Not dead. Not even hurt," Griffin said. "Except for a dislocated shoulder."

"They were willing to kill you," Malachai said solemnly.

Jac shivered.

Malachai turned to her. "I'm so relieved you're all right." Then, almost as an afterthought, he asked, "And what happened to the pottery?"

"Robbie wouldn't let go of it," she said. "He has it still."

Malachai leaned toward Jac. Put his hand on her wrist. Felt for her pulse and then concentrated. His touch was welcome. She didn't mind at all that someone was concerned about her and wanted to take care of her. She could still feel Ani struggling beneath her, still see the random images of their trek through the tunnels. The shifting bones. The wall of names.

Letting go of her hand, Malachai said, "You're still stressed." He stood and walked toward the kitchen. "Let me get you some hot tea laced with some of your brother's fine brandy."

"My father's brandy," Jac corrected. "Robbie likes wine."

"Well, your father has excellent taste in brandy."

Jac didn't answer.

As Griffin watched Malachai leave the room, he was frowning.

"What's wrong?" Jac asked.

"Nothing." He shook his head.

"I wish we hadn't left Robbie down there alone. Are you sure they can't get out of that well?"

"I can't imagine how they could. But even if they did, Robbie's long gone. Hiding deep in some cavern. He's safer there than anywhere else."

"Because of you. Because of what you did. You saved our lives down there."

Jac still felt the ache across her torso where Ani had held her. The woman would not have hesitated to kill her. Jac knew that without doubt. From the way she'd looked at her. Talked to her. Strangely, from the way the woman had smelled. She'd had no humanity. Her scent was cold. It was the same scent as the rapist's scent.

The nun's accomplice would have killed them, too. Thinking of him, she remembered something else. Wincing, she pulled her knapsack off the floor and up on the couch. She took the napkin from beside Malachai's cup and saucer, reached into her bag, and pulled out the gun. She held the butt carefully away from her. As if it were alive and might spring back on her and strike. "There are fingerprints on this that could help the police figure out who was following us."

"The police?" Malachai said as he came in carrying the tea things and a bottle of brandy. "Are you going to call in the police?"

"There are fingerprints here. Clues to who those people are." She got up and walked to the bombay by the fireplace. Opening the top drawer, she placed the gun inside.

"If only Robbie would sell me the pottery. We could bring this dangerous adventure to an end."

"After tonight? I'm convinced nothing is going to change his mind. The closer he gets to delivering it to the Dalai Lama, the less likely that becomes," Jac said. "He believes so strongly in what he's doing." She heard how wistful her voice sounded. "I'm afraid you came all the way here for nothing," she said to Malachai.

"I came to help you."

She was going to argue, but there was a sincerity in his voice that stunned her.

"You know what I don't understand," Griffin asked Malachai. "Don't you already have methods to regress patients? Even if the shards were impregnated with enough fragrance to induce a past-life experience, why would another method be so valuable?"

"We use hypnosis, and it does indeed work most of the time," Malachai replied. "But the memory tools are more than a way to regress someone. They're a piece of the history of reincarnation. The stuff of legends. Surely you, Griffin, of everyone, would understand why that is so enticing."

"Knowing the past, knowing who you were—you can make it *too* important, can't you?" Jac asked.

"Too important? We live in darkness. We stumble and fall. We don't know which way to go. Memories of the past would light the path to the future . . ."

As he spoke, Jac was seeing the labyrinthine corridors they'd been trekking through all afternoon. Smelling the shadowy corners and dry dust of millions of bones. The damp, dead world. The false exits. The cave-ins. Edges falling off into darkness.

"If someone said, 'This is who you were, and this is the mistake you made then,' you'd have a choice not to make that mistake again," Malachai continued. "And by not making it again, you will be freed from the burden of it in your next life. If somebody offered you that chance at peace, wouldn't you take it?"

His voice was soothing. She remembered how he used to sit and talk to her at Blixer Rath and how much he'd helped her. She didn't believe in reincarnation. Didn't care about past-life karma. But she wanted his assistance. Desperately. Maybe if she told him that the terrible psychotic episodes had returned, he would save her again. Guide her to understand what the hallucinations symbolized. But if she admitted what was going on, she'd return to the person she'd been then. Different from everyone else. Never fitting in. The girl on the outside looking in.

Malachai was studying her. "Jac, you've had moments of envisioning the past, haven't you?"

"So you think we're absolutely fated to repeat our past?" She asked a question instead of making a confession.

"No. We have free will. We have choices. But if we had a map, we could make more educated choices. We could help ourselves to make this turn rather than that turn. We could do better in each life."

The images that had flown at Jac while she was with her brother and Griffin in the underground caverns were returning now with no inducement. Brushing up against her, their ghostlike wings grazing her skin.

Jac shut her eyes.

"You must be exhausted," Malachai said. "That's not good for you. It's a trigger."

She glanced over at Griffin. He'd picked up on the comment. Damn. "Is there something wrong, Jac?"

"No," Jac answered before Malachai could say anything.

"What did Robbie mean when he asked you if you saw something in the tunnel?" Griffin asked.

"Saw things? In the catacombs? What happened, Jac?" Malachai's tone was urgent. When Jac didn't answer him, he asked Griffin. "What happened down there?"

"When Jac took the pottery from Robbie—she had a reaction. Her eyes went glassy. She didn't hear what I was saying for about thirty or forty seconds. She was just looking off into space as if she were looking at someone or something that wasn't there."

"Stop it!" Jac screamed as she stood, stunning everyone in the room. "Nothing happened to me! I'm no different from you." She turned from Griffin to Malachai. "Or you. I'm fine. It was just frightening. Robbie's used to it—he's been exploring those caves since he was a teenager." She turned back to Griffin. "You've been crawling around in Egyptian tombs most of your adult life." Now her gaze returned to Malachai. "You see the machinations of my brain as clues to some mystery you're forever trying to figure out. There's nothing going on. Nothing is wrong with me except for the horrible fact that my brother's life is in danger. Someone who no one can identify died here five days ago, and two people just attacked us and tried to steal some worthless ancient pottery Robbie found in the mess my father made of our lives."

Griffin and Malachai were both watching her with concern and care. She hated their intensity. Their scrutiny. Her father used to look at her just like that when she was young. When she saw things and heard things that weren't there. When she was, to use her mother's word— the word she used to describe both of them—"ca-*ra*-zy." Audrey would laugh when she said, it too. "Ca-*ra*-zy." Making three syllables out of a two-syllable word and laughing. As if it were wonderful to be different. Not the disaster of her life.

"I have to take a bath." She drained the teacup. "We need to go to the Buddhist Society tonight," Jac said. "Robbie gave us the name of a lama there. The man Robbie's been studying with. He'd been in the process of setting up the meeting. He'll make it happen. And then we can all go back to our normal lives."

She left the room and headed for the staircase. She was fine, she told herself. In control. She just didn't know why her voice had cracked on the word *normal*.

As Jac walked upstairs, her legs felt so heavy each step was an effort. Her back ached. She gripped the handrail like an old woman.

In the bathroom, she turned on the faucets and added a healthy dose of scented bath salts. Then added more. She had to get the stink of the catacombs and the perfume from the pottery off her skin.

As the crystals hit the water, their fragrance slowly rose up to envelop her like a caress. She hadn't looked at the bottle. It was Rouge. Her mother favored Noir. But Jac loved Rouge. The first important fragrance from the House of L'Etoile. Created by Giles L'Etoile. Inspired, her grandfather told her, by his trip to Egypt in the late 1790s. Rose and lavender mixed with of one of the most mystical scents that existed, civet.

For thousands of years, the musky ingredient had been harvested from the small mammals of the same name. Recently, animal rights groups protested, and perfume companies switched to a synthetic version. Most people couldn't smell the difference. Jac could. But not in the bath salts.

Then something curious occurred to her. In her hallucinations, Giles L'Etoile died in Egypt. Marie-Genevieve had been heartbroken. It was why her father tried to arrange another marriage. Why she'd run away. Why she'd gone to the convent. So how could this scent have been created by Giles after he came back from Egypt?

Jac sat on the edge of the tub. She took off her shoes and socks. Why was she giving any credence to these daydreams? She was sick. The illness was back. She couldn't trust what she imagined now any more than when she was fourteen. She slid out of her pants. Pulled her shirt over her head. Stripped off her underwear and then bunched up the whole pile. Shoved it in the knapsack, zipped it up, threw it in a corner of the bathroom and then sniffed the air.

She could still smell it. Under the odors of the dust and the stone, and Ani's juniper, under the smell of mold and mud, she could still catch the ancient perfume from the pottery shards.

Naked, she pulled on a robe and grabbed the knapsack. Opening the door, she walked out into the hall and bumped into Griffin.

"What are you doing? What's wrong?" he asked.

"I have to take these filthy things out of here. To the kitchen. I can't stand the stink of them. Of those tunnels. It's in my skin, my hair . . ."

Griffin took the knapsack from her hands and headed down the stairs. "Take your bath—I'll get rid of it for you."

Jac returned to the bathroom, steamy with the hot, fragrant water. She breathed in deeply as she slipped into the tub. Breathed in again. She smelled what was here now. She took the scents deep into her nostrils. Wisps of myrrh. Tempered by benzoin. And roses. Lush blossoms of immeasurable sensuality.

The water would have been too hot if not for the long day and the dirt and the stench.

Jac shut her eyes and soaked, hovered in a half-asleep state that deep exhaustion and sudden relaxation can bring on. And she kept her eyes shut even when she heard the bathroom door open and close and felt his hand on her skin, soaping her hair, massaging her scalp, then her neck and her shoulders. Kneading all the tension out of her muscles.

Griffin's hands were like silk on her body. Wet silk that stroked her. Replacing the exhaustion with exhilaration. The mysterious incense-imbued rose was all she could smell. The steam was all she could see. It was as if Griffin wasn't real. He was mist and memory and scent and sorcery.

He wasn't one man making love to her—but several. Griffin, yes, but also the men from her hallucinations. The young French perfumer with whom Marie-Genevieve had been in love. And Thoth, the strong Egyptian priest who worked in Cleopatra's perfume factory.

Jac couldn't be sure whose hands she was feeling, whose breath was on her neck. It was all sensation now and an intoxicating mixture of exhaustion and intense pleasure and excruciating longing. A desperate need to stay with him longer. Destiny or circumstance—it didn't matter which—had kept them apart again and again. Yet they were complete only together. As they were in this beautiful moment.

He was in the water with her now. His hands holding hers. Their fingers intertwined. She'd never let go. Never again. Nothing could force them apart anymore. Jac was melting in his heat, in the heat of the water. They would be melded together forever. Their lifelines commingling in her blood. They could die like this: wrapped up in each other, surrounded by each other . . .

In the midst of the waves of pleasure, she suddenly saw the Egyptian priest, with his lover, in a tomb, holding each other, fighting off sleepiness. Saw how they had drugged themselves. A joint suicide. Dying in each other's arms, sharing a last kiss and all without fear because Thoth had promised . . . he had promised her . . . in their next life they would know each other again. And again and again and again.

"Jac . . ." Griffin whispered.

Her name sounded foreign. It brought her out of her dream. Sent shivers down her spine and sparks off inside her.

"Jac . . ." He said her name again, and then there was nothing, not air and not water, between them. They were together in a timeless dance that their bodies knew and their souls embraced. This was who they were. Even if it brought disaster. Or death. This was worth all of that. This was worth all.

Fifty-one

Robbie sat in the dark cavern, leaning against a rock wall. He had turned off his helmet light. His eyes were shut. His mind was opened. Tired. Worried. Nervous. He listened to droplets of water hit a pool in the distance. Adjusted his breathing to the steady, even rhythm.

The well was eight feet away. The two people inside of it were quiet. He didn't think they knew he was here.

Ani had obviously told them the truth about marking her passage through the catacombs with infrared ink. Her companion had followed the identifying marks.

"That means," Griffin had cautioned before they'd all split up two hours ago, "that there could be someone else following the trail. Don't go back. All right?"

Even before Robbie could agree, Jac had made him promise he'd stay away from the area near the well.

He'd promised he wouldn't come back here. But he had. It was all right, though: he had an exit path mapped out. He was only two yards away from the warren hole that would provide passage away from this chamber.

Robbie had friends who'd become lovers. Lovers who'd remained friends. Was with more men than women because he was able to choose men who suited him better and made him happier. They were usually intellectually curious. Adventurers like his grandfather.

But the women he was drawn to had rips in their souls. Rebellious, angry, half-crazy women like his mother. His sister. They were always women who needed healing but couldn't be healed.

Like Ani Lodro.

Every summer, Robbie attended a Buddhist retreat a few hours outside of Paris. Six years ago, she'd attended during the same two weeks he did. Fraternization among the students wasn't encouraged. Meals were silent. There were no group lectures or activities. But he saw her everywhere he went, as if they were following in each other's footsteps. She was always leaving the temple when he was going in. He was always outside at the same time she was. He'd be walking down to the river, she'd be walking up. For the first week, they didn't speak to each other. She always kept her head down. He kept to himself.

Then one afternoon, while they were both walking the circular meditation path in the garden, a sudden and violent thunderstorm broke. Each of them took shelter in the peaked-roof gazebo.

While rain poured down all around them, Robbie finally looked at her and was stunned by the pain he saw in her wide, almond-shaped black eyes. He could sense the demons that sat on her shoulders. Saw the tension in the ropes of muscles in her neck. He felt her dire need to find peace. Without saying anything, they came together during the storm. Lying on the floor, smelling the cedar wood and her clean skin, Robbie made love to her. He'd always enjoyed sex. Luxuriated in it. He'd studied tantric sex—the Hindu discipline that is based on the worship of a man and woman coming together and experiencing bliss without orgasm. But he'd never experienced true tantric coupling until that day.

Robbie stood. Walked over to the well. He didn't turn on his lamp. Didn't want to really look into her eyes and see all that pain again.

"I searched for you," Robbie whispered into the blackness.

He heard Ani sigh.

"What happened? Why didn't you contact me?"

"I was in training."

"Not to be a Buddhist nun?"

"No."

"Training for what, then?" Robbie asked.

There was no answer.

"Ani?"

Silence.

"Who was the man who died in my workshop?"

"I didn't want you to be there that night. I wanted him to break in and steal the pottery."

"Who was he? Your lover?"

"My mentor. Like a father to me."

"He was going to kill me," Robbie said. "Did you know that?"

Silence from the hole. In the distance, the droplets of water continued their endless dripping. There was a faraway snap. A bone breaking? A rock falling?

Robbie stepped right up to the edge. Peered down. In the darkness, he could just make out the two figures. Only one staring up. Robbie would never be sure, but he thought it was Ani looking up at him from the shadows.

Fifty-two

Xie could hear snippets of conversation echoing from under umbrellas. English, German, and Spanish. Art lovers and tourists waiting outside in the rain for the Orangerie to open. Most of them, he guessed, were there to see Monet's famous *Nymphéas*—the eight water-lily murals the painter had created at the end of his life. They would stumble on the exhibit of calligraphy only if they went downstairs.

Last night the Monet rooms had been closed, and everyone in the museum was there for the reception. Lan had said it was the most exciting night of her life—to have her work shown in Paris. In the Orangerie. Fifteen feet below masterworks of Impressionism.

Xie had agreed. Even though his stomach had churned and sweat dripped down the back of his neck. Even though he'd spent most of his time concentrating on his surroundings. For him, the reception was a dress rehearsal for today. He'd memorized the security checkpoint, the exits, the windows, the restrooms, the doors, the elevators, and the stairs. He studied the traffic flow through the galleries. Paying attention to everything he saw as if his life depended on it. Because it did.

This morning at breakfast, Professor Wu had suggested they return to the gallery.

"It can be helpful to see how people react to your work when they aren't aware of your identity," he'd said. "It gives you perspective."

Now they waited with the rest of the crowd. Xie looked at the other students. At Lan. At Ru Shan. At the tourists. No one here has any idea about what is planned to happen here today, he thought. At least he hoped not.

When it was their turn at the security desk, Xie stepped up and held out his hands. He wasn't carrying anything. Without a briefcase or knapsack, he was able to walk though. Unlike at the airport, there was no metal detector. Xie could have a knife or a gun or plastique explosives on him, and no one would know.

That meant Ru could have a weapon on him.

A wave of nausea rippled through Xie. He was an artist. The most dangerous things he had ever done were hiding messages in infinitely small print in his artwork and asking Cali to send cryptic messages over the internet. How could he carry this off?

"I didn't get a chance to visit with Monet's famous *Water Lilies,*" Wu said to Xie, Lan, and the other eight artists assembled in a tight band. "Would any of you care to join me?"

The whole group followed Wu into the first oval gallery.

"He was going blind when he painted these," Wu explained, gesturing to large murals gracing the walls. "He deeded them to Paris—in exchange for their promise to build a museum for them."

Despite Xie's acute awareness of why he was here and what lay ahead of him, the power of Monet's work stunned him. Two of the murals were at least six feet tall and over thirty feet long. The other two were as tall but half as long. Standing in the middle of the oval room, the paintings curving around him, Xie felt as if he were lost in the master's garden. The other people in the gallery disappeared. Cool blues and greens, lavenders and warm pinks were all he saw. The abstracted ponds and sky, flowers, trees, and their reflections filled Xie with a beauty that made him stand still. Hold his breath with wonder. For the second time since he'd come to Paris, he felt tears welling up inside of him. These paintings were pure and perfect expressions of the beauty of nature. The communication he was having with an artist who had been dead for almost ninety years was as profound as anything Xie had ever felt.

Xie knew he had a job to do as Panchen Lama. And if he was lucky, he would be given a chance to fulfill his destiny. But he had to find a way to incorporate art into his new life. Yes, his calligraphy was unimportant compared to Monet's work, but competing wasn't the reason to be an artist. Cali had told him that. She said it was the energy you gave to the universe when you were creating that was all that mattered. The positive, powerful energy that replenished the earth.

Ah, Cali. How she would love to see these murals. How moved she would be. How he would miss her. Was it all worth it? Forsaking her and his professor and his work?

"We're going in the next room," Lan said. "You coming?"

"I'll catch up."

Lan walked ahead, leaving Xie alone with a crowd of strangers. Or so he thought at first. Then Xie spotted Ru on the other side of the room. The Beijing student seemed as lost in the paintings as Xie felt.

But Xie doubted Ru was lost. He doubted Ru was even looking at the paintings. He was sure he was just watching him.

Fifty-three

9:56 A.M.

Jac and Griffin stepped out of the mansion on Rue des Saints-Pères together. A soft rain was falling. Each opened an umbrella. Then they turned left toward the Seine. Nothing about their pace suggested they were in a hurry.

They walked along the river. Raindrops troubled the river's surface—sluggish green-brown without the reflection of a blue sky. The vehicular traffic was heavy, but because of the rain, there weren't many people strolling on the wide boulevard.

"Do you see the police?" she asked Griffin.

"Yes."

But it wasn't the police that they cared about this morning. "Anyone else?"

"I'm just not sure."

They'd talked about it with Malachai the night before and again early this morning. When Ani and the man with her hadn't reported back to whomever they were working for, other plans must have kicked into effect. They all needed to assume they were being stalked, listened to, and spied on.

As they continued to walk, Jac pictured the map Robbie had shown them. By now he should have emerged from the manhole in the sixth arrondissement and be on his way.

At seven that morning, she and Griffin had snuck outside, descended down the tunnel, and met Robbie in the first chamber. It was still one of the safest places he could hide. They brought him clean clothes and instructions from the lama at the Buddhist center.

When she asked him how the night had been, he just shrugged.

"Did you talk to Ani?" Griffin asked.

"Not for long."

"Did you learn anything?"

He shook his head. Jac's heart hurt for her brother. She could see the betrayal in the dark shadows under his eyes. In lines around his mouth that seemed to have deepened overnight.

Jac and Griffin reached the Pont de la Concorde, the bridge that connected the Left Bank to the Place de la Concorde. They'd mapped this route the night before. Halfway across, Griffin took Jac's arm and pulled her over to the balustrade. They stood and looked down at the river.

"We could be tourists," she said.

"Or lovers," he said and kissed her.

For show? To confuse anyone following them?

"I don't want to let you go," he said when he finally pulled back.

Griffin had said he and his wife were separated. But a separation isn't a divorce. And whenever he spoke about Therese and Elsie, something in his voice made Jac wonder if a divorce would really be the result of their time apart.

"We have things to talk about, Jac. Once Robbie's safe and back at home."

On the other side of the bridge, they strolled down the Rue de Rivoli, protected from the rain by the arcade. When they reached the Hotel de Crillion, Jac pointed to the building. "Why don't we have some coffee?" she said as if she'd just thought about it. Not as if she and Griffin and Malachai had stayed up past two in the morning planning how to get to the Orangerie without being followed.

A half hour later, finished with their *petit déjeuner,* Griffin paid the bill, and they sauntered into the lobby and onto the elevator.

Inside, Jac pressed the button for the lower level.

The doors opened onto a hub of activity. Waiters, chambermaids, carpenters, painters and a variety of other service personnel hurried back and forth, carrying food trays, laundry carts and piles of sheets and towels.

"Which way?" Griffin asked.

There hadn't been any blueprints on the internet. And Jac had been here only once when she was thirteen years old. She remembered the day but not where the exit was.

A famous musician and his wife had ordered a vast array of perfumed items from the shop—everything from soaps to candles—and asked for it all to be delivered. L'Etoile knew his daughter loved the British rock star. So he made the delivery himself and brought Jac with him.

Father and daughter had entered via the lobby's main doors—the only entrance Louis knew. But the concierge refused the delivery. He didn't even let Louis finish explaining. He showed them to the door and told her father where the service entrance was.

Louis was furious. Cursing under his breath, he stormed out of the hotel, Jac struggling to keep up with her father. By the time they were around the corner at the hotel's back entrance, he had calmed down.

He knocked on the door of the celebrity's suite. Jac was mesmerized by the tall, craggy-looking man whose music she adored. His autograph—scrawled on the House of L'Etoile bill of sale—was framed and still hanging in her bedroom in the mansion.

"To Jac—never stop listening. You never know what you'll hear."

The memory was interrupted by a portly woman in a housekeeper's uniform who asked, "Can I help you?" Her voice was on the edge of gruff. She seemed to be holding back just in case they were lost guests.

"We just made a delivery," Jac improvised, "and got turned around. Which way is out?"

Following the housekeeper's directions, they exited the hotel on the Rue Boissy d'Anglas, a quiet street around the corner from the busier Place de la Concorde.

Even though they were fairly certain no one had anticipated

their coming out here, they proceeded cautiously to Rue St.-Honoré. Maintaining a window-shopping pace, they went to the next corner, took a right onto Rue Royale, and from there circled back to the Rue de Rivoli. In front of WHSmith bookstore, they crossed the intersection and entered the Jardin des Tuileries. From there it was only a couple of minutes walk to the Orangerie, where they got in a short line outside the museum. Neither Robbie nor Malachai was there. Yet. Or else they were already inside.

The plan was for all of them to arrive by eleven-thirty. It was only eleven-fifteen.

The queue moved slowly. Museums were crowded on Saturdays. Seven minutes later, they were inside on another line—this one to buy tickets.

Jac had often come to this museum with her mother, who loved the Monets. But it had been renovated since she'd last been here. Instead of the dark and slightly dingy interior, the entryway was flooded with morning light. The unfamiliarity was disconcerting. Jac's heart banged against her rib cage. She buried her face in the white scarf she'd wound around her neck that morning. She'd sprayed it with her mother's perfume. Wanted her with her on this very difficult day.

This line moved slowly, too. Jac looked around. Still no sign of Robbie or Malachai. "Where are they?" she asked.

Griffin put his arm around her shoulder. "It's going to be fine."

But she couldn't stop worrying. "What if Robbie's recognized before he gets here?"

"Everything is going to go smoothly."

"You can't know that."

Griffin shook his head. "I can. Your brother has proved he's resourceful. He's managed to arrange all this from a hundred feet underground."

They were finally next in line. In front of them was a woman with her two teenage daughters. They were speaking to one another in Dutch. Jac bent her head. Inhaled the scent impregnated in her scarf.

Maybe it would be better if the police did find Robbie first and put him in custody. At least then he'd be safe.

"There's nothing going on here—wouldn't there be more guards on duty if the Dalai Lama was expected? Some indication a VIP was visiting?"

"I'm assuming there's some serious undercover security."

They bought their tickets, walked through the cursory and not very thorough security post, and into the first gallery.

She looked around, scanning the crowd for Robbie and Malachai.

"They aren't here," she said.

"I know, Jac. Don't worry."

"Funny," she said. "Impossible and funny."

She glanced at her watch.

"Don't," he said.

"What?"

"We're at a museum. People at museums aren't usually nervous. Slow down. Look at the paintings."

She bristled and started to argue.

"Take a deep breath." He took her arm. "Look at the paintings. The beautiful paintings. Everything is going to be fine."

Slowly they circled the room. She tried to do what he said. Really examine the murals. Monet's colors did, in fact, have a calming effect.

Jac and Griffin stopped beside a group of schoolgirls looking at the last painting before the exit. Their conversation was about shoes, not the swirls of blues and greens highlighted with violet.

A guard, rocking on his soles, watched the teenagers with a small smile playing on his lips.

Griffin led Jac around the girls and through the door. She didn't mean to, but Jac glanced at the guard as they walked out. He noticed and followed her with his eyes.

Fifty-four

The driver met Malachai at the mansion's front door. Holding his umbrella aloft, he protected the psychologist from the drizzle. As they walked the few steps from the street to the car, Leo tipped the large black silk umbrella forward, transforming it into a shield, and whispered, "That detective insisted he wait for you in the car. I had no choice."

They'd reached the Mercedes. Leo opened the door.

Malachai slid onto the soft leather seat and feigned bewilderment when he saw Marcher. Since he'd arrived in Paris, he had anticipated the possibility of an encounter like this. Hoping against hope that he'd be able to avoid it, he was mildly surprised it had taken this long for the French authorities to ambush him.

"Inspector Marcher. Usually you visit with Jac. To what do I owe the pleasure of your company?"

"Good morning, Dr. Samuels," the detective said in his accented English. "I was hoping to catch up with you. I've asked your driver to take us to my office."

"It's not a good time for me. I have an appointment," Malachai said. "Is this official?"

"I apologize in advance, then. You might be a bit late." He avoided answering the question.

Malachai started to protest but was interrupted by the detective's phone. Pulling it out of his pocket, Marcher looked at the number. "I'm sorry. I have to take this."

The drizzle intensified. The traffic came to a standstill. Malachai stared out the window and listened to the detective's one-sided conversation. Tried to translate. He was certain the police had found a witness to a crime in the Marais. But he doubted that the woman was requesting the police buy her a monkey in exchange for cooperation. Despite everything, Malachai chuckled at his mangled translation.

Swollen raindrops hit the window and blurred the scene.

The detective hung up. Shrugged. "I'm sorry, but I have to follow up on that call. I'll be with you in a moment."

As Marcher punched in the number, Malachai glanced at the clock on the dashboard. They'd gone five minutes out of their way. Now they were stuck in traffic. This was a disaster. The plan he, Jac and Griffin had worked out last night required Malachai to get to the museum by eleven fifteen. It was going to be his last chance to talk L'Etoile into selling him the memory tools instead of giving them to the Dalai Lama.

If he was late, Malachai would have lost yet another chance at the golden ring. How many more chances would there be?

His nerves were getting the better of him. Pulling a deck of playing cards out of his jacket pocket, he shuffled the deck. No matter that the cards were worth thousands of dollars, they were made to be played, appreciated, enjoyed. As he manipulated them, their golden edges sparkled.

Malachai glanced at the dashboard again. Another minute had evaporated. The traffic was still congested. The detective was still jabbering away.

The reincarnationist swallowed a sigh. He had no more patience for gendarmes and Interpol inspectors, FBI agents, Art Crime detectives and New York City policemen. Since 2007, he'd been on the receiving end of far too much attention from the authorities. But once you were on their radar, you couldn't escape.

Possessing one of the memory tools would be the culmination of Malachai's career. So he'd followed the rumors wherever they'd led him whenever a potential tool surfaced. And even though he wasn't the only one to covet the ancient artifacts, over and over he'd found himself at the center of international incidents and investigations. He couldn't blame them that he was often the first to be suspected and the last to be exonerated.

Once more, Malachai checked the clock on the dashboard. Two more minutes passed. He had only ten left before he had to be at the Orangerie. How long would Marcher's questions take? How much was there to ask him? He hadn't done anything illegal since arriving in Paris. Hadn't seen anyone but Jac and Griffin. Leo the driver. No crimes he knew of had been committed since he'd been here. He'd been in New York the night Robbie had disappeared and the murder had occurred.

For once, Malachai was almost thankful that the FBI had his residence and office under surveillance. They'd probably already confirmed he'd been safely ensconced in his apartment and hadn't left America until forty hours later.

As Leo navigated the sluggish traffic, Malachai checked the time yet again. What if he just opened the door and ran out? Left the stupid little detective in the Mercedes. Catch a cab—no, no cabs in the rain. Could he get to the Orangerie on foot?

Outside, the sky darkened. The charcoal clouds thickened. What was left of daylight disappeared and was replaced by an ominous gloom.

Leo turned a corner. The stone buildings on the narrow street were cast in shadows. A boom of thunder. A heavy wave of raindrops hit the rooftop with enough force to reverberate inside the car.

Even for someone who believed in the impossible, Malachai knew he was too far away and it was too late for him to make it to the museum on time.

The detective closed his phone. "Since we didn't get a chance to chat at all, I'd like you to come upstairs with me."

"Do I have a choice in the matter? Speaking to the police wasn't on my agenda for this morning."

"Yes, you mentioned you had somewhere to be. Would you like to tell me where your appointment is?"

"Was. Where it was. I'm too late to make it now."

"Where was the meeting?"

"It's a private matter."

Marcher's eyebrows rose. "That makes it sound suspicious."

"No, it makes it sound private. I'm not a French citizen. I haven't been involved in any crimes committed while I've been in Paris. At least to my knowledge. Or am I wrong?"

"You are in Paris because Robbie L'Etoile is missing, correct?"

"Yes, because both he and his sister are friends of mine, and I wanted to offer support."

"Robbie L'Etoile is a prime suspect in a murder."

"That happened days before I arrived."

The chauffeur inched ahead.

"I'm going to have to insist you come upstairs."

"Even though I just told you I am in Paris offering support to a dear friend."

"I'm sure your support is of great value to Mademoiselle L'Etoile. But the murder was a result of a robbery attempt that does have something to do with you."

"I think you are mistaken."

"The fragments of ancient Egyptian pottery, which are now missing along with Monsieur L'Etoile, are inscribed with poetry that references reincarnation."

"Just a coincidence," Malachai said and smiled sadly. Let the detective believe that. Malachai knew better. There were no coincidences.

Fifty-five

Jac spotted her brother in the second of the Monet galleries. Standing in front of one of the blue-green murals, he was writing in a small notebook. He'd cleaned up and was wearing the clothes she and Griffin had brought him early that morning. But he hadn't been able to disguise the bruises on his cheek.

Since they were all supposed to look like visitors, she tried to focus on the painting Robbie was studying, but couldn't see past her brother's bowed head as he scribbled notes. There were about twenty other museumgoers in the room, some of whom appeared truly absorbed by the artwork, while others walked through barely giving the masterpieces more than a glance.

No one looked suspicious. No one seemed to be watching her or Robbie. And Malachai was nowhere to be seen.

Robbie put the pen and notebook in his pocket, turned, and walked out of the gallery.

After sixty seconds, Jac and Griffin followed.

They found Robbie on the lower level, in the suite where the temporary show hung. The signage here was in both French and Chinese. Jac translated for Griffin. "New Masters of the Ancient Art of Calligraphy."

The predominantly black-and-white pen-and-ink drawings were in stark contrast to the soothing blues and greens, lavenders and pinks and lemons of the Impressionist masterpieces on the floor above.

Malachai wasn't here, either. Where was he? Could they orchestrate all this without him? They'd planned on having three of them in place to help her brother make his donation without interference from the police or anyone else.

While they waited, Jac looked at the calligraphy, examining the foreign letters. Even in her nervous state, she recognized they were beautifully rendered, elegantly spaced. It didn't matter if she didn't understand the words, she knew they were poetry and for a moment found some respite in that.

Jac felt eyes on her. Looked up.

Across the room, seven or eight young Asian men and women stood in a group. Curiously, none of them was inspecting the artwork. Instead all of them were watching the crowd. Who were they? Why were they here? The Dalai Lama's visit hadn't been announced to the public, so they couldn't be here to meet him. One of them was watching her.

He bowed his head. Then looked from her to the drawing she was studying, then back at her. He smiled. His expression exuded so much innocent joy that she knew without any doubt that he was the artist whose work she was examining. Peering at the legend under the frame, she read his name:

Xie Ping

Nanjing, China

She glanced back at Xie. Now he was staring at a spot behind her, his joyous expression replaced with anxiety. Jac felt a chill pass over her.

Turning, she saw a tight formation of a dozen men, all wearing similar dark uniforms, coming through the entranceway. These weren't visitors; their faces were expressionless, their stance cautious but in control. Their eyes scanned the room. Missing nothing.

Beside her, Griffin was watching them too. Jac glanced across the room. Everyone, including her brother, was focused on the approaching phalanx.

As the circle entered the gallery, they split apart. A bespectacled, bald-headed man wearing saffron robes emerged from inside their protection. Before he examined any of the artwork, His Holiness bowed to the crowd. His smile never waned. Then, starting at the beginning, he scrutinized the exhibition.

Griffin stood still. On alert. Watching. Jac could feel the tension in his body and his concentration. He was scanning the crowd. So was she. Looking for anyone paying attention to Robbie. Or to them.

If anyone here had discovered their plan, he or she would be especially careful. But there was no way anyone could have found out, was there? Even Robbie hadn't known the time and place of the meeting until early this morning.

The Dalai Lama spent at least thirty seconds on the first drawing. Leaning in, then stepping back. Gesticulating, he pointed to the upper-left corner and then said something to one of his companions. His Holiness radiated pleasure so pure, Jac felt it all the way across the room. For a moment, she actually thought that everything was going be fine.

She stole a glance at Robbie. He smiled at her. He felt it too.

The monk from the Buddhist center had given her and Griffin simple instructions:

"Wait until His Holiness finishes looking at the paintings and begins to talk to the visitors. Tell your brother to approach then. Give His Holiness his name. The Dalai Lama and his Dhob-Dhob guards will be aware of him and know Robbie has a gift for him. One of the guards will take it from him."

The elderly but spry holy man continued around the gallery, examining and delighting in the artwork. His mood was infectious, and most of the crowd watched him with smiles on their faces too. Only among the group of Asian calligraphers did Jac notice discord. Two of the young men were scowling. And one of the women looked horrified. The elderly man standing beside Xie Ping watched the Dalai Lama in awe.

When His Holiness had completed his perusal of the artwork, he strode into the center of the room. Facing the crowd, he put his palms together and bowed. He then rose, smiled, and walked toward the first person on the right of the room: a woman so in shock, she didn't move.

"I don't bite," the Dalai Lama said to her in French, laughing as he reached out and took her hands in his.

As he moved on to the next visitor, two bodyguards flanked him and followed his every step. Three others stood behind him, covering his back. The rest of the team faced in different directions, watching the room.

As the Dalai Lama continued mingling with the crowd, two things happened simultaneously.

Robbie stepped out from where he stood on the left side of the room, and Xie emerged from the knot of students in the middle. From different directions, both men approached the Dalai Lama. Xie moved tentatively. Robbie was more self-confident.

The guards watched, aware of both men.

"Something is wrong," Jac said to Griffin.

"What do you mean?"

"I don't know. I can smell something." She looked around. Scanned the crowd.

Close by, behind a heavyset man in his fifties, Jac spied the couple. For a second, she wasn't sure. The man was wearing a windbreaker and a Disney baseball cap. The woman was slight. She was wearing black slacks and a yellow rain slicker and had a camera around her neck like any tourist. Her thick, shining black hair hung down past her shoulders. Shoulders she held stiffly, as if she was in pain. Jac could smell the woman's skin. Knew the scent. Recognized the spice of it. The hair was too shiny. A wig. It was Ani and the intruder, whom Jac had last seen in a well in the catacombs.

She elbowed Griffin. Looked over. He followed her glance.

"I'm going to go around the other side to try to cut them off," Griffin whispered. "You stay put. We can't let on we know they're here."

Then he was gone. Jac couldn't bear just standing there and watching. What if Ani and her companion noticed Griffin? If one of them took off after him while the other tried to intercept Robbie?

She tried to work her way out of the crowd. The couple in front of her wouldn't let her through. She asked them to move. First in French. When they didn't understand, she tried in English. Still no recognition that they understood. She pushed through. Headed toward her brother. Went as slowly as she could so that she wouldn't draw any undue attention.

"Robbie?"

He turned. "What are you—"

She interrupted him. "Ani. That man. They're here. Someone must have followed them into the tunnel. Got them out. Griffin's going to try to keep them from getting to you. But we can't take a chance. I'm going to stumble. Grab me. Hold me like you're helping me. Then slip me the pottery. No one will see what you're doing. Quickly. I'll get it to him. I promise."

She slumped. Robbie grabbed her before she hit the ground. Put his arm around her back then tucked the pouch into her pants pocket.

"Now walk away," she whispered. "Go away from the Dalai Lama."

Jac took a step toward His Holiness while Robbie went in the other direction. She couldn't see where he was going. He was behind her now. Jac took another step. Were the guards going to let her talk to the Dalai Lama?

From the right, Jac saw the young Asian man approaching. The guards were watching him. But not suspiciously. They seemed to be expecting him.

Maybe . . . picking up her pace . . . *maybe* . . .

Jac bumped into Xie Ping. "*Je m'excuse*," she said as she slipped the pottery into his pocket.

He gaze was deep and penetrating. As if he was seeing far into her and recognized something in her.

"*Pour le Dalai Lama, s'il vous plaît?* Please give it to his Holiness. Please?" Jac begged in a low voice.

She didn't know if he spoke French. English? But he closed his eyes, then quickly opened. As if in response.

Jac was close enough to smell him. His scent was so familiar. As if she'd smelled him before once, in a dream. Now his aroma was mixing with the scents coming from the pottery.

The scented air waved and crashed around her.

Through the shadows, Jac watched as Xie reached the Dalai Lama. Bowed. Whispered something. The Holy Man reached out and pulled

Xie to him. Instantly the bodyguards surged forward, surrounded them both, hid the old man and young artist from view.

From behind, strong arms grabbed Jac.

"Give it to me," Ani said in Jac's ear as she shoved a gun in her side.

Jac shook her head. "I don't have it."

"Give it to me!"

Then someone shoved Jac so violently, it broke Ani's grip. Jac tumbled to the floor. Then smelled the cordite at the same instant she heard the gun. The odor was bitter and cold as it mixed with the scents still in her memory: Xie's scent and the scent of the ancient perfume. Then both were overpowered by the aroma of rich, sweet blood.

Fifty-six

Xie bowed his head and whispered his name to the Dalai Lama. He felt the venerable man's hand under his chin. He lifted up Xie's face, smiled brightly, and put his arm around the boy's shoulder. His Holiness turned, whispered something to the guard closest to him. In seconds, the cadre of guards had closed ranks around them.

Suddenly the room exploded. First there was a popping sound. Not too loud. But ugly. Screams. The bodyguards tightened even more. Xie heard someone shouting his name. He peered through a sliver of space in the human shield and saw Lan rushing toward him. At first he thought she was worried. Then he saw the flash of the ceramic knife in her hand, slashing her way through the crowd.

A melee had broken out. Visitors screamed. Museum security guards shouted. Held guns up in the air. Fought to control the hysteria, to hold the crowd away from the Dalai Lama's guards.

Xie watched as Ru, the student he'd suspected was spying on him, grabbed Lan by the hair and efficiently threw her down in one expertly executed martial arts move.

As the Dhob guards pushed Xie and the Dalai Lama toward the exit, Xie was able to look back once more. The students he'd traveled with were watching—some in shock, others in horror. Only Professor

Wu was observing the scene with equanimity, his face impassive except for the single tear slipping down his weathered cheek.

Outside, along with the Dalai Lama, Xie was hustled into a waiting limousine. From the backseat, through the window, he saw the dark-haired woman with the bright green eyes who'd spoken to him. There was a red stain on her white shirt. More red—the color of the ink he used on his stamps in his calligraphy—dotting the scarf around her neck. Her skin was as white as its fabric. Ghostlike, she moved as if in a trance, following a stretcher.

She wasn't crying, but her face was ravaged with grief.

Xie wanted to get out of the car. Talk to her. See if he could help her. Soothe her. Then he remembered the packet and her desperate plea.

Please give it to His Holiness. Please?

Xie felt strange. Not pain. Not confusion. Not fear. It seemed as if he could see further and more deeply than he'd been able to see since he was a child. When he'd remembered things that hadn't happened to him as Xie. But before this life. When he was a ninety-year-old monk living by a waterfall in the shadow of a tall mountain. And the man he'd been before that. Remembered a whole dreamscape of beings. Past embodiments.

Reincarnation was part of the fabric of what he had been taught. But there was a difference between learning and doing. Between imagining and knowing.

As the car took off, the Dalai Lama took Xie's hands in his and told him how glad he was to welcome his spiritual son back.

"How long it has been. How much you have suffered. But you have been brave and done well, and we're very proud of you."

Xie was too moved to speak.

"The last time I saw you, you were just six years old." His Holiness smiled. "A very impetuous six, with the soul of a much more educated man than me."

"That's not possible."

"I think it is." The holy man's smile was expansive. "Do you have something for me?"

Xie nodded. Took the packet out of his pocket. "There was a woman at the gallery; she wanted me to give you this."

The Dalai Lama looked at it. "I'm so pleased both efforts proved a success."

"What is it?"

"I think you already know. I can see it in your eyes."

"Something to help you remember?"

"So it is said. You are remembering, aren't you?"

Xie, who now, for the first time in twenty years, didn't have to hide what he knew and felt and saw, nodded. "Are you?"

"No," replied the Dalai Lama. "But that doesn't worry me very much. One of us is remembering. You are. And you are enough."

Fifty-seven

SATURDAY, 7:00 P.M.

Jac hadn't expected so many tubes and bandages. She gripped the door frame. Willed her knees to keep her standing. Forced herself to take in the worst of it.

Behind her, Robbie gasped, "Oh, no!"

The first thing that steadied her was the slight rise and fall of Griffin's chest under the thin white sheet. The second was her brother's hand in hers. Together they crossed the threshold and entered the hospital room.

They each took a chair on either side of the bed and began their vigil.

Griffin had taken the bullet Ani's comrade had intended for Jac. It had gone into the fleshy part of his upper arm. He'd lost some blood, but the doctors had been able to remove the bullet without any trouble. The wound wasn't life threatening.

His fall had been.

The gunshot's impact had sent Griffin reeling. He'd cracked his skull against a bronze sculpture. The past six hours had been a nightmare of sketchy information, consultations with doctors, surgery to relieve some of the swelling in his brain, staples to hold his skull together, and, finally, a drug-induced coma.

While Griffin was in the operating room, Inspector Marcher arrived at the hospital. Debriefed Robbie. Took his statement and Jac's. He told them there'd be a formal inquiry, but Robbie was no longer suspected of murder. His actions had clearly been taken in self-defense. Ani Lodro, also known as Valentine Lee, and her companion, known as William Leclerc, were in custody. Along with the pseudo-journalist found dead six days before, François Lee, they'd been identified as members of the Chinese Mafia. Hired to keep the pottery from getting to the Dalai Lama.

Jac and Robbie sat quietly. The lights in the room were low. Machines blinked red and green. Beeped and hummed. The medicinal odors filled the air. Clean. Crisp. Like the linens on the bed.

"What do we do now?" Jac finally asked her brother.

"We wait."

"I remember Griffin telling me about seeing the artifacts from King Tutankhamen's tomb," Jac said. "How monumental the sarcophagus was. How much gold had been used. How brightly it shone. Griffin said by the time he saw the actual mummy, he'd forgotten that the king was a real man."

The hydraulic hinge whooshed as the door opened. They both turned. Malachai came in, accompanied by a nurse who told them that only two visitors were allowed at a time. Robbie offered to get some coffee.

Malachai didn't sit. Not yet. He stood behind Jac and looked down at Griffin.

"How is he?"

"It's too soon."

He shifted his gaze to her.

"And how are you?"

She shrugged.

He pulled the chair around so he was sitting next to her instead of on the other side of the bed. "What happened in the museum?"

For the next few minutes, she recounted the events that had occurred during that tense, life-changing half hour. While she spoke, they both watched the still figure on the narrow bed.

Jac tried but couldn't discern Griffin's scent over the antiseptic smells. It was the first time since she'd met him fifteen years before that she couldn't smell it.

After all the fear, anxiety and terror of the past week, not being able to smell him was what broke her. She put her head in her hands. And sobbed.

"How I wish I could do something to help you," Malachai whispered as he put a tentative hand on her shoulder.

For a moment, they stayed like that. She cried, and he tried to console her.

Finally, she said: "Griffin always said I put too much pressure on him. That I thought he was better than he was. Except in the museum . . ."

"What he did was very brave," Malachai said.

"But look at him. This is my fault."

"Your fault? I don't understand."

Jac didn't answer.

"The scent affected you, didn't it?"

"What scent?"

"Jac," he reprimanded. "Coyness doesn't become you. Griffin couldn't smell anything on the pottery. Your brother could just sense it, but it didn't do anything to him but give him a headache. You have the more sensitive nose. You could smell it, couldn't you? It helped you remember other lives? All this time, what you thought were psychotic incidents were past-life memories."

"I don't believe that."

"Even now?"

"I have hallucinations that seem to be induced by olfactory triggers."

"Still so cynical."

She shrugged.

"One day, you'll outgrow that." Malachai smiled.

She picked up her head. Straightened her shoulders. This conversation wasn't going to help. Not Griffin. Not her. "Let's not do this, okay?"

"I've worked with so many people who've had past-life memories. Some perceive them but never fully comprehend them—nevertheless, they learn from them. Grow from them."

"I know you want to believe that's what's been afflicting me, but you're wrong."

Robbie came through the door holding a tray. "I waited till the nurse was looking the other way," he said as he handed each of them a cup. "I saw one of Griffin's doctors downstairs. He seemed optimistic."

Did Robbie sound as if he were trying to convince himself?

"That's wonderful," Malachai said.

Robbie walked around the bed and leaned against the windowsill. "This wouldn't have happened if I'd just sold you the pottery," he said to Malachai.

"No one wishes that more than me. But sometimes things happen for a reason. These events played out this way for a purpose. Have either of you seen the news?"

Jac and Robbie said they hadn't.

Malachai pulled out his cell phone, tapped a web address into it and then handed the device to Jac. She was looking down at the front page of the *Herald Tribune* international edition.

"There are stories like this on every major news TV station and website. The young man who went off with the Dalai Lama isn't just a Chinese art student named Xie Ping. He's a Tibetan Panchen Lama who was kidnapped when he was six years old, taken to China and completely brainwashed. It's quite a harrowing story. For the past twenty years, his family and the Buddhist community thought he was dead."

Jac clicked on the photograph of the artist standing next to the Dalai Lama and made it full screen. His Holiness was beaming. Xie looked like a lost soul who had finally found safe harbor. She handed her brother the phone.

"The Panchen Lama and his story will bring a fresh wave of sympathy to the Tibetan cause," Malachai said.

Robbie nodded. Something in him, Jac thought, was finally at peace.

"There's a mention in the article about you," Malachai said to Jac. He held out his hand for the phone, and she gave it back to him. He scrolled through the story, and when he found the part he was looking for, he read aloud.

"'Miss L'Etoile and her brother exhibited amazing bravery in getting a package to us,' the Dalai Lama said in an interview after the incident. 'In it are thirty-three shards of Egyptian pottery inscribed with hieroglyphics. A translation by Griffin North was enclosed. It explains the jar once held an ancient perfume that induced past-life memories. It's a precious gift. We hope with all our hearts that the far more precious gift of someone's life was not lost in the effort to get this treasure to us.'"

Fifty-eight

SUNDAY, MAY 29

Jac, Malachai and Robbie had held vigil at the hospital all evening, but at midnight she insisted they both leave her and go home. Robbie hadn't slept more than an hour or two at a time in the week he'd been in hiding, and he was falling asleep in the chair. Malachai's driver was going to drop off Robbie. Then the reincarnationist was going back to his hotel. He was leaving in the morning.

"If you need me, please, call," he'd said to Jac as he pulled her toward him in an embrace. In all the years she'd known him, he'd kept his distance, at most touching her on the shoulder. "Anything at all," he said as he let her go.

She nodded.

"Even if it's just to talk about what—"

"Thank you," she interrupted. Jac didn't want Malachai to bring up the hallucinations in front of Robbie. She wanted to forget about them. Wanted not to discuss them. With anyone. Not again.

Once they left, she found herself alone with Griffin in his hospital room for the first time. All the lights were off. Only electronics illuminated the cubicle.

The doctors had said it was important for Griffin to know someone was with him.

"I never asked you what your favorite myth was," she said now. "Isn't that strange? Mine is Daedalus and Icarus. Would you like to hear me tell it?"

Jac began the time-honored, age-old way. "Once upon a time . . ."

But she was tired, too tired. It would be all right if she rested for a few minutes, wouldn't it?

She lay down her head on her crossed arms. Closed her eyes.

A nurse woke her at six in the morning when she came in to take Griffin's vitals.

A half hour later, when his team of doctors arrived, Jac went downstairs. She bought a cup of coffee and took it outside. Leaning against the building, she sipped as slowly as she could, resisting rushing back to his room. She knew they wouldn't let her in while they were examining him.

After what seemed like fifteen minutes, she checked her watch. Only five minutes had elapsed. Watching the people come and go, she was able to tell who worked at the hospital even if they weren't dressed in nurses' or doctors' uniforms. The staff's faces didn't tell a story. There were no vestiges of fear etched on their foreheads. No grief in their eyes. Their lips were not pursed in anxiety.

When Jac went back upstairs, there was a new nurse on duty who stopped her from going in to see Griffin.

"Is he all right?" Jac asked, looking toward the door.

"He's fine." The nurse smiled. "I'm Helene by the way. I'll be on duty until five. Are you Mr. North's wife?"

"No, not his wife, no. His cousin. I'm his cousin."

Robbie had been the one to lie to the hospital when he and Jac came in with the ambulance. If he hadn't said they were relatives, they might not have been able to stay with Griffin. When she asked how he knew that, he smiled sadly and told her how many gay friends had been kept out of hospital rooms because blood trumped love.

"Why are the doctors taking so long, then?"

"Mr. North is out of the coma. They are doing some tests."

"Is there any brain damage?"

"I'm not supposed to—"

Jac grabbed the nurse's hand. "I know you aren't. And I won't ever tell you did, but I'm going crazy. Please tell me, is he all right?"

The nurse leaned in a little. Jac smelled lemon, verbena and something sweet mixed up with the medicinal smells. Helene's heart-shaped lips slid into a smile. She wore bright-pink lipstick almost the color of bubblegum. That must have been what smelled so sweet.

"I was in there for a lot of the tests," Helene said. "It looks like he's going to make a complete recovery."

Like a warm wind, relief wrapped around Jac. Cosseted her. She knew she was standing still, but she felt as if she were spinning. Before she realized it, she was sitting in a hard plastic chair, Helene beside her, holding out a paper cup.

"Take sips," the nurse said.

"What happened?"

"You got a little light-headed, I think."

Jac nodded. "Relieved. So relieved."

"I know, dear. I know. Now just rest here until the doctors are done. One of them will want to talk with you."

Helene started to walk away. Jac reached out and grabbed her hand. "You actually saw him awake?"

The nurse nodded. "I did."

A half hour later, Griffin's neurosurgeon reassured Jac that he was going to make a complete recovery and would probably be in the hospital for only another two days or so. "Mr. North is sleeping now," he said. "He'll probably sleep off and on most of the day. But you can go in."

All of the tubes except for one intravenous line were gone. Griffin was lying on his back, his mouth open slightly. His color was almost back to normal. The bandages across his upper shoulder had been changed. There was no blood seeping through. Just hours ago, there had been blood all over.

Then she saw it was still in his hair. Dried dark brown coating the silver. It made her shiver.

Jac stood beside his bed and looked down at him. Looked down at Griffin, the man who had so long ago brought her to life. And now had saved her life. It seemed too great a thing to even contemplate. Too complicated to comprehend.

Leaning down, she kissed his forehead, hoping that her lips would wake him the way it happened in fairy tales. But he didn't open his eyes. Didn't shift in the bed. He didn't react to her touch at all.

She didn't know how long she stood there, but at some point, the nurse with the bubblegum-pink lipstick came into the room.

"You might want to go home for a while. He's going to sleep now for most of the day. You can take a shower and get some rest." Helene smiled. "Change your clothes. Come back later, perhaps at dinnertime? He might be more alert by then."

Jac looked down. There were splashes of blood on her shirt. On the scarf. On the top of her right shoe. She was wearing the same clothes she'd left the house in yesterday morning.

Yes, she should go home. She started for the door. Reached it. Put her hand on the handle, but then couldn't pull it. She listened for what he always said when they parted. All she heard was his steady breathing.

Could she really leave him now? Leave him again? They had too long a history of leaving. From the time she first met him till he'd finally walked away from her that day in the park, they'd said good-bye so many times she could hear him in her memory now.

Except Griffin never actually said good-bye. Instead he'd tilt his head to the right, a hint of a smile would lift the corners of his mouth, his voice would dip a little, slide into a lower register, and in a hoarse whisper he'd say, "Ciao."

The first time she heard it, she wondered if he was a little affected.

"*Ciao?*" she'd asked.

"In Italy, it's what you say when someone arrives—not just when they leave. Isn't that better? What could be good about us being separated? We can pretend that you just got here and we have the whole weekend ahead of us."

Jac turned, walked back, sat beside the bed, leaned over, and laid as much of her upper body beside his as she could. She closed her eyes.

Gave in to a thought that she hadn't allowed herself for more than fifteen years. She wanted to be with him.

Jac could never get her mother back; she could smell her perfume and hear her voice. But that wasn't real. It was a daughter's desperation. But Griffin was real. How many people did she have to lose? How many times did she have to lose this one?

At first, the touch of his fingers on her cheek was so natural that she didn't realize what it meant. He was wiping away her tears. "You know you can drown in that much sadness," he whispered.

She opened her eyes and looked at him. No words came. There wasn't anything to say. There was just this man whom she'd never stopped loving. And whom she couldn't say good-bye to again. Ever.

Fifty-nine

At home, Jac took a shower and then tried to take a nap. But it was only ten in the morning. And she couldn't stop her mind from reliving the past few terrible days.

Barefoot, with her hair still wet, wearing the same terrycloth robe that she'd worn as a teenager, she left her bedroom. On her way to the kitchen, she stopped at her brother's room. She wished he was awake, but his door was shut.

Downstairs Jac made herself a cup of Etoile de Paris tea. Her grandfather once told her Mariage Frères created the blend just for him. But she never knew if that was true. As she watched the dried leaves tint the water green, Jac breathed in the scent. Vanilla wrapped around mint. And a flowery thread. She sniffed. Familiar but elusive. Peppery and sweet at the same time. Very green.

Lotus.

In those few seconds in the Orangerie, after she'd taken the pouch from Robbie, as she hurried to Xie Ping, she'd smelled the scents impregnated in the ancient pottery with a clarity that had eluded her in the catacombs. Even in the midst of the commotion, for those few moments, she'd recognized all of the individual essences.

Frankincense and myrrh, blue lotus and almond oil, and—

There was another, but now she couldn't remember what it was. How could that be? She'd known it in the museum.

What was it?

Not sure why it mattered so much but determined to remember, she left the house, crossed the courtyard, and entered the workshop.

The scent that Robbie called Fragrance of Comfort suffused the studio. No one had been in here for at least two days. Dark and provocative, the perfume of time long gone—of regret, of longing, maybe even of madness—had intensified.

Here in this room, generations of her ancestors had blended elusive essences and absolutes from flowers, spices, wood and minerals. They had mixed elixirs to tempt patrons. Constructed perfumes to delight emperors and empresses, kings and queens. Created magic potions that no one could resist.

Here she'd discovered she was different from everyone else. Here she had suffered the most. Here her mother had ultimately failed them all. And Robbie, in saving his own life, had ended someone else's.

Here in this terrible and wonderful room, secrets had been lost. And found. And lost again.

Jac stared at the instrument she hated and feared. Maybe it was time to finally welcome the conscious nightmares instead of fighting them and accept that she had an illness she couldn't always control.

Jac sat down at the organ. Inhaled the cacophony of smells. Hundreds of threads. A whiff of rose. Jasmine. Orange. Sandalwood. Of myrrh. Vanilla. Orchid. Gardenia. Musk. Could there be so many, many smells in one place anywhere else in the world? A richness of odor. A treasure of it. Each individual scent a story. A tale that went back in time. Instead of interpreting myths, she could spend the rest of her life tracing them.

The glass bottles were lenses. The liquid in them prisms. Her vision was wavering. In the gold and bronze and amber, pictures were coming to life. Jac could pick out the individual threads that made up her mother's perfume. Her father's cologne. She remembered, when she was little and things were still good, she'd sit on her father's lap, here at the organ, and he'd tell her the story of the book of lost fragrances that their ancestor had found. She'd close her eyes and see the scenes play out. Her own private theater of the mind.

Sixty

Marie-Genevieve had agreed to accompany her husband because she couldn't think of any reason to say no. But she didn't want to make the trip from Nantes to the place where she'd been young. Memories weren't always her friends. Often they woke her at night and held her hostage. The brutal revolution that had begun in that city had robbed her of all her family. Her mother and father, two sisters. All imprisoned. Then killed.

In Paris, all the ghosts would be there to greet her. She'd have to walk down streets she'd traversed as a girl. She'd have to see the specter of her past. Of Giles.

But her husband wanted her to go. And she had no excuse to refuse him. He was a kind man. He'd saved her life when he found her—mostly dead, half drowned—on the shore of the Loire River. The priest she'd been bound to had used his last bit of strength to untie them and to give her a chance to survive.

Without his dead weight, Marie-Genevieve had risen to the surface. Sputtering, choking, she gulped in air. Took in water. If not for the current, she wouldn't have lived. But the river had pushed her onto the shore.

The first two days in Paris were not as emotionally trying as she'd expected. There had been so many changes in the past fifteen years that Marie-Genevieve's memories were mitigated by the shock of the new.

On the third morning, she was so relaxed that when their carriage crossed the Seine at the Pont du Carrousel, she was watching a young woman trying to control her three little children and didn't focus on where they were. Or ask where they were headed.

Then the carriage turned onto Rue des Saints-Pères and pulled up in front of the building.

Marie-Genevieve turned to her husband. "Where are we?"

"A surprise."

Except she'd never told him anything about L'Etoile.

"I don't understand!"

Couldn't he hear her panic? Why was he smiling?

"I've heard they make the finest fragrance in all of Paris here. I wanted to buy you something to remember the trip by."

"It's too dear. We've spent enough money." She was looking at her husband. But over his shoulder, through the window, she could see the door to the perfume shop that she used to go in and out of a hundred times a week. The door opened. Someone was coming out. At first Marie-Genevieve thought it was Jean-Louis L'Etoile. Tall. Gray hair. Eyes so blue she could see them from here.

He noticed the carriage. Glanced in. Right at her.

There were ghosts here after all. Giles had died in Egypt when she was still a girl. He was long dead.

Except the man who was looking in at her, staring at her as if she were a ghost too, was very much alive.

Their gazes met. For a few seconds, Marie-Genevieve forgot she was married with two children and sitting in a rented carriage with her husband. The sound that escaped from her lips was a sob blended with a laugh.

"Are you all right, *ma chérie?*" her husband asked.

"I don't feel well . . ."

That night, once her husband was asleep, Marie-Genevieve stole out of the hotel room. It was only ten blocks to Rue des Saints-Pères. The streets weren't dark and dangerous. She wasn't a forty-two-year-old woman with streaks of gray in her hair anymore but seventeen again. She didn't lumber, she flew.

The door to the store was unlocked despite the hour. Even though they hadn't made contact, hadn't arranged for the rendezvous, he was there. Sitting in the darkened boutique. Waiting.

"How did you know I would come?" she asked.

"Where have you been all these years?"

They both started talking at the same time, but before either of them finished, he reached out for her. They were in each other's arms until the first rays of the sun set the bottles of perfume alight.

Marie-Genevieve managed to return to her hotel before her husband awoke. While she dressed, she tried to behave like herself. But it seemed as if she'd lost twenty years of her life. She didn't recognize the man she'd married. She had forgotten the life she'd been living.

They had four more days in the City of Lights. Each night, she pretended to fall asleep quickly and then lay beside this stranger and waited for his breathing to slow. Then she'd get out of bed, dress and steal away.

The dark was her ally. Assignations of the night were so common in Paris she was invisible. She disappeared into the shadows and ran into her lover's arms.

Her last night, after they'd made love, as she was still lying in his arms on the settee in the workshop, Giles told her he wanted her to leave her husband and stay in Paris.

"You and I are both married, we have children!" she cried.

"You can bring your babies. I will buy you a house. I'll live with you there and work here."

She shook her head. *"Ce n'est pas possible."*

He got up and went to a cabinet. Opened it and extracted something. Marie-Genevieve's eyes were so full of tears, she couldn't tell what it was.

"You don't have a choice," he said.

"I don't understand."

"The Egyptians believed in destiny. In fate. We are each other's fate." He held out a leather pouch and emptied its contents into his palm. "Smell."

She looked down at the pottery that he held in his hand, and the world began to swim. At first she was terrified. It was the way she felt in the Loire so long ago. Black. Cold. The stink of mud and slime. And then small, gentle hands of scent pulled her away from Nantes. Back, back to someplace she'd been before. These scents were purples, deep maroons, velvet navy, and starlight. A man with dark skin sat beside a woman with raven-wing hair, holding out a jar to her.

Like seeing her reflection in the Palace of Versailles Hall of Mirrors, Marie-Genevieve was looking at herself—except she was seeing Iset, head bent over her lover's hand, smelling the unguent he held.

The man, Thoth, was speaking in a language Marie-Genevieve had never heard before and yet understood. He was speaking the same words that Giles had just uttered.

"We are each other's fate."

Then she heard her name cried in a voice that was of the present. It yanked her out of her dream. Her husband's voice. The kind, gentle vintner who had saved her life was standing in front of her, his eyes wild with anger. He held a pistol. His hand shook.

The dawn light shone through the windows and glinted on the hilt of the weapon. If Marie-Genevieve thought her gentle, God-fearing husband was capable of using the gun, she would have thrown herself in front of Giles. But it was inconceivable.

"I won't let you take the only thing I ever wanted!" he shouted at Giles and then, without any hesitation, pulled the trigger.

A fortnight later, at home in Nantes, Marie-Genevieve read in the newspaper that Giles L'Etoile had died of a gunshot wound. She couldn't eat or sleep. Didn't speak to the man she was married to. She took care of her children in a fog. She was focused only on the bedside of the man she'd loved since she was a very little girl. Who'd held his hand? Who'd whispered words of comfort as he slipped away from this world into the next?

If only she had not gone to Paris, Giles would still be alive. He had died because of her. But Giles had said they belonged together. Two children who had been inseparable since childhood—almost, Marie-Genevieve's mother used to say, as if one was the right glove and one was the left.

Sixty-one

Jac tried to force herself to get up and get away from the organ. To break the pull and escape the grip of the memories that weren't hers yet were as real as if she'd lived them. But she couldn't. There was more sitting on the edge of her consciousness. Something important she had to understand. The story wasn't over. It hadn't even begun.

Jac inhaled. Found the thread. Of the hundreds of bottles of essence and absolutes, she could read only some of the labels. She was lost in possibilities. Of all these ingredients, which ones combined to create her hallucinatory nightmares?

One by one, she looked at each label. This one? This?

Frustrated, she banged on the organ with clenched fists, like a child demanding attention. Bottles rattled, glass tinkled. Banged again. Under the perfume maker's music she heard another sound that made no sense—an echo.

The organ was a solid mass of carved wood. How could it be hollow?

One by one, Jac removed every bottle from the organ. Soon there was no room to walk. Four hundred bottles—some dating back to the seventeen hundreds—covered the floor in a three-dimensional fragrant rug.

The organ was empty. A coffin. Years of oil stains had left an abstract design on the wooden shelves. Pressing and prodding, Jac knocked against each section until finally she found it.

A hidden recess.

Carefully she pried up the wooden square, revealing a fragrant, dark cavity. The fountainhead of the scent. Robbie's Fragrance of Comfort. Jac's nightmare.

Reaching in, she felt for what she couldn't see. As she lifted it out, dozens of flecks of amber-stained linen cracked off.

It was a scroll. This was the source of the dangerous, exotic, mesmerizing scent.

Jac wasn't sure she should, but she unrolled it. Inside was a pottery jar. White glaze. Turquoise and coral designs. Black hieroglyphics. This was an undamaged version of the shards that Robbie had found. She felt inside with the tip of her forefinger. There were vestiges of wax still lining its walls.

The air waved. The imagines beckoned. The scent embraced her in a horrific grip, wound around Jac, and pulled her in.

Sixty-two

Censers burned in each corner of the room. A cloud of the finest incense hung over the wooden chests, the finely carved and gilded chairs and chaises. The ceiling was painted with a rich lapis lazuli and a silver astronomical star chart. Cut into the walls were several doors, one larger than the others. Delicate and detailed murals, beautifully rendered in earth tones, decorated the walls. The stylized motif of water lilies that bordered the crypt and framed the paintings illustrated Thoth's favorite flower, the blue lotus.

In the center of the chamber was a black granite sarcophagus, five times the size of an ordinary man. Its polished surface was carved with cartouches and inlaid with a turquoise and lapis portrait of a beautiful, catlike man with blue water lilies around his head. He was Nefertum, the god of perfume.

"You have to be very careful, Iset. If your husband becomes suspicious, you won't be safe." Thoth was trying to tell her what he wanted her to do once he was gone, but she could barely listen.

It was her fault that Thoth had broken his promise to the queen. Iset had begged him to let her smell the fragrances he was creating despite his promise to his sovereign that they were for her nose alone.

Now his treachery was going to cost him his life. Cleopatra was to have him publicly executed in two days time—a lesson to anyone else who thought about betraying her.

But Thoth was not going to wait to be humiliated. He was going to take his own life. He was a priest. A perfumer. Had all the herbs and plants needed to mix up a fatal poison.

"I've made two of these jars. This one is for you. Leave instructions that it's to be buried with you, as mine will be buried with me. As long as we take this perfume with us into the afterlife," Thoth said, "we'll always be able to find each other."

Iset took the jar from Thoth. Felt its smooth roundness in the palm of her hand. Cupped it. Closed her eyes. Iset breathed in the scent. Thoth had told her what was in it. Frankincense, myrrh. Honey. Blue Lily. Persimmon from the groves Mark Antony had imported and planted for his bride.

Once she'd found out about the scent of soul mates, Iset was relentless in getting Thoth to let her smell it. Together they shared visions of the past. Of the people they had been before. Long before. When they were together in another life, as Thoth explained.

Now because of her greed and curiosity, she was going to have to say good-bye to him and live without him.

It was unthinkable.

The draught of poison that he'd prepared sat on a small wooden table. The cobalt-blue glass shimmered in the candlelight. Was cold to the touch. On her fingers. And then on her lips.

"No!" Thoth shouted as he reached for it and grabbed it from her.

A trickle of poison slid down her chin.

Thoth examined what was left of the liquid.

"Did I drink enough?" Her voice was light. She wouldn't be left behind. She would go with him.

"More than enough. Do you understand what you did, you fool? There's no antidote. I can't save you." Then, lifting the glass to his mouth, he put his lips where hers had been. And he drank.

"No one knows where I am. I've disappeared from my husband's home. My death will be a secret. As long as I can be buried with you, that's all that matters. Leave instructions for your embalmers."

"Why did you do this? You could have lived. You weren't in danger. Your husband didn't know."

"What's going to happen?" She ignored his remonstrations. "Will it hurt?"

"No. We'll just go to sleep. Hold each other and go to sleep in this beautiful place . . ."

"Kiss me now."

He took her in his arms. She tasted the bitter poison on his lips. Happy, she thought, I'm happy here in this man's arms. Then she felt something wet on her cheeks and pulled away. The tears weren't hers; they were his, coursing down his face. She didn't mind leaving this world for the next. He was her world. Without him, she wouldn't have wanted to live. But not so for Thoth. In his eyes were regrets.

"What is it?"

"My work isn't finished."

It was all her fault. She'd caused his misery. What she had done to him was unforgivable. If only she could take it back. If she could do it over. If she could change his fate.

Iset wanted to kiss away the sadness in his eyes but knew she couldn't. She put her lips back on his. At least they could kiss their way to death.

Sixty-three

The precious artifact was wrapped in a sheet of ordinary bubble wrap and secured in Jac's pocketbook. It was a good one that she'd bought years ago and still used. The more battered the leather, the better it looked. Like Griffin, she thought. He was bruised, wounded, stitched up, and stapled but had never been more special to her.

He'd been moved from the intensive care unit to a regular room. Was sleeping. Had been since she'd arrived a half hour before. She was waiting for him to wake up. Because she needed him to do something.

Jac was going to ask Griffin to sniff the residue of pomade in the Egyptian jar. If nothing happened to him, she'd know Malachai had been wrong. Her hallucinations weren't past life episodes—she was crazy after all.

But if Griffin had hallucinations and remembered the two of them in the past . . . if the scent provoked his memories and he could recollect them loving each other through time . . . then they had to be *âmes soeurs*.

"Once upon a time," she whispered to Griffin, retelling the story she and Robbie had been told by their father, "in Egypt in 1799, Giles L'Etoile discovered an ancient book of fragrance formulas. One for an elixir that enabled people to find true soul mates. After he'd smelled the scent, he was never the same. The book and the fragrance have been lost, but once upon a time in the future another L'Etoile will find them and—"

Griffin opened his eyes and smiled at her.

"What were you saying?"

"I was telling you a story."

"Will you tell me again? I missed most of it."

She nodded. "Later."

"Did you go home and sleep?" he asked.

"I tried."

"How's Robbie?"

Jac reassured Griffin that her brother was fine and would be coming over soon. She'd seen Robbie before she left but hadn't told him about the jar she'd found. Or the scroll. There'd be time for that. First she needed to find out what was happening to her. What the images meant. Whether she was having memories or was crazy again.

Griffin's cell phone rang. He looked down at the LED readout. Smiled. "It's my daughter."

"Take it. I'll get some coffee."

As Jac walked to the door, she heard Griffin answer. Listened to the catch in his voice as he said his Elsie's name. She shut the door with a shaking hand. Leaned against it. Jac was remembering her father saying her name. She was thinking about her parents' separation. Her loneliness. Robbie's unhappiness. The way her parents' bitterness ripped apart their days, cast their lives into shadows.

"Where is the chapel?" Jac asked one of the nurses bustling by.

For the few minutes it took to get from Griffin's room to the simple chapel on the lower level, Jac didn't think about anything. She willed her mind blank. Simply put one foot in front of the other and propelled herself forward. Only when she reached the small stone sanctuary and sat down on one of the wooden pews did she let the torrent of complicated thoughts twist into her consciousness.

At the feet of a lovely and serene marble Madonna, a dozen votives burned in small ruby holders. On either side of her, vases of lilies lent their perfume to the paraffin scent. Afternoon light poured through the cobalt stained-glass windows, casting melancholy reflections of the same sad blue that always filled the mausoleum where her mother was interred.

You know what to do.

The voice came from the shadows of the dark little prayer room.

Jac hadn't expected her mother's voice here. She'd never heard it outside of the Sleepy Hollow Cemetery.

And it's the right thing to do.

"You don't know anything!" Jac shouted. Shouted it before it occurred to her she was speaking out loud. She'd never spoken to her mother's ghost. Never allowed that the manifestation was anything other than her imagination playing tricks.

There was nothing wrong with asking Griffin to smell the pomade. If Jac was crazy, then Griffin wouldn't remember anything. If she wasn't, then he'd remember the things she had. They'd find out they'd been together before.

But in both of those lives, he died for you. As Giles, when Marie-Genevieve's husband discovered them together early that morning in Paris. And as Thoth, in Egypt, by swallowing his own potion.

"So what?" Jac asked.

The chapel, filled with the scent of sadness and prayers, was silent.

Jac went over it again. Thought it all through. He'd died for her twice in the past. And just two days ago, Griffin had almost died for her again. If reincarnation was real, if they had lived these lives by each other's sides, they were in a karmic treadmill.

Twice she had taken him as a lover when he wasn't free.

Twice he had died because of her.

Griffin was off the phone when Jac returned to his room.

"How is Elsie?" she asked.

"They landed in Paris. She'll be here in an hour."

Jac gripped her purse to her chest.

"She'll be so happy to see you. And it will be so good for you to see her."

Griffin nodded and started to say something.

Jac interrupted. "I'm going to go . . ." She gripped the bag tighter. She loved this man. Wanted him still. But she knew what she had to do. "I think I should—" she broke off. How could she say good-bye?

She stared into Griffin's eyes. Tried to speak without words. She knew she was failing.

"Thank you for everything. For helping Robbie and me. For saving my life. I can't ever . . ." Her voice quavered. She squeezed her bag tighter, heard one of the bubbles pop. "Go home with your wife and your little girl, Griffin. You told me yourself you weren't sure it was over. Give it another chance."

"But—"

She knew what he was going to say and interrupted. She didn't want to hear it.

"You can't figure anything out with me around. And you need to. Not so much even for Elsie's sake or for your wife's. For yours, Griffin." Jac wanted to reach out and take his hand and feel his flesh, but she knew if she did, she would never let go.

"Ciao," she whispered. He had saved her life. Now she had to give him a chance to save his own.

Sixty-four

The room was bright and sunny, filled with furniture, books and artwork from the house on Rue des Saints-Pères. Her father sat in a leather chair by the window; Claire sat beside him.

Jac was surprised by how lovely the small apartment was. How beautiful and green the view was. How sweet the air smelled and how peaceful her father appeared.

He'd turned to see who'd come in. Studied her as if he were trying to place her. But couldn't. There was no recognition in his eyes.

"Hello," Claire said softly. "It's good of you to come. Is Robbie here?"

"Outside. In the car."

"I'll go say hello and give you some time with your father."

Jac almost stopped her. She didn't know if she wanted to be alone with him.

She sat down in the chair Claire had vacated. Her father wasn't as frail as she'd expected. He still looked like himself. He didn't look lost— even if he was lost to her. But she was used to that. Since her mother died, he hadn't been able to deal with her. A therapist had suggested she reminded him too much of the woman he hadn't been able to protect and keep safe. Jac didn't care what the reason was. The facts hurt too much.

"I'm Jac, Father," she said.

"Jac?" He said it as if he'd never heard the name. "I'm sorry. I don't remember people that well anymore. How do we know each other?"

Jac opened her pocketbook. Took out the small package and unwrapped it. She'd told Robbie what she planned to do. He'd agreed. They'd examined the scroll. Everything her brother needed to enable him to work on the scent was written there—including the names of the ingredients. A quick internet search had pointed out the greatest problem. One of the main ingredients was extinct. Cleopatra's ancient persimmon fields had been so valuable the Egyptians had burned them to the ground rather than let the Romans profit from them. A group of botanists was currently working in the desert in the area where the fields had been, hoping to one day find ancient seeds and regrow the plant. Perhaps if they did, Robbie could recreate the scent. He'd sniffed the jar she'd found over and over, but it only gave him a headache.

An olfactory trigger to psychotic episodes or a memory tool? Robbie couldn't help her unearth the truth. She called Malachai and asked him if everyone could be regressed.

"No," he'd said with so much sadness in his voice that she could hear it over the phone. "Why are you asking?"

She hadn't told him the truth. He'd only want the jar, and she and Robbie had decided that it wasn't theirs to give away. It belonged to someone else. Even if it meant selling Rouge and Noir. It wasn't a sacrifice, Robbie had told her. It was the past, and they had the present to take care of.

Jac knelt by her father's chair. Looked into his face. Searched his eyes. Hoped he could hear her.

"You found this, didn't you?" she asked.

He looked down at what she was holding.

Recognizing it, he nodded his head. "Yes. In the organ. Where it was hidden."

"Robbie and I want you to have it."

He took it from her. Bent his head toward it. Inhaled deeply.

When he raised his head, he looked right at Jac. His blue eyes smiling.

"I'm sorry," he whispered.

"For what?"

"I didn't keep you very safe, did I?"

She wasn't sure what he meant. When he took her to the doctors in Paris? When he sent her to Blixer Rath?

"What do you mean?"

"I should have realized that you were still in love with Giles. Not arranged for you to marry another. If I had listened to your mother, you never would have run away to the convent. Never been tortured . . . They said you drowned . . ." A tear escaped his eye and ran down his cheek.

He took her hand, clasped it in his, lifted it to his mouth and kissed it.

"It was my job to keep my daughter safe. I failed."

"No, Papa," Jac said, knowing somehow that this was what Marie-Genevieve had called her father. "No, Papa, you didn't fail. See? I am safe. I am. They tried to drown me, but I survived. Married. I had children, Papa."

"Married Giles?"

"No. Someone else. We named our oldest daughter after Maman."

He smiled down at her, remembering things that everyone else but the two of them had long, long ago forgotten.

And then she buried her head in his lap, and while she wept, he stroked her hair, and she did what Robbie had said she would do one day. She forgave her father.

Glossary

of

M. J. Rose's Research

M. J. Rose has been researching history and reincarnation for more than two decades. In addition, in preparation for this book she spent more than two and a half years researching the world of fragrance. She spent time with leaders in the perfume industry, reading ancient treatises on perfumery and alchemy, traveling to flower farms and conventions, as well as studying with fragrance architects, famous noses and niche perfumers.

This glossary offers a glimpse into the author's research and provides some factual information about some of the topics, locations, theories and legends discussed in the novel.

Some of the rarest perfumes Rose collected during her research. Pictured are Shalimar (left) from the 1960s, Coq d'Or (middle) from the 1940s and Mitsouko from the 1950s.

When she starts a new novel, Rose creates a journal for her main character—this is a page of L'Etoile's impressions of Paris upon returning home after several years.

A

absolute   A highly concentrated aromatic oil harvested from plants using solvent extraction techniques such as enfleurage. Absolutes are often favored for perfume formulation, as the low temperature used in the extraction process does not damage the delicate fragrance compounds. As a result, absolutes often smell truer to their botanical source than oils produced through extraction methods requiring higher temperatures, such as steam distillation.

ancient perfume   Rose relied heavily on the history of perfume in this novel and was greatly inspired by her research. The art of perfumery and perfume-making is said to have emerged from Mesopotamia, with earliest recorded accounts dating from around the second millennium BCE. Numerous ancient cultures used incense, perfumes or aromatics in ceremonial rituals and worship. These include the Ancient Egyptians, Ancient Greeks, Romans, Chinese Taoists, Australian Aborigines and Native Americans.

Egypt   Perfumed preparations were originally used in Egypt chiefly by the priesthood, who would burn incense in the temples to worship their deities. Perfumed smoke was inhaled and allowed to imbue one's clothes, as it was believed this act would bring one closer to divinity. Perfume oils were used in bathing rituals and in ceremonial rites; and incense preparations such as *kyphi,* allegedly containing psychoactive ingredients, were burned nightly to produced a tranquilizing smoke (see hallucinogen). Plutarch writes:

> *Every day they make a triple offering of incense to the Sun, an offering of resin at sunrise, of myrrh at midday, and of the so-called kyphi at sunset.*
> —Plutarch, *Isis and Osiris*

As perfume pervaded Egyptian culture, entire gardens were cultivated to produce perfume-bearing plants, which were then processed in some of the first primitive perfume factories of the ancient world. Perfume was considered an integral part of their civilization in both life and death. Clay pots of perfume oils were buried with ancient queens and Pharaohs to be enjoyed for all eternity. Bas-reliefs Rose saw at the Musée International de la Parfumerie in Grasse depict the entire process of making a fragrance—from harvesting the ingredients to extracting their essence.

A bas-relief, sculpted on an Egyptian tomb presents the various stages in the process of making perfume in the Musée International de la Parfumerie.

Greece   Perfume was central to ancient Greek culture, both in mythology and in real life. According to Homer, perfume was bestowed upon man by the gods of the Olympic pantheon, and it played a pivotal role in worship to win their favor. Incense and aromatic plants were burned by the oracle priestesses of Delphi and summoned visions that were interpreted as prescient (see hallucinogen). In ancient Greek civilization, perfumed oils and libations were applied to the skin of athletes, suggesting a consciousness of their therapeutic and healing properties. Perfume was used to commemorate life—to mark milestones such as births and marriages—and to memorialize a person in death. Bodies were anointed with perfume and wrapped in perfumed shrouds, which were believed to bring happiness in the afterlife.

C

catacombs   Under the city of Paris is another city. A necropolis known as the catacombs. This ossuary is comprised of more than 200 miles of subterranean tunnels located in what were once Roman-era limestone quarries. The tunnels and ancient chambers, which have never been fully mapped, hold the skeletonized remains of more than six million people who were moved there from aboveground cemeteries for sanitary reasons in the eighteenth century. The use of these quarries as a resting place was established in 1786 by the order of the Lieutenant General of Police, Louis Thiroux de Crosne and the Inspector General of Quarries, Charles Axel Guillaumot.

The catacombs run under seven distinct arrondissements, but only one mile under the fourteenth is open to visitors. This mile is the museum *Les Catacombes de Paris*, which is on the Left Bank. It can be accessed by traveling 130 steps down into the tunnels and climbing eighty-three steps back up to ground level.

Robespierre discarded the bodies of prostitutes in the catacombs of Paris in what are sometimes referred to as the "Crypts of Passion." During the Second World War, both the Resistance and German SS troops had headquarters in the twisting mazes of tunnels but never found each other's hiding places. The catacombs have been featured in many works of fiction, including *The Phantom of the Opera* and Victor Hugo's *The Hunchback of Notre-Dame*.

Carefully arranged bones of some of the more than six million bodies reburied in the catacombs in Paris, France.

M. J. Rose on her visit to the catacombs. Paris, France 2010. This is the entrance before you get to the miles of skeletons.

cataphiles People who illegally explore the miles of catacombs closed to the public. Cataphilia is practiced by spelunkers, some of whom are artists who use the tunnel walls as canvases or carve sculptures into the stone. Others stage plays in the catacombs. Some show movies on the chalk cemetery's walls, and others engage in black magic or hazing type rituals. Some cataphiles bring wine and food on their midnight forays that they often cook in the twelfth- and thirteenth-century rooms. People have even used the quarries to grow mushrooms.

Chinese law on reincarnation In 2007, fifty years after invading the small Himalayan country of Tibet, the Chinese government passed a law banning reincarnation of the Dalai Lama and other Buddhist monks without government permission. The Tibetan government claimed the law was aimed at wiping out its identity and culture, that indeed, China's motive was to cut off the influence of the Dalai Lama, Tibet's exiled spiritual and political leader. The Chinese claimed the law would institutionalize the management of reincarnation, but the prime minister of Tibet, the Venerable Samdhong Rinpoche Lobsang Tenzin, said the law was an attempt to end the major Tibetan Buddhist institution—the leadership roles of the Dalai Lama and the Panchen Lama.

Chypre Chypre is an olfactive classification referring to perfumes featuring citrus top notes (usually including bergamot), floral middle notes (traditionally including jasmine and rose), and a base of oakmoss, musks, labdanum and patchouli.

Chypre is the French word for the Greek island of Cyprus, also known as the Island of Venus. Cyprus is a rich source of labdanum and of the hesperidic (citrus) components found in chypre perfumes. Famous chypres include Guerlain's Mitsouko, Chypre de Coty and Femme by Rochas.

Cleopatra's fragrance factory Cleopatra (69–30 BCE), the last pharaoh of Ancient Egypt, was fascinated with—some say obsessed by—scent. Marc Anthony built her a fragrance factory that was erected in fields planted with now-extinct flora, including groves of balsam trees (important in the creation of perfume at the time) that he had confiscated from Herod.

In the 1980s a team of Italian and Israeli archaeologists believed they unearthed the factory at the south end of the Dead Sea, thirty kilometers

Another journal page: Egypt and her mythology
play a big part in the main character's life.

from Ein Gedi. Residues of ancient perfumes along with seats where customers received beauty treatments were found there.

Cleopatra's lost book of fragrance formulas   Cleopatra was said to have kept a recipe book for her perfumes, entitled *Cleopatra Gynaeciarum Libri*. The book has been described in writings by Dioscorides, Homer and Pliny the Elder. No known copy of the book exists today.

D

Djedi   1. A powerful ancient priest and magician referred to in the fourth story of the Westcar Papyrus texts from the twelfth dynasty of the ancient Egyptian Middle Kingdom. Djedi was said to have lived in the fourth dynasty, dying at 110 years old. It was said he could consume 500 loaves of bread, a side of beef and 100 jugs of beer each day. It is alleged he possessed the ability to reattach the severed heads of animals and bring them back to life and that he predicted the births of the future rulers of the fifth dynasty. 2. A perfume created by Jacques Guerlain in 1927. Launched on the heels of Howard Carter's historic discovery of Tutankhamen's tomb in 1922, Djedi paid homage to ancient Egyptian civilizations. Interestingly, Jacques Guerlain chose not to celebrate the opulence and splendor of the Golden Ages of Egypt in his olfactory interpretation, opting instead to memorialize the demise of the dynasties that were lost to the sands of time. Djedi's aroma is a unique and compelling narrative of decomposition and disrepair. One of the most rare and sought-after perfumes from the revered House of Guerlain, it is still highly coveted and desired by collectors today.

E

enfleurage or cold enfleurage   A time-honored method of essential oil extraction, in which odorless animal fats are used to collect the fragrant compounds exuded by botanical matter. Traditionally, glass panes are smeared with fat, and then the delicate blossoms are layered over the fats. The perfume diffuses into the fat over several days, after which the spent flowers are replaced with fresh ones. The process is repeated until the fat is supersaturated with the floral scent. The fat is then soaked in ethyl alcohol to draw the fragrant molecules into the alcohol. The alcohol is later isolated and filtered to produce an absolute.

essential oil   A concentrated aromatic oil obtained from botanicals using either expression or distillation extraction methods. Expression or "cold pressing" is used to obtain citrus oils. This method involves piercing the peel so that the essential oil found in the tiny pouches over the skin can be released. The whole fruit is then pressed to isolate the juice and oils from the pulp. The essential oils rise to the surface of the juice and are separated and filtered through centrifugation. In distillation, raw plant matter is placed inside a distillation apparatus called an alembic, which itself is placed over water. The water is heated, and the steam produced rises through the botanical material, vaporizing the volatile compounds.

This vapor travels through a coil and in doing so, cools to a liquid again. This liquid (the perfume oil) is collected in a receptacle as it leaves the coil. The high temperatures required to extract the oil can sometimes prove destructive for more delicate botanicals, in which case alternative extraction processes, such as enfleurage, are preferred.

F

factice   A perfume bottle, usually filled with colored water, that is chiefly used for display or promotional purposes. Factices are usually oversize replicas of the original perfume flacon.

flacon   A perfume bottle. Derived from a Middle French word for "bottle," flacon has become a term used widely in the global vernacular to describe a receptacle for perfume, particularly one of exquisite beauty or craftsmanship.

For research (which wound up being a labor of love) Rose bought hundreds of perfumes. This is a collection of some her favorite inspirations including scents from Guerlain, Frederic Malle, Serge Lutens, Oliver Durbano, Van Cleef and Arpels, Sophia Grojsman, Joya, Jar Parfums, Jo Malone and more.

G

Grasse   A town in southeastern France that is considered to be the traditional and modern capital of perfume. Rose spent time there researching; the fictional perfumers at the heart of her novel have a home and factory there.

In the middle ages, Grasse was perhaps best known for its tanneries. "Grasse" itself is a French word meaning "fatty." In the seventeenth century these tanneries began production of perfumed leather goods, catering to an increasing demand for scented gloves and accessories, which were popularized by Catherine de' Medici. Grasse's thriving perfume industry could be credited, in part, to its warm sheltered microclimate, which provided the ideal conditions for flower farming.

Nowadays, the region is particularly well known for its jasmine, lavender, roses and violet leaves, and it has attracted a vast number of factories that process the raw perfume materials. Grasse's cornerstone perfumeries include Fragonard, Molinard and Galimard.

On display in Musée International de la Parfumerie, nineteenth-century copper alembic stills used in the distillation process of extracting scent from flowers.

Outside the Musée International de la Parfumerie in Grasse, a sculpture of a seventeenth-century perfumer selling his wares.

H

hallucinogen   A substance, usually inhaled or ingested, which produces hallucinations. Chemical compounds found in certain plant species can affect the central nervous system when ingested, resulting in adjusted brain function, which can ultimately alter mood, consciousness and perception. A number of fungi and cacti species and many other psychoactive botanicals have been used in folk preparations of hallucinogens for millennia, and many cultures have a recorded history of their use for medicinal, religious and shamanistic purposes.

The ancient Egyptians worked with botanicals like blue lotus (a water lily that contains psychoactive compounds), to which Rose refers in her book. Other hallucinogenic compounds were added to incense preparations, mixtures of natural ingredients that were rolled into balls and placed onto hot coals to release a perfumed smoke. In folk culture, messages received through visions, hallucinations and altered states were regarded as prophetic and/or divine.

I

incense   A blend of aromatic botanical components that release a perfumed smoke when burned. Incense has been used in purification, meditation and religious rituals since the dawn of time. Many incense preparations in the ancient world had hypnotic properties or a narcotising effect (see hallucinogen). Incense is said to carry prayers to the heavens, to ward off negative spirits, and to bring joy and peace to the soul. Burning it brings positive energy and a balance to our emotions. It is a used in many cultures as a meditation tool and to promote spiritual healing with its tranquil aromatics (see ancient perfume).

K

karma   A spiritual law that concerns cause and effect. In a reincarnation belief system, it is thought that souls are brought back to life to atone for or rectify sins, repay psychic debts or to complete unfinished tasks. In essence, one has to return to the mortal world to satisfy one's karmic responsibility.

M

maceration　A method of extracting fragrant oils from botanical materials by steeping or soaking them in either a cold or a heated solvent solution. Maceration can take from several days to months, depending on the desired outcome. Aromatic compounds gradually pass into the solution, the plant matter is removed, and the perfumed solution is later filtered of impurities.

N

niche perfumes　A perfume created by a boutique or artisanal studio, whose production and distribution are on a much smaller scale than that of mainstream or designer perfumes. Perfumes have also been classified as being either niche or mainstream based upon the number of retail outlets they are supported in. Niche perfumes often tend to be preferred by serious perfumistas, as they offer the uniqueness and hands-on craftsmanship that a lot of mainstream scents are lacking. Rose met several niche perfumers, notably the amazing Olivier Durbano, and was inspired by their artistry and talent. In the book, the character Robbie L'Etoile is an homage to these men and women.

Olivier Durbano, architect, jeweler, niche perfumer extraordinaire, and M. J. Rose. Olivier was the inspiration for one of the characters in the book.

Gedhun Choekyi Nyima   In 1995, the Dalai Lama identified the next reincarnated Panchen Lama, a five-year-old boy named Gedhun Choekyi Nyima. Months later, the child disappeared. The Chinese government admits to taking Nyima but claims he is alive and living with his family in Tibet. His whereabouts, however, remain unknown and no foreign party has been allowed to see him since his disappearance.

O

Oud   A fragrant oil extracted from the resinous heartwood of the aquilaria (agarwood) tree, which grows in abundance in India and Southeast Asia. Aquilaria trees are susceptible to blight by way of a fungus that causes a rich, dark resin to form within the heartwood. This wood is then harvested and distilled to produce pure Oud oil, which has a very unique odor profile. One of the world's most expensive perfume ingredients, Oud is also prized for its spiritual and esoteric value.

P

perfume and the afterlife   In ancient times, scent was aligned with religion and the afterlife. The soul was believed to travel to the next life on the stairway of smoke from the burning incense. Ancient Egyptian tomb paintings, which the author studied in the Metropolitan Museum of Art, show Egyptians wearing perfumed cones on their head.

perfumer's organ   The central workspace at which the perfumer is seated, which is surrounded by ascending staggered rows of small shelves that are laid out in an amphitheatrical arrangement. These shelves hold numerous small bottles of oils and absolutes, each of which is within easy reach of the perfumer while he or she is composing a fragrance. The complex, tiered appearance of the workspace resembles the console of a chapel organ.

Rose traveled to France to learn more about the perfume industry and history, and it was seeing one of these organs in Paris that inspired the antique one in the novel.

The laboratory of a great perfumer, on display in Paris, France.

pyramid The basic structure of a traditional perfume, comprising top notes, middle notes and base notes. Top notes are those components that you can smell upon initial application. Traditionally, these comprise of lighter citrus oils and tend to evaporate rapidly. Middle notes are the essences that emerge after the top notes have faded. They represent the heart of the perfume. Generally florals, spices and herbaceous components reside here. Base notes are the foundation upon which a perfume is built. They are traditionally comprised of heavier or muskier notes that act as the perfume's backbone. These include woods, resins, mosses and animalic facets such as civet or ambergris. Base notes linger on the skin after the top and middle notes have vanished.

R

reincarnation The word derives from Latin and means "entering the flesh again." A synonym, "metempsychosis," means "transmigration of the soul." Reincarnation is the belief that after death the soul returns to a new body—usually without memory of the previous life. The doctrine is incorporated into almost all Indian religions, including Hinduism and Buddhism. But reincarnation doctrine appears in the beliefs of certain

Jewish, Christian and Islam sects as well, including followers of the Cabbala, Catharism, the Alawi, Gnostic and Esoteric Christianity and the Druze. Reincarnation is also part of Native American, Greek and Norse mythologies.

Pythagoras, Socrates, Plato, Plotinus, Hermes, Raymond Lully, Nicolás de Cusa, Leonardo da Vinci, Edmund Spenser, Shakespeare, and Milton and Yeats all explored and wrote about rebirth in their work. Spinoza and Leibniz, Voltaire, Benjamin Franklin, Thomas Paine, Walt Whitman, W.B. Yeats, Ralph Waldo Emerson, Henry David Thoreau, General George Patton, Kant, Herder, Lessing, Hume and Carl Jung all believed in or wrote about the idea of rebirth.

> *The tomb is not a blind alley: it is a thoroughfare. It*
> *closes on the twilight. It opens on the dawn.*
> —Victor Hugo

S

sillage   The lingering trail of perfume that remains behind, particularly after the wearer has left the room. *Sillage* is the French word for wake.

soul migration   The belief that a soul returns to a very specific and tailored set of circumstances in order to rectify a previous sin.

Dr. Ian Stevenson (October 31, 1918–February 8, 2007)
Dr. Stevenson was a biochemist and professor of psychiatry who headed the Division of Perceptual Studies at the University of Virginia. He spent forty years studying more than 3,000 cases of reincarnation in children. Stevenson believed that reincarnation might help both modern medicine and psychiatry in understanding certain behaviors that had no other explanation. He wrote several books, including *Twenty Cases Suggestive of Reincarnation* and *Reincarnation and Biology*. His work is carried on today by Dr. Jim Tucker.

T

Tibetan reincarnation   In Tibetan Buddhism, a *tulku* is a person who has been identified as a reincarnation of a great master. A *tulku* can choose the manner of his (or her) rebirth. Tibetan Buddhists believe that the Buddha is said to exist in three bodies. One of these, the *nirmanakaya* is the earthly, physical body, which manifests in the world to help bring all beings to enlightenment. Since 1193, hundreds of living masters have been identified. The Dalai Lama and the Panchen Lama are the highest ranked.

Different religious methods are used to help identify a reincarnated *tulku*. Among these are oracles, retreats, portents, searches for mothers who've had unusual dreams and children who process certain knowledge without receiving training.

triads   Originally Triads were Chinese resistance forces who opposed the Manchu rule. In the 1760s they formed the Heaven and Earth Society in order to overthrow the Qing Dynasty. The society then branched out into many smaller groups, adopting the triangle as their symbol, and going on to exert influence throughout China. In reference to that symbol, the British colonial authorities in Hong Kong coined the term "triad" to describe organized crime syndicates.

In 1949, when the Communist Party came to power in China and law enforcement became more stringent, the triad society members began to migrate. Since the 1880s they have been engaged in counterfeiting. Today, they are active in many regions with significant Chinese populations. They are known to engage in prostitution, extortion and money laundering.

tulpa   A mystical concept of a being or object that materializes through willpower, based on the ancient idea of mind transmission. The term originated with Alexandra David-Néel, a Belgian-French explorer and spiritualist who entered Tibet when it was forbidden to foreigners. She claimed to have created a *tulpa* in the image of a monk who eventually took on a life of his own and needed to be destroyed.

Written by M. J. Rose and Dimitri Dimitriadis,
author of the acclaimed blog *Sorcery of Scent*
http://sorceryofscent.blogspot.com.

Author's Note

As with most of my work, there is a lot of fact mixed in with this fictional tale.

Cleopatra's love of fragrance was legendary and she did in fact have a perfume factory. Archaeologists believe they found remains of it in the Dead Sea, thirty kilometers from Ein Gedi. According to Dioscorides, Homer and Pliny the Elder, the Egyptian queen kept a record of her favorite fragrances and cosmetic formulas in a book called *Cleopatra gynaeciarum libri.*

No known copy of the book exists today.

Napoleon, who was sensitive to scent, did go to Egypt in the late 1700s and while there explored the pyramids with an army of savants; there is no record of a perfumer having accompanied him.

The history of perfume and the fragrance industry past and present, the Triads, the methods by which lamas are found and how monks study and live are all based on research.

That's also true of Tibetan beliefs and rituals having to do with reincarnation, which are sadly being threatened by China's rules requiring people to register to reincarnate.

Unfortunately, Xie's story is rooted in history. In 1995, the Dalai Lama identified the next reincarnated Panchen Lama, a five-year-old boy named Gedhun Choekyi Nyima. Months later, the child disappeared. The Chinese government admits to taking Nyima and claims he is alive and living with his family in Tibet, but his whereabouts remain unknown and no foreign party has been allowed to see him.

While there is no Phoenix Foundation, the work done there was inspired by work done at the University of Virginia Medical Center by Dr. Ian Stevenson, who studied children with past life memories for more than thirty years. Dr. Bruce Greyson and Dr. Jim Tucker, a child psychiatrist, continue Ian Stevenson's work today.

And then there's Paris. I'll never be able to do her justice. What a magical city. If you visit, do voyage down to the catacombs. They are moving, fascinating and yes, a little frightening. Afterward, stop at Café Marly for a glass of wine and then on to L'Orangerie—Claude Monet's paintings are truly breathtaking.

Acknowledgments

To my editor, Sarah Durand, an author's dream: insightful, wise, patient and sensitive.

To my agent, Dan Conaway—for so many reasons—this wouldn't be *The Book of Lost Fragrances* without you.

To my sorcerer of scent—the blogger Dimitri—who opened the doors of the mysterious world of perfume. Thank you for your generous advice and all the vintage samples.

For the inspiration: thanks to the iconic Sophia Grossman, one of the great living perfumers, and the inventive and poetic Olivier Durbano.

To Frederick Bochardy for his wonderful fragrances, spirit of adventure and willingness to share his scents with me and with this book.

To the whole team at Atria Books—those I know: Hilary Tisman, Lisa Sciambra and Paul Olsewski, as well as all the people who worked on this book whom I haven't had the chance to meet yet—I'm honored to be working with you.

To everyone at Writers House—from the always calming Stephen Barr to the charming Michael Mejias (one day I will open the right door!).

To the dream team—when you're stuck with a plot point, character or just losing confidence—they're incomparable and great friends all—Lisa Tucker, Douglas Clegg, C.W. Gortner and Steve Berry.

To readers, booksellers and librarians everywhere who make all the work worthwhile.

As always, to my dear friends and family. And most of all, Doug.